BLOOD AND STARLIGHT

Sonata of the Astral Seas

E.K. MacPherson

CHATTAN

First published in the United States

Copyright © 2024 E.K. MacPherson

All rights reserved.

No part of this publication may be reproduced, distributed, or transmitted in any form or by any means, including photocopying, recording, or other electronic or mechanical methods, without the prior written permission of the publisher, except as permitted by U.S. copyright law.

The story, all names, characters, and incidents portrayed in this production are fictitious. No identification with actual persons (living, deceased, or undeceased), places, buildings, and products is intended or should be inferred.

ISBN HB: 979-8-9916966-0-9; PB: 979-8-9916966-1-6; eBook: 979-8-9916966-2-3

Library of Congress Control Number: 2024921352

1st edition 2024 published by Chattan, LLC

chattanrecords.com

Nashville, TN, USA

Cover art © 2024 E.K. MacPherson

Map © 2024 E.K. MacPherson

CONTENTS

Overture   1
Tribunal of a Witch

Movement 1
Death's Hand

    1. The Vale   9
    2. The Drowned Horde   22
    3. The Haunting of Skylark Manor   35
    4. The Last Vampire   50
    5. A Quest   60
    6. Isle of the Gods   67
    7. Hurricane Smile   78
    8. Animal   99

Movement 2
A Fool's Errand

    9. Once More With Feeling   104
    10. Temple of the Horned God   112

11. Festival of Haunts	127
12. Doctor of Lost Letters	152
13. Bad Behavior	176
14. Woman in White	191
15. Ad Astra	214
16. Road to Ruin	235

Movement 3
Winter's Bones

17. The Coming of Night	262
18. Ballad of the Daughters of Parris	269
19. Miracle Aligner	289
20. The Septus Seal	304
21. Fallout	318
22. Meanwhile	326
23. The Trick of Kindness	341
24. Midnight Sun	360
25. Blood and Starlight	379
26. Enter the Chorus	394
27. The Light at Dawn	423

For my parents, always my biggest fans.
For Colleen, to whom I dedicate the dashes of spice.
For the monsters who simply want to be loved.

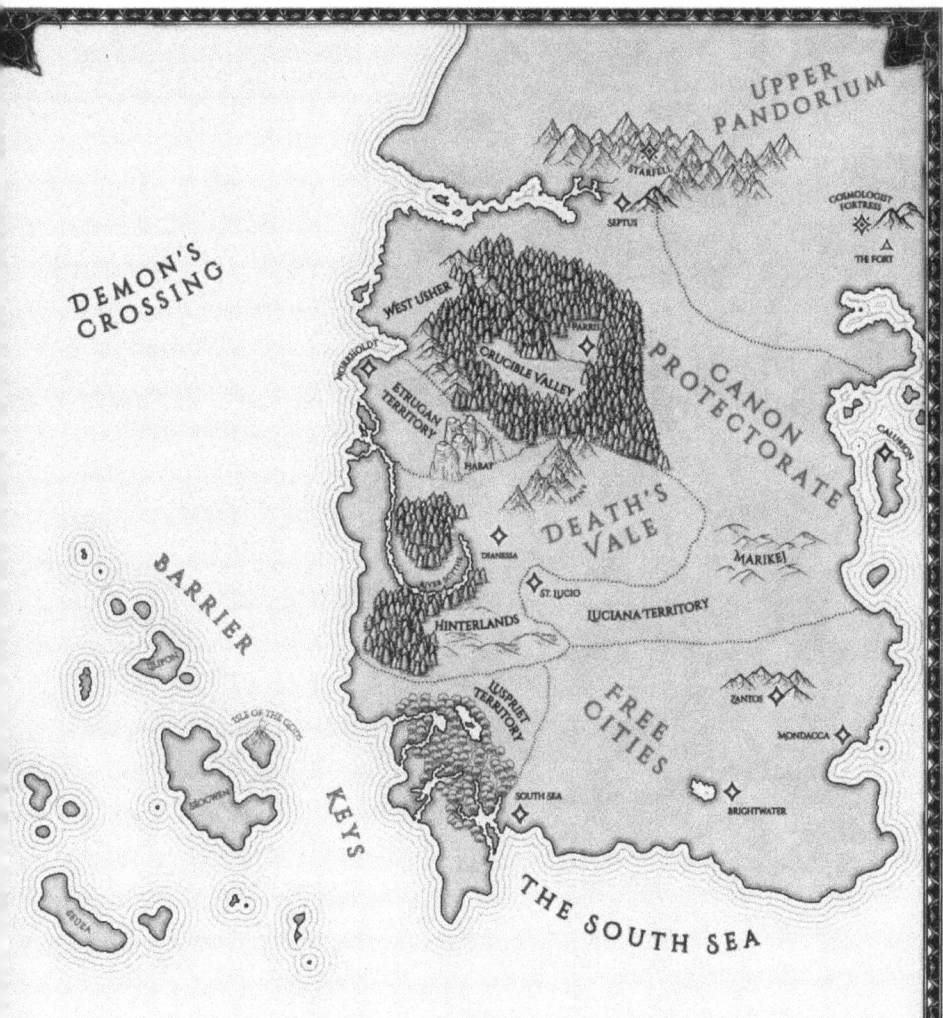

MAP OF THE EASTERN HEMISPHERE

OVERTURE

TRIBUNAL OF A WITCH

Silence crouched like a hunting beast over the packed chamber. All eyes strained toward the figure in chains at the foot of the cleric's dais. From the high platform, grim-faced members of the tribunal glared down at the small boy trembling before them.

"Elyssandro Santara Ruadan, you stand accused of the capital crime of witchcraft," Cleric Kraul's voice boomed from the vaulted ceiling.

Ely kept his eyes fixed on the white-robed figure looming above. An iron gag clamped tight over his mouth. The cleric drew breath to continue his proceeding when the chamber doors burst open with a clang.

"Stop this madness!"

Ely's heart skipped to a note of hope. Uncle Misha would save him. He was the king's brother. They had to listen to him. Didn't they?

The prince limped toward the dais, his cane cracking thunder bursts against the stones. Red-hooded templars crossed blades before the platform, barring his path.

"Free him at once," Prince Misha bid.

Cleric Kraul peered down the length of his nose, a formidable scowl on his face. "No one is permitted to interfere in the tribunal of a witch. Your authority ends at the threshold of this chamber."

The prince drew up, helpless in his fury. Ely's limbs began to tremble. Creeping cold whispered beneath his skin.

Not now, he begged.

The ice subsided, bending to the full concentration of his will. No one knew his secret. If he could only keep it hidden, they would let him go home.

"The House of Ruadan recognizes the authority of the Holy Canon, your Eminence," the prince said, "for a credible accusation, but this is preposterous. My nephew is not a witch. He's just a child."

"You may rest in comfort knowing the tribunal of the One does not convict absent proof," the cleric replied.

"And what proof do you have?" Prince Misha demanded.

The cleric gestured to a templar at the small side door of the chamber. Ely inhaled sharply, knees knocking again as he took in the slender figure escorted to the witness stand. He was bloodied and bruised, one eye swollen shut but recognizable all the same.

"State your name for the tribunal," the cleric commanded.

"Al...Alexei...Prince Regent Alexei Santara Ruadan," came the stammered reply.

Ely stared at his brother, pleading silently.

"State the accusation which you bring against Prince Elyssandro," the cleric prompted.

"Ely..." Alexei faltered a moment. "Elyssandro used death magic to raise our mother...Terésa Santara's corpse from the grave."

"Your Eminence, it is clear that lies have been beaten into his mouth!" Prince Misha's exclamation rang, but a faceless templar restrained him.

"He has Death's Gaze across his ribs on the left side," Alexei continued.

The cleric motioned with his hand, and the templar seized Ely. His heart clanged in his chest. He froze. Unable to think. Unable to resist. The templar produced a knife and slit Ely's nightshirt, jerking the folds from his shoulders. Another forced his arms up as high as the shackles permitted. The crowd gasped at the raised scars revealed. A triad of stars standing out stark and pale against his copper skin.

Hisses exploded through the chamber.

"Witch!"

"Demon!"

"Monster!"

Fear rushed in once again, and the flicker inside him burst to full anarchy. This time he could not contain it. His eyes rolled toward the back of his skull, and he saw only a haze. Icy blackness slithered around his arms, shearing through his shackles and unlocking the gag. Freedom!

The gathered men screamed as he leaped from the platform. Vacuous darkness spewed from him like smoke from flame. The doors of the chamber burst open with a flick of his hand.

Ely charged into the cobblestone streets. His sight cleared as Death's presence dissipated about him. He rounded a bend and collided with a figure that sent him toppling to the ground. Scrambling to his feet, he found himself face to face with his uncle.

They stood immobile. Eyes locked. Ely's heart sank as he thought he saw Prince Misha reaching for the sword at his hip. Instead, his uncle tugged loose the buttons of his jacket and held out the garment. It draped to his knees as Ely threw it about his shoulders. His uncle removed his sword belt where rapier and dagger both clung. This too he offered. As Ely reached for the weapons, his uncle's hand closed about his wrist.

"Run," he commanded.

"Uncle–"

Prince Misha squeezed his wrist, the pressure painful. "Do not stop until you find the other side of Death's Vale."

"Death's Vale?" Ely protested. "No one can cross–"

"You can," Prince Misha insisted. "If anyone can survive the Vale, it is you. Do not look back, Elyssandro, do you understand me?"

"Yes, Uncle," he replied.

The prince released him. A tear shimmered in his eye, but he blinked it away.

"Go!" he barked.

Ely obeyed, securing the belt around his waist as he ran. Beyond the city walls, past the last watch tower, the dead waste greeted him with a howl of wind and a swirl of dust.

Eerie light spilled through the clouds onto stones twisted and crushed beneath thorn-ridged vines. Nothing stirred. Not a bird in the sky or a crawling insect. Perhaps it was the calm after the storm, or perhaps this land truly did not grant passage to the living.

Ely had fled deep into the night, fighting the raging wind until he collapsed under the cover of a crumbling wall. After a fitful sleep, he wandered on, driven by terror of every shadow. It was near dusk when he began to hear the sounds of the dead. At first a rustle on the stones behind him. Then groans drifting from derelict ruins.

A lurching collection of corroded flesh rose up from the ground before him. Ely drew his uncle's rapier from its sheath. He detested sword lessons, but the years of forced repetition might save him now.

With an unbalanced vault and thrust, he dispatched the ungainly monster. Or so he thought. It rose once more with a chilling moan. Ely cut it down again, now breaking into a run toward a stone archway. A snarling corpse blocked his path, strips of thin, withered skin stretched taut over bleached bones.

Ely dodged the monster, tripping over a loose stone and striking his head on the hard ground. Pain vanished. Vision dimmed. Something else, something cold and vast, flowed into him. The monster sprang, bony fingers grasping. Ely raised a hand. The skeleton stopped, its arms dropping to its sides. It stood motionless. Waiting.

Ely flexed his fingers, a silent command rippling between them. The corpse turned, its bones creaking as it walked away.

"It's been a thousand years since your kind have walked the Vale," hissed a voice like rusted, scraping metal.

A figure emerged from the shadows clad in a hooded gray cloak. Ely stood rooted in place, watching it draw closer. Though every instinct screamed to run, he could not bring his body to obey.

Throwing back her hood, the stranger gazed at him through pale, milky eyes. Her waxy skin, mottled gray and green, looked half-decayed. Long silver hair draped her shoulders like cobwebs.

"You're just a child," she observed. "What is your name, warm blood?"

"Elyssandro Santara Ruadan," he replied.

"Ruadan, is it?" the stranger mused. "Won't someone be missing you? I can return you to Saint Lucio if you've lost your way."

Ely shook his head. "I can't go back there."

The stranger nodded. "I am Dr. Selene Faidra."

"Good to meet you, Dr. Faidra," Ely said with a stiff bow.

The stranger laughed, exposing a row of sharp teeth, eerily stained red. "Such a polite little prince you are, Elyssandro Santara Ruadan."

"Are you a witch?" Ely asked.

"I am a scientist and a scholar," Dr. Faidra replied. She regarded him for a long moment, then finally commanded, "Follow me."

"Where are we going?" Ely asked.

"You will be safe with me at the University," she said.

"And what do you need in return?" Ely asked, wary.

"In time," Dr. Faidra replied with an unsettling smile. "Do we have a bargain?"

Ely inclined his head. "Yes."

"Good. Then follow me, warm blood."

MOVEMENT I
Death's Hand

CHATTAN

Chapter One

THE VALE

Ely woke underground.

  Steam hissed in his ear, and sulfurous fumes stung his nostrils. He sat up slowly, head fuzzy. Above, he could only just see the sky from the opening down which he had fallen. He was lucky to be alive. As he glanced at the fire spitting from a fissure in the stone, he realized just how lucky.

How had he lost his balance in the first place? He usually excelled at climbing.

The voice, he thought.

Halfway down the wall, he had heard someone speak his name as clear as if they clung to the rocks beside him. Perhaps he hallucinated it. That was entirely possible. He was, after all, hovering over an interspatial rupture. Where two places leaned against one another, bending and folding and melding, strange things were bound to happen.

Ely passed his fingers across his face. A swirl of midnight ether took shape, forming a contoured mask over his nose and mouth. Protection against the dangerous miasma that leached from temperamental ruptures. He approached the flaring gap in the stone with practiced caution.

Dr. Faidra had brought him to view these phenomena in his first months as the only living resident of Death's Vale. He had perfected, over the past twenty odd years, a method for stabilizing troublesome ruptures like the one he now sought. Like sutures in a wound, a coil of death magic could knit the edges of the aperture together. The procedure left scars and occasionally burst open again, but for the most part, he was able to calm the tremors and noxious smells. This particular rupture had caused a violent earthquake that shook him from his bed and demolished a portion of the University roof in the north wing. Dr. F had easily located the source of the quake with her well-tuned instruments.

As he squatted down to the opening, the steam cleared just enough for him to view the frayed edges of the rupture glowing crimson. Before he could work out how to maneuver closer, a pair of jaws jutted from the vent, snapping at him with crooked teeth. Ely leaped back. The beast appeared to be an enormous, long-snouted gar. Then its scaly body scuttled into view over a multitude of insectile legs.

Ely crouched low. Darkness spiraled around him, sliding over his body as armor. The beast screamed like a steaming kettle, then it charged, stabbing a clawed leg. Ely rolled beneath the flailing limbs.

A twist of his fingers conjured an obsidian lance in his hands. When the creature struck again, its prey bit back. Not a skilled maneuver, but nevertheless, a fiery geyser spewed magma where the lance plunged deep. Ely leaped out of the way as the creature stumbled. A rivulet of the molten blood struck him. He growled in pain, clutching his wounded shoulder.

The scaly head turned. Its gaping jaws seized him and tossed him high into the air. Ely collapsed. Breath scattered. The beast reared up again. An icy surge rushed through him, and his eyes clouded over. Death's infinite void permeated his every cell. His hands raised without conscious direction. Black ether burst free, coiling around the beast's multitude of limbs. He felt the power sinking into its pores to the molten core of its body. With an echoing shout, he retracted the force, and the beast erupted, its blood frozen into a basalt shower.

With the danger past, Death receded, and the milky veil lifted from Ely's sight. His armor dissolved in a spray of violet embers.

"A machnid," he panted, once again in control of his faculties. "Fascinating."

He hated to kill a creature so primordial, but according to the University texts, machnids infested a healthy mantle, eventually fracturing the crust and causing violent volcanic eruptions.

Ely edged closer to the vent once again. His shoulder screamed as though a hot iron pressed against his skin. The fabric of his tunic appeared to be unscathed. At least the conjured armor had been good for something. It was a nice tunic. He would have loathed to lose it. The damage to his arm? Probably substantial. It would be best to make the climb out of this hole before he lost use of it entirely. Still, he could not leave the rupture unattended.

Ely reforged his mask, groaning as he stooped near the opening. He knew it would be unwise to reach in without conjuring full armor, but he felt his inner resources perilously near spent. Taking a breath, he dispersed ether like ice through the heated vent. It steamed and stilled, but it would not hold for long.

Ely stretched his arm inside the opening, threading darkness between the edges of the rupture until it was rendered suitably closed. A shimmer still trembled in the air like a beam of light escaping through a canopy. It would have to suffice.

The climb back up the rock wall proved far more difficult than anticipated. By the time he collapsed into the dust at the top of the ravine, his throbbing arm refused to move. Dr. F would fix him up, no doubt with a lecture on being a fragile, careless mortal.

The undead doctor had first brought him this far out into the wilderness when he was still new to Death's Vale. Winter was approaching. He wore a cloak with a thick fur-lined hood, boots cuffed in the same gray hide, and over large gloves. He surely cut a comical figure in garments meant for a full-grown man.

The doctor scrabbled over sheer rock faces. Deft as a spider. She did not slacken her pace for the young human struggling after her. By the time he caught up to her, Ely found her preoccupied with a strange machine tucked away in her pack.

A cave opened into the rock wall. At least he thought it a cave until he got a better look. Light poured from inside. The edges pulsed as though the opening were drawing breath.

"Don't get too close," the doctor cautioned. "This one needs to be stabilized."

She tuned her instrument, and it hummed as she set it on the ground just beyond the lip of the glowing aperture. It rippled and sputtered, shaking the cliffside so that Ely reeled back. He caught himself before tumbling over the chasm. The doctor bared her razor teeth and swiped her fingers across a set of dials on the machine. A stream of azure light projected from a curved lens at the end of a copper tube. The light formed into glyphs which rose into the air, shifting in a ring about the tear in the stone wall. The quaking ceased. Slowly, the light dimmed.

Ely peered through the opening, a jubilant grin on his face.

"Now, remember what I told you," Dr. F said. "The nest will be high. Likely on the cliffs. I only need one feather. If you see even a shadow, find cover."

"I remember," Ely beamed.

He summoned his armor as she had made him practice, then stepped into the rupture.

A breeze caressed his cheek, cool and salted. When his vision cleared, he saw golden sands washed by fervent ocean waves. He freed himself of his winter furs and ran through the foamy surf, splashing and howling like a wolf pup.

A shout rang from up the shoreline. Weapons clashed. Ely caught sight of templar red, eye and blade insignia gleaming alabaster. Death usurped all thought as he rushed toward the fray, gathering black magic in his palms.

The templars fell swiftly to his unanticipated attack. They had been too focused on the band of shackled children to notice the lone shadow that now hunted them. When the last of the crimson-clad warrior priests lay still, Ely freed the captives of their chains.

They were garbed in colorful patterned fabric accented by polished shells and shimmering feathers. To the Canon, the Séoc of the Barrier Keys were pirates, but elsewhere they were hailed as paladins of the waves. One of the liberated prisoners stepped forward. He was not the tallest among them nor the broadest, but his presence named him unmistakably the leader of the group.

"Thank you, diakana," he said, his easy smile brushed with good humor at the dimpled corner. He spoke in heavily accented Lanica, the language of the Free Cities. Not Ely's native tongue either, but a good common ground.

The Séoc boy continued, "I am Kailari Novara. Kai for friends." He pointed to a sturdy girl at his elbow. "This Salía. Cousin. This Yamon. Mirit. Baby cousins."

More chuckles from the pirates. Yamon and Mirit both stood a head taller than their older kin.

"I am Elyssandro Santara Ruadan."

Kai laughed and said something to his crew in the Séoc tongue.

"What do friends say for you?" he asked.

"Ely."

"Much better," Kai beamed. "I wonder how you get here, Ely? They say diakana fall from sky."

"What does *diakana* mean?" Ely asked.

Kai's brow ruffled in thought. "Star hands?"

Ely smiled. "Then, yes, something like that."

"What brings you to Séocwen?" Kai asked.

"Do you know of Cocatl? I'm to bring back a feather," Ely said.

Kai frowned, looking at him thoughtfully. "The sky snake."

"The doctor says it nested here," Ely said. "Dr. Faidra is my..." He thought a moment, trying to puzzle out what she might be called. "My family."

"Cocatl disappear long ago," Kai told him. "But maybe feather stay in nest. We go look, yes?"

"You know where it is?" Ely asked.

"Come," Kai gestured.

Ely followed him down the beach to the mouth of a creek where the young Séoc crew had moored their vessel. It was not a ship exactly. More a narrow sloop with a single sail and a small shelter with enough room for two to lay comfortably side by side. Still, Ely gaped in awe at the smooth mirrorwood hulls that reflected water, sand, and sky.

The crew pushed the sloop into the sea. Ely stood at the bow as they sailed along the shoreline. Porpoises leaped from the emerald water, crystal waterfalls unfurling from their tails.

He returned to the shore salt-kissed and exhilarated. While the rest of the Séoc crew stayed with the boat, Ely and Kai hiked inland to where shifting sands hardened into soaring cliffs. Kai assembled a system of ropes and spikes to aid them as they scaled the pockmarked rock. As they ascended higher, the enormous crenulated edges of a nest peeked at them from a plateau above. Ely's excitement lent a burst of speed. His feet slipped from the narrow ledge, and he tumbled into open air. The line pulled tight around his waist. He slammed a shoulder into the stone, but he fell no further. Kai shouted down to him, and when he waved with a pained smile, the pirate hauled him back to his side.

At last, they reached the cliff where the monolithic nest had been woven into the rock from tree limbs, strips of bark, and the curved rib bones of some bovid animal.

Kai approached the base. A tar-like substance crusted the walls. The pirate tested his weight against the woven branches. When they held, he scaled the side with practiced ease. Ely followed. Unsteady but determined to keep up.

Inside they found petrified bones and fragments of eggshell thick and heavy as slabs of turquoise stone. No feathers.

They returned empty-handed to where the Novara cousins had lit cook fires on the beach. Ely had never tasted anything so delicious as the fire-blistered fish slapped into his hand as he collapsed in the sand.

They watched the blood orange sun plunge beneath the ocean waves. Kai rose and beckoned Ely.

"Come with me, diakana."

Ely followed him to the boat's prow. He had not noticed the carving that adorned the ship's face. A serpent with curved fangs and a forked tongue.

Kai pried loose a leather thong from a hook set in the figure's neck. It was braided with scalloped shells, carved beads, and one long, lustrous feather of deepest emerald green. The pattern at the base looked smooth, almost scale-like before flaring into downy curled ends.

"Cocatl?" Ely asked, staring in awe at the shimmering plume.

Kai nodded, a roguish sparkle in his black eyes. "They say the Novaras come from Cocatl. My...how you say mother of mother?"

"Grandmother?"

Kai nodded. "Yes, grandmother. She find this. She is king of Séocwen."

He held the feather talisman out to Ely. "Take it. For your family."

"What? I couldn't do that," Ely gasped.

"You save *my* family." The pirate prince pressed it into his hand. "Take it..."

Ely blinked away the waking memory. Delirium must be setting in if he was thinking about Kailari Novara.

He raised himself to his feet with a groan and set out across the bleak landscape. Bodies lay sprawled in various states of decay. Unlike the cursed dead, these lay inanimate, never to rise. Some were refugees from Canon lands, but most wore the crimson cloaks of the templar order. The templars carried out the will of the Canon, holy warriors with the sigil of the eye and blade emblazoned on their chest plates. For all their violent piety, they did not stand a chance against Death's domain.

This barren wasteland had once burgeoned pristine woodlands and rolling fields outlying the greatest city known to mankind. Dianessa.

Scholars the world over came to Dianessa to study the art and science of magic. Naturalists and physicians had come to immerse themselves in the wonders of the surrounding landscape. Now the forests stood cemeteries of charred, naked trees. Persistent weeds, scrubby bushes, and creeping vines eked out a parched existence along the stony hills. Here and again a trickle of a stream slipped through the dust. Ely stopped to fill his canteen. The glyphs inscribed about the vessel glowed red. Many travelers through Death's Vale met their ends drinking the water without a spell to cleanse poison.

Dusk draped shadows over the valley. Ely pressed on. If he stopped now, he would not be able to start again. His arm was beginning to go numb. More alarming by far than the constant throb.

As he walked, he lifted his fingers and coaxed starlight into his hand, siphoning the light into a flask secured to his belt. When the shimmering opalescence reached the brim, he unhooked the flask and drank from it. It was cold and spiceless, satisfying the need for nourishment but not the craving to eat.

As pale morning light kissed night's brow, Ely saw the walls of the dead city silhouetted on the horizon. Nearly home. A gaping ravine made up the metropolis's eastern border. Only the jagged tip of a spire could be seen from the blackness below, but if Ely closed his eyes and cast awareness down, he could feel the echoes that still clung to the ruined walls. It was once known as the Tower where the Order of Cosmologists harnessed the powers of the night sky and unlocked the secrets of Death. One day he would venture down. One day. The thought of the perilous climb and combing through the ruins sent chills rippling through him like he stood on his own grave.

The buildings nearest the aperture that had swallowed the Tower all those centuries ago had collapsed, but a mile or so beyond, cobbled streets, stone apartments, and spacious shops remained. Weathered but intact.

Despite containing no breathing beings except Ely himself, Dianessa was anything but quiet and still. Skeletons in tattered garments strolled about their business. A sizable group crowded around a marble table in the market square. Two sat opposite one another, white skulls bowed over a Caj board sliding painted tiles between numbered squares. The gathered spectators moved bony hands wildly, shouting their predictions to one another as the moves progressed. Somehow they could see, hear, and speak despite the absence of any of the necessary organs. Ely never questioned why the different flavors of magic worked as they did. He simply learned the quirks and adapted accordingly.

Ely waved to a nearby skeleton dressed in a diamond-patterned vest, a silk ascot, and a magnificent feathered hat. A rapier and dagger girded his hip bones. Sir Ambrose Quinn. Knight errant in life and death.

"Who's winning?" Ely asked.

"Lily Duchess for now, but you know how Caj is," Quinn replied, shaking his head.

Ely chuckled and patted Quinn on the humerus. "Keep me posted."

Quinn saluted and turned back to the Caj table. Ely left the marketplace behind, traipsing between crumbling dormitories. Two ghouls bristled at the front steps of the University. They turned away with disinterest as Ely jogged up the soaring stone steps.

The heavy front doors had not budged in centuries. He wasn't even sure they *could* be opened at this point. Instead, he followed the outer wall to a small side door that let in between a cluster of offices.

Today Dr. F haunted her underground lab, christened the Oubliette, which contained its own forge as well a number of cells outfitted with bars and shackles. The latter were left over from dark ages past when the scholars conscripted criminals and prisoners of war to serve in their research. Now every conceivable manner of smithing hammer and chisel hung neatly from hooks set in the wall. Dust gathered in puffy clouds around the perimeter. Ely sneezed the moment he walked through the arched doorway.

"You've come back," Dr. Faidra's rusty voice emerged from a screened partition at the back of the room.

She sat at her low desk. Thick square-framed glasses over her milky eyes. Stylus poised delicately between her withered fingers. The other hand held a small cylindrical bit of copper, hollow and hammered eggshell thin. Each precise motion of the stylus etched fine lines that glowed white then cooled into permanent glyphs whose meanings Ely still had not learned. To the undead doctor's eternal irritation.

When she had finished setting the characters, Dr. F laid down her stylus and looked at him with narrowed eyes. "You smell like a seared pig. Are you injured?"

"It's nothing," Ely shrugged.

He bottled the swell of pain into a low grunt that he hoped escaped the doctor's notice. It did not.

"Hm," she observed, baring her pointed teeth with displeasure.

Dr. F rose from her seat, setting her dense encoding glasses on the desk beside the copper cylinder and stylus. No doubt she would return through the late hours of the night to finish infusing spells.

"Come, warm blood. Let's visit the infirmary," she said.

They ascended the cobwebbed staircase from the Oubliette to the doorway behind the staff commissary. Then down the corridor to yet more flights of stairs. The infirmary was on the fourth floor.

Rows of beds, corners pinned in eternal tucks, lined the walls. Clay pots sprouting with all manner of plants and herbs gobbled up sunlight from the windowsills.

Dr. F motioned Ely to sit on a stool while she illuminated a bright column of translucent crystal with a touch of her fingers.

Ely unfastened the buttons on his tunic. Polished brass carved like intricate flowers studded the right side of the garment shoulder to hip.

He had found it in a chest in an abandoned apartment off the square. It was a little short in the arms, but it nearly fit. Close enough.

"What have you done to yourself, Elyssandro?" Dr. F chided, peeling the fabric back from his blistered skin.

"There was a machnid," he grinned, unable to contain the burst of excitement at his fascinating near-death encounter.

"You need to work on your basic conjury," Dr. F observed, far less amused.

"I held my own," he countered.

Dr. F grunted and poked his shoulder again. Something squelched, and Ely grimaced.

"This is infected," the doctor diagnosed. She pursed her lips in thought, a twitch of a smile at the corner. "I'll need a sample."

"Ah, now you're excited," Ely grumbled.

"Analytical," she corrected.

Dr. F procured a mirrorwood scalpel, humming to herself as blue lightning skittered around the handle to the blade. Ely sighed and looked away. She was done with a stinging flick of the wrist. Ely found a bit of cotton gauze to staunch the bleeding while she secured her sample.

When she returned, she held a glazed pot overgrown with white-veined ivy, its bizarre creepers twisting every which way. Ely set the bloodied gauze on the neighboring table and took a deep breath. He lifted his hand on the uninjured side. Where his fingers ended, his senses stretched on in elongated tentacles, drawn to the radiating presence of life.

It was easy, in this place, to perceive the warm spark of a living being. The clerics of the Canon would have called it the soul, but years spent among the spirited dead revealed dogmatic definitions to be an oversimplification. It was energy, all of it. The beautiful vibrance that stirred flesh, bone, leaf, and stem came in many forms. Life was but one aspect. Death another. Undead another still. The shooting, tenacious aura of the ivy felt altogether different from the spirit of an animal. Regenerative. Perfect for healing.

Ely moved his fingers, reaching his awareness to coil around one single length of vine. Though he was gentle as a whisper of wind, he felt the immense gravitational pull trying to escape his grasp. It would wither the whole plant to dust if his careful control slipped even for a second. With surgical precision, Ely channeled a trickle of honey-hued light until it hovered over his palm. From the corner of his eye, he saw a single leafy ringlet slump, blackened.

Dr. F coaxed the wayward sliver of ivy soul into her hands, twisting and shaping it expertly between her clawed fingers until it resembled a glowing spider's web. She hummed softly, sketching glyphs across the surface with her thumbnails before laying the gossamer filaments over his wounded shoulder. The pain ceased in an instant, followed by the tingling itch of mending muscle and skin.

"Don't make it too perfect," Ely said.

Dr. F clicked her tongue in exasperation. "I know exactly how you want it, Elyssandro. Intriguing and mysterious but not unsightly." She shook her head. "Vainest creature I've ever met."

There was only one story he wished he could erase from his skin. Each forearm bore a deep, concave indentation ringed by branded glyphs. Nothing he tried would convince them to fade. Instead, he wore long sleeves even in the sweltering heat of summer. Not that he ever forgot them. Not for a moment.

The undead doctor cut off the spell with a pinch of her fingers.

"Many thanks, Dr. F," Ely said, stretching and rotating his arm.

The new skin was still a little tight, but the pain had disappeared. Satisfied, he replaced his tunic.

Darkness had claimed the campus, though Ely hardly noticed. He knew the twisting stone corridors with eyes shut. He first visited the bathhouse, an underground spring that had been redirected to flow through a pipe set in the wall. The water filled a wide stone pool before disappearing through a channel at the far end. Dr. Faidra had carved glyphs all the way around the pool which cast gilded light from the walls and low ceiling. The spells not only cleansed the poison from the water but warmed it to steaming.

With the dust and grime of Death's Vale scrubbed clean, Ely moved on to the eastern wing which he had claimed as his own. He had amassed a collection of clothing scavenged from the dormitories and uninhabited domiciles of the surrounding city. Everything was looking a bit worn.

Colors faded. Hems frayed. He hadn't found any exceptional threads in quite some time. Not since the brass-buttoned tunic.

When he had dressed in passable attire, he kindled a fire in the hearth of what was long ago a common room for students of Applied Magics. The chattering flames cast a cheerful glow on the chamber. Bookshelves hugged the walls, and ancient furnishings stood in comfortable arrangements around the hearth. In his youth, Ely liked to imagine the lively discussions and late nights of study that must have taken place in this room. Now, he savored and lamented the solitude.

He opened the shutters, admitting silver starlight and the ghoulish grin of the full moon. The window overlooked a courtyard where stone figures surrounded an ornate fountain that sprayed a playful but deadly geyser.

Inspired by the clear night sky and his newly healed arm, Ely hurried to a shelf to retrieve his violin case. His mother had begun his music instruction when he was very small. Behind closed doors. Away from the disapproving ear of the Canon. He had found this instrument years ago while exploring the University. Dr. F allowed him to keep it as she said the practice was excellent for death magic. It kept the fingers nimble.

Ely returned to the window seat and tuned his violin, its voice a sweet, silvery soprano. He played a dreamy opening. A smile, all mischief and mystery, glancing up to meet an awestruck gaze. The flutter of a foolish heartbeat. The flirtation of greeting. The thrill of lively conversation. His sonata rose to an exuberant crescendo. Then the tempo slowed. A parting. In closing, a heartbroken soliloquy.

As silence overtook the room, a shiver prickled from his neck down his spine like ghostly fingers. Ely looked up, a shimmer in the air catching his eye. It wasn't a shadow. Nor was it a solid shape.

"Hello?" Ely called.

The phantom moved from the fireside toward the window, undulating as though it were trying to assume corporeal form. The voice emerged muffled and distorted but with clear enunciation. "Elyssandro."

"Yes?" he replied.

His heart battered against his ribs. It was the same voice that had startled him into falling as he attempted to climb down into the cavern.

Whatever it was, this being had followed him through Death's Vale and back home.

The shimmer brightened, and the voice emerged again. "Help me."

Ely stood, setting his violin on the window seat.

"Who are you? How can I help you?" he asked.

The phantom shuddered again and vanished. Ely looked about the room, but he no longer felt the other presence.

Chapter Two

THE DROWNED HORDE

Ely met Sir Ambrose Quinn outside his stuccoed apartment building near the square. The balcony overlooking their secluded portico overflowed with magnificent blooms in shades of blue, violet, and black. They were cultivated by the famed Evangeline Clay who still tended her garden despite being dead some thousand years.

They sat at a little round table with a worn Caj board between them. Today, Quinn wore a fine burgundy doublet and a jaunty cap with an exceptionally plush gold feather. Ely imagined he cut quite a romantic figure before the Curse rendered him in this skeletal form. His voice was the sort of smooth baritone that would make a lion purr, and he had an undeniable flair for the poetic.

Quinn divided the tiles between them. Then they took an extended silence as they worked out possible combinations.

"Feel free to start if you have a move," said Quinn, jaw bone flexing in the memory of a smile.

Ely laid his opening set. Not a glorious hand, but a rather clever beginning.

Quinn tapped a fingerbone to his chin. He rearranged a few of his concealed tiles then revealed his own opening. Ely winced. Perhaps he had been hasty in applauding himself.

He paused to rethink his arrangement and laid a new set. Quinn pushed his tiles into place on the board, collecting enough pieces to leave Ely's set looking like a broken-toothed mosaic. Ely grunted. He rearranged his tiles and added three more to the board. Quinn inclined his bony head and eliminated all three of Ely's fresh tiles along with two more for good measure.

"You seem out of sorts today, Elyssandro. Are you fatigued?" Quinn asked.

"A little. I didn't manage to sleep last night," he said. Not the reason for his poor playing but as good a scapegoat as any.

"Troubling dreams?" Quinn continued.

Ely shook his head. "Have you heard of any spirits haunting the University?" he asked.

Quinn considered a moment. "Only the lower dormitories. Not the campus itself. Have you had a visitation?"

Ely narrated his encounter with the incorporeal being. Quinn listened with interest, tilting his skull to the side and folding his phalanges together.

"It isn't a ghost. I'm almost certain," Ely concluded.

"It sounds like a casting," Quinn remarked.

"Casting?" Ely echoed with a frown.

"Projecting one's mind across physical distances," Quinn explained. "It was a useful form of communication for the magically inclined back in the old days. Startling, to be sure, but not uncommon."

"Interesting," Ely mused.

"I'm sure Dr. Faidra can recount the finer points for you," Quinn said. Then he wiped Ely's set from the board, dealing a swift defeat. "Rematch?"

After losing twice more, Ely returned to the University. He drained the dregs of distilled starlight from his flask on the walk, wondering what he wouldn't give for a full board of heavy tavern fare. Roast duck. Lamb with mint. Summer squash and charred garlic. Mincemeat pie.

"What are you brooding about, Ruadan?" The disembodied voice nearly stopped his heart. "I've been waiting three fucking hours in the dark."

No, not a phantom. The snarl belonged to a familiar and thoroughly solid figure striding toward him down the hall with a razor-toothed smile. Rión Twin Axes.

At the moment, her eyes shone red as rubies, signifying she was alert but comfortable. As with all members of her race, the outer surface of her eyes were black not white, and the color of her irises shifted between a scintillating array of hues that mirrored her emotions. Her hair, stone gray like her skin, was braided high in the center of her head and shaved at the sides to display lines of glyphs tattooed along her scalp. As her name suggested, she bore twin axes at her hips.

"Riri!" he grinned.

"Starshine!" the Etrugan warrior boomed as she engulfed him in a bone-cracking embrace. She was a head taller and pure muscle. Ely didn't mind the pain in the least.

"God's tits, it seems ages since I've seen your face," Rión said, releasing him.

"I could say the same of you," Ely beamed. "Have you gotten taller?"

"New boots," Rión replied, holding up her leather-clad foot for his admiration. "I can walk a hundred leagues without a single shiteating blister. Get yourself a pair, and you might almost meet me at eye level."

The Etrugan burst into throaty laughter like a thunderstorm.

"Pour me a fucking drink, little brother. It's been a long journey, and I am thirsty."

Rión hailed from Fjarat, a rocky fortress near the border of the Vale. Though Etrugan villages predated human civilizations by several millennia, mankind still came to believe they held some divine right to this continent. The Canon Protectorate had originally formed to drive out the Etrugans and establish human reign. Free from demons. Free from magic.

The pair made their way down winding flights of stairs to the ground floor of the University. Whatever else it had destroyed, the Curse had not touched the liquor stores. They took their bottle out to the courtyard.

An enormous beast met them as they emerged. She resembled a wolf carved from smoke, eyes glowing with pale fire. Where Rión journeyed, Sigranja often followed. The firewolf had been no more than a pup when Ely first saw her, but now she all but knocked him from his feet as she rubbed her great head across his chest, yowling and grunting.

"Good to see you too, Siggy," he laughed, scratching the beast behind the ears.

Ely and Rión sat by the fountain with its magnificent, poisonous blooms. He poured them each a generous dram. They drank, and he poured another.

"How are your daughters?" Ely asked.

Her eyes shifted from crimson to rich, pride-filled purple as she proclaimed, "Strong. Ariadna fights better than others twice her age, and Brindle can weave spells from no more than dust motes in the air. They would send human children running in fear."

Ely smiled. "I would expect no less. What brings you to Dianessa then?"

"The spellwork has worn off my best battleaxe. I left it with Dr. Faidra," she replied.

"It really has been a long time, then," Ely remarked.

"It's tasted a lot of templar blood since I saw you last," Rión replied, eyes now engulfed in lethal jade. They shifted to entreating gold as she continued, "We need the stars on our side."

Ely glanced back at the University walls. "Is that why you're here?" he whispered.

Rión gave a nearly imperceptible nod. Standing, she said, "Shall we take a walk? I would like to get a look at the city."

Ely stood. Siggy trotted in front of them, waving her smoky tail as they left the University grounds. Embers sparked from her lolling tongue.

They remained in silence while still in sight of the looming campus. Ely couldn't guess how many times they had taken this route over the years. Rión had been visiting Dianessa since they were both children. Back then she came with her mother, Xaris the Hammer, who brought her gargantuan weapons to have their spells replenished. The pair of them had their run of the campus while Xaris shared news with Dr.

Faidra or holed up in the University library. When they needed to exchange secrets, the fast friends stole down into the city, losing any unwanted ears in the maze of alleyways.

"Tell me what's happening out there," Ely said at last.

"The Canon has taken to raiding our villages, stealing children for their work camps," Rión spat. "The Séoc tell us that the seas are teaming with templar vessels. They say the Council of Free Cities still refuses to acknowledge the Canon as anything other than a radical cult. That cock of a nameless god is of little concern to them."

"They think it is a problem for Fjarat and the Barrier Keys," Ely commented.

"In truth, they would be happy to see us fall," Rión growled. She looked up at him. "Every day the eye and blade moves closer to Fjarat. They no longer fear us."

"You think I could change that?" Ely asked.

Rión shook her head. "Not you, little brother."

Ely nodded, understanding. The Etrugans believed it was Morgata, goddess of death and the night sky, that took hold of him when he no longer remained in control of the flow of death magic. As far as he knew, it was true. Something else did move through him, guiding the destruction that followed. He felt the other presence reverberating inside his skull. Part of him, yet separate. Always at the ready. It whispered in his ear. A multitude of voices chorused in one. He feared them. Perhaps that was the human in him. The Etrugans respected and welcomed his power as mankind never had.

"She won't let me go," Ely said. "You know how she is when it comes to the Canon."

Dr. Faidra took all pains to keep him far away from the templars when they came sniffing through the Vale. He liked to think it was her way of showing affection.

"You're a grown man. Must you ask her fucking permission?" Rión hissed.

"Don't you remember what happened the last time I thought I could turn the tide against them?" Ely demanded.

"It wasn't the Canon that–"

"I know!" Ely snapped before she could finish.

His vision clouded, and he felt himself begin to slip away. He clenched his hands into fists and drew slow, measured breaths.

"I'm sorry, Riri," he murmured.

"No, I should learn when to hold my fucking tongue. I know what it cost you." Rión laid a gentle, calloused hand on his arm. "You don't have to come to Fjarat, although you are missed, little brother. I thought about it on the journey. Even a whisper of Morgata's presence would be enough to give them pause."

"I can send effigies back with you," Ely mused. "They won't last long, I'm afraid."

Rión gave a grateful smile, her eyes ruby red with excitement. "They don't need to. I'll take whatever I can get."

Ely's mind throbbed as they plodded back to the University. Thoughts stirred into a frenzy. It wasn't Rión's fault that he had almost lost control. His injury-induced fever had already released memories he kept under lock and key. He had not realized how near the edge he stood until that moment.

Rión, who had already deposited her luggage in the east wing, unpacked a rainbow assortment of dried fruit, salt-roasted nuts, cured meat, and some kind of hard cheese suited to survive an apocalypse. Ely broke out another thousand-year-old bottle of zaqual, and they laid out their feast in the common room. Siggy curled up before a roaring fire, sitting up every now and again for a scrap of food or a scratch behind the ears.

"I know the dead aren't exactly silent, but don't you ever miss having warm-blooded companionship?" Rión asked, leaning back to look at him. "Eating? Drinking? Fucking?"

"Of course," Ely said. "But you do get used to it after a while."

"I sure as shit wouldn't. When was the last time you left Death's Vale?" Rión demanded.

"You know when," he answered, not wanting to trouble this subject.

She fell silent, face sober. Cautious.

Ely stared at a scuff on the floor, jaw tight. Finally, he replied. "My place is here, whether I am content or not."

Rión watched him. Her eyes shifted between hues before she decided to lay the matter to rest.

"Whatever you say, Ruadan," she shrugged.

Rión sprawled out on a sturdy chaise, hands clasped behind her head. "I'll just have to travel this way more frequently to see that you're fed."

"You've become your mother at last," Ely laughed.

"I should dream as much," she replied, settling back and closing her eyes. "My mother is a fucking legend."

Xaris the Hammer was tall and broad as a mountain, silver braids shot through with cobalt. One leg, cast of steel, was etched with powerful glyphs and carved in the likeness of a cloven hoof. A tribute to Zygos, the horned god of war and fucking. Whenever Ely had been fortunate enough to sit at her table, she prompted him to "Eat, scrawny human!" until he was certain he would burst.

Ely chuckled at the memory. He glanced at his companion, but she was already fast asleep. He had just drifted off himself when a whisper jolted him back to consciousness.

"Elyssandro."

He sat bolt upright and surveyed the empty room. Siggy was already on her feet, fiery eyes fixed on a viscous shimmer that floated in the air. It stretched and bent, assuming a near human shape.

"Who are you?" Ely asked.

The phantom lifted its hand and motioned him to follow before disappearing through the door. Ely rushed into the corridor. Siggy bounded after him. The phantom glided swiftly in front of them, its light flickering along the stone walls. They entered the second floor library. It was cold as a winter midnight, and the air smelled earthy and tomblike.

The phantom wavered, then vanished.

"Wait," Ely called.

Siggy barked at the empty air.

Thud.

Ely turned to the book that now lay on the floor beside him. He set it on a table, wiping thin, filmy ash from its binding. It appeared to contain at least a thousand pages of tiny handwritten text. The scholar that had inscribed this volume seemed to be more concerned about speed than ensuring their scribbling could be deciphered later on.

"If there's some clue hidden in here, you're going to have to do better than this," he said.

Siggy yipped a warning, and Ely ducked just in time. The projectile turned out to be a scroll of heavy drafting paper. He unrolled it and examined the schematic. The diagram showed a branching figure like a great tree with roots of gears and levers.

"If you want help with engineering, you're better off asking Dr. Faidra," Ely said to the darkness.

He heard a growl of annoyance and muffled swearing.

"My apologies," Ely chuckled.

The book flipped open. Pages fluttered. When they settled, he read:

Transcribed letter from Abbess Mary Chastity to Magistrate Gaius Cassius:

Your Eminence, I must regretfully inform you that your request could not be fulfilled as desired. You have asked to be apprised of the whereabouts and activities of the Necromancer Ariel Marcellus, but no such person exists. Of course, I am familiar with Prator Tiberius Marcellus, or more particularly with his violent death. I searched the name records. There was a Petros Marcellus born to Tiberius and Lucretia Marcellus in the Summer of the Thousand Martyrs. Petros was to inherit his father's position and property in Saint Laurel as the Prator's only son. Early on, he showed promise as a worker of Miracles and was sent to train at the Seminary in White Spire. I had to request access to the Forbidden Archives to obtain any

> surviving records. It is reported that he was the most gifted student ever to attend White Spire. "He has the makings of a High Apostle." Those are the words of Cleric Cyrillus under whose leadership the school stood at that time. Indeed he was an inducted Apostle. He served in Marikej and trained with Apostle Galan Prosperus at Calurion. He commanded legions in the Western Wars. Why does he have no Epistle? Since we have no record for Ariel Marcellus, I assigned Sister Anointia at Watch for Petros. She says he lives, but he cannot be located.

"So who am I speaking with?" Ely asked. "Are you a Watcher?"

Vestal Watchers were rumored to be the eyes and ears of the Canon. A sisterhood of spies who meditated into a trancelike state that let them peer in on the lives of whomever they chose to track.

The silence seemed peeved at his guess, and he swore he heard a despairing hiss in the shape of, "Idiot."

"This story is about you, then?" Ely conjectured. "Petros?"

Something flew across the room and struck him square between the eyes.

Ely rubbed his forehead. "No? Then you're the one that doesn't exist. Ariel Marcellus."

"Finally!" The exclamation echoed from the walls.

Siggy howled in alarm.

"Pleasure to meet you, Ariel," Ely said dryly. "So, if this account is correct, you're like me."

Silence, but no objects thrown.

"Are you dead?" Ely asked.

The air glittered and rippled as the voice replied, "Trapped."

"Where?" Ely asked.

The phantom faded, and the voice distorted. He could not make out what it said. Then something in the air changed. She was gone.

Ely took the book and the rolled up schematic back to the east wing. He sat in the window seat to read. Siggy curled up next to him, laying her hazy bulk on his feet.

After a hundred pages of the scribe's excruciating penmanship left him no closer to learning more about his phantom visitor, he found the sun peering in through the window.

"What are you doing, Ruadan?" Rión yawned, sitting up and stretching.

"Solving a mystery," Ely said. "Or rather, *not* solving it."

Rión bared her teeth, squinting against the dawn light. "Are you going to tell me what the fuck that means, or shall I just put the coffee on?"

"It's a long story."

Rión shrugged and fetched a package of ground coffee from one of her knapsacks. The thousand year old press left behind by some sophisticated student of magic still worked wonders after all this time.

As they sipped their brews from cracked mugs, Ely recounted the tale of the earthquake, the voice in the wilderness that followed him back to entreat his help, and the previous night's visitation.

"Well, starshine," Rión assessed. "If this story is old enough to be written down by a scholar and tucked away here in the library, then it is a millennium old at least. You are dealing with another poor soul cheated out of her life by the Curse."

"She's like me," Ely said.

"Weren't they all like you? The Cosmologists?"

Ely frowned. Of course. The Tower. He always felt something crying out from the darkness of the ruins. Perhaps these visitations were the remnants of a Cosmologist trapped in astral form after the Curse. What had Quinn called it? A casting.

"You're right," Ely nodded. Leave it to Rión Twin Axes to snatch the simplest explanation out of the air.

After a leisurely breakfast and a visit to Sir Ambrose Quinn, they found Dr. Faidra waiting for them with Rión's enormous battleaxe.

"It was in very bad shape," the doctor chided. "You're lucky it didn't shatter."

Rión shifted from foot to foot, voice tense as she replied. "Yes, ma'am. Thank you, Dr. Faidra."

Ely held back a chuckle. It was a rare sight to see the fearsome warrior so nervous, but Dr. Faidra never failed to put the fear of named gods in her.

"Give your mother my regards," Dr. Faidra croaked, then stalked away.

Rión stayed the night, then she and Ely set out just before sunrise, leaving the dead city behind. Their journey took them into the petrified ruins of an ancient forest. Now and again a pile of bones resembling a deer or a rabbit scrambled up from the ground and followed them. They were harmless, attracted by the lure of death magic. Siggy growled and batted away squeaking rat skeletons that ventured too close. Once, they caught sight of an eagle soaring overhead, its wing feathers intact but rib bones gleaming white.

A great river, wide and deep enough to accommodate half a dozen ships, cut a muddy swathe through the forest. The River Scythe ran all the way from the stormy sea, curving around the western lip of the Vale and coming to rest near the fringe of the dead city. Long ago a highway for shipping goods in and out of Dianessa, the River Scythe's poisoned currents were now as deadly as its name.

The broken hull of a Canon ship protruded from the water, shredded crimson sails draped like blood over a splintered mast. Ely knelt on the shore out of reach of the water and sank his fingers into the silt bank. Connected to the earth, he sent a gentle pulse that returned echoes as it bounced from the multitudes of bones lodged in the depths of the riverbed. Death reared to escape his grasp. Hungry in the presence of their own handiwork. Ely relinquished control. White clouds consumed his vision, death magic flowing like roots into the ground.

The lazy current began to ripple and boil. Rounded skulls, slick with moss, appeared above the water. Then bodies wrapped in ragged templar red emerged, marching to answer Death's summons. They lined up in three ranks on the shore, standing at attention. The effigies were not alive. Not even undead. Just puppets awaiting their new captain.

Ely held out his hand to Rión who gripped it without fear or hesitation. The tether that connected the animate corpses coiled around her wrist, sinking into her gray skin and leaving a jagged black ring like a thorny bracelet.

"All yours," Ely said, struggling to catch his breath as his eyes cleared.

She raised a fist. The effigies stamped their feet as one, shouting the Etrugan war chant above the din of the river. Rión nodded, satisfied with her new toys.

"A million fucking thanks would not be near enough, starshine," she declared.

Ely watched his friend disappear around the bend, her gruesome battalion marching behind her. It would be years, he knew, before he saw her face again. He tried not to dwell on it, but it was all he could seem to think about as he began the journey back to the University. It was hardly lonely back home. In fact, it was often overcrowded. Still, the brief reminder of life among the living reignited too many desires that had been suppressed.

Twilight overtook him while he was still a considerable distance from the city. He didn't want to go back just yet. In fact, his path had somehow deviated north. In the distance, flat plains shipwrecked against the jagged bones of a mountain ridge. The Spine it was called.

"Odd," he commented to a corpse that had just sat up from among the rocks. "I must have confused the way."

The decaying creature snuffled at him, bloody eyes absent spark. One of the reasonless, hostile dead common in these outlying wastes. It jerked to its feet. Unnatural electricity radiated from it, projecting volatility. Pain.

"Rest," Ely said as he flexed his fingers.

A mantle of black ether billowed around the feral corpse. It stopped, blinking in confusion. Then its eyes slid closed, and it sighed in relief before collapsing motionless on the ground. Ely turned a pondering eye back to the Spine. For whatever reason, the craggy range was ripe for ruptures. Most had healed well and now provided entry to a collection of fascinating places.

"But where to go?" Ely mused.

Somewhere from which he had yet to be banished. Not Marikej. Far too hot and a recent acquisition of the Canon Protectorate. Definitely not Coldwater Forge. They would ready a fire to burn him at the stake the moment they caught sight of him.

"There's always the Zephyr," he said.

His favorite establishment, the Zephyr Tavern, lay in the seediest edge of the sprawling city of Mondacca. It was owned by Daysha Osai, a formidable woman with the warmest smile and the coldest scowl. She roasted whole pigs in pits and smoked juicy fowl and racks of ribs in fire-blasted metal contraptions she constructed herself. Her wife, Esperanza, baked bread in a clay oven and made stews and curries in a steamy little hut adjacent to the cook yard. Ely could rent a room above the tavern for a few coins taken from the corroded safe in the dean's office. He always carried some out of habit. No one recognized the mint, but they didn't seem to care. Gold was gold.

"So it's decided, then," he declared and set out toward the Spine.

Chapter Three

The Haunting of Skylark Manor

The moon swelled full over the jagged ridges. Brush and vine twisted a violent chokehold about the stone, the air thick with dust and sweet mildewed decay. Ely pressed on well after nightfall. It was more than just the promise of food and merry company that lent vigor to his stride. He had almost forgotten the way the stars whispered here. The air shivered with magic.

The way to Mondacca lay halfway up the second ridge at the edge of a dreamy lagoon. Ely recalled his first glimpse of that rupture, glimmering like a haunted mirror where pale spirits drew up from the inky depths to gaze at the hazy shadows of the city beyond. Seventeen. Maybe give or take a year. Still headstrong and audacious to the brim.

"What's beyond the shimmer?" an ethereal voice trembled in the air.

The being it belonged to appeared as no more than a white mist that swirled above the surface of the lagoon, making gentle ripples in the black water.

"I don't know yet," Ely said. "But I'll tell you what I find."

The spirit made a sound like a gasp as he summoned his black armor about him.

"You're shiny too," they laughed. "Tell Fiera all you see, conjurer!"

Ely stepped through. One foot landed in refuse heaped in a dingy marketplace alley. He took in the cacophony with grinning wonder. Wading among stalls, he dodged bawling hawkers and gaily painted women beckoning from street corners. This seedy, sinful port was unlike anyplace he had laid eyes on.

When he returned, he found Fiera waiting, eager to hear every detail about the food, the pleasure houses, the Caj tables. Gaudy women flaunting voluptuous merchandise and rough characters that drew pistols at the slightest disagreement.

It was a balmy spring night upon his next visit. He strode through the red-trimmed doors of a brothel, carrying a knapsack full of ancient gold. No one seemed to observe the nervous flutter of his hands or the subtle tension in his brow. Raw nerves hidden behind a mask of vigor. Corseted beauties, shining hair aflutter, bosoms overflowing, surrounded him, all eager to befriend the young man with the overburdened purse.

"What's your name, handsome?"

"Elyssandro? Sounds foreign. Are you from up north?"

"You like what you see, brown eyes? You'll like it better unlaced."

"Who's that playing? Sure thing, sugar. Charlaine! Give this fine gentleman a serenade."

The raven-haired siren with the green tiger eyes caught his gaze from her seat at the piano. She delivered the rest of her song to him like she meant every word. Then she left her instrument and approached. A cat stalking very willing prey.

Her smile worked potent, unfamiliar magic that brought blood to his cheeks. He followed her upstairs to discover a new kind of spell. Fiera listened to the story, fascinated, though they didn't quite grasp the concept of physical sensation.

Ely returned to Mondacca often, widening his radius of exploration at the insistence of his spirit friend. The swollen Gateway River divided the city into two distinct walks of life. On Portside, tumbledown shanties and open air markets stretched all the way to the bay, wrapping about the coastline as far as the eye could see. Across the bridge stood Kingsbank where decadent villas peered out over the gulf from the bluffs. Below, elegant shops, restaurants, and theatres bustled with a well-dressed patronage. There Ely collected tales for Fiera of princesses and promenades. Grand balls. Horse races. Operas.

Wherever he turned up, people welcomed his presence, a little too warmly at times. A curious side effect of death magic. In one memorable incident, a baker's wife lured him into the back kitchen with the promise of pie only to drop her dress by the blazing oven. In another, a wealthy baron with a penchant for painting promised him a villa by the sea if he would stay and become his muse. Fiera laughed and laughed when Ely told them the stories.

Then one day, Ely approached the Mondacca rupture, and Fiera did not appear. He called to the other spirits that stirred lazily beneath the surface of the lake. They ignored him. He closed his eyes, mind submerged in the dark water. Fiera was not there. They were gone.

"Where is Fiera?" he demanded.

He sent blasts of sparking ether into the lagoon until finally a voice hissed, "Fiera went through the shimmer."

Ely's blood ran cold. The city of Mondacca stood completely modern. It had no room for the unexplained. In all his travels there, he had not encountered even a whisper of magic save for the stars. He hurried through the portal, tuning out the noise and bustle as he searched for his friend. Had they even survived the rupture? Were they lost in the fold between?

Then he felt it. The slightest tingle of a familiar presence.

Ely set out, searching, calling their name until the road changed from hard-packed dirt to pristine pavement at the bridge. He caught a ride across to Kingsbank on a cart of filigreed panels just offloaded from a ship and ready for delivery to a spice merchant's mansion.

His quest led him along a meandering road to a palatial house far removed from the city. Each wing was constructed of a different material. South corner: rustic wood. East wing: thin layered shale. West cupola: tan stucco. North suite: red brick caped in thick green ivy. A gleaming metal dome protruded from the central hub, its polished surface reflecting the sunlight like a great beacon. With their fixation on all things shiny, it was no wonder Fiera had found their way here.

Ely marched up to the sprawling domicile's front door and rang the bell. A young woman with a sweet round face, eyes like sapphires, and hair as red as a summer sunrise answered.

"Not who I was expecting, but you'll do," she said, then ushered him inside.

He found himself in a grand foyer with marble floors and columns. A skylight high above streamed vibrant light through stained glass.

"I'm Leanora," she said, bell-like voice echoing.

"Elyssandro," he returned, swiveling his head to take in the statues, plants, and curiosities that filled the cavernous space.

Leanora led him through an angled doorway into a dim, lamp-lit hall. No, not lamps. Glass-enclosed lights that burned without flames. They looked like the magic-fueled crystals that Dr. Faidra illuminated back home, but they hummed with strange currents that vibrated in his teeth. Lightning? Electricity! He remembered talk of electric lights in the ballet box.

They entered a library with shelves spanning rounded walls. Leanora led him up a spiraling staircase to a platform where a long brass telescope adorned with gears and nobs extended toward a high, sunny window.

"I have all the calculations, but I can't reach the blasted lens cap," she fumed. Despite her bold demeanor, the top of her head barely reached his chest.

Ely smiled and unscrewed the cap. She laughed with delight then adjusted the telescope, gasping as she looked into it.

"There it is! It looks close enough to touch. Come see!"

She pushed Ely to the eyepiece. He broke into a grin at the sight of the silver comet, its glorious flag ablaze behind it.

"Incredible," he exclaimed.

"Corrigan's Comet," she said, once again peering into the telescope. "It can only be seen by the naked eye every ninety years, but from where it is presently in its orbit, I was able to tune the scope for a perfect view. It just needed a few adjustments."

"Remarkable," Ely smiled.

"So." She straightened up. "What brings you to Skylark Manor? A friend of Victor's, perhaps? He said he was inviting a few from South Sea, but I didn't think they were arriving until next week."

"Victor is your...?" Ely led.

"Brother. Can't you tell? Are you a student?" she questioned.

Ely nodded. That was true enough.

"What subject? No. Don't tell me. I have a knack for reading people." She scrutinized him carefully. "Fashion forward. Too avant-garde for science. Literature? Philosophy? I'll sniff it out. Your accent is interesting. You're not from Mondacca, but you don't sound like a midlander either."

"I–" he began.

"Don't tell me, Elyssandro."

He chuckled. "Alright then, tell me about you."

"I am an Astronomy Fellow at Jade Hill," she told him.

"Where is that?"

"You're joking." She waited for him to laugh. "You're not joking. You really are from far away. Good gracious, you're from the Protectorate aren't you?"

"Saint Lucio," Ely nodded.

"I knew it!" she crowed. "Well, then, my foreign friend, Jade Hill is the premiere institution for scientific research on the continent. It's located in the heart of Zantos about six hours by train."

Ely was about to ask her what "train" might be when the doorbell clanged.

Leanora beamed. "Excuse me a moment, Elyssandro. I have Fellows to greet."

Ely followed her back down the stairs. When her footsteps died away in the hall, he called out quietly, "Fiera?"

He closed his eyes, seeking their presence in the vast house.

"Come on, Fiera, this is no place for you!" he hissed.

No response.

Ely sighed then occupied himself with the rows upon rows of books all neatly cataloged by author and topic. It reminded him of the University library, except far less dust and not a single mention of magic.

Voices buzzed in the hallway, and Leanora reappeared with four companions, all young, bright-eyed, and neatly dressed.

There were Étienne and Javier who studied Art and Literature respectively at the Classics Academy in Mondacca. They appeared as flamboyant peacocks in bright satin and patterned silk. Ada and Yves attended Jade Hill with Leanora. Ada was pale as Yves was dark, but with their matching gray suits and contemplative expressions, they resembled one another more than they did the other guests. The arriving Fellows eyed Ely with curiosity as they entered the observatory.

"Elyssandro is a guest of Victor's," Leanora explained.

"Where is Victor?" Étienne asked before Ely could set her assumption straight.

"He'll be along. He stopped in Brightwater to see some girl," Leanora replied with a roll of her eyes.

"Damn, is it serious?" Étienne inquired, taking a neatly rolled cigarette from a gold case.

"Victor is never serious. Don't smoke in here, Teensy. Father will have my head."

The bell jangled again, and they were soon joined by another group of Fellows. Jamien, Hannah, and Roan studied at Jade Hill. Nireen, Gregoire, and Clara hailed from the Judicial Academy in Montalbany.

As their discourse soared, Ely sensed the frantic pulse of a frightened spirit. Fiera had never been around so many fleshly beings before, much less the din of conversation. The study lights began to flicker. No one noticed at first, but as the flashing grew more insistent, all eyes turned upward.

"Looks like you have a ghost, Lea," Teensy tittered.

"I'll have to get Stephens to see to the wiring," Leanora commented.

With that, the Fellows disbursed, floating off to pursue conversation in more intimate corners.

Leanora caught Ely's eye and shook her head with a good-natured smile. "Ghosts indeed. Can you imagine? That's an Art Fellow for you."

Ely laughed, unsure what else to say in response. She was charming, and he did not want to dampen her smile with the news that she did, in fact, have haunted wiring.

"Of course it would happen on my turn to host the Fellows," she lamented. "We haven't had a spot of trouble even during the storms."

"Fate has a sense of humor, they say," Ely offered.

"Fate," Leanora snorted. "You're funny, Elyssandro." Her eyes narrowed in thought. "Which means you're not a Fellow of Arithmetics."

Ely shook his head, confirming her deduction.

"I'm sorry my brother isn't here to keep you company," Leanora continued. "Typical Victor. I'll find some way to entertain you once I've called Stephens for this electrical disaster."

"I'll be fine," Ely assured her.

She scrutinized him again. "Independent and confident. Histrionics? No, you're too reserved. I will figure you out."

Ely watched her flutter away, her kitten heels tapping on the marble floor. His smile faded to a sigh as he considered that she probably would figure him out all too soon.

A blinking light caught his eye near one of the bookshelves. Ely approached.

"Fiera?" he whispered.

The light sputtered then fell dark.

"Fiera, flash twice if you can understand me."

The light blinked to life then fell dark, then again once more.

"Fiera, this place is not safe for you. You have to come back with me."

The light shuddered and flashed as though desperately trying to tell him something.

"Are you stuck?" Ely asked. "Flash twice if you're trapped."

Blink. Blink.

Ely nodded. "Alright. Stay calm. I'll figure something out."

The light buzzed so violently that the glass burst. Ely threw a hand in front of his face. A shard stung his palm. When he opened his eyes again, he caught sight of a distinct trail of flickers racing away down the hall.

"Damn it all," he hissed.

"Everything alright, Elyssandro?" Leanora's voice spooked him.

"Yes, fine," he replied, forcing a smile. "That light shattered. It was...startling."

"Oh dear, you're bleeding!" she exclaimed, taking his hand.

"Just a nick," he shrugged. "I've had worse."

"Have you?" She eyed him. "Culinary Arts?"

Ely laughed. "I wouldn't test that theory."

Leanora flashed a saucy grin. "Come on, let's get you fixed up, shall we?"

She took him to a cozy study and sat him in a stiff-backed chair. After a moment's disappearance, she returned with a walnut case that contained bandages, ointments, and various medical supplies.

"It looks like there's still a bit of glass in here," she assessed.

Leanora found a pair of tweezers in the case and gingerly probed the cut.

"Does that hurt?" she asked, brow furrowed with concern.

"Not at all," he replied, chuckling to himself at how gentle a nurse she was compared to Dr. Faidra.

Leanora plucked out the glass shard and wrapped his hand in a bandage.

"There," she said. "I apologize for my misbehaving lights. I'll make it up to you, I promise."

"That is very kind of you," Ely smiled.

They returned to the Fellows, most of which had gathered in a spacious parlor with a full wall of glass windows overlooking a magnificent garden.

Ely found an unobtrusive spot, seeking Fiera once again. He caught snatches of their presence, hovering just on the edge of awareness, then disappearing. Gradually, he found himself watching the youthful Fellows interact with confident ease. Leanora fluttered between them, a butterfly drifting from flower to flower, sampling conversation like nectar. She caught him watching her and waved him over.

With a tilt of her head she told him, "Javier says that of all the wonders of the world, there can be nothing more valuable than Art, but Hannah here considers Science to be the nobler pursuit. What do you think, Elyssandro?"

Ely looked between them, contemplating a moment. "Is there really a choice to be made?" he asked. "No matter which way you look at it, you can't have one without the other. A painting is shape and form and the chemistry of color. Music is waves of vibration. Magic is..." he stopped.

"Magic is what?" Javier prompted.
"Science unexplained," he managed to finish.
"Well put," Hannah commended.

Leanora just smiled with an approving nod. His contribution made, he was allowed to recede to a mere listener with no more accidental mentions of the metaphysical.

A short while later, they were taken to the dining room for delicate cucumber salad, the daintiest pheasants ever plucked, roasted summer vegetables, and to Ely's delight, mint ice cream. Then they all gathered again in the parlor for cards and more talk. Ely had just remembered he had a wayward spirit to track down when Leonora beckoned him to her.

"Can I show you something that will change your life?" she asked.

"With an offer like that, I can't very well refuse, can I?"

She beamed and took his hand. Leading him down a corridor and up a flight of stairs, Leanora drew a key from her pocket and turned the lock on a set of heavy, ornate doors.

"After you," she said, ushering him into the pitch black room and securing the doors behind them.

A switch on the wall brought the colossal space crackling into light. The room was circular with a ring of elegant chairs surrounding a deep hollow like an orchestra pit. Leanora led him around to a set of narrow steps that wound down to the nadir.

At one end of the pit, a drafting table collected a jumble of unfurled charts. Ely smiled at the calculations scribbled among the margins in blotted blue ink. The all too familiar trappings of a mad scientist.

An astounding display of mechanical implements ringed the perimeter of the pit. Leanora approached a metal contraption with layer upon layer of buttons and dials. She set to tuning them expertly, like a maestro at the piano forte. Instead of music, the rumbling echo of turning gears sounded at her command.

"My father built this," she said. "I helped with the calculations."

She turned to Ely, motioning him over, aquiver with excitement.

"Do you see that lever there?" she asked, pointing to a tier just out of her reach. "If you would kindly pull it to the second notch..."

Ely did so, and she continued, "And the black dial there, no not that one. Yes, that. Set it to seven. Good."

Leanora hurried to another control board. Her fingers swept across the surface. Then she ran to an enormous switch, pulling with both hands to wrench it into place. The lights shut off with a groan. Then she looked upward expectantly, panting from the exertion. Overhead, the ceiling shifted and split into neat sections, peeling away to reveal the night sky.

No. Not the night sky.

Ely knew the stars like his own skin. These were unfamiliar. He gasped, unable to draw breath as he gazed at the glittering expanse. The stars' light, magnified by the curved dome above, rushed over him, into him, their song filling every atom. Ely gazed up in awe. He wanted to reach out and grasp the silver beams, feel them glide through his fingers, but he resisted.

A warm touch on his arm brought him back to the earth.

"It's Dianessa's Raiment," Leanora told him. "You can't see it from anywhere else except the Skylark observatory."

"It's beautiful," he breathed.

"I didn't take you for an Astronomy Fellow, but now I think I might have been mistaken," Leanora said.

"You're not," Ely replied. "I could never keep the math straight."

Leanora laughed.

"You were right," he said, turning his eyes to her face. "It is life changing."

Her smile of quiet pleasure eclipsed the song of the heavens. Their gazes lingered. She drew a bit closer but hesitated.

Then she murmured, "I have to set this room straight or father will have my head."

Ely watched her reset the telescope, chest tight. It was strange this feeling. Hope. Dread. Excitement and terror. Frantic hummingbirds trapped in his stomach.

She caught his gaze, then grinned and pointed to the lever and dial too high for her to reach. He fixed them back in place. Leanora locked the doors behind them as they exited the observatory. They made their way back to the party, taking turns pretending not to steal a glance.

"And where have you two been?" Teensy's smirk met them as they entered the parlor.

"Looking at stars," Leanora replied.

Teensy rolled her eyes, turning a conspiratorial eye to her companion. "The tragedy is she's quite serious."

Leanora ignored her. "It's so gloomy in here. Let's put some music on, shall we?"

She strode to a brass-plumed phonograph, flicked a switch, and dropped the needle. A lively orchestra filled the parlor. Teensy dragged a bewildered Law and Justice Fellow to dance. Others followed their lead.

With her guests distracted, Leanora drew Ely to a secluded window seat with plump gold cushions. She leaned against him, listening to the music unfold. Her hand rested lightly on his knee.

"I've finally figured it out," she mused, raising sparkling blue eyes to his face. "Why nothing about you makes sense."

"Oh?" he asked. "Why is that?"

"You're undeclared," she determined with a triumphant smile.

"Aren't you clever then?" he murmured.

"Exceedingly," she whispered.

Her lips found his, all silk and Syrah. The nervous fluttering wings in his stomach turned to flames. The gentle caress of her tongue. Her fervent fingers tracing his face. Here she was doing magic without even knowing it.

Then suddenly the phonograph crackled and skipped. Its music distorted and slowed. The dancing ceased. Everyone turned toward the struggling machine.

"Still don't think you have a ghost?" Teensy asked with a nervous giggle.

Leanora shot her a withering glare. The phonograph crackled and spun again, but instead of orchestral tones, a high, panicked voice croaked, "Ely! Elyssand...! Hel...help me! Ely!"

Now all eyes veered to him.

Leanora sprang to her feet, her face scarlet as she eyed him with scathing suspicion. "Is this some sort of joke?" she demanded. "Did Victor send you ahead to play pranks?"

"No, Leanora, I–" he protested, but she was already storming about the room.

"Victor! Victor, show yourself at once! You've had your fun at my expense. Come out!"

Now the lights flickered again. Every bulb burst at once, plunging the parlor into darkness. Someone shrieked. Exclamations rose in a thundering avalanche. Teensy blubbered from somewhere nearby.

"Be quiet, all of you!" Leanora stomped into their midst carrying a lantern that emitted friendly warm light. "It's an electrical surge, nothing more. Now, there are candles and lanterns in the cupboards across the hall. Teensy, fetch the broom. Everyone lend a hand, and for goodness sake keep your heads."

With that she waved the Fellows off to set lights and sweep up glass. Ely edged toward the phonograph. It was no use. The spirit was gone.

Leanora approached, lantern swaying in her grasp. "I'm sorry," she said.

"Well, it was certainly alarming," he replied. "I can hardly blame you."

"I liked you, so I panicked."

"Liked?" he questioned.

She narrowed her eyes, humor returning to her face. "Pressing your luck, are we, sir?"

Shrill annoyance interjected, "I got the broom, Lea, what do you expect me to do with it?"

Leanora glared at Teensy, who continued to stare at her in obstinate defiance of the hint.

"I can sweep up the glass," Ely offered, holding his hand out for the broom just to break the tension.

"Aren't you a gentleman? Thank you, Elyssandro." Teensy gave him a coquette smile as she passed him the broom, to Leanora's audible irritation.

Teensy turned as if to leave, then paused. "Did you ever figure out why the phonograph knows your name?" she asked him.

"Honestly, Teensy, you're working my last nerve," Leanora growled.

Teensy ignored her. "It's funny, he shows up, a mysterious foreigner that no one seems to know, except, quite conveniently, Victor, and now we're haunted."

"If I hear one more mention of ghosts or ghouls or haunted phonographs, I'll feed your tongue to my fish!" Leanora barked.

Teensy cackled at her threat. In the same instant, misty white light rushed from a shattered wall fixture and directly into her gaping mouth. Teensy gasped and sputtered. Her body contorted, her skin rippling in unnatural waves.

"Fiera," Ely warned, trying to calm the panicked spirit.

Teensy shuddered. Her head flung back, and an ear-splitting howl tore from her throat. Her body rose, levitating above the ground. Then she shot across the room, hitting the door frame with a dull thud before she disappeared down the hall.

Ely raced after them, leaving Leanora behind in the parlor. He followed Fiera's sparking presence to the study where Leanora had fixed up his hand. Teensy quivered on the floor. Her arms and legs lay like snapped twigs. Blood streamed from her nose and mouth. Her chest heaved.

Ely knelt down beside her and touched her forehead. The human girl was no more than a fading ember, barely detectable behind the terrified sprite that wracked her body.

"Ely..."

The gasping voice that emerged was Fiera's.

"I'm scared, Ely. I hurt her," Fiera whimpered. "I *feel* her hurt."

"It's alright," Ely soothed. "I'm going to get you home. Trust me. Just be still."

He closed his eyes, quieting his thoughts. Assessing. There would be no saving the poor Art Fellow.

Rising to his feet, he held his hands out in silent command. The first soul slipped easily from its broken shell. Ely released Teensy into Death's care to make her journey to the stars. The second passenger proved more difficult. Fiera, unsuited for flesh, was lodged tight in the crush of cells. The body rustled and jolted, its hands and feet drumming against the floorboards. Hopeless. Death, still close at hand, sank a hooked claw into his frustration.

Let us, the pressing force said.

Ely surrendered. His eyes clouded. His fingers twisted, threading waves of death magic until the mangled corpse was engulfed in black shades. Fiera howled, then burst loose, curling into a ball of white light in Ely's hand. He unhooked his empty starlight flask from his belt and siphoned Fiera into the vessel. Death receded as the lid clanked shut.

Ely sighed, swaying on his feet. He felt hollow. At least it was over. Fiera would be safe.

An explosion echoed behind him, dropping him to his knees. Agony followed. His left arm fell useless at his side. Ely managed to keep hold of the flask in his right hand. As he looked up, he met Leanora's blazing blue eyes. She leveled a pistol at his face.

"Get away from her!" she shrieked.

Hot rivulets oozed down his arm. He was near to losing consciousness. He should leave while he had the chance. Looking up at her tear-drenched face, why did he still want to explain?

"Lea..." he pleaded.

She fired the pistol at the ceiling. "Get out, or I will kill you right here. You demon! You monster!"

The words struck deeper than the bullet. No matter how he wished otherwise, that was all he would ever be. Ely stood with a grimace. Clutching the flask, he stumbled to the door...

Prickling alarm along the back of his neck brought Ely from his unpleasant reverie. It had been foolish to wander off into memory so deep in the Spine.

A voice, smooth and dark as the night itself, called from the mountainside. "You should watch your step. You're very close to the edge."

Ely turned, death magic gathering in his palms. It seemed to be coming from above, except there was nothing that way but a sheer cliff face.

"Show yourself," Ely called.

A shadow diverged from the rock wall. It sailed overhead and made a graceful landing on the path. As the stranger stepped into the light, he appeared effervescent white as the moon overhead. Dark hair made chaos about his face. Black circles underlined wild eyes. His aural emanations felt bizarre yet so familiar. This was life arrested mid-breath. Crystallized into perilous and exquisite immortality.

"Are you well, conjurer?"

Ely withdrew his gaze.

"Forgive me. I've never met a vampire before," he said with an apologetic smile. "I'm Elyssandro Ruadan."

"Ravan Aurelio," the vampire replied, moonlight glinting from exceedingly sharp eye teeth.

"Pleasure," Ely smiled.

The vampire just blinked.

"Does Death own all the world now?" he asked.

Ely frowned. "You don't know about the Curse?"

"I've been locked in the dark. I can't say for how long," Ravan said. "A tremor in the earth set me loose some days ago."

"The rupture," Ely mused.

Ravan tilted his head, watching him with an unblinking gaze that made Ely shiver. Restless waves coursed through him like unsettled lightning.

"Can you feel me as I do you?" Ravan asked.

"Yes," Ely answered. A bit breathless, if he was being honest.

In a heartbeat, the vampire was beside him, alarmingly close. He smelled of ice and pines and something ethereal that could not be placed. If he chose to taste blood now, Ely would not resist.

No fanged sting followed, only a frozen whisper in his ear, "So strange. I felt your presence the moment I returned to this world."

The vampire restored a more comfortable distance. He looked over his shoulder like an animal alerted to danger. "Dawn is near. I'll see you again."

Then he was gone, joining the shadows as swift as a gust of wind.

Ely let out his breath. He knew death magic had its potency, but this he had never imagined. It was like passing a pipe around Etrugan solstice fires or draining a bottle of zaqual in one gulp. The sudden absence left him dizzy.

Earthquakes, phantom visitations, and now vampires?

Perhaps this was not the time for a holiday after all.

Chapter Four

THE LAST VAMPIRE

"Back so soon?" Dr. Faidra's dry voice greeted him at the doorway. The Oubliette seemed especially dirty today. Coarse metal dust heaped in mounds around her work bench. It appeared the doctor was building something new.

"I was only sending Rión on her way," Ely said. "What are you working on?"

Dr. F grunted, not pausing her stylus strokes. "Something to monitor our excessive seismic activity."

Ely pulled up a chair to sit.

Dr. F looked up over her glasses with undisguised irritation. "Is there something you need, warm blood? Are you injured again?"

"What do you know about vampires?" Ely asked.

"They were allergic to sunlight and fed on human blood," Dr. F intoned, more acrid sarcasm than usual.

"I met one," Ely said.

This caught her attention. She even set down her stylus and looked up at him with milky, bloodshot eyes.

"You what?"

"Last night. I was walking in the Spine–"

"What were you doing there?" Dr. F interrupted.

"Reminiscing," Ely replied. "He said he's been trapped all this time and that the tremor set him loose. The one that caved in the north wing."

"Did he have a name, this vampire?" Dr. F asked.

"Ravan Aurelio," Ely said.

Ely had never before seen Dr. Selene Faidra look rattled. Teeth bared. Chest heaving, drawing breath not out of necessity but pure shock.

"You know him?" Ely asked.

"Yes. He is very dangerous, Elyssandro. You're going to need protection."

Her chair screeched on the floor, and she began rummaging through her shelves.

"He seemed...odd but reasonable," Ely commented. "A little inconsiderate of personal space."

"The only reason you are still alive is because a thousand years of imprisonment will have weakened him," Dr. F stated, then returned to rummaging.

"What did he do?" Ely asked.

"Ravan Aurelio wreaked bloody terror on Dianessa," Dr. Faidra told him. "He slaughtered babes in their cradles and women at their work. The Cosmologists finally trapped him and locked him in the caves deep in the Spine. Ah, here."

The doctor brought an ornate ebony box inlaid with silver back to her work bench. She carefully opened the lid. A glassy mirrorwood stake lay nestled in blue velvet. She handed it to Ely.

"Keep this with you," she instructed. "Aim for the heart. Anywhere else will only enrage him."

Ely frowned at the instrument. The strange markings carved from handle to point were not common glyphs used in Applied Magics. These were sharp. Lethal. Death magic in written form.

"You didn't make this," Ely observed.

"No," she shook her head. "The Cosmologists carried them as a rule. I didn't think there were any vampires left after the Curse. It would appear that Ravan's imprisonment saved him. A most unfortunate turn of events."

Ely rolled the smooth stake over in his hand, revisiting the encounter in the Spine. He remembered the intoxicating thrill of the vampire's presence, the underlying danger in his soothing tones, but not the devious evil with which Dr. Faidra seemed to equate him. He certainly didn't want to use this implement on a being that was the last of his kind.

From the look on Dr. F's face, she would not be receptive to his reluctance, so he placed the stake in his inside coat pocket and said, "Well, you've given me a great deal to ponder. But first I'm going to get some sleep. Enjoy your project."

Dr. Faidra's voice followed him toward the door. "You've never been in company with vampires before, Elyssandro. They are cunning with motives behind their motives. Remember that."

Ely nodded and exited the Oubliette, for once relieved to regain his solitude. Weariness set in as he returned to the east wing common room. He had not slept the previous night, and the sun was once again preparing its descent.

He kicked off his shoes, threw his coat around the back of an armchair, and collapsed on the chaise. Despite his exhaustion, sleep evaded him. He tossed and turned, mind awhirl with the events of the past few days. Who could have guessed that the tremor that shook him from his bed would turn his entire world on its head?

With a sigh, he rose and fetched the book that Ariel Marcellus had hurled at him. Perhaps he would have better luck tonight finding the answers hidden in its dusty pages. An hour's labor proved his optimism misguided.

He exchanged the book for his violin. Music cleared the cobwebs from his mind and eased the tension headache that had been creeping on.

Ely paused to yawn, and his stomach rumbled. A few days of real food had undone years of disciplined abstinence. He set down his instrument, trying to decide if he should eat the remainder of the provisions Rión had left behind or collapse into bed.

"That was beautiful."

The languid voice over his shoulder sent his heart leaping into his throat. He knew the intruder before he turned. Ravan had taken up residence on the armchair. His feet were bare. In fact, his entire costume was exceedingly simple. Earth-toned linen with a plain high-collared jacket.

"You don't mind do you?" the vampire asked. "The window was open. I never could resist music."

"Not at all, Ravan," Ely said, setting his violin back in its case.

"It's Rav, please," the vampire corrected. He looked almost alive when he smiled.

"Rav," Ely echoed.

His thoughts strayed for a moment to the stake resting in the coat draped behind Rav's head. He wondered if the vampire had selected that seat on purpose.

"I saw the Tower lying in ruins at the bottom of a chasm," Rav continued. "What of the Cosmologists? Are you all that's left, or are there others?"

"Just me, that I know of, though I'm no Cosmologist," Ely said. "You knew them?"

Rav avoided his gaze, a shadow overtaking his expression. "I did."

"Did you by chance know an Ariel Marcellus?" Ely asked, not sure why the phantom visitation and the vampire's appearance felt connected.

Rav looked up at him in surprise. Ely opened the book to the page his phantom visitor had recommended.

Rav inclined his head, face pensive. "She came to Dianessa from the Protectorate. Like you."

"How do you know where I came from?" Ely interjected, intrigued.

"Your accent," Rav replied.

"Of course," Ely said with an ironic chuckle. "Dr. F says my tongue is hopelessly tainted by Paxat. I suppose it is still true even after all this time."

Rav continued, "Ariel was an exceptional conjurer. Not a studied scholar like the Cosmologists of the Tower. She possessed raw power such as none of them had ever seen. She could change shapes. One could often spot her as a falcon soaring above the highest precipices of the Tower under the light of the moon.

"She was not welcomed with open arms by those in authority. They feared her. Envied her. She was like the wind and the sky and vast galaxies teeming with stars. They could not fathom her."

The vampire's seething intensity crackled electric through the air between them.

"You loved her," Ely remarked.

"Love?" Rav repeated. "Humans have beaten that word into something so bereft of meaning."

There was pain in his voice and rage at whatever violence now played out within his recollection. If the vampire had slept all this time, then to him these memories were still fresh.

"What happened to her?" Ely asked.

Rav's glittering eyes lifted to his face. "I don't know," he said. "I was locked in a stone sarcophagus and left to rot."

"Why?" Ely asked.

Rav's voice grew quiet. Tense. "I discovered their plans. The atrocity they had built for her. I tried to stop them."

Ely's brows raised, his skin prickling. He reached for the scroll that Ariel had thrown at his head. "Does this look familiar?"

Rav bared gleaming fangs, elongated from their reposed position with his mounting rage. "How did you find this?"

"Ariel," Ely told him. "She's been...haunting me, I suppose, for the past week. Though she's unlike any ghost I've ever encountered. I think the quake that woke you may have disturbed her too. She said that she's trapped."

"She's alive," Rav all but whispered.

"I think so," Ely frowned.

Relief brought life into the vampire's face, followed by dawning horror. "They did it, then."

"Did what?" Ely asked.

Rav tapped the schematic. "What you see depicted here is a prison built for a single inmate. If she is alive, that can only mean that they succeeded."

Rav stood.

"I have to go."

"I could go with you," Ely said, also standing.

He had no idea why those words had tumbled out of his mouth, but now that they had, he wanted to follow through on this quest.

Rav shook his head. "No. I have to move quickly, and you should rest. You're nearly spent."

"How do you...?" Ely started.

Rav set a mesmerizing gaze upon him. "I told you. I can feel you."

He lifted his hand, and Ely's stomach dropped as he realized that the vampire held the mirrorwood stake balanced between his pale fingers.

"You shouldn't leave this lying about," Rav said. He slipped the stake into the empty sword loop on Ely's belt. "There are monsters on the loose."

The vampire grinned. Then he vanished through the open window.

Dr. Faidra was dragging a heavy box full of metal scraps across the floor when Ely reentered the Oubliette. She nearly jumped out of her skin at the sight of him, sending odds and ends clattering over the dusty stones.

"Now look what you've made me do," she blustered. "Leave that be, Elyssandro!"

Ely stopped mid-stoop and left the copper coil in its resting place. In all his years in Death's Vale, he had never seen her in such a state. Distracted and irritable, certainly, but never so perilously taut. He did not know what might happen if she finally snapped.

"Dr. F, maybe it would be best if you took a rest?" he suggested, unsure if gentle concern would help or hurt the situation. "Get some fresh air. Sunlight."

"Do I look like a houseplant to you, warm blood?" she hissed.

"Perhaps a neglected one?" he smiled.

Dr. Faidra offered a scathing look in response. She was immune to charm of any kind, but most particularly his. Still, his foolish demeanor did seem to set her at ease.

"Have you come to pester me with more questions, then?" she asked.

"Just one," he replied.

"Out with it then."

"What happened to Ariel Marcellus?" he asked.

The metal cylinder in her hands rang like a cymbal on the stone floor.

"I take it you know the name," he observed.

"The question is, how do you?"

"A book," he replied. "She used death magic notably enough to be hunted by the Canon, but she wasn't a Cosmologist."

"No," Dr. F confirmed. "She did not learn her craft at the Tower. She came to Dianessa seeking sanctuary. We granted it, and she betrayed us."

"How?" Ely asked.

"What does it matter, warm blood?" Dr. F evaded. "She belongs to another time."

"Why not answer the question if it's just a history lesson?" Ely pressed.

"She is the reason that Dianessa and the Vale are cursed," the doctor croaked.

Ely eyed her, sinking unease in his stomach. "You told me you didn't know what caused the Curse."

Dr. Faidra raised bloodshot eyes to his. "Because you weren't ready to know."

"Why wouldn't I be ready?" Ely demanded. "What difference would it make if I knew who was responsible?"

Dr. Faidra snarled in exasperation. "I didn't want you asking these questions, Elyssandro. You are forever asking questions, and this one could be your undoing."

"Why?"

"Because you are exactly like her!" Dr. Faidra barked.

A low, quiet voice interjected from the doorway. "That is a compliment, Elyssandro, even if she spews it like an accusation."

Dr. Faidra tensed, eyes narrowed as she rose to her feet to meet the intruder. "Ravan."

"Selene." The vampire stepped forward, gaze unblinking. "I see at long last your face matches your soul."

"Rav," Ely intoned with warning.

The vampire bared his fangs, not taking his eyes off Dr. Faidra. "This doesn't concern you, conjurer. She knows why I'm here. Tell me how to free her, Selene."

Dr. Faidra gnarred. Her full set of crimson, razor-pointed teeth made Rav's bite look delicate. Of the two, Ely didn't know which might prevail in a fight.

"The keys are gone," Dr. Faidra growled. "And you will never find them."

In a howling blur, Rav knocked Ely from his feet and seized the doctor by the throat, slamming her into the stone wall hard enough to rattle the rusted shackles.

"Where are they?" he hissed.

"Everyone who knew the answer to that is dead," the doctor gasped.

Rav released a pained bellow. Ely regained his feet and drew the stake from his belt. He pressed the point to the vampire's back, aimed for his heart. Rav went rigid, and Ely felt the shimmer of fear rush through him almost as if the terror were his own.

"Release her," Ely commanded.

"She's not worth your loyalty," the vampire murmured.

"Don't make me kill you, Rav."

Rav remained intent upon the doctor for a moment. Then he loosened his grip. Ely waited for Dr. F to stalk across the room, clawed hand clutching her throat. Then he took a step back, stake still poised.

Rav turned to glare at him. The disappointment in his eyes struck hard as a physical blow. The vampire left them, a hurricane tearing up the stairs.

Ely turned to the doctor. "Are you alright?" he asked.

"Fine, warm blood," she croaked. "Are you?"

Ely nodded. His speeding pulse betrayed the lie at least to himself. He set the stake back in the sword loop. His hands felt shaky.

"What was he talking about, Dr. F? What are the keys?"

"To open the Hollow," Dr. Faidra rasped. "That is where Ariel Marcellus is imprisoned. We designed it together. Myself, my colleagues in Applied Magics, and the Cosmologists. The keys to the Hollow are not lumps of metal that you carry in your pocket. They are mechanical devices."

"Where are they?" Ely asked.

The undead doctor eyed him, a shadow in her septic eyes.

"You really think I'm going to betray you?" Ely asked.

Dr. Faidra glared at the tools on her work bench. Finally, she said, "We hid the keys. No one knew where each device was to go except the scholar who carried it."

"Which one did *you* carry?" Ely pressed.

"Leave me, Elyssandro. I need to clean up this mess."

Ely wanted to insist further, but he knew better than to push his luck tonight. Confusion set in as he made the journey back to the east wing. She had lied to him about the Curse. Lied to him because she did not trust him with the truth. Not through any fault of his own. No. She saw in him echoes of another. All these years, he considered Dr. Faidra to be his mentor. His family. Was she simply keeping an enemy close?

He was not surprised in the least to find Rav waiting for him as he walked through the common room doors.

"What hold does that creature have on you?" the vampire demanded, naked fury in his eyes.

Ely's fingers made a reflexive circle around the stake at his waist. Rav caught his wrist, trapping his hand in place. He could break bones with hardly more than a twitch. This was a cosmos of power harnessed into the likeness of a man.

"She saved me," Ely grimaced. "I escaped into Death's Vale when I was ten years old. They would have executed me for witchcraft."

"Why?" Rav frowned.

"I brought my mother back from the dead," Ely said, voice toneless, nearly inaudible.

Rav relaxed his frozen grip, taken aback. They moved a few paces apart, the silent truce rippling between them.

Ely continued, "I could not go back to Saint Lucio, and I would not have survived another night in Death's Vale. Dr. Faidra took me in. She taught me to turn to the stars for sustenance. She healed my wounds when I found misfortune. I owe her everything."

"Have you ever asked yourself why she did it?" Rav questioned.

The vampire winced. His neck contorted as though he found himself suddenly uncomfortable in his waxen skin. Thin, sweltering lines like glowing fissures etched themselves along his cheekbones, sputtering and searing. Rav grunted in pain.

"She changed the wards," Ely realized aloud.

Intricate spellwork protected the University from unwanted intruders. Rav had been able to enter only because Dr. Faidra had thought vampires extinct. Now, it seemed, she had corrected her mistaken assumptions.

"You should go while you still can," Ely said.

The vampire fled through the window. Ely heaved a sigh and sank into the window seat. Rav would not be back without an invitation. He wished the notion were a relief, but the betrayal in the vampire's oceanic eyes gnawed at him. Perhaps it was simply death magic clouding his judgment. Still, the sick feeling persisted long after the dizzying presence had faded. What was he to do?

It was the doctor's voice that provided clarity this time. *"You are forever asking questions."*

"Perhaps you're right, Dr. F," he murmured.

So first inquiry, then. Where might one find the Hollow?

Chapter Five
A Quest

Sir Ambrose Quinn answered the knock at his door in a satin dressing gown. His finger bones were ink-stained, and he carried a bejeweled goblet.

"Are you alright, Elyssandro? What's happened?" he asked.

"Oh, yes, fine. I had a question, but...what is that?"

Quinn followed his glance to the goblet. "Ah, this. It's just a prop." He tipped it toward Ely to reveal its contents nothing but air.

"Did you want to come inside?" Quinn asked.

"If you don't mind," Ely replied, looking over his shoulder.

He did not expect Dr. Faidra had followed him, but his nerves remained raw all the same. Quinn stepped aside, holding the door wider.

"It's a mess at the moment," Quinn mumbled apologetically.

Ely had never seen the inside of Quinn's apartment. The skeleton chevalier usually met him on the portico for Caj or elsewhere in the city. He did not seem keen to share his private space. Inside, a narrow entryway paused at a coat rack before flowing on into a cozy sitting room with a cheery fireplace and a curtained window.

Shelves lining the walls held an assortment of thick folios and stacks of loose pages tied with twine. In the center of the room, a candle dripped wax on a table laid out with longswords, daggers, dining utensils, colorful fans, and other oddities. Another candle winked from a small desk where a half-written page lay beneath the downy white plumes of a writing quill. An ink bottle sat uncorked beside the stack of finished manuscript pages.

"You're a writer?" Ely asked.

Quinn inclined his head. "I dabble. The props help me set the scene," he explained, placing the goblet back on the table.

Ely tried not to grin too wide. He had felt it impolite to ask what an immortal skeleton might do with his abundance of time. This seemed very fitting for Quinn.

"So, what brings you knocking at this early hour?" the skeleton asked.

"I thought you might be up for a quest," Ely replied. "But I'd hate to interrupt."

"The only thing you're interrupting is a terrible case of writer's block," Quinn declared. "That's exactly the inspiration I need. A good quest. I'll go get changed."

With that, the skeleton chevalier disappeared through the bedroom door. Ely sat in a faded armchair near the fireplace, resisting the temptation to peek at some of the manuscript pages.

"Will it be warm or cool, this quest?" Quinn called.

"Will it make a difference to you?" Ely asked with a frown. Then quickly added, "No offense."

"I like to dress appropriately," Quinn snapped.

"Dress for a steep climb," Ely answered.

"Excellent!" came the reply.

A few minutes later, the skeleton emerged in black linen, a tailored leather vest with a multitude of pockets, and sturdy green hiking boots.

"So, what daring adventure are we seeking today, my friend?" Quinn asked.

"Do you remember my ghostly visitor?" Ely inquired.

"Of course."

"Why don't I explain the rest on the way."

As they walked, Ely recounted the newest chapter of his strange tale. Quinn had not heard of Ariel Marcellus or Ravan Aurelio.

"I never dallied in the academic or political circles," the skeleton knight explained. "I am, however, quite familiar with the rumor that vampires plagued the streets of Dianessa. Disappearances. Puncture wounds. There was certainly a convincing body of evidence. I never saw a vampire myself, though I was quite intrigued..."

By the time Ely reached the previous night's events, they had come to a halt at the mouth of the treacherous ravine overlooking the ruins of the Tower.

"So, this is our steep climb?" Quinn asked, peering over the edge into the darkness below.

"You can wait up here if you'd rather," Ely offered.

"How dare you even suggest it," Quinn huffed. "Have you brought a rope?"

"Better," Ely beamed, lowering his pack from his shoulders.

Inside, he had tucked away a set of climbing harnesses. He demonstrated their assembly to Quinn who let Ely adjust the straps. They fit a bit loose over his bones, but it would do.

With the harnesses in place and the first anchors and ropes set, the two adventurers began their descent.

"Can you see the bottom yet, old chap?" Quinn called. They had been climbing for hours, the sun long since past its noon arc.

"Nothing yet," Ely answered, voice ragged.

He feared they might be plunged into darkness with no way to reach solid ground.

The skeleton knight repelled down the rock wall, his boots breaking bits of debris loose. When he stood safely on the narrow ledge, Ely unknotted the rope and pulled it free from the metal loop fixed in the stone above. They continued without assistance as the next incline proved gentler.

"It's not that I'm worried for myself," Quinn continued. "Don't mortals have to eat and sleep?"

"I'll be fine," Ely assured him.

He was, in fact, bone-achingly weary, and he was sure the rumbling in his stomach would cause an avalanche any moment. Damn Rión and her knapsacks of food. It had been years since hunger had struck him so hard.

"So what do you think we will find in this bottomless pit?" Quinn questioned.

"I'm hoping an answer or two," Ely said. "At the very least, I plan to see if I can coax Ariel into materializing long enough to ask where she's locked away."

"Suppose she doesn't know?" Quinn pointed out.

"Then we're back to square one with an excruciating climb ahead of us," said Ely with a pained grimace.

"The luck of the quest, eh?" Quinn shrugged. "Is that a battlement I spy?"

"Yes!" Ely exclaimed.

He sidled to the nearest ledge. The bottom of the rocky ravine stood solid and fully visible below. Too far to jump, but one last repel might bring this leg of the journey to a close.

"Thank the named gods!" Quinn cried, then added hastily, "Not for me, for your sake."

"Of course," Ely nodded with a sideways grin.

The one final repel turned out to be far more difficult than anticipated. The cliff face near the bottom of the chasm was weathered and weak. It crumbled away at the touch and would not hold an anchor.

"Plan beta then?" Quinn proposed.

Ely nodded, calculating the distance. He did not generally use magic to solve problems of physics. That was Dr. Faidra's domain. In this case, there seemed no alternative.

"Alright, Quinn. I'm going to lower you down first. It will be a bit of a drop at the bottom, but I think you'll manage."

Quinn nodded. "Who's going to lower you down?"

"Me. Theoretically."

"Ah, yes. Conjury," Quinn nodded. "Have you attempted this before, whatever stunt you have up your sleeve?"

"I have?" Ely replied with an upturned voice.

"Very convincing," Quinn remarked.

"I *have*. Technically. But I wasn't the one in control of the situation," Ely admitted.

"Ah. We shall let Death take the reins then," Quinn said with a nod of his skull.

Ely fixed up Quinn's harness straps again and lowered him toward the flat expanse below. He was surprisingly heavy for a pile of bones. Ely tried not to grunt with the exertion. When he dangled as far down as the rope would allow, Quinn counted him off, and Ely let the lead slip. The skeleton landed lightly on his feet in a puff of dust.

"You alright, Quinn?"

"Kittens and daisies, old chap," Quinn called with a salute.

"My turn then," Ely murmured to himself.

He closed his eyes, relaxing his mind. The infinite host that usually lingered close by ready to seize control stood conspicuously absent.

Do it yourself if you're so clever, they seemed to say.

Ely sighed, then drew his armor tight around his limbs. It would not save him from a fall at this height, but it felt a comfort all the same to have its familiar protection in place.

Closing his eyes once again, he reached for the memory of the power that had shimmered through him on a long ago day. He had stood beneath the eaves of a black hurricane. As Death enveloped him in misty ether, he rose into the storm with arms outstretched. He felt as though he were part of the raging wind. He was the wind. He was the storm...

Ely's stomach lurched. His feet were no longer touching the ground. He wrenched his mind back to focus. Slowly, he directed the flow of death magic. His body glided through the air toward the bottom of the ravine. He nearly reached jumping distance when his concentration slipped.

Quinn shouted a warning as he wobbled and shook in midair. Then he plunged for the ground, landing in a heap. He sat up, head ringing.

"Well, that's one way to do it," Quinn said.

Ely groaned and stood, dusting himself off. When his swimming vision steadied again, he surveyed their surroundings.

Gargantuan slabs of black stone littered the ravine floor. The remnants of spiked turrets and crumbled battlements soared higher than any edifice that Ely had ever seen. At the far end of the chasm, the great Tower stood a doorless monolith, its spire like an unsheathed blade pointing to the heavens.

Ely stared transfixed at the ruins. Chest tight. Revenant magic trembled and cavorted about him. It was hard to breathe down here. Hard to think.

"I'd forgotten how impressive it was," Quinn said. "You could see the Tower from any point in Dianessa. If ever you were lost, it would help you find your way as surely as the Polestar."

"Did you ever go inside?" Ely asked.

Quinn shook his skull. "This daring adventurer and amateur scribe did not attract their notice. They kept their eyes ever fixed to the stars. Their minds forever beyond this world. You can see their dark and lofty ideals reflected in these gothic stones."

"They must have been as asinine as Rav said if they didn't hire you on spot to pen their story," Ely said.

"Did your vampire say anything about where we might begin looking?" Quinn asked.

Ely shook his head.

The skeleton nodded and began scouting the perimeter of the ravine. Ely closed his eyes, endeavoring to shut out the noise. The echoes. There was nothing down here that felt like Ariel.

Quinn called out from ahead, and Ely jogged over to him.

"Look at that."

He pointed toward the foot of the Tower. Nearly swallowed in shadow, Ely made out the limbs of a tree jutting up from a crack that split the ground like a wound. The tree's thick boughs twisted and stretched as though trying to haul itself from the depths of the earth. Its leaves seemed to pulse and sway. Gasping for breath in the gloom.

Ely shivered. The sight of the gnarled limbs scraped against his mind, jarring as claws on metal. He wanted to run. Yet he knew as surely as if it spoke its own name. This was the Hollow.

A vicious buzzing like a swarm of angry hornets droned in his ears. He tried to tear his eyes away, but the hypnotic swaying leaves held him captive. Ely stepped closer, drawn in by an inescapable force.

"Elyssandro, stop!" Quinn's warning sounded as if from underwater.

It was too late. His next step tumbled through thin air. He was falling.

E.K. MACPHERSON

Down.
Down, as the earth swallowed him whole.

Chapter Six

ISLE OF THE GODS

Ely opened his eyes to glittering ocean. A ship's deck swayed beneath his feet, ropes creaking on the mast, sea breeze stroking its sails. Wasn't he just elsewhere? Aching pain rippled through him, and for a moment he felt his faraway body stir. Gentle waves undulated in a soothing rhythm. Like hypnotic breath.

"What are you thinking about, diakana?" The lilting tones rooted him back to the ship's deck. He turned, heart crashing against his chest.

"Kai," he breathed.

The pirate prince looked at him inquisitively. His long black hair was braided back, and he wore a loose russet tunic unlaced at the neck. Why did this moment seem so familiar? Had this day already happened?

Kai leaned against the polished mirrorwood railing.

"Seasick, my friend?" he asked in his rolling accent.

"Maybe a little," Ely replied with a wry smile.

"We're almost there," Kai chuckled, patting him on the shoulder. "We will stop in Séocwen for a few days before we go on to the Isle of the Gods. A hot meal and solid ground will help."

Ely nodded, remembering all at once what they were doing here. Rión had carried a message to him in Death's Vale, entreating him to come to the aid of her allies. A rupture in the heart of a long dormant volcano threatened the ten thousand souls that lived on Séocwen and its neighboring islands.

Ely came at once, traveling first to Fjarat, then on to the cold, rocky coastal village of Norrholdt. Kai met them there, no longer helming his little sloop but captain of a sleek, full-sailed ship. The Marisola. That was the name of this vessel. How could he have forgotten?

"Thank you for coming, Ely," Kai said, quiet and sincere.

"Of course. I'm glad to help," Ely smiled.

"*Melór!*" someone called.

"What is that?" Ely asked.

"Land," Kai grinned.

The ship exploded to life as the crew prepared for their return to shore. The Séoc coastline drifted into view. Pristine golden sands and waving palms. Ely turned to lend a hand, but the sudden burning in his chest doubled him over...

Ely woke to blind pain. His sternum felt as though it had crumpled inward. His leg should not be lying at that angle. When he managed to peel open his encrusted eyes, he found nothing but a tangle of thick black bark above him. The Hollow.

Ely stirred, but root and rock pinned him into the crevice in which he had fallen.

"Help," he rasped, his voice no more than a whisper on dead air.

"Elyssandro!" Quinn's muffled shout resounded from high above. He strained to look for his friend.

"Here!" he wheezed. "I'm here..."

The hive of angry hornets began to buzz again, and the roots of the biomechanical prison shuddered. Pulsing. His head fell back. Mind adrift...

"Wake up, Ely."

He lay on a comfortable cushion in the open air of a shady balcony overlooking the sea. Kai's bungalow. That was it. They had disembarked at the port yesterday and journeyed out of the bustling coastal city through the jungle to the pirate prince's secluded cove.

"What did you say?" Ely asked, still groggy.

Kai laughed. "Come on, get up. We have to beat the sun."

Ely nodded, rising with a groan. What had he been dreaming about? A tree with evil roots choking him.

"Leave them," Kai commanded as Ely reached for his boots. Ely hastened after him, still blinking the dream away.

"Take this."

Kai thrust a bucket in his hands and headed out the door.

The blast of a salted breeze revived him. Kai led him past the beach's silky sands to porous rock formations shaped by volcanic eruptions. The Séoc set out across the sharp, wet rocks without a flinch. Ely grunted, trying not to appear too slow and tender-footed. Kai glanced back once or twice just to chuckle at him.

They stopped where shellfish clung to the rocks amidst the ocean spray.

"*Patescado,*" Kai named them.

Crouching down, he drew a knife from the belt at his waist. He demonstrated the technique to dislodge a patescado shell from the rocks, then handed the knife to Ely. He mimicked Kai's motion, attempting to lodge the tip of the knife between the shell and the rock. The first three attempts proved fruitless, but the fourth saw a periwinkle shell detach with a pop and sail over the edge of the rocks into the water.

"See? You got it," Kai said with an encouraging smile, then drew a knife of his own to harvest the bounty before them.

They worked in silence. Ely managed to hold onto his next few patescados long enough to toss them into the bucket with Kai's swiftly growing pile.

The sun climbed from the embrace of the sea, scattering warm, blushing light. Ely paused to watch the play of color. Never before had he seen such rich hues as the deep blues, lustrous golds, and fierce pinks that burst across the Séocwen sky.

They returned to the bungalow with a full bucket. Kai set a fire in his outdoor cooking pavilion. Then they sat on the steps while the pirate prince taught Ely how to use the knife to open the shells, revealing the translucent treasure inside. He tipped the contents of the shell into his mouth. Ely followed suit. It was slick and salty, not for the faint of stomach but oddly exhilarating.

The rest they saved for their meal. Kai sent him to fetch water, garlic, oil, and a few other necessities while he finished shucking. Then the pirate prince manned an enormous steel pan that sat over open flames. He set Ely to work mixing gritty nut flour with salt water then showed him how to shape the dough into folded rounds to steam. They feasted at a driftwood table overlooking the ocean, retiring after to braided hammocks under breezy palms.

They were awakened by Kai's trio of cousins—Salía, Yamon, and Mirit—who arrived carrying fresh-caught fish tied to poles. Kai stoked the pavilion fire. Taking up a paring knife, he fileted the enormous red-scaled fish, removing head, bones, and innards with a single motion. These he piled in their own pot, doused with water, and hung over the fire on a hook to boil. He moved on to slice mounds of onions, garlic, and colorful vegetables that smelled of earth and spice. The knife blade sang, moving with terrifying speed.

More friends arrived, bringing their own food offerings. Spirits were poured and fragrant smoking herbs passed. Ely noticed they all greeted their prince with embraces and hearty laughter. Their smiles faded, and they lowered their gazes when Ely approached. They were quick to move from his path with stiff nods of acknowledgement and mumbles of, "Diakana."

As evening arrived, Ely found himself sitting alone near the water, watching the foaming waves roll. Kai joined him, passing a glazed cup overflowing with zaqual.

"How do you find Séocwen?" he asked.

"It's beautiful," Ely replied with breathless sincerity. "The water, the sky, the feel of sand. And, of course, there is the food."

"They don't feed you where you're from?" Kai laughed.

Ely shook his head, and the pirate prince's smile faded as he realized that his companion meant no jest.

"How do you live?" he asked.

"The stars," Ely replied.

"Of course. You are diakana," Kai nodded. "Rión Twin Axes told me you dwell among the dead in Dianessa. Is that true?"

Ely confirmed with a nod, reticent to speak of his home. Perhaps it was because the dingy cobwebs and macabre company would seem a horror compared to the paradise that surrounded them. Perhaps it was the way the others had been avoiding his gaze.

"Do I frighten them?" Ely asked, inclining his head toward the bungalow where the others sat laughing around a purring campfire.

Kai pondered a moment, considering his words carefully before he replied, "They are cautious. And trying to be respectful. You are a legend made flesh, and they do not yet know what to make of you."

"So they *are* frightened."

"Maybe that is not such a bad thing, diakana. With awe and wonder, and yes, a little fear, you allow them to believe that you can save them."

Ely sighed. "As long as *you're* not afraid of me."

Kai turned a quiet smile to his face. "I have seen you snatch a man's soul from his body, freeze blood in veins, and pierce flesh with shadows. You'll have to do better than that to frighten me, Elyssandro Santara Ruadan."

Ely turned misted eyes to the sea. No human had ever offered more than curses after knowing what he was.

"Have I offended you?" Kai asked, concern in his voice.

Ely shook his head. "No. When others find out my secret, see it with their own eyes...I don't blame them, but I'm not used to being looked at as anything other than a nightmare."

Kai met his eyes, regarding him with a soft, earnest gaze that made Ely's cheeks flush hot. "Without you, I would be a slave behind the mast of a Canon ship. I wake drawing free breath, and I thank the named gods for you."

"It's no more than anyone would have done," Ely murmured.

A rumbling tremor shook the ground, confusing the tide and sending flocks of birds screaming into the sky. Ely and Kai both stood, eyes fixed seaward where a billowing column of black smoke streamed high into the air.

"The rupture?" Ely asked.

Kai nodded. "It is angry again."

"How long will it take to get to the volcano?"
"We should leave now."
The furious ache was spreading again. The beach and the pirate prince faded away...

Hypnotic roots tightened their embrace as consciousness returned. Ely could no longer feel his leg. A small relief. Probably a very bad sign.
Sleep.
The Hollow buzzed in his ear. Ely fought to wrest his eyes open.
Sleep...

Splash!
Ely's feet plunged into shallow water. Kai waded ahead of him through the shoals toward land. They dragged a small canoe between them. How had they gotten here so quickly?

Beyond the thin sand bar, a green tangle of jungle trees overgrew the uninhabited Isle of the Gods. In the distance, the great volcano rose, a fortress of gray stone crowned in a coronet of smoke.

They took an ancient path through lush forest. The Séoc of old came this way to make sacrifices to appease angry gods. The practice of blood offerings had been determined outdated in the last generations, but the Séoc still held the island sacred and did not set foot on its shores without purpose.

"Tell me more about this rupture," Kai called back to him as they walked. "Would it lead us to unknown lands like the ones you spoke of in Death's Vale?"

"With the tremors and smoke, it is more like an infected wound," Ely said. "It will need to be closed and hopefully it will heal in time."

"So, it would not lead the way to the land of the dead," Kai observed.

Ely shook his head. "Even if it did, you should not try to pass through. The rupture can shear a human in two."

"Are you not human?" Kai asked.

"I have armor to protect me," Ely explained.

Kai nodded, delighted by this revelation.

"I hope you will show me one day, this place you call home."

"It is nothing like here," Ely told him.

"All the more reason to see it," Kai replied, left side dimple winking over his shoulder. "I envy your freedom, Ely. I fear my adventures will be called to a close before I get the chance to see even the half of this wide world."

"Why do you say that?" Ely asked.

"My mother would rather I stay on the island with her to study king craft. She says I will never find a wife wandering about like a common sea dog." Kai sighed and shook his head. "I do not want a wife, I tell her. A king must have children, she says. I owe it to our people. What of my heart? I ask. What of it? she replies. I lost it long ago, I tell her. Even if I could find it again, it would not please you to know where it is."

"Why?" Ely interjected.

"It would be *tapána*," Kai said.

"Which means?"

"Forbidden."

"What is forbidden to a future king?" Ely questioned.

Kai turned an amused smile to his face. "Many things, diakana."

Ely accepted this with a nod, too short of breath to press further. The trail must be steeper than he thought or the day deceptively hot.

After a short silence left him a bit less winded, he asked, "So does this person know they've stolen the heart of a pirate prince?"

Kai kept his eyes trained on the steepening path ahead. "I don't know," he said, voice pensive. He halted and turned back to Ely, melancholy vanishing as he declared, "I don't think I will reach the top of this mountain without a break from the heat."

"What do you propose?" Ely inquired.

"A swim!"

With that the pirate prince broke from the trail, charting a course through the undergrowth. The roar of a waterfall grew louder, and at last they came into sight of a crystalline pool so clear Ely could see straight to the silt at the bottom.

Kai left his clothes on the shore and dove in, resurfacing to float on his back. Ely squatted among the pebbles in the shallows, splashing his face and neck with cool water.

"Come in!" Kai urged.

"I can't swim," Ely answered with an apologetic smile.

"Over here."

Kai kicked to where a collection of boulders lay beneath the pool. He planted his feet.

"Come on, Ely, I won't let you fall in," he coaxed with a dripping grin.

The water did look tempting swirling about the pirate prince's muscled torso. And the heat seemed to have doubled yet again. Ely undressed, wading into the water. Kai was right, it felt like heaven.

"Better, yes?"

The pirate prince splashed him and paddled away laughing. Ely watched him dart like a fish under the water, diving deep to scoop something from the bed of the pool. He swam back over to Ely's boulder and took his hand, dropping three glittering diamonds onto his palm.

"Don't these belong to the gods?" Ely asked.

"You're helping their people. They owe you something," Kai insisted.

Ely shook his head. "Anything I can do for your people I would do freely."

Kai held his gaze, brow furrowed, expression somber. "I wish they knew that like I do. Maybe then..."

He trailed off, letting the rest of his thought sink beneath the water. Ely watched his face, heart throbbing so painfully.

"We should keep going," Kai said, then returned to the shore.

They dressed and made their way back to the path toward the ruptured volcano. Ely continued the trek in contemplative silence. Questions begged to escape his lips. He contained them to his worrying fingers, tracing the rough little gems that rested in his pocket.

The incline steepened as the final ascent to the mountain's peak began. Kai pressed the pace, pausing only to glance over his shoulder to reassure himself that Ely still followed. At the end of the rise, they could see down into the basalt valley below, ridged with ancient lava flows, long cooled.

There were no live vents in this volcanic basin. The smoke beacon that had risen high enough to be seen all the way from Séocwen was coming from the yawning rupture whose jagged edges burned red in the cratered ground. It looked wide enough to swallow a city whole.

"How is this possible?" Ely gasped.

For all the ruptures he had healed in his years, he had never seen anything like this one.

"I thought you'd have the answer to that," Kai said.

Ely knelt down and placed his fingertips against the ground. Seething energy radiated from the monstrous breach. It would take everything in him to mend it.

"I need to get closer," he said. "You should wait here."

"I'm staying with you," Kai replied.

Ely shook his head. "Remember what I told you about ruptures? Stay here. Please."

Kai nodded reluctant agreement. Then Ely flexed his hands, his armor slithering up his arms, wrapping about him like coils of night sky.

"Ely!" Kai called after him. "Be careful."

Ely gave him a reassuring smile, far more confident than he felt. Then he continued on the descent, calling an ether mask about his face to block the fumes.

As he walked, he relaxed his mind. Listening to the rupture. Getting its measure. The ground rumbled, and a spray of slivered stone gusted high into the air. Ely ducked, waiting until the growling rift grew still again. He continued on until he stood at its edge. This close, he could not even see across to the other end. He extended his hands, threading death magic about the vast perimeter until the two ends met out on the other side of the wavering horizon. Sweat beaded his brow, and his breath grew tense. The rupture resisted, pushing back as he tried to draw the great cavern closed.

A roar like a primeval beast escaped from the fold. The ground quaked, porous lava rock splitting asunder out toward the surrounding mountain. Ely lost footing, careening forward toward the gaping maw. His eyes clouded. Death took hold.

When he could once again see clearly, he stood at the center of a destructive spiral that blasted the volcano's basin all the way to the slopes of its crater walls. The rupture was gone. Not even a shimmer remained.

Turning back the way he came, Ely's stomach dropped. The mountainside where he left Kai had crumbled away in a landslide. Setting out at a run, Ely skirted newly torn fissures and leaped over fractured stones.

"Kai!" he shouted, praying desperately for a response.

He saw the motionless form half-buried at the base of the crater. Ely dug frantically, panic lending strength enough to hurl away the slabs of stone. At last, the pirate prince came loose. He lay still, face masked in blood and ash. Ely did not need to search for a pulse to know Kai was dead.

He heaved a gasping cry, cradling the pirate prince's body, wracked with sobs. Then he fell still, every muscle tense. Closing his eyes, he felt as though he had vacated his body, spinning through the dark until he collided with the vast presence that had carried his friend away in their swathe of destruction.

Give him back, he demanded.

Death's hiss bent and stretched as if legions spoke with a single voice. *You dare use our power against us.*

Take anything you want from me, he pleaded. *Take my life in exchange, but you will not take him.*

A hurricane raged about him, rushing through him until he thought he would shatter. Then the tempest stopped. He opened his eyes. Kai sat up from the rocks, blinking and coughing.

Ely threw his arms around him, crushing him to his chest as tears streamed down his face.

"*Elyssandro, wake up.*"

The whisper shivered over his shoulder. Ely looked up. He knew that voice.

Ariel's command echoed louder, more urgent. "*Wake up, Elyssandro.*"

Kai gazed at him, lips forming words, but Ely could not hear. The pirate prince faded as though all the color had suddenly drained from the world.

"*Elyssandro, wake up. You have to fight it...*"

Ely gasped. Searing, wrenching pain revived him as the root that held him pinned lifted. Granite arms circled him, and he felt wind rushing past his face. Then he was laid gingerly on the ground. Throbbing nausea overtook him as he shifted.

"Don't try to move." Rav's smooth, quiet voice sent shivers of alarm through his body. "Your leg is broken, and your breathing is...wrong."

"You saved me?" Ely managed to gasp.

"It wasn't me that saved you," Rav replied.

"Ariel," Ely murmured, eyes falling closed.

Chapter Seven
Hurricane Smile

When Ely returned to consciousness, he lay on a lumpy mattress covered by a faded patchwork quilt. A sewing machine rested on a sturdy workbench. Long reams of colorful fabric and bits of unfinished costumes provided a clue as to where he found himself. Safely returned to Sir Ambrose Quinn's apartment.

Ely groaned, dragging himself upright despite his body's protests. A tightly bound splint braced his left leg, and each breath felt like a fight only to inhale fire. The skeleton chevalier appeared in the doorway.

"Good morning. Or afternoon now," Quinn said, a pleasant veneer spread thin over his worry.

"How bad?" Ely asked.

"Your leg is broken in two places. You've cracked several ribs. Apparently a lung has collapsed. And you've taken a nasty blow to the head. In short, you have rather outdone yourself, my friend."

"Well," Ely grunted. "Nothing a quick jaunt to the fourth floor can't cure."

"About that," Quinn sighed. "I paid a visit to the University the first moment I could bring myself to leave you. She said...Dr. Faidra said that perhaps leaving you to discomfort will convince you to do as you're told."

Ely's heart dropped. In other words, she knew what he had been up to and was letting her displeasure be known.

"I hope you don't mind the company then," he wheezed with the most gamesome expression he could muster.

"Not in the least, old sport," Quinn replied, jaw bone lifted with the intended smile. "Here, these might be of use."

The skeleton knight brought him his canteen and starlight flask which had miraculously not been lost in the fall. Ely took a sip from the flask. The cool diffusion soothed the burn in his chest. Perhaps he could make real headway on his recovery after nightfall.

"What happened?" Ely asked.

"Well, old bean, you walked right into some kind of trap," Quinn told him. "By the time night settled, I had despaired of ever finding a way down to you. Then who should turn up but your vampire. He swooped down into the blasted tangle of roots and sailed back out again in a hailstorm of debris."

"How did we get back here?" Ely asked.

"Kind fellow gave us both a lift," Quinn replied. "A good thing too. That would have been a hell of a time trying to climb out of there myself."

Ely lay back, exhausted.

"Why don't you take a rest, old chap. I'll be in the next room if you need anything."

Quinn left the door cracked, and Ely closed his eyes with a sigh. This was not the first time Dr. Faidra had chosen to punish him for defiance.

He found his thoughts wandering back to that cloudy fall morning when he heard a familiar voice calling his name from the courtyard below the east wing. Sure enough, when he peered out the window, he found Kailari Novara standing by the fountain.

Ely hurried down to meet him, heart soaring and quaking. How could Kai be here? No human had made it this far into Death's Vale apart from himself.

"Ely!" The pirate prince rushed to embrace him.

When Ely greeted him in halting Séoc, Kai beamed with delight. He launched into a lilting stream until Ely shook his head.

"Not so fast," he laughed. "I only have a book for a teacher, and I'm a slow study. How are you here?"

"I found an old chart in the monastery library. There's a river that feeds straight from the sea to Dianessa," Kai explained.

"You sailed the River Scythe?" Ely gasped.

Kai inclined his head. "Yes, and then a talking skeleton pointed the way to the University."

"They spoke to you?" Ely gaped.

"It seems that Death has left its mark on me," Kai replied. "That is not why I've come."

"Why have you come, mortal?" Dr. Faidra's voice scraped over the courtyard stones.

Kai and Ely both jumped. The pirate prince surveyed the startling figure with interest. "You must be Dr. Faidra," he said with his most dashing smile.

Dr. Faidra glowered at him, unmoved.

"Kai is a friend of mine," Ely explained, hoping to diffuse her irritation.

"So, this is the reason you've been useless since you returned," Dr. Faidra rumbled. "Let you out of my sight for one second and you start collecting pretty strays."

"He is the future king of Séocwen, and really, Dr. F, would it kill you to be civil?"

Dr. Faidra eyed him, replying dryly, "I'm already dead, Elyssandro."

She turned to Kai. Something flashed in her eyes, and she tilted her head to the side, observing the pirate prince more closely.

"You have a touch of Death about you," she croaked.

"I've seen the other side of it before," Kai replied.

She turned narrowed eyes back to Ely. He could see the calculations scratching across her mind.

"What business brings you to Dianessa?" she questioned at last.

"I would rather discuss it with Ely," Kai answered in an even tone. "Respectfully."

Dr. Faidra bared her stained teeth. "This is my domain, mortal prince. You want an audience with my ward, then state your business."

Kai looked between them, confidence wavering. "I need his help," he said. "The Séoc need help. The Canon has been encroaching on the Barrier Keys. They will take Séocwen if we cannot turn the tide."

"And what makes you think Elyssandro is the one to do it?" she demanded.

"He saved our islands before," Kai answered, this time turning his seeking gaze to Ely. "Will you come with me?"

"Of course!"

His words were drowned out by Dr. Faidra's snarl. "No. I forbid it!"

Ely glared at her. "Kai, can we have a moment?" he asked.

Kai gave them some distance.

"What's the matter with you?" Ely hissed. "You've never given a damn where I wander."

"I do when the Canon is involved, you know that well, Elyssandro."

"I can't just stand by and watch Séocwen fall into their hands." Ely met her milky, bloodshot eyes. "I'm going. You can't stop me."

"Alright, go then," she spat. "Just remember no matter what you do for them, it will never be enough to make them forget you are a monster."

"Many thanks, Dr. F," he muttered, then turned to rejoin Kai.

"When you come crawling back with your own beating heart in your hand, don't expect any pity from me," she shot after him.

The day's end saw him climbing aboard the single-sailed vessel Kai had piloted up the noxious River Scythe.

"We will meet the Marisola outside of the inlet," Kai told him. "My cousins are waiting for us there."

Ely had never seen Death's Vale from this vantage. Flowing past a dreamlike phantom realm.

"It is beautiful," Kai said. "Your home."

"You think so?"

Ely turned to him, watching the angles of his face as the pirate prince gazed out at the ghostly landscape. He had changed. Aged. Not in body but in spirit.

"Kai, are you well?" Ely asked.

"Everyone keeps asking me that," Kai answered with a quiet chuckle. "I never told anyone what happened on the Isle of the Gods. They know you saved them. But not how you saved me."

He paused, thoughtful.

"I am not unwell, Ely. I was in the stars. I saw the vast reaches of all that is. There is so much beyond what I ever dreamed. Then I returned to realize that the time we share on this earth is so short. And yet here we find ourselves once again at the mercy of those who want to squander *our* lives with hate and bloodshed. It fills me with such rage..."

The mirrorwood railing groaned under his grip. Then he relaxed, turning to look at Ely again.

"I want to put an end to the Canon," he said. "I want my family, my people to be free to live this life to its fullest so that when they return to the stars, they will be content to journey on."

"And what about you?" Ely asked. "Will you be content?"

He turned to meet Ely's eyes with a cryptic smile. "Yes. I think I will be."

They arrived in Séocwen under a honeyed sunrise. A convoy met them as they disembarked. A broad-shouldered man, auburn beard interwoven with shells, hailed Kai.

"The king will see you, Prince Kailari," he said, voice gruff and deep. His eyes flicked to Ely. "Both of you."

"Thank you, Balor," Kai said.

Balor's company escorted them to a pale limestone palace adorned with sculped lava rock. Feathery trees and vivid flowers skirted the front walk. Salía, Yamon, and Mirit waited outside in the walled palace garden. The king's guards stood at attention as their prince approached. They turned their faces away from the diakana.

King Tennoc sat on a throne woven from thick fronds of fragrant grass. She wore a purple mantle trimmed in sunset orange. Feathers adorned her white-streaked hair. She did not rise as they approached, only looked down on them with sharp, appraising eyes. Kai's eyes.

"I expected someone older," she pronounced.

The king spoke in Séoc, and Ely was not sure if she expected him to understand.

Kai made his introduction quietly and quickly. Ely followed as best he could.

"Mother, this is Elyssandro Santara Ruadan. He is the diakana...Isle of the Gods. He also...saved us...Templars...beach...I called him to...Canon...Séocwen..."

The king listened, eyeing her visitor with keen interest. Then she addressed him in precise Lanica. "Welcome, Elyssandro. My son tells me we owe you a great debt."

"It is nothing that wasn't offered freely," he replied.

Her eyes narrowed. The answer displeased her, though he could not discern why.

"And now you return to our aid as we face the Canon incursion," she continued.

"Yes, *che'alta*," he confirmed, using the Séoc word for addressing a king.

"What do you expect of us in return for your service?" she asked.

"Ely is not–"

Tennoc lifted her hand for silence.

"He will speak for himself, Kailari."

Ely straightened his shoulders and met her gaze.

"The Canon slaughtered my mother's people and crushed my father's kingdom underfoot. I want no other reward than to see their tyranny put to an end."

The king considered his words. She seemed more satisfied with this response.

"I have called together the kings of the Barrier Keys. We will convene at dawn tomorrow to let the Council decide what our next stand will entail. Kailari, you will attend at my side. I trust your young guest will manage without you for a day."

Kai inclined his head respectfully. "Yes, Mother."

She gave a sharp nod, signifying the audience to be at its end. As they turned, she called, "Kailari."

He looked back to her. She spoke in Séoc, but Ely understood.

"Be careful. There are eyes watching."

They left the palace. Kai's cousins rose from where they lounged under the latticed shade of fruit-laden vines. They made their way down the packed path back toward the port city.

"They've called the Council together," Kai told his cousins. "We will need all hands at watch on the Marisola."

Unspoken tension rippled through the Novara crew. Salía nodded, dark eyes wary. "Yamon and Mirit can see to that. I will go with you."

Kai shook his head. "I need you to stay with Ely."

"A diakana can look after himself," Salía argued.

"Please, cousin," Kai asked. "For me."

Salía accepted his request with a nod and a sigh. The others departed. Ely breathed in the moist jungle air, delighting in gentle birdsong on the journey to Kai's bungalow. He visited this place so often in his dreams, but it was never this alive. Just a muted echo.

"What did your mother mean about eyes watching?" Ely asked as they walked the sanded path.

"I am to be king after my mother, and because of that, I have enemies," Kai explained.

"What enemies?" Ely asked.

"Lesser kings who would control the Barrier Keys. They are always watching, waiting to sniff out some sign of weakness in Séocwen."

"Why the reminder today?" Ely pressed.

"Because I have not been myself since I returned from the Isle of the Gods," Kai answered, tense. "And she told me not to ask for your help."

"Why?"

"That is a complicated question. She is a very wise king, and she is right about many things, but in this I know that I have taken the best course."

Ely frowned, far less sure. Closing ruptures and putting the fear of Death in pious templars he knew. Politics and intrigue? That strayed far outside his realm.

Kai's grin quieted his doubts. "It would seem we are both the rebellious sons."

Ely laughed. He was sure Dr. Faidra would be less than amused at being named his parent.

They reached the bungalow just before sunset. Kai set a fire in the cooking pavilion, and they pieced together a simple feast. Then they lit dancing lanterns on the balcony and sipped zaqual, listening to the ocean's purr. When the stars emerged, they lounged side by side on the cozy balcony cushion, gazing skyward. Kai packed a wooden pipe, passing it first to his guest before imbibing himself.

Ely leaned back, watching fragrant smoke curl over his head.

"I could spend every night like this," he said. "Until we're old men with white hair and hobbled knees."

"Why don't you stay then?" Kai asked.

"I thought you said you weren't one for the quiet married life," Ely laughed.

"I only said I didn't want a wife," Kai replied with a pointed look.

"You'll settle for a friend then?" Ely smiled, heart suddenly roaring louder than the ocean below.

"Ely," Kai chuckled softly. "You can't look at me that way and call me a friend."

"Tell me a word for it then," Ely replied.

Kai shifted to gaze at him, the lantern's glow casting a gentle spell over his face.

"Tapána," Kai murmured.

Forbidden.

"I've thought quite a lot about what you told me on the Isle of the Gods," Ely said, turning his gaze back to the heavens. "Every time I closed my eyes, in fact. Part of me hoped you really did mean it was me. The rest of me hoped it was someone long gone. That what I am didn't matter at all."

Kai took his hand, tracing the lines gently. "I would not wish for you to be any way other than as you are."

His fingers brushed the inside of Ely's wrist. Traveled his arm. Moved aside his shirt to trace his collar bone. Ely turned his face as Kai caressed his cheek. The pirate prince leaned forward, unable to resist any longer. Ely kissed his lips, hot and spiked with zaqual.

Kai pressed closer, stealing his breath until he saw stars. Ely's hands slipped under Kai's tunic, the soft warmth of his skin setting him alight. The pirate prince shrugged off the hindering garment and freed Ely of his own for good measure.

Then Kai drew away with a questioning gaze.

"Is this not what you want?" Ely asked.

"Of course it is. But I am forever terrified of what I want." Kai stroked his face with strong, tender hands. "No, not of you, diakana. Of the way that I am."

"But you're perfect. As you are." Ely brushed a finger to his lips and bent once more to claim them.

He set a trail of kisses from Kai's throat down his chest and torso, then leaned back to catch his lantern lit gaze as he reached for the fastener at his waist. He found the pirate prince roused to straining passion beneath the sea-worn trousers. Kai shuddered a low moan as Ely strummed his fingers along the length of him. Bent to taste him with a worshipping tongue.

They lay lost to time with only the night sky and the swelling sea to witness their trespasses.

Ely woke alone on the balcony covered in a light blanket. From the look of the sun, it was past midmorning. Kai would be long gone to the Council by now. He heaved a sigh, apprehension at war with contentment.

He found Salía outside by the cooking pavilion, four fish smoking in the iron pot. She nodded to him, good humor in her brown eyes. Unlike most of the Séoc, she did not flinch from his gaze.

"You're awake," she said. "Kai kept you up late, did he?"

"A bit," Ely replied, wrangling his smile before it exploded into a grin.

"Come get some food while it's hot," she ordered.

Ely obeyed gladly. He hadn't noticed his ravenous hunger until that moment.

"Can I ask you something, Ely?" Salía inquired.

She had been watching him in silence for a while, but he was too hungry to offer a penny for her thoughts.

"Of course," he said.

"Did something happen to Kai on the Isle of the Gods?"

Ely frowned, unsure if he should reveal what Kai had chosen to keep to himself.

Sensing his hesitation, she continued, "He's seemed different since his return. Distant. I am not the only one to notice. I'm asking you because I need to know how to protect him." She held his gaze, eyes probing. "What happened to him?"

"He died," Ely said. Voice low. Heavy with the memory.

Salía looked up at the billowing palms, stricken. "You brought him back?"

Ely nodded.

"But he is himself?"

"Yes. He remembers what is beyond. That leaves a mark."

Salía eyed him, appraising. "You love him?" she asked.

"Yes," Ely answered.

"I do not doubt it," she said. "He loves you too. I've known it always. You are his one weakness."

Ely frowned. "You think I should leave?"

Salía leveled stern eyes. "I am asking you to stay watchful of the danger. He will not."

Ely inclined his head, not trusting his voice. Though there did not seem to be any animosity under her words, Ely wondered if she believed the superstitions about diakana and their entrancing effect on humans. There was truth to those fears. He had seen it often enough. Was it even by his own will that Kai endangered himself and his position?

It's different with Kai, he thought

There was no manic gleam to his desire when he gazed on him nor a breathy catch to his voice as though something compelled declarations from his lips. It was not death magic that bound them together. Of that he was certain. But yet...

Kai's voice interrupted his troubled thoughts. "Please tell me you've left some for me. That circus can leave a man famished."

"There's plenty," Salía assured him.

He beamed at Ely, dimpled smile raising fluttering wings in his stomach. If anyone was working spells, it was the pirate prince. Kai paused to kiss him, not concerned with Salía's eyes on them. His cousin had been his right hand since they were children. He trusted her with his life, and she guarded him fiercely. Her words bore no ill will. She was merely protecting her captain and prince.

Kai moved on to pile a bowl high with food.

"You're back early," Salía observed. "What happened?"

Kai shook his head, irritation shadowing his face. "You know the kings. An argument broke out within moments of their gathering. Mother ended the Council until tomorrow to hope for cooler heads."

"Who's causing the trouble this time?" Salía questioned.

"Who do you think? Morag of Seúza. He says he will not join the fight against the Canon unless he is granted *Sémar Esanto*. As you can imagine, that did not sit well with Jian."

He paused to explain to Ely, "Jian is married to my mother's younger brother. She is king of Lilipon to the north. Yamon and Mirit's mother."

"Any fool could see he spoke out of turn," Salía said. "What claim could Seúza have to *Sémar Esanto*?"

"He brought up his help expanding trade on the mainland, and made some outrageous demands."

"Such as?" Salía pressed.

"It doesn't matter. Mother does not humor tantrums," Kai evaded. Salía caught his tone and asked no more questions.

"We are adjourned until tomorrow," he continued.

"I will leave you, then," Salía nodded.

She said farewell to Kai in Séoc and departed.

Kai turned to Ely, soft smile curved over his lips. "I'm sorry to have left you, but you would not be roused from your dreams."

"I slept like a stone," Ely laughed.

"Have I worn you to tatters, diakana?" he asked with a dizzying grin.

"I think I've recovered," Ely said.

"Good. Come then."

He set off down the beach. Ely followed, curious. They took a new path through the lively trees. Kai paused at a branch heavy with sweet-smelling fruit. He plucked two blushing bulbs, tossing one to Ely before continuing the journey. Ely took a bite of the plump fruit, tart juice exploding on his tongue.

They came to a lazy stream captured in a rock-lined basin before trickling on toward the sea. Kai undressed and climbed into the pool.

Ely followed, enjoying the cool lapping water. Kai sought his lips, nimble hands quick to heat his blood.

By the time they returned to the bungalow, he had forgotten Salía's warning. The day passed a delicious cycle of longing, ecstasy, and contentment. They recovered their strength in the cooking pavilion, then bathed in the sea only to taste the salt on each other's skin.

Darkness' descent found them resting comfortably in Kai's bed. The pirate prince turned to him, caressing his hair with a smile.

"Will you come with me tomorrow?"

"To the Council?"

Kai inclined his head. "I think it would help the others to know that we do not need Seúza to send the Canon crawling back to the Protectorate."

"If you think it will help, then of course. I will do anything you ask," Ely said.

Kai kissed him. "Thank you."

He looked as if he had something more to say but settled back instead. Ely closed his eyes, drifting off into the dreamless sleep of perfect bliss...

"You're almost as bad as when I left you," Rav's voice roused Ely from his fevered visions. It seemed the vampire had made his entrance through the open shutters.

"I'm only human, I'm afraid," Ely breathed.

"But you don't have to die like one," Rav intoned. "I'd have thought she would have fixed you by now."

"She thinks she's teaching me a lesson," Ely groaned.

The effort to speak seemed steeper than a sheer cliff face.

"That you live and breathe at her whim?" Rav snarled.

"Why did you save me?" Ely grunted.

"It was Ariel that fought off the Hollow," Rav deflected.

"But you pulled me out," Ely countered.

"Do you think I'd leave you there to suffer?" Rav asked.

"I don't know," Ely answered. "Dr. Faidra said you butchered women and children. Then you turned on the Cosmologists."

"I think your doctor may have the details confused after all this time," Rav said. "It was the Cosmologists of the Tower that demanded blood, and they sent my kind to collect it."

"Why would the Cosmologists need blood?" Ely asked.

"For the Hollow, of course," Rav said. "Nothing so twisted could grow from water and sunlight."

"What does that make you then?" Ely asked.

Rav turned a scathing look on him. "The stories they told about vampires preying upon humans were meant to provoke fear. We cannot live off of human blood any more than you could cake or wine. Enjoyable at a party? Yes, but a slow death in the long term. In truth, we are made in your image. What is starlight but the last lifeblood of celestial bodies trickling down through the darkness of the universe?"

Ely watched his face in silence, and as he digested the vampire's words, the truth seeped from them.

"When you say the Cosmologists sent you, you had no choice in the matter, did you?" Ely asked.

Rav shook his head. "We were to them no more than machinery. If we did not play our parts, we were thrown in a box and locked away to rust."

Ely watched him, throat tightening. Rav looked up sharply as though Ely had spoken aloud. The vampire flexed his teeth, rage bursting like a runaway breaker about him.

"I didn't come here for your pity, Elyssandro."

"Then why did you come?" Ely shivered. Fever was setting in.

"You must drink the stars, conjurer. It is slower than healing spells, but it will save you," Rav said.

Ely lifted his hand toward the window, but he could not muster the strength to draw the light into his grasp. Rav moved to his side in a wail of wind, lifting Ely's head gently in one hand and siphoning icy light to his lips with the other. Ely drank in desperate, unfiltered rivulets. When he lay back on the pillow again, the fight to draw breath felt just a little bit easier.

"Sleep," Rav commanded.

Ely could not open his eyes, but he felt the vampire's departure as surely as if he had watched him glide away through the window.

What had he been dreaming about..?

The summit of island kings took place in Tennoc's palace throne room. Chairs had been brought in and placed in a deliberate hierarchy. Kai brought Ely forward, introducing him to the gathered nobility with an incomplete recounting of the events on the Isle of the Gods. Muffled whispers and curious looks accompanied the story, but in all, they seemed willing to accept Death's aid in their campaign against the Canon.

Relieved to have completed his part, Ely sat with Salía and the rest of the Novara clan. As the proceedings commenced, she whispered the names and origins of the speakers, translating the more interesting pieces of dialogue for him.

A ruckus at the door admitted a tall, wiry man dressed in a flowing cape with a feathered collar.

"King Morag of Seúza," Salía whispered.

He addressed King Tennoc with an impenitent apology as he stalked to the empty chairs reserved for his entourage near the back of the chamber.

The Council resumed.

Finally, King Morag rose to speak. "You ask us to send our ships and our warriors to defend your shores with nothing given in return. Our island has never seen even a rumor of red sails."

"Do you think that will not change should the Canon occupy the remainder of the Barrier Keys?" demanded a noble-visaged woman sitting among the Novaras.

"The templars may have no trouble navigating your gentle waters, Jian, but ours are untamed," Morag declared. "Even if they manage to get close, the reef will take care of the rest."

"If you do not count yourself as Séoc, why did you come?" Jian questioned.

Morag raised resentful eyes to the gathered company. "It is you that have always treated my people as outcasts. As though our shores do not break the harshest storms before they wreck your great cities?"

"Did we not all sail to your rescue when the monsoons struck?" another king asked.

"We sent shipwrights and builders and mirrorwood," Jian added.

"Food, livestock, fresh water," put in another.

"All shared with contempt," Morag spat. He turned narrowed eyes to Tennoc. "We have rebuilt tenfold since your meager aid was supplied. You want our might at your back? I have named our price. We will take nothing less than First Seat. The Séocwen prince is yet unmarried, and I have seven daughters, all strong and healthy. Take whichever suits your liking, but we will join the Novara line."

It was Kai that rose to answer. Ely frowned as he heard his own name spoken. Kai turned toward him, and with his address, all eyes in the chamber followed. Ely looked to Salía, waiting for a translation, but she just stared at her cousin.

"What did he say?" Ely whispered.

"I cannot offer my hand to your daughter because it has already been offered to Elyssandro Santara Ruadan."

Ely blinked at her, not quite sure he had heard her right.

Kai continued, voice unwavering. Salía translated in a hushed monotone, "Séocwen would share allegiance with Death's Vale whose prince has done more for the Séoc people than Seúza or anyone else that sits at Council."

The room buzzed with shock and outrage. Ely looked between the flushed faces, chest tight. With some of the glares cast his way, he feared he might be forced to defend himself. Salía's hand poised on her cutlass hilt confirmed she expected the same.

King Tennoc's voice rose above the din. The protests fell to a dull roar as the kings of the Barrier Keys began to disperse.

"She has adjourned the Council," Salía told him. "We should go."

They left the chamber, avoiding the departing monarchs. Kai met them under the trees in the courtyard. He caught Ely's eyes, looking sheepish. Nervous even.

"The next time you decide to incite a riot, give us a warning, cousin," Salía scolded.

"I'm sorry. I did not know what I was about to say until it left my lips," Kai said.

"Did you mean it?" Ely asked, a foolish, hopeful grin escaping.

Kai nodded, smile just as wide. "Yes."

"This is not the time, you two," Salía hissed, snapping the back of her hand against Kai's arm.

"Kailari!" Tennoc's enraged shout boomed.

The king swept toward them with eyes like an inferno. Seeing Ely, she rounded on him. "Is this the price you demand for your freely offered help?"

"Ely had nothing to do with it," Kai intervened, placing himself between them. "He was as shocked as everyone else."

"Salía, your father wants a word with you," said the king.

Salía and Kai exchanged glances, then she nodded and left them.

"What were you thinking?" King Tennoc demanded in Séoc.

"I was thinking we need not...a greedy fool...let us all burn...his own ends."

"You are no better...Morag...gone...Others will..."

They continued to argue in tense Séoc. Ely caught only pieces of the conversation, but he understood the shape of it. The Council and its allegiances were in chaos because of him. With a final growl of rage, King Tennoc stormed away.

"What will happen?" Ely asked as they traded the city for the jungle path back to the bungalow.

"There will be shouting and hand waving," Kai replied. "But we will prove them wrong."

The pirate prince paused, turning to take in his apprehension.

"Are you angry?" Kai asked, searching his eyes.

Ely shook his head. He wished he was. It would feel better than the sinking feeling of a fool's hope.

"They will see it our way, Ely. When the tides have turned, they will see it our way."

The look of determination on his face would not be swayed. Ely followed, heart aching as he thought of Salía's entreaty. She was right. Kai would not pay heed to the peril that followed their hearts into the daylight. Even if he were to do his part against the Canon, would the Séoc people ever see past a storied monster? Would Kai's mother?

The Novara cousins met them in Kai's cove. They spoke in Lanica as much to confuse any listening ears as for Ely's benefit.

"My father says I am to stay off the Marisola and away from you," Salía said.

"Our mother says the same," Yamon added.

"Are you going to do as they ask?" Kai inquired.

Salía glared in defiance. "You are our captain. Not them."

Yamon and Mirit nodded their agreement.

"So, what is our next move?" Salía asked, arms crossed.

"There is a blockade of Canon ships encroaching on Lilipon," Kai said. "Jian told the Council they lurk but do not move to attack. I say a blockade *is* an attack. Were we to clear the way, they cannot deny that everything I told them is true."

The others listened intently, considering his mad proposal. It was suicide, surely, setting off five against named gods knew how many. Yet Ely felt Death's vigor singing through his veins, begging for release.

"What do you say, diakana? Can you sink a few Canon ships?" Kai asked.

Ely inclined his head. "Get me close enough, and I can."

"Good." Kai looked to each of his crew on turn. "We are all on board for this mutiny, then?"

"Yes," they said as one.

They set out under the cover of night, though they did not make for the docks and the Marisola. Instead they journeyed to a cave where Kai had secured the old, single-sailed sloop with the carving of Cocatl at its prow. The same boat they sailed the day Ely met the Novara cousins on the beach.

While Kai and his crew charted their course by the stars, Ely sat high in the crow's nest drinking in their light. Dawn approached. Canon ships dotted the horizon, crimson sails aloft. More than a few.

Ely stood, hands raised, focus fixed on the eye and blade that waved its banner at the forefront of the fleet. A shout skipped across the water. They were seen. A warning shot sprayed a geyser a hundred feet from their hull.

"Keep steady," Kai's voice commanded below.

Ely closed his eyes, mind plunging beneath the waves down into the darkest depths. He had felt it there when traveling this way before. The bones of an ancient beast, vast as a mountain. It rumbled a reply to his gentle call. His target locked, Ely weaved a net of black ether and cast it into the sea. He felt the beast stir. Heave. Split the ocean floor.

A roar echoed from the deep. The ocean seemed to rise into the sky in a solid wall of water. Ely gazed at the primordial beast, its bones crusted with barnacles and draped with seaweed. Then it crashed down again, pulverizing the foremost line of Canon ships to splintered shards. Kai shouted orders, frantically trying to pilot their vessel away from the aftershock.

The surviving templar ships veered away, panicked shouts rising in a maelstrom across the water. With a twitch of his hand, Ely called the beast back around. It obeyed, loyal as a steadfast watchdog, gathering speed for another charge. Before it broke the surface, a blast of blinding white light burst across the horizon, knocking Ely from his feet. When his vision recovered, he saw boiling bubbles where his pet had been, but it did not emerge. He could no longer feel it. The blast had severed the connection.

"What was that?" Salía called.

"I don't know," Kai said, peering out toward the remaining Canon ships with apprehension.

"We should go," Salía said. "We've made a point they won't soon forget."

"No," Ely said. "Take me closer."

It was not his own curiosity compelling him forward but the insistent whispers of the presence beyond the veil that drove him toward the figure that had unleashed the light.

"It's an Apostle," he whispered.

He had never seen one of the Canon's legendary invokers of Miracles. Few living ever had.

Death rustled within him, seething to escape. Black clouds formed above their vessel, thundering and flashing. Ely struggled to keep control, but a howling wind surrounded him, bearing him up into the tempest.

Surrender, death's legion intoned.

Still he resisted, fighting as the storm raged about him. He stopped as he came face to face with a figure cloaked in white from head to toe. He floated with effortless grace among the clouds, not troubled in the least by Death's storm.

He smiled, a sinister light in his gray eyes.

"Hello, Morgata," he laughed.

Though he spoke softly, his voice carried over the wind, muting it.

Ely flinched away from the voice. That was all the opening needed. His eyes glazed over, and he knew no more until he sat up, gasping and retching seawater on the Novara's deck. Kai bent over him, dripping wet, breath heaving.

"Are you alright, Ely?" he asked.

"Fine," Ely managed. "What happened?"

"You did it," Kai said, awe in his voice. "The Canon fleet is gone. I was afraid we'd lost you."

Ely lay back, vision hazy. Kai helped him into the shelter of the small cabin. He slept fitfully, waking in the late afternoon heat as they once again neared Séocwen.

"So, you don't remember any of it?" Kai asked him when he returned to the sun-drenched deck.

"Only one thing," Ely replied. "It was an Apostle that made the light. He met me in the sky. Spoke to me. Well, not to me. To Morgata."

"Interesting," Kai remarked, "that an Apostle of the Canon would address a named god."

Ely nodded. "Very interesting."

They pondered the strange, unnerving occurrence as they sailed to shore. The cousins left together while Kai and Ely walked the beach back toward the bungalow. Already long shadows were beginning to drape over the sand

Ely's limbs dragged. He felt too drained to speak. He could not have conjured even a dust mote if he tried. Death had wrung every drop of power from his body and tossed him like a husk into the sea. Perhaps if he had a shred of strength left, he would have sensed the trap.

Before he could cry out or draw a breath, they were surrounded. Ely's knees buckled, kicked out from under him. Someone hit Kai in the temple with the haft of a spear. Ely threw out a hand toward him, but heavy metal clamped about his wrists, biting into his skin. The manacles glowed red then white hot, illuminating a circle of glyphs that sizzled and burned. He cried out. Someone tied a gag tight around his mouth. Four men held Kai while two more bound his hands behind his back. It was not until they were both restrained that Morag of Seúza emerged from behind his henchmen.

"You will pay for this," Kai growled.

Morag loosed an ugly, gleeful smile. "I have already been paid. Not to worry, young prince. King Tennoc told us *you* were not to be harmed."

The Seúzans laughed.

"Bring them," Morag commanded.

The rogue islanders gagged Kai and marched them off into the jungle trees. Ely closed his eyes as they walked, reaching for any spark of death magic. He felt it knocking at his hands, but he could not channel it. The manacles. Of course. They were forged for a diakana.

Dusk settled in purple shades. They reached a cliff overlooking a punishing ocean current. The Seúzans forced Kai to his knees while Morag's men dragged Ely toward a mangled tree that stood a white-limbed corpse on the cliff's edge. Kai shouted through the gag, struggling to no avail.

The Seúzan mercenaries scaled the tree, dropping down ropes to bind Ely by the arms, hauling him up into the petrified heights. Someone stretched out his arm. The heft of a hammer drove a bolt through a round opening left in the manacles. It pierced his forearm, biting into the wood on the other side. Ely screamed. He tasted blood as his teeth ground his cheek. Another bolt nailed his other arm to the tree.

"He is yours!" Morag shouted to the star-blistered sky. "Take him back!"

Then the Seúzan horde dragged Kai away, leaving Ely alone, his blood staining the bone-pale bark.

He did not know how long he hung on the cliffside, waiting for Death to come to his rescue. He thought the rustle in the woods was another fever dream. Salía, Yamon, and Mirit wrested the bolts free and cut him down. They did their best to bind his wounds and bore him between them back through the jungle. More darkness. More fever dreams haunted by the Apostle who threw discs of burning light to sear his flesh from the bones.

The Novaras delivered him into the Etrugan's care. Rión sat with him for many nights until, at last, his fever receded. He found his hands shook when he tried to stir, and his fingers would not move to his command.

"I will take you back to Dr. Faidra when you're out of danger," Rión promised.

"Where's Kai?" Ely asked.

"They said that he is safe," Rión soothed. "You must rest now, little brother."

It was another week before Rión took him back to Dianessa. The journey was slow and perilous. Without Death's raiment about him, the dead did not recognize him and tried to hinder their passage. They fell to the Etrugan warrior's axes, but the journey to the University took much longer than it should have.

Dr. Faidra examined his wounds, observed his useless hands.

"I told you what would happen, warm blood," she croaked.

She left him in the east wing to heal at nature's pace. It had taken weeks to regain the use of his hands. Weeks more to recover magic. The last he had heard of his pirate prince was that he had married a princess from Lilipon. The scars left by the burning manacle glyphs and the spikes that nailed him to the bones of a tree remained. A story he wished to forget.

Chapter Eight

Animal

A day passed. Then another. Rav did not return. The doctor did not appear. The pain did not subside. Quinn brought him warm tea spiked with zaqual.

"It's been in the cupboard a long while, but it can't hurt you much more than you've hurt yourself, old man," he reasoned.

With the medicinal beverage, the hospitable skeleton brought a pile of his handwritten manuscripts filled with knights and adventurers and a rather satirical depiction of nobility in old Dianessa.

"Are they true?" Ely asked.

"The names and places are plucked from history or legend," Quinn replied, "but all just pretty fiction."

The stories certainly did pass the time. For all the daring do and intrigue, it was the skeleton knight's flair for slow-burning romance that kept him wrapped up in the ink-blotted pages.

The nights were the worst when the pain kept him up, but he found that if he consumed starlight straight from the source and not first filtered through his spell-carved flask, the healing effects magnified. Why had Dr. Faidra so strongly cautioned him against this practice? Had she really meant to keep him weakened? No. Surely, it was simply to keep him safe when such potency was not required. Surely.

A week passed.

The tower of manuscripts grew thin. So did the pain.

When he could sit up comfortably, Quinn carried in a rickety table and set his Caj board between them. As they laid out their sets, it became swiftly apparent that Quinn's mind remained preoccupied.

"What's bothering you?" Ely asked.

Quinn scratched his bony pate, heaving a sound like a sigh.

"Elyssandro," he said, eye sockets trained on the board. "I think it may be time for you to consider leaving the Vale."

"Leaving?" Ely frowned.

"There must be somewhere among the living you may happily settle," Quinn said.

"The living will not happily let a necromancer settle among them," Ely replied.

"Do you not have Etrugan friends?" Quinn pressed.

"Why are you so adamant about this?" Ely asked. "Have I worn out my welcome in my invalid state?"

Quinn shook his head. "Never, my dear fellow. You have reminded me how fragile it is to be alive. And…"

He paused, considering his words.

"I don't like how this episode has played out. It isn't right. Leaving you here like this when something could be done."

"It's my own fault, Quinn," Ely insisted. "She told me not to touch the fire, and I set my hand straight in the flames. I think she's just hoping this time I'll get the message through my thick skull."

"I doubt your skull is any thicker than standard, old bean," Quinn replied.

Then he swept the board in a final triumphant coup.

Another two nights of pure starlight saw Ely walking again with hardly even a limp. On the third, he felt a familiar presence as he sat at the window.

"You can come in," he invited.

Rav slipped between the shutters from his perch on the apartment wall. He appeared dusty and windswept like he had just returned from a long, arduous journey.

"You look much better," the vampire observed.

"The stars work wonders, so it would seem," Ely said.

"Did you not drink from them before?" Rav frowned.

"I live on them," Ely said. He held out his flask for Rav to examine and explained, "Dr. F taught me to filter it first to consume it safely."

"And I take it you can't read glyphs," Rav said with a sideways glance.

Ely stammered, "Well, I'm not the best at it, but...no, not well. Hardly at all, really."

"You're being poisoned, conjurer," Rav informed him.

"Poisoned?"

Rav tapped a pale finger to a series of characters. "That has watered your starlight down to exactly one tenth of its potency. These have made your blood thin and prone to hemorrhage. And these..." Rav's brows raised in bewilderment. "These I've only ever seen used for animals."

"Why? Why would she do that?" Ely whispered.

"Render you weak and docile? I couldn't imagine how she might benefit from such a thing," Rav scoffed.

Ely sat down on the bed, feeling suddenly tired and achy.

"You don't need her anymore, Elyssandro," Rav said.

Ely looked up at him. "So, what do you propose?"

In an instant, the vampire was at his side, breath like ice as he whispered, "Help me free Ariel from the horror of the Hollow, and you will no longer be alone in this world."

Rav dropped the flask into his hand. Ely stared at it, sickness welling in the pit of his stomach. Rage followed. He raised his eyes to the vampire's face.

"Where do we begin?"

MOVEMENT 2

A Fool's Errand

CHATTAN

Chapter Nine
Once More With Feeling

Ely took the University steps at a fraction of his usual speed. The cane, borrowed from Sir Ambrose Quinn's prop collection, rapped a hollow cadence against the weathered stone. These stately walls had never before looked sinister to him, but today the University frowned down like a wrathful monarch ready to dole judgment.

He slowed his pace, leaning more heavily on the cane. Nerves had made him forget his part for a moment.

"You're going to have to really sell it, my boy," Quinn had told him. "Give it the old stagecraft panache, eh?"

Ely remembered the way his uncle wielded his cane, as though it were a mighty staff that lent him authority despite his youth and limited mobility. He would have to handle his crutch with far less flair than Uncle Misha.

"You might," Quinn advised, "try imagining the exact spot where the aching fracture throws a hitch in your step. That's how we did it in my old theatre days."

"You were a player?" Ely asked him.

"I dabbled," Quinn shrugged. "There's not a maiden fair or worldly wise matron that can resist a thespian."

"Of course," Ely chuckled.

His mirth subsided as he recalled that it was neither maiden nor matron he had to convince with his performance. Dr. Faidra knew him better than he knew himself. She would certainly catch any tell he might convey. Whether he realized it or not.

"I'm not sure this is such a good idea, Quinn," he said, feeling suddenly queasy.

"Nonsense. You've soldiered on through far more harrowing adventures. This is nothing. Now, show me your walk once more..."

The doctor hunched at her workbench, a soldering iron in hand as she bent copper wires into place on a small sheet of metal.

Ely's heart convulsed, doing its damndest to threaten him with untimely collapse should he continue putting one foot in front of the other. He took a breath, stooping his shoulders, leaning into the cane. Quinn was right. The prop helped.

"So, you've finally crawled out of bed, have you, warm blood?" she croaked with a smug note.

Ely nodded, lowering his head, trying to appear contrite. Anger erupted at the sight of her putrid face. The cold, voracious power within him, grown healthy again fed on raw starlight, demanded release.

Focus.

"I trust you have learned a lesson you will not soon forget?" she asked.

"I have," he replied. "But I had hoped since I have done my penance you would allow me the chance to explain."

Dr. Faidra set aside her tool and folded her clawed hands on the table. "I'm all ears, Elyssandro."

Ely drew up a chair, taking care to allow a groan and a wince to escape as he sat. He did not have to feign a struggle. Quinn had trussed up his leg in the splint again, so the stiff discomfort required no further theatrics.

"Ravan Aurelio paid me a visit after our little standoff. He was trying to get more information out of me. If you hadn't fixed the wards, I'm not sure what would have happened."

"I fail to see how that justifies the utter stupidity of your behavior," Dr. Faidra growled.

"I'm getting to that," Ely said. "He mentioned something about how the Cosmologists would have answers, and that set me thinking he must be planning to make a visit to the ruins of the Tower. I wanted to stop him before he could find anything that might help him get to Ariel."

"And did you?" Dr. Faidra asked with undisguised interest. "Stop him?"

"I fought him off until I lost control. I don't know what happened to him after. Sir Quinn said he carried me to a great height and let me plunge. He said also that the vampire appeared to have been injured as he retreated."

"Sir Quinn, yes," she mused, eyes narrowed. "So, the vampire has not troubled you since?"

Ely shook his head. "I haven't seen so much as a creeping shadow. Which has me worried enough to drag myself all the way here."

"You think he knows something?" Dr. Faidra questioned.

"Evidence suggests," Ely replied.

He looked up, hoping he would not give away his intent the moment he met her glazed eyes.

"Dr. F, the only way we will know for sure he cannot get to her is if we are the ones protecting the keys."

The undead doctor grimaced, but she did not refute his reasoning.

"I saw what your wards did to him," Ely pushed. "They would be safe here."

She drummed her claws on the table. "I told you before, I don't know where they are."

"You know where to find one," Ely countered. "That's a start."

Dr. Faidra studied the wire-ridden scrap of metal before her. Finally, she nodded.

"I gave my key to the Etrugans," she said. "If we were to recover it, I could use it to find the next. We built them in such a way that the keys point to one another so they might be recovered if the need arose."

Ely beamed with excitement, nearly springing to his feet before the cane and splint reminded him of his staged injury.

"It's too dangerous for you to go as you are," Dr. Faidra declared. "And there is no guarantee they will still know where it was hidden after all this time."

"It's just a short jaunt along the Demonhead. I've traveled it before in worse condition," Ely reminded her. "At the very least, it will be therapeutic to stretch my leg."

He tamed his grin, asking earnestly, "If you don't want me to go, then I won't go. May I have your permission?"

Dr. Faidra scrutinized him, milky eyes unblinking.

"You may go, warm blood," she intoned at last, clearly pleased with the change in him.

"Many thanks, Dr. F," he replied, letting his voice turn breathless as if with relief. He braced the cane and heaved himself to his feet. "I'd like to pay a visit to the east wing, then I'll be on my way."

She inclined her head. Was there a hint of a smile on her bloodless lips?

Ely limped for the door. No need to imagine an ache in his chest to stoop him over. He paused, turning back to the undead creature that had been his only family since he lost his own. She was already back to tinkering.

"Dr. F?" he began.

She looked up, scowl not quite so deeply lined as usual. Who knew it took a cowed, subservient aura to inspire such fondness in her?

"Yes, what is it, Elyssandro?"

He shook his head. "Nevermind. I'll see you when I return."

She nodded. "Look after yourself, warm blood."

He departed the Oubliette, making a slow plod to the east wing common room. Blinking back mist, he tried to swallow the tightness in his throat. Doubt settled as he looked about his comfortable, familiar space. What if Rav had been wrong about Dr. Faidra? Or worse? What if the vampire had lied to sway him to his side?

His mind wandered back to the first time he had set eyes on this place. He was cold and exhausted from the long journey through the wastes. Dr. F had lit a fire for him in the hearth, and he sat in awe of the mystical azure streaks that cavorted gently through its flames.

"You will be safe here, warm blood," she told him, speaking still in Canon Paxat. He had not yet revealed he knew Lanica, his mother's native tongue and the doctor's as well. "No one will hunt you. You will find the dead of Dianessa are more agreeable than in the Vale."

"Is there anything to eat?" Ely asked, with the famished whine of a child.

She brought him a draught of something that quieted his hunger and left him contentedly drowsy as he huddled in his uncle's overlarge jacket by the fire.

When he woke, she provided him scavenged clothes near his size and a few provisions left by an Etrugan visitor. He scarfed down the lump of cheese and packet of dense wafers like a starving pup. With his mortal needs addressed, the doctor listened intently to his story of persecution and narrow escape.

"Was it true?" she questioned at last. "What they said about your mother returning from the dead?"

Ely stared at his knees, hands clenched into fists. Death spilled icy tendrils through his veins, threatening to overtake him if he raised the memory of that night.

"I can't talk about it," he said through clenched teeth.

"There is no shame in whatever you did, child," she said.

"They say I am evil," he murmured.

"So, you're evil," the doctor shrugged. "So am I. So is everything they cannot grind underfoot."

He looked up at her. For the first time since his mother died, the knot in his chest loosened just a little.

"Would you like to see more evils, warm blood?" she asked, leaning forward with an eerie smile.

He nodded, grinning.

Dr. Faidra led him through winding, dank-smelling corridors and up flights of cobwebbed stairs to a windowless chamber at the peak of the University. She lit no candle, instead pressing her fingers to a prismatic crystal fixed to the wall. Ely gasped as the crystal glowed soft white at its heart. She beckoned him onward to a low circular platform enclosed by a corroded metal rail. Opening a latched gate, they stood in the center of the platform where a rectangular box sat fixed to a pedestal jutting up from the boards. Dr. F clacked her claws across the collection of switches and buttons arranged in a neat grid on its surface.

The platform shuddered, and a bass hum murmured through his bones. Gossamer lines like threads of spider silk projected from one side of the platform to the other, weaving together overhead. The lines converged on flickering, multicolored nodes that varied in size and brightness. Strange characters written in ochre light appeared and faded among the branching threads.

"What is it?" Ely asked.

"A map," Dr. Faidra replied. "I can see all that passes in the Vale. This is how I found you, warm blood. It is how I will protect you from everything that would do you harm..."

Ely shook off his stupor. Any spark of caring from the doctor had been a carefully acted play put on for a lonely lost boy. The recollection of her living map, however, raised a matter of imminent concern to his current plans.

Ely found his knapsack and packed his least threadbare clothes along with an ample supply of gold coins. He took also the violin in its case. His fingers ached to play it, to release some of the melancholy from his soul.

Shouldering his pack, he said one last goodbye to his haunt of all these years. Then he let the doors swing shut on that epoch of his life with a resounding clang.

Dusk approached by the time he returned the cane to propmaster Quinn. The skeleton chevalier unbound the splint, poured him a generous dram of zaqual, and wiped invisible tears from his eye sockets while Ely played a tune on his violin. As he had hoped, the wistful vibrations released some of the anguish that had built to a crescendo in the past few days.

When he laid down his bow, Rav silently joined them. Ely had sensed the vampire lingering out of sight near the window, but he was not going to interrupt his rhapsody in the middle without reaching a satisfying conclusion.

"So?" Rav inquired.

"She gave me a starting point," Ely said.

"Where?" Rav pressed, shadowed eyes eager.

"I'll get to that. There is something else of which my visit to the University has reminded me. Something that could spoil our plot before it begins."

Rav eyed him impatiently, lips drawn into a tight scowl.

Ely continued, "The doctor has a device. A whole loft, really, in one of the University towers devoted to a machine that tracks the movements of everything in the Vale. It tells her where there are ruptures or when templars venture too deep into the wilderness. It told her where to find me when I fled Saint Lucio."

"You're certain it can track *anything* in the Vale?" Rav asked.

"So she says," Ely nodded.

"But you can't read glyphs, so you have no idea for sure what exactly this contraption tells her," Rav said with blunt irritation.

"She has used it accurately enough for me to know we cannot risk hoping for a blind spot," Ely answered, pretending he could not feel the jab of the vampire's contempt for his technical illiteracy.

"What exactly are you hinting at, Elyssandro?" Rav asked, pronouncing his name in lethal staccato.

"I think I should go alone to fetch the key," he said.

Rav glared, fangs flaring. "You would still be trapped in the roots of the Hollow if not for my help."

"I know that, and I am grateful," Ely said.

It was difficult to remain calm with gusts of fury rushing over him from across the room. He wondered if this was what it was like when others stood at his own side.

"I will not entrust Ariel's release to a mortal, conjurer or not," Rav spat.

"If Dr. Faidra suspects that we have conspired against her, we don't stand a chance."

"You've overestimated her cunning," Rav glowered.

"I have friends among the Etrugans," Ely went on. "They will help me recover the key."

Rav cocked his head to the side, and Ely realized his mistake too late. "So, it's with the Etrugans, then."

"Yes, but—"

The vampire shot through the window like a bullet from a pistol chamber.

"Well done, old man," Quinn said, patting him on the shoulder.

Ely rubbed his burning eyes with a sigh.

"Shit."

Chapter Ten

Temple of the Horned God

The entrance to Etrugan territory lay at the feet of a gray stone monolith known as the Sleeping Giant. Its great crags jutted high in geometric blocks carved from eons of punishing wind and water.

Ely found the narrow shoulder that gave passage through the Giant's base. It was not particularly hidden, but the tight squeeze discouraged any but a most determined traveler. Beyond the corridor, a labyrinth of rock formations towered skyward in bizarre shapes that seemed to defy gravity. After a short stroll in the strange stone garden, it soon became apparent that some did just that. Entire slabs of jagged earth hovered above the ground like crumbled islands adrift in the air. Ely picked his way between the floating monuments. With such wondrous distractions, it was easy to miss the drab staircase hidden in plain sight on a large but otherwise unremarkable formation rooted to the ground.

The steps wound back around to a new arrangement of sculpted cliffs, some anchored to the earth and some fixed upon the sky. Though there was not even a stirring of dust, he knew he was being followed. It was not until his deliberate path made clear that he was no lost traveler that a figure, gray as the landscape, emerged, irises a warning shade of green surrounded in ebony pools. He did not recognize the guard that met him, nor did the Etrugan betray any sign that she knew the stranger trespassing in the heights.

"I am Elyssandro Santara Ruadan," he said in the sharp Etrugan tongue. "I am a friend of Rión Twin Axes."

The Etrugan warrior scrutinized him closer, eyes muting ever so subtly from jade to turquoise. "You are Morgata's messenger," she determined. "I saw the marching dead. You sent them?"

Ely nodded. The Etrugan did not smile, but her eyes shifted to purple delight.

"Rión Twin Axes said you might come. I will take you to Fjarat."

"You have my undying thanks," Ely beamed, using the dramatic Etrugan declaration of gratitude. "What are you called?"

"Sora Wolfheart," she replied.

"Sora Wolfheart, glad to meet you."

"And you, night magician," she nodded. "Follow me."

They ascended another steep staircase and crossed a thin stone bridge onto a levitating leviathan.

"What holds them up?" Ely had once asked Rión as they made this very same hike long ago. He had been half his height back then, and the climb seemed more arduous.

"I have no fucking clue, starshine," Rión exclaimed. She called ahead to Xaris who had left them behind with her long stride. "Mother, why do the stones float?"

The hulking warrior glanced back at them with shades of amusement. "That is the kind of useless question that sends shiteating humans scrambling to break the gods' mysteries."

Rión waited for her mother to walk on before she leaned close and whispered, "She doesn't know..."

They crossed two more bridges to even more dizzying altitudes before they reached the stone isle where Fjarat lay hidden among the mist. The final overpass came to rest at an ashen gate with feral figures carved in relief in its heavy granite.

Sora raised her fist and signaled with her hand. The Etrugan language extended beyond spoken speech to intricate gestures. Rión's younger daughter, Brindle, spoke only in sign. Ely had learned the best of what he knew from her during his visits to Fjarat. The young Etrugan had grabbed his hands with tiny gray fingers and molded them like clay into the right shapes until he could tell her his name, his favorite foods, and his favorite animals. Yes, I would like to be friends. No, I would not like to eat raw fire peppers. My eyes stay the same because I am human, and we are boring.

Rión's elder daughter, Ariadna, preferred to leap, snarling, on his back and use his arms and legs as tree limbs. A little jungle cat that left claw marks wherever she landed. The girls were twins, but the five minutes between them could not have forged more different people. Ely wondered how old they would be now. He had not been himself on his last visit, and even that was years past.

The gate rumbled and split, swinging inward to admit the newcomers to the darkness of a tunnel. Several Etrugans met them on the other side carrying glyph-carved lamps. After a brief exchange, Sora bid him farewell, and a cheerful Etrugan with moss-green skin led him onward.

Ely blinked in the bright sunlight as they emerged from the tunnel into a long corridor lined with ornate stone columns. A low wall ran along the passage, protecting against a nauseating fall into the square below. He thanked his guide and continued on alone. He knew his way.

A dozen levels of pillared walkway ran the perimeter of the stronghold. At intervals, sets of staircases led to upper and lower levels, then eventually down into the open square. Etrugans of many shades–stone gray, moss green, slate purple, indigo blue–went about their daily business with more civility than in human cities but equally bustling.

Rión resided in a spacious townhome at the top level with stunning views from her clifftop terrace. The door was answered by a lavender-complexioned Etrugan with a round face, neatly plaited amethyst beard, and full belly wrapped in a leather apron. Jorig the Beloved, Rión's mate of sixteen years.

He slapped Ely's shoulders in greeting then ushered him into the foyer, bidding him to wipe his feet on the mat. They had redecorated since his last visit, adding a large painted wolf mask to one wall, new furniture expertly lathed, and several happy-looking potted plants.

"It keeps me busy," Jorig shrugged at Ely's compliments, ever humble.

Rión had made no secret of pining over Jorig in their youthful years. He had been even shorter and rounder back then, already gaining notoriety for his perfectly braided solstice loaves and sturdy wood carvings. Rión had confided lamenting doubts over catching the eye of such a rare and magnificent Etrugan specimen. As if Rión Twin Axes ever settled for anything less than exactly what she wanted.

"Uncle Ely!" Ariadna galloped across the room and slammed into him, a hurtling mountain. She nearly matched his height now, her hug as bone-crushing as her mother's.

"Hi, Ari," he gasped, patting her on the back as much to cry for mercy as to express affection.

She released him, eyes bright lavender to match her skin. "Mother's not here, but I'm sure she won't be long." She turned on Jorig, demanding, "Father, why haven't you brought him something to eat?"

"I'm fine," Ely laughed.

"You're too thin," she pronounced, looking the very echo of her grandmother and mother before her. "Sit! I'll be right back."

Then she lumbered off, footfalls like hammer strikes to an anvil.

"Where's Brin?" Ely asked Jorig.

"The garden."

Ely thanked him and stepped through the side door to the spacious terrace where raised beds and sculptured lattices overflowed with vegetables. In one corner, hens muttered and clucked in their coop. A goat nibbled scrubby grass in another pen.

Brindle knelt in a garden bed, eyes closed. She had stone gray skin and hair like Rión, though she was smaller and softer in stature like her father. She raised her hands. Gentle golden light spilled from her fingers, coaxing a withered fern back to health. Ely watched in wonder as the leaves recovered their emerald hue then slowly unfurled toward the light.

She opened her eyes. They glowed bright gold until she took in her visitor. Then her irises turned first to exuberant purple, then pale, aching blue. She moved closer, gaze transfixed.

"You are okay?" she signed.

He nodded. Brindle took his hands, turning them over to examine them. She folded back a sleeve, touching the scars on his forearm that refused to fade.

"Mother wouldn't talk about it," she continued, hands speaking quickly. "I thought maybe you had died, and she did not want to tell us."

"If I died," he signed. "I would come back as a ghost and tell you myself."

Her eyes slipped to laughing lavender then settled to comfortable red.

"Was it templars that hurt you?" she asked.

Ely shook his head, replying, "Humans but not templars. It is..." He frowned, searching for the sign. "Complicated."

"Can you still use magic?" she asked.

Ely smiled and held out his hand. A dusky swirl shaped into a black dahlia in his palm. Brindle picked up the ether bloom, touching its arched petals in fascination.

"For you," he signed as she made to hand it back to him.

Brindle slipped the death magic trinket into her pocket. Then she threw her arms around him. She was far more gentle than her sister but her embrace just as earnest.

Ariadna bellowed from the doorway, calling them inside. The young Etrugan had apparently pulled everything out of the pantry and heaped it on the dining room board. Ariadna crowded in next to him on the bench, and Brindle sat across. Jorig brought him a mug of foamy dark beer.

"Brewed it myself," he said.

"Yet another reason you are called the Beloved," Ely grinned.

By the time he was uncomfortably full and a touch fuzzy-headed, Rión returned looking frayed at the ends. Her scowl vanished when she saw Ely at the table with her family. The bone crushing did not hurt nearly so bad after Jorig's pints. Siggy bounded between everyone in the room, sparks flying from her panting snout, smoke tail billowing back and forth. She settled finally at Brindle's feet.

Rión paused to thoroughly kiss Jorig. Ariadna's gagging and retching went unacknowledged. Jorig took Rión's weapons, and she sat down at the table, digging into the plentiful fare.

"Did you find the shiteating bastard, mother?" Ariadna asked.

"Watch your tongue, Ari," Jorig chided, returning with two fresh mugs. He set one before Ely and the other before his mate.

"God's tits, this is delicious!" Rión declared. "Your best yet, my love." Jorig's eyes shone with such pride that it overflowed into a smile.

Rión turned to Ariadna and said, "No, he's too fucking fast even for Greta the Swift." She looked to Ely, explaining, "We have a strange and very irritating intruder. He is holed up in the distilling caves. Whatever he is, he moves like lightning."

"Rav," Ely groaned.

Rión raised her eyebrows. "Oh, you know him. Good. Maybe you can get him out of Kristor's barrels."

"I doubt it. He's angry with me," Ely said, sipping his beer. "But I'll give it a try."

"Excellent!" Rión boomed. "I knew it was a good omen, you turning up."

"Don't be too hasty on that," Ely said with a pointed look.

Rión caught his undertone and inclined her head. "You can tell me all about it on our way."

"Can I come?" Ariadna chirped.

Rión shook her head. "You are going to stay here and clean up this mess."

Ariadna growled but was silenced by Rión's louder, fiercer roar. When the warrior had finished eating, she fetched her axes once again.

Brindle tapped Ely's arm, signing, "Will you say goodbye before you leave?"

"I promise," he replied.

As the two friends walked the columned city perimeter, Rión told him about how she had marched the effigies raised from the river against raiding templars. Every one of the nameless god's soldiers had dropped their weapons and run in dread. The death magic had faded soon after, and the Etrugans set the inanimate templar corpses on spikes along the border of their more vulnerable outer villages. Not a sign since of another assault.

Her story finished, Ely took his turn recounting all that had transpired since they last parted. While Rión was furious at the revelation of Dr. Faidra's treachery, it did not surprise her in the least.

The distilling caves lay at the other end of Fjarat on a smaller, separate isle inconveniently connected by a flimsy rope ladder.

"Had a few too many, Ruadan?" Rión called dryly as he clung to the yielding rungs.

"Up in a minute," he panted, waiting for the sky to stop spinning.

Closer to five minutes later, he made it to the top.

"So, this vampire is looking for some kind of mechanical device in Kristor's barrels?" Rión asked.

"My guess is he's hiding out in the caves to avoid being roasted to ash by the sun," Ely replied.

"And he is your friend or not?" she continued.

"Still to be determined. I'd rather not kill him."

"You'll have to fight Kristor on that point," Rión said, "but understood."

They entered the lower caverns where the master distiller kept his empty barrels and spare parts. Paved tunnels made a crisscrossing highway back to the caves where Kristor worked his magic, deriving potent spirits from succulents and roots.

Ely paused, a shiver passing through him. Rav was near, tired and hostile. A cornered beast. Ely signaled Rión to wait while he walked ahead.

"Rav?" Ely called, voice echoing in the vaulted cavern.

Smashed barrels lay like wrecked ships among a sea of pale green liquid.

"So, you finally managed to catch up," the voice resounded from above somewhere among broad stalactites.

"You can come down," Ely said. "They just want you to stop destroying their best vintage."

"It's not their best. It stinks of vinegar," the vampire hissed.

"Come on, Rav," Ely coaxed. "I'm sorry I bent your nerves. Let's start fresh, shall we?"

The vampire dropped from the shadows, face dirt-streaked, hair electrified.

"You look awful," Ely commented. "Come with me, and we'll get you cleaned up. Then we can talk with my friend about where we might start our search."

Rav seemed to be considering his proposal when a meaty arm swung a club toward the vampire's head. Rav darted away in a whirl of screaming wind, and Ely ducked just in time to avoid losing his teeth.

The husky Etrugan snarled a curse.

"Kristor!" Rión shouted. "Put your fucking weapon down, you lout!"

"Two hundred years of fermentation fed to the stones!" Kristor howled. There were tears in his eyes, bright blue with anguish.

"Call it a sacrifice to the named gods," Rión consoled him.

Ely closed his eyes, seeking Rav's movements. He felt nothing. Night had fallen, and the vampire was gone.

"Sorry, little brother, I've just never heard of a magical key being hidden in Fjarat or anywhere else in our territory."

Rión propped her feet up on the hearthstones, relaxed in a cushy chair with a mug in hand.

Ely threw one arm over his eyes, trying to keep his head from floating away like an Etrugan rock island. Seven pints more had not helped matters, but they had fortified his nerves.

"What about your mother?" he asked. "Might she know something?"

Rión grunted. "You know Xaris. She will tell us some tale about a god fucking a sea scallop and shitting out a pearl shaped like the key. It will waste several hours in the telling and get us no closer to finding anything."

They lapsed into despairing silence until he heard snores rolling from the direction of the Etrugan's chair. Ely too balanced on the brim of unconsciousness.

"Elyssandro."

"Yes?" he grumbled before he realized it was not his friend's voice that addressed him.

Ely opened his eyes to find viscous light taking form in the middle of Rión's living room. Siggy growled, sitting up from her bed by the fireplace.

"Ariel!" Ely exclaimed, upsetting his chair.

Rión sprang to her feet, hands balled in fisted cudgels. She squinted at the woman-shaped light. Ariel held up a lambent hand then rushed toward the front door, passing straight through.

"Get up, starshine! Your ghost wants us to follow."

"Right now?" Ely asked, rubbing his bruised hip.

"God's tits, you need to sleep it off first? Useless shit of a magician."

"No, no, I'm coming."

Ariel waited for them by the front steps. As they emerged, she swept off into Fjarat. Siggy charged after her. Rión and Ely followed, a little worse for wear. They stole between the darkened avenues, looking over their shoulders as though they were still naughty children about to get their hides shredded for unruly behavior.

Ariel led them above the topmost peak of the city where fragments of floating rock gazed down on the Etrugan stronghold. These were ancient temples of the named gods, abandoned long ago when their foundations began to crumble and entrance became too dangerous even for the occasional offering. They caught up with Siggy beneath the largest and most remote of the temple outcroppings.

"Is that where we almost died in a cave-in?" Ely asked, tilting his head to take in the lopsided edifice.

"Do you mean the Temple of Zygos that mother threatened to kill us for desecrating?" Rión asked. "Yes, it would appear so."

The land bridge that had once connected the temple to Fjarat had broken away, its stones still afloat but drifting apart.

Ariel flickered on the other side of the bridge by an idol of the horned god. Rión made the leap to the first segment, still nimble enough on her feet. Ely eyed the distance, wondering when the bridge had doubled its width. No time for stupid questions. Rión and Siggy were already halfway across.

Ely squeezed one eye shut, bringing the two smeared bridge halves together, then he took a running leap. Bit of a hard landing but no plunge into the void. Now, just seventeen more.

Luckily, Jorig's frothy brew instilled more than enough confidence to hop from stone to stone, maybe more frog-like than cat-like, but who was keeping score? The final jump to the temple's mouth turned out to be longer than it looked. He struck the edge of a half-tumbled staircase, scrabbling desperately for a hold. Rión seized him by the collar and dragged him to more stable ground.

"That was the easy part," she growled.

Siggy whined, and they caught a glimpse of their guiding light drifting onward through the domed entrance.

"Maybe it was true after all, what you said about the god and the sea scallop," Ely chuckled.

Rión roared with laughter, and the two walked mirthfully past disapproving statues into the temple.

"I suppose we should have brought a lantern or something," Ely remarked, blinking in the pitch black.

"Well, at least it is very easy to see your ghost," Rión pointed out, setting off toward the wavering light that brought a section of debris into focus. "Just watch your step."

While they had been fully sober when last they trod this sacred ground, they had been in the throes of teenagedom. A condition arguably worse for the equilibrium.

Ely recalled the spiked pillars and endless carvings of the horned god in every configuration imaginable. Including a few disturbingly phallic depictions he was quite glad it was too dark to see now. Rión had found a hidden passageway into a stuffy chamber where a circle of body-shaped mounds surrounded glyphs etched deep in the stone.

"Blood sacrifices?" Ely asked, with the shuddering fascination of youth.

"No, orgies," Rión corrected matter-of-factly. "Our gods like fucking not slit throats."

"Oh."

She pointed his attention to sculptured figures frozen in explicit poses for all eternity. Or at least until Ely tapped one with a curious finger. Its base quaked, and the lude figures tumbled down on their heads. They raced back down the passage, the walls collapsing behind them. Diving headlong into the main sanctuary, a wave of rubble broke, at last, against the foot of Zygos's altar...

"Where has that shiteating ghost gone?" Rión growled.

They were deep in the maze of the temple now where the priests had squirreled away offerings and treasures among a multitude of chambers. Ely managed to conjure a black-hearted lantern that emitted just enough light to survey their surroundings.

Siggy barked and pawed at a section of wall that appeared solid even on close inspection.

"Ariel?" Ely called, setting down the lantern and laying his ear against the rough rock to listen. It felt very good to rest his head.

Rión kicked him. "Wake up."

"Sorry."

Rión picked up the lantern, shaking her head. Something creaked, and a gap appeared a few paces away.

"Many thanks, Ariel," Ely grinned.

He traipsed through the opening without thinking to duck down. His head struck a sagging post on the other side. Shaking followed. When he sat up coughing in a cloud of dust, the entryway was blocked.

"Riri?" he called.

The muffled answer came from the other side, "Fine, starshine. You in one piece?"

"I think so," Ely said. "Go back to the main entrance. I'm going to find another way out."

"Fucking gods. Alright. We'll meet you outside."

Ariel's light waved at him. He noticed now that this room housed a collection of relics artfully displayed on ornate sculptures. Ariel hovered beside a vaguely womanish statue with hands cupped around an unremarkable black lump. An egg, maybe? A fruit? No time for interpreting ancient abstract art.

"What am I looking at?" he asked the light.

Ariel rippled. Faded. Her voice emerged at last, crackling, "The key. The key. Right there in front of your face."

"What, this egg thing?" Ely asked, picking up the black ovoid. It was heavy as lead but otherwise unimpressive.

He looked around, hoping to catch sight of something that looked a bit more promising.

"Take it," Ariel insisted.

"The egg?"

"Yes. Sure. The egg. Take it."

Ely put the key or egg or fruit into his pocket. He swore he heard a sigh of relief come from the direction of the fading light.

"Alright then. If that's it, maybe you could point the way out?" Ely asked.

Ariel buzzed and flickered. Then she was gone.

"Many thanks," he muttered.

Conjuring his own light, he discovered an unobstructed doorway leading from Zygos's art museum into yet another hallway. There were only so many branching pathways and chambers, he reasoned, before one of them had to lead back around to the sanctuary. Or perhaps not. Perhaps if he just laid down by this statue for a few minutes...

"Are you hurt, Elyssandro?"

Rav's outburst of worry roused him like a dousing of cold water. He sat up.

"No, I'm just...resting," he mumbled, regaining his feet unsteadily.

"Are you drunk?" Rav inquired with a sniff.

"Very," Ely nodded. "But I found the egg. The key, I mean. So, if you know a way out, that would be excellent."

Rav glared at him. "Give it to me, conjurer. You are in no condition to carry it."

Ely sighed. "If I do that, you're just going to run off with it before I have the chance to explain to you—"

Rav sprang at him, sweeping him off his feet and pinning him against one of Zygos's cloven hooves. Ely gasped for breath, air knocked from his lungs.

"That's the problem, Elyssandro," the vampire hissed in his ear. "You are forever explaining things to me which you know nothing about."

Rav broke away, disappearing once again in a cyclone of dust. Ely groaned and reached into his pocket. The key was gone.

He swore and kicked a chunk of stone. It thunked against a pillar, and a great rumbling shook the ground beneath his feet. Stomach sinking, Ely searched for an exit. He looked up, dodging streaming wreckage. Above, the open sky glittered through the growing hole in the ceiling. Death's whisper, which had been blessedly absent since around his fourth mug, rose up so suddenly he had no chance to dispute its control. His vision went white. When it cleared again, he stood on the far side of the scattered bridge. Across from him, the Temple of Zygos was no more than an airborne field of crushed stone.

Rión and Siggy trotted to meet him. At least they had made it out. The Etrugan clapped him on the shoulder.

"It was bound to come down eventually," she said, peering out at the ruined temple. "Why don't we keep this little visit between us?"

Ely nodded as he watched a disembodied horn drift past. "Yes, that's probably best."

The empty-handed plod back through the Vale dragged without a driving purpose. Ely wondered if perhaps the doctor could use her machine to help him find Rav, but the burn of her betrayal grew more raw the closer he came to Dianessa. He was not yet ready to go back.

"Mother wishes you could stay with us forever," Brindle had signed as he sat with her in the garden on his final morning in Fjarat. *"I wish you could stay too."*

"Thank you, Brin," he replied. *"Maybe someday..."*

Darkness claimed the Vale. Ely pressed on until he spied a pleasant nook where he could listen to the soothing chirr of undead crickets. He lit a campfire and took out his violin. There had been no chance to play it during his eventful trip to Fjarat, but out here in the moon-drenched woods, time stood still enough for a little music.

He looked up expectantly as the last notes faded. Rav stepped into the circle of firelight. The vampire sat with legs crossed, looking at him with shadowed, feral eyes. Then he set the heavy oblong device they had taken from the horned god's temple onto the ground between them.

"What do we do with it?" he asked.

"Dr. Faidra told me each key points to the others," Ely told him. "We need her to convince the device to give up its secrets."

"So, without the doctor, it is no more than a useless lump. One might say...an egg," Rav concluded with a tilt of his head.

"In my defense, I was not expecting to leave the house that night," Ely blushed.

He paused to observe his companion's face, take in the swell of emotion that radiated from him. Frustration. Weariness. Anxiety. On top of subtler fluxes beneath.

"I know you don't like the answer, Rav, but you're going to have to trust me."

The vampire's lip curled across his pointed fangs. "How can I trust you? For all your power, you are so excruciatingly human."

"Maybe Ariel can tell you what to do with it, then," Ely suggested. "We would never have found it without her help."

"She does not speak to me," Rav murmured, pained.

"Why?"

The vampire glared at the ground. "I failed to protect her. And now she is trapped in the Hollow."

"You were locked away. It hardly seems fair to hold that against you," Ely said.

Rav looked up at him, the slightest hint of amusement twitching at the corners of his lips. He stood, leaving the key nestled in its indentation in the dirt.

"Take it to the doctor," he said. "Find out where we're traveling next."

Ely nodded. "I'll meet you in the Spine."

"Why there?" Rav asked, a bit edgy about returning to the site of his imprisonment.

"There are so many ruptures, it confuses her instruments. She won't be able to see us there," Ely said.

Rav inclined his head. "Alright, Elyssandro. Be careful in the spider's web."

When he was gone, Ely picked up the oblong key, turning it over in his hands. It was perfectly smooth, not a crack, indent, or engraved glyph. Was Ariel so sure this was the instrument of her salvation? Was he so sure he hadn't imagined her? What if it was, after all, just an egg?

Chapter Eleven
FESTIVAL OF HAUNTS

Dr. Faidra eyed Ely with keen interest as he strode into her workshop.

"You're looking healthy," she commented.

"Etrugan food and doctoring," Ely smiled, stomach squirming. He had forgotten the elaborate play acting of his last visit. No matter. She would be too distracted in a moment to wonder about it.

"Did you find it?" Dr. Faidra asked.

Ely set the heavy egg on the table. Her look of instant recognition assured him he had found the right artifact. Dr. Faidra fetched a box from a locked cabinet hidden behind a heap of scrap metal. Inside lay a set of styluses, some short and squat, others long and slender. She selected a delicate instrument that looked as if it were made of blown glass. Orange light pulsed from a hollow tip. Dr. Faidra directed the light over the key. It shivered as though stirred from a deep sleep. A thin crack appeared in the center. Then more tiny fissures fractured along the fulcrum. The onyx crust flaked away. Like an eggshell. Beneath, a polished silver sphere emerged, rising into the air until it hovered, bobbing just above the table. Pale, rolling mist swirled across the surface, gathering about a circle of faceted gold light that peered out like an eagle's eye.

"Welcome back," Dr. Faidra said. "You've been in stasis for quite some time."

A voice emerged from the sphere, chopped and mechanical, yet expressive. "Hello, Dr. Faidra," it droned. "How may I be of service?"

"We are initiating protocol five-one-nine. Full recovery. Please state the location of your sister node."

"To initiate protocol five-one-nine, the prime glyph must be entered."

Dr. Faidra raised her glass stylus and drew a pattern in light across the key's misty storm. The clouds whirled. Then the eye focused again.

"Thank you, Dr. Faidra. You will find my sister with the Seeker of Letters."

"Ah, yes, of course," Dr. Faidra nodded.

"Who is the Seeker of Letters?" Ely asked.

"An associate of mine, Dr. Ortiz. You've read his writings."

Ely nodded. Dr. Juan Ortiz was a historian and naturalist that devoted much of his life to documenting the strange and wondrous. Ely had read his tome on machnids from cover to cover.

"So where is he, then?" Ely asked.

"Probably in his grave," Dr. Faidra rasped.

"Oh, yes, he would be very old by now," Ely realized. "Can that gadget take me to wherever the sister key, or whatever you call it, is at present?"

"I can," the key answered. "I feel her."

"Oh. Sorry, I didn't know you understood me," Ely stammered.

"That's alright. Most humans don't. I'm Nix."

"I'm Elyssandro. Nice to meet you, Nix."

"You as well, Elyssandro," hummed the sphere.

"Is she alive?" Ely asked, turning to Dr. Faidra.

"My program understands and reasons like a living person," Nix offered. "Some might argue—"

"That will do, Nix," the doctor snapped. "Please shut down."

"As you wish."

The orb shuddered and lowered back to the table, a motionless silver ball once again.

"How do I wake her?" Ely asked, reaching for the key.

"You can't take it with you," Dr. Faidra objected.

"Why not? As you said, Dr. Ortiz is almost surely dead. Nix can track the other key. I need her."

"It," Dr. Faidra barked. "You need *it*. The interface is an elaborate encoding. Very effective, but it is not a being, Elyssandro. It is a tool."

"Yes, Dr. F," Ely replied, doing his best to meekly lower his head. "Alright."

She scooped up the silver sphere and laid it gingerly in his hand.

"Speak its name when you wish to wake it. Direct it to shut down when it is not in use. I will see you when you return."

Ely nodded and left quickly. He cradled the key in his palm, careful not to squeeze too tightly for fear of hurting Nix. Whatever Dr. Faidra might say, she could not hide from him what churned beneath the swirl of clouds. Spirit. Life.

Rav waited for him amidst the skeletal ridges of the Spine just above the ledge where they first met. From his frantic vibrations, Ely got the impression he had spent his wait revisiting his thousand year confinement and doubting his choice to trust a human.

Ely had gone first to visit Sir Ambrose Quinn and tell him the tale of his latest adventure. The skeleton chevalier found a sturdy leather pouch for Nix amongst his props. It now replaced the starlight flask on his belt.

"I was beginning to doubt–" Rav began.

"Yes, yes, we've already established I'm a slow, irritating human. Let's skip to the interesting part."

He drew the silver sphere carefully from the pouch, unwrapping it from a harlequin patterned handkerchief the skeleton knight had supplied.

"It *was* an egg!" Ely grinned. "Dr. F made it hatch with an odd glass stylus."

Rav blinked, a note of alarm escaping.

"What? What is it?" Ely asked.

"That is a spirit encoder," Rav told him. "As its name suggests, it is used for manipulating spirits."

"Ah, yes. That makes sense. Watch this."

He balanced the key in his outstretched palm.

"Nix?"

The silver ball rumbled and whirred, gliding above his hand as misty clouds gathered around her gilded eye.

"Hello, Elyssandro," she modulated.

"Hello!" he piped, a little too loud perhaps. "Hi, Nix. Nice to see you. I hope you've been comfortable enough."

"Oh, yes. Thank you. Much better than the shell," she told him.

Rav watched the key bob and ripple, eyes narrowed like a cat readying for the pounce.

"Put it away," he glowered. "I don't trust it."

Ely groaned. "Damn it all, Rav. You don't trust anyone."

Now the vampire turned his glare to him. "It's a helyx. Do you know what that is?"

Ely shook his head.

"Of course you don't."

Rav snatched Nix out of the air, pausing to snarl at the illuminated eye before he continued, "There is a demon trapped inside."

"Demon?" Ely blinked.

"Yes. An unpredictable being notorious for providing unreliable information."

"My programming does not allow for such inconsistencies," Nix sniffed.

"That's exactly what a demon would say," Rav growled.

"Well, maybe she could..." Ely paused. "Nix, is it alright if I use *she* for you?"

"Yes, I like that very much, Elyssandro. Thank you," the helyx purred.

Rav glowered at him.

"Maybe she could prove her good intentions by showing us the way to the next key."

"I can do that," Nix stated. "If the vampire would kindly let me loose."

"Rav?" Ely prompted.

Rav grumbled his protest, then freed Nix, who drifted over to Ely. Points of light emerged from the helyx, arranging in flowing arteries and markers. A map.

"She is sleeping, but I feel her somewhere near here."

Radial green flashed on the map along a crescent bay.

"It doesn't look familiar," Ely frowned.

"South Sea," Rav identified.

"Have you been there?" Ely asked.

Rav nodded. "We collected blood from a borough there. By direction of the Tower and by request of city officials. They wanted the rabble cleaned out."

"Ah," Ely nodded, not sure how else to respond to government sponsored murder. Maybe just sweep it under the rug. "Nix, is it possible to get a broader view of the map? If you don't mind."

"I don't mind in the least, Elyssandro."

Nix adjusted the map, and Ely made out more familiar landmarks.

"That's better. It looks like the closest starting point will be Mondacca. We can take the highway there. Maybe three days? Four?"

"If you are traveling on foot, the journey from Mondacca to South Sea will take approximately seventeen days not counting stops for human necessity," Nix informed him. "On horseback five. By boat four to six, weather dependent. By train two and a half."

"Oh, train, yes," Ely nodded. "I forgot about those."

He had yet to climb onto the back of a steam-belching land dragon that chugged between the Free Cities.

"I can be there before sunrise," Rav interjected.

"Well, unless you're suggesting you carry me on your back, I'm stuck going the long way," Ely said.

"I'm suggesting that this task is better suited to someone not confined to the ground."

"I'm not going with you," Nix informed him, dissolving the map.

"You don't have a choice," Rav shot.

Nix darted behind Ely's shoulder. "You won't let the vampire take me, will you, Elyssandro?"

"No, of course not," Ely assured her.

"Thank you. May I go back in my pouch now?"

"Certainly," Ely soothed. "Do you want the handkerchief?"

"Yes, thank you, Elyssandro. You're so kind."

He wrapped the silk around her and tucked the key into the pouch on his belt.

"You didn't shut her down, conjurer," Rav rumbled.

"Oh. Nix, will you please shut down?"

"As you wish," the muffled voice emerged. A whirr and a click. Then silence.

Rav leaned too close for human comfort and pronounced in a low hiss, "You have to be more careful."

"And you might try adding a hint of sugar to your approach so that just maybe a demon will be inclined to do as you ask," Ely replied in a hushed tone.

He patted the vampire on the shoulder and restored a more respectable distance.

"I've always wanted to ride the train. What do you say, Rav? Up for an adventure?"

Rav sighed.

Ely looked up from his reading as a breathy whistle serenaded the joy of locomotion to the gentle green slopes. He sat alone in the dining car, a puddle of syrup all that remained on his breakfast plate, morning paper in hand. Outside the window, bursts of yellow blossomed on emerald hills. Cattle grazed lazily without a care in the world. Here and there a thatch-roofed cabin puffed smoke from a chimney stack. A woman with a bubbly smile and a frilly pink frock refilled his coffee. What a way to travel. Rav had certainly missed out.

In the end, it was not the prospect of dodging daylight locked in a trunk or the overwhelming crowd that swayed the vampire's final refusal to board the Coastal Express. It was the suggestion that he wear shoes.

"I'll meet you in South Sea," he had snarled, then disappeared.

Perhaps it was for the best. This way he could sip his coffee and enjoy his newspaper without worrying that someone might rearrange the luggage and accidentally set Rav's trunk to catch fire in a rogue sunbeam.

Ely gave his newspaper a flick and skimmed over something about coldhearted bankers. Bad year for sugar. Travel on the highway growing hazardous. Community production of The Solicitor's Demise an unexpectedly stirring success. Midnight Haunts Gala to be hosted by the Society of Lost Letters.

"Interesting," he remarked to the empty seat opposite him.

He read on:

The Society of Lost Letters will hold its annual fundraiser gala at midnight on the thirteenth night of Haunts. The masquerade extravaganza, with admittance by invitation only, has generated much interest among the wealthy elite across the Free Cities. Little is known to the public about the origins and activities of the Society. If you have been fortunate enough to receive an invitation or know where one might be procured for the press, please contact Cecilia Stone at 333 Morningstar Lane.

Nix did say the key was with the Seeker of Letters. It seemed more than a coincidence, that name. And if their search happened to start at a grand Haunts party, well...

"Excuse me, miss," Ely called to the woman in pink. She shimmied over, carafe in hand. "Do you know South Sea at all?"

"Born and raised," she chirped.

"Excellent. Do you know where one might get outfitted for an event such as the one mentioned here?"

She leaned over him in a cloud of floral perfume. "Hm, black tie. Barley and Baker maybe. They can get you fixed up with a respectable suit," she offered.

"I was hoping for something with a little flair," Ely countered. "It's Haunts but once a year."

The woman in pink gave a delighted nod. "You'll be wanting Madame Toulouse then. I'll write down the address for you," she promised with a wink.

"You're an angel. Thank you!" he beamed.

Address in hand, he retired to his cabin. A single gold coin had bought him his own private compartment with a curtained window and two seats that folded together into a bed. He stretched out on the cushion, propped up on a pair of firm pillows. Taking Nix from her pouch, he called her name, and she blinked awake.

"Hello, Nix. I was hoping you could give me another look at that map."

After getting better acquainted with the layout of South Sea, he politely requested the demonic device go dormant again, then settled back for a nap. The gentle motion of the train soon lulled him to sleep. He woke to ominous tapping on his window. With the opening too narrow for entry, Ely sent Rav around to the back of the car, glancing about to ensure they were not observed before admitting the vampire. He was covered from head to toe in dirt and grass. Ely ushered him quickly to his compartment, making him wait in the hall while he separated the bed once again into benches.

"You'll not be ruining my bedsheets, thank you. What have you been doing? Exhuming dead bodies?"

"Yes," the vampire replied acidly. "Mine."

Ely paused, staring at him. "You sleep underground?" he asked.

"There is not much cover from the sun in these hills," he muttered.

Ely shook his head. "And to think you turned up your nose at my oversized trunk idea."

"I'd rather be in a shallow grave than locked in a box," Rav growled, awash with panic.

"Yes, I can see why you might feel that way, Rav, I'm so sorry," Ely apologized, kicking himself for his insensitivity.

Rav grunted and looked away.

"While you've been out digging holes, I've been busy sleuthing," Ely said, hoping to distract him. He fetched the newspaper and pointed to the article about the gala.

"Are you joking?" Rav asked.

"Not at all. I've had a look at the map. Sure enough, the address for this gala affair is within the same radius as the second key. I think the Society of Lost Letters is exactly the place to start. Have you ever been to Haunts?"

"Haunts?" the vampire questioned.

"The Festival of Haunts? No? They must not have had it back in your day. It's glorious. It's like every city in the free world is throwing one wicked, raging month-long party all devoted to the dead."

"Why, then, would you even bother leaving home, I wonder?" Rav asked dryly.

"You'll love it, Rav. You can walk among them, fangs flying free, and they'll never know the difference."

"I prefer the solitude of the empty woods," Rav grumbled.

"You're going to be a scintillating date to the masquerade, aren't you?" Ely smirked.

"I'm not going to any masquerade, and neither are you," Rav informed him. "It says by invitation only."

"Yes, I'm still working that out," Ely sighed.

Rav left before sunrise to find a suitable place to burrow. Ely returned to the dining car as a lemonburst of light heralded the day. The woman in pink, now the woman in navy polka dots, Gladys as she was known every day, poured him a cup of coffee. She supplied also a list of establishments in the city where one might rent a room on short notice. It would be difficult to find a vacancy during Haunts season.

"I'd give you the keys to my place, but my sister isn't too keen on letting strange men crash. I won't have a day off until the weekend."

"Maybe next time, Gladys. I'm meeting someone in the city. He prefers a reliable hotel. You wouldn't happen to know a good barber would you?"

"Sure thing, hon. I'll write down his address. You swing both ways, you and your friend?"

"What? Oh. Um...well, I'm entirely unhinged, but it's not that kind of visit. He's very devoted to his wife. One could only dream of such undying love."

"That's sweet. No harm asking, right? Here, I put my address down too, in case you're still in town on Saturday. More coffee?"

"Certainly, thank you, Gladys."

It was dinner time when he disembarked at the station in South Sea. He waited at the bistro across the street, enjoying harvest squash soup, pork loin with sautéed mushrooms and roasted potatoes, followed by pumpkin spice cake. This time of year, it was darkness that brought a city to life. He watched through the window as the lamplighters set about their work. Costumed Haunters began trickling out to the streets, faces painted white with black hollows under their eyes. Some carried pumpkins carved with grinning ghoul faces, others lanterns with colored glass that shed spectral light.

Ely noticed the barefooted figure on the train station steps, surveying his surroundings with alarm and distaste. He paid his bill, leaving a generous tip, and crossed the street to meet Rav.

"I don't think this is going to work," the vampire breathed.

He sounded like he was sweating, despite being beyond such human functions.

"Come on, you'll feel better after a shower."

Ely guided his disgruntled companion through the cavorting crowd, getting swept up among dancers and stopping to wave at rowdy revelers shouting overhead from balconies. Rav stalked among the macabre painted faces and bizarre masks, the only real shadow in the night.

"If they knew what we are, they would either run in terror or seize weapons to drive us out," the vampire pronounced.

"Of course," Ely smiled. "They're human, and they only want to–"

A coquette skeleton in a lacy ensemble took him by the collar and planted an absinthe soaked kiss on his mouth. Then she ran off cheering and spinning.

"Flirt with Death," Ely continued.

Rav hissed at a Haunter that ventured too close with a sloppy smile.

"Come on, Rav. Lighten up. Can't you enjoy the madness even a little?"

He sensed the vampire coiling tight as a spring. Rav turned and cornered him against an alley wall, fangs protracted.

"Ariel is trapped in a torture chamber, her only hope of rescue a monster that must waste the daylight and a drunken fool of a conjurer too concerned with feeding the glut of his humanity to have a care for the urgency of her plight. No, Elyssandro, I cannot enjoy one second of this."

"Rav, I–" he started.

"Excuse me, sir, is this man bothering you?" a gruff voice interrupted.

"Not at all. We're fine. Carry on," Ely waved with a smile. Looking back to Rav, he continued, "You can let go now. You've made your point. Let's just get to the hotel. You can clean up, and we'll make a plan."

Rav stepped back, letting him loose. They continued their trek in silence. Ely did his best to remain subdued, but the lively street musicians made it near impossible. Even Rav paused a moment to listen to a saxophone wail.

The Hotel Lioncourt stood a bourgeois castle in the heart of the city. Haunters here wore sleek silks and sparkling rubies like elegant blood droplets. The concierge eyed the dirt-encrusted vampire as they approached the desk but quickly handed over the key to the executive suite when Ely set down a handful of Dianessa gold.

Ely ushered Rav straight to the spacious bathroom and turned the shower to steaming. The vampire hissed at the rattling stream. He distrusted this too, apparently.

Ely slid the curtain closed and walked to the door. "Just get in, scrub off all that dirt. There's a towel on the rack. I'll find you some clean clothes."

"I'm not wearing–"

"We're burning your filthy prison rags, Aurelio. Go."

Ely slammed the door behind him, then rummaged through the tragic assortment of clothes in his pack. His errand to Madame Toulouse's shop could not be put off. Selecting a faded shirt and trousers, he set them folded on the bed.

Rav joined him some time later wrapped in a luxurious towel and looking revived almost to living. With the high-collared tunic and layer of dirt stripped away, scarred markings appeared etched in relief around his throat. Ely turned his eyes aside. He knew the burn of restraining glyphs all too well.

"We were fitted with collars to keep us under control," Rav told him, though he had not asked aloud.

The vampire pointed to the complex sigil tattooed on his chest. Not common glyphs but sharp death magic script.

"These set my heart beating again. If you wish to stop it, that's where the stake is meant to strike. There's a second one here in case it is more convenient to stab me in the back."

Ely took the stake from his belt and offered it blunt-end forward to the vampire.

"No one is going to hurt you, Rav," he said.

Rav nodded but made no move to take it. "You keep it, conjurer. Eternity is a long time. It is comforting to know you are the one carrying an end to it."

Ely returned the stake to its loop. Then he put a few paces between them to dilute the bleak flood that spilled from the vampire's gaze.

Rav dressed and drew the drapes tighter to block out a tiny tendril of morning light probing for entry. He collapsed on the mattress and bunched the pillow under his head.

"You're not going to sit there and watch me all day are you?" he asked.

"No, I've got to pay a visit to the couturier," Ely replied. "They won't let us into that party looking like paupers."

"They won't let us in without an invitation," Rav reminded him.

Ely sighed, rising to his feet. "I still haven't figured that part out. But we have some time yet. Sweet dreams, Rav."

"I don't dream," came the reply as he walked out the door.

Daylight found the streets of South Sea tamed and lazy. Most Haunters would now be sleeping off the night's indulgences and preparing for another round. How they survived a full month of this could only be explained by youth or a lifetime of practice.

He located Madame Toulouse's boutique with some difficulty. It was set up in the back of a novelty shop selling charms, crystals, and spells without a whisper of magic. Ely bought a stamped medallion as a souvenir for Quinn.

Madame Toulouse looked up from her mannequin, cigarette clutched between hot pink lips along with a few pearled pins. She wore a dazzling sequined dress, cherry red hair wrapped in a scarf.

"You picking up an order, hon?" she asked, voice smoky as her shop.

"No, but–" Ely started with a bright smile.

"We don't take requests during Haunts," she dismissed.

Ely moved over to a collection of vibrant suits on display. "Are these for sale?" he asked.

"Barley and Baker is just down the street," she said.

"We're not going to a funeral."

"Baby boy, I am busy. Come back after the winter holidays."

"You see," Ely pressed. "I've received a last minute invitation to a masquerade. A once in a lifetime kind of affair."

Madame Toulouse looked up mid-stitch. "You're with the Society?" she asked.

"Newly inducted," Ely replied. "I'd like to make an impression."

Madame Toulouse crushed her cigarette in a crystal tray, set down her pins, and rolled aside the mannequin. "Right this way, pumpkin pie."

She beckoned him deeper into the screened partitions and rolls of fabric.

"There is no time to make something new," she said, fetching a measuring tape. "Stand here. Jacket off. I have a few pieces that I am sure will be the talk of the town. Arms out. What do you think of chartreuse? No. No. You need the lilac."

"I'm taking a friend," Ely said. "He's a bit more...reserved, shall we say? I have a feeling he'll do best in classic black and white."

"You have his measurements, shug?" Madame Toulouse asked, sweeping a jacket onto his shoulders and setting pins.

"Mine will be close enough."

She nodded. "I have something."

Ely left with hands full of bags and a parting command, "Tell every head you turn that you are wearing Madame Toulouse."

He stopped for lunch at a café, then paid a visit to the cobbler and the barber. Loitered for a leisurely dinner. Detoured for a drink with a couple of locals. It was past dark when he walked back through the Hotel Lioncourt's gilded lobby.

He found the suite deserted.

"Rav?" he called, though he didn't feel the vampire anywhere near.

Ely turned on a lamp and set down his bags. Sure enough, no Rav. Since there was nothing to do but wait, he hung up the fresh suits in the wardrobe, kicked off his shoes, and laid down on the bed to close his eyes for a moment. The pillows smelled like a frozen forest at midnight, and he realized as he drifted off what it was, that ethereal perfume that clung to the vampire. Starlight.

The breeze through the window woke him, and he knew without opening his eyes that Rav had returned. Ely sat up, head pounding. He could have used another twelve hours or so. But what else was new?

"Where have you been off to?" Ely asked.

Rav dropped a cream envelope embossed with gold on the bedside table. Ely drew out the heavy card inside. It bore a printed illustration of a woman in a red gown, face made sultry by an elaborate feathered mask. He skimmed over the invitation, then looked up at the vampire.

"Are you playing the countess or shall I?" he asked.

"A thank you would suffice," Rav evaded.

"Where did you get it?" Ely pressed. "Don't you think it will be missed?"

"They won't be missing anything, I can assure you," Rav replied.

Ely eyed him sternly. "Rav, did you eat the Count and Countess of Belle Heights?"

"They made their fortune trading slaves," Rav growled.

"Oh. Well, good riddance, then." Ely glanced at the invitation once more and slapped it against his palm. "I can work with this."

"And?" Rav prompted with a crook of an eyebrow.

"And thank you."

Rav let a twitch of a smile escape.

Ely yawned. "What time is it?"

"Dawn," Rav replied.

"Right." Ely scooted to the far edge of the bed and pushed a pillow to the other side. "Hop in. I'm not quite ready to be up and about yet."

Rav looked displeased but checked the curtain and laid down. Ely curled on his side, ready to drop like a stone back to sleep. He soon found the vampire's restless brooding kept him from finding his dreams again. He rolled onto his back, staring up at the wood-paneled ceiling. Waiting.

"I can't remember being alive," Rav confided at last.

"Nothing at all?" Ely frowned.

"Sometimes a scent or a sound will stop me for a moment. But when I reach for the memory, it's distorted. Faded. A wisp of smoke. Being in the presence of so many humans is...disorienting."

"Where did you come from?" Ely asked.

"The Hinterlands below the Dianessa Vale," the vampire murmured. "In the end, I was a criminal condemned to death."

"Something we have in common there," Ely said.

"Treason. What precisely that means they never told me. Only that I was executed and revived to serve my sentence to the delight of many. I do not imagine I was a human you would have wanted to know."

Ely looked over at him with a pensive frown. "If I know anything about laws, it is that they favor a few greedy tyrants and grind the most vulnerable into the dirt. Whatever you did to displease them, it could never justify enslavement."

Rav remained motionless, but Ely felt him relax just a little.

"You have a lot of sympathy for devils, Elyssandro," he remarked.

"I've been dragged before a tribunal, beaten, shackled, nailed to a tree and left for dead," Ely said. "Maybe I know a thing or two about what it's like to be a devil among men."

He had not realized he was worrying at the scars on his wrists until Rav took hold of one arm and drew back the sleeve. The vampire touched the glyphs lightly, recognition in his eyes.

"How do you dance through the streets with them like they have never done you harm?" Rav puzzled.

"*They* haven't," Ely said. He took back his arm, covering the scars again. "And maybe it's selfish to do it. I bring Death to walk among them. I fascinate them and terrify them and steal their willpower. It's just a game, Rav. It's only when I get lost in the fantasy that I get into trouble."

"I'm beginning to think it is simpler to be a vampire."

Ely smiled. "I like my dreams. Most of the time. And memory can be a beast, but I wouldn't part with it. Sometimes it's all I have. Sometimes, when I'm alone in the Vale, it is only the recollection of a sea breeze on the prow of a ship or the taste of fresh baked bread that keeps me sane."

"Do you remember your life before the Vale?" Rav asked.

"Saint Lucio? Yes. I remember my father. Stern. Distant. But gentle. My brothers. Orlando was older. He didn't bother much with me. Alexei liked to read and daydream. My Uncle Misha. He walked with a cane and told the best stories in the dark of winter when it was so cold you could not get the chill from your bones even if you sat in the fire. My mother..."

He stopped.

His breath caught as her face rose before his mind's eye. Dark curls tamed into braids. Deep brown, laughing eyes. A smile whose ghost he still saw in the mirror. Cold stole over him, white mist dimmed his vision. Rav's hand closed over his, and Death receded.

"The dead do not always come back as expected," Rav said.

"But she did," Ely whispered. "Warm and loving and fully alive."

"So, where is she?"

Ely blinked. Tears fell.

"I can't talk about that."

"Don't then," Rav murmured. He brushed a cool finger to Ely's temple. "Rest, conjurer."

Ely closed his eyes, descending to still, dreamless sleep.

When he woke it was near dark again. Ely glanced at the motionless vampire and rose quietly.

"Where are you going?" Rav asked as he pulled on his shoes.

"Just downstairs for a bite. It should be about time to get dressed when I get back."

Rav nodded and rolled over. Ely found him unmoved upon his return, so he showered and shaved. By the time he had finished, the vampire sat by the open window, starlight dripping from his long fingers.

Ely laid out their evening attire while Rav eyed the tailored jackets as though they were snakes with rattling tails. Handing the vampire his suit, he pushed him toward the bathroom. Satisfied that the tap was indeed running, Ely donned Madame Toulouse's debonair lilac costume with sheer pleasure.

Rav's voice emerged from the bathroom along with his resounding misery. "I can't do it."

"Can't do what?" Ely asked, straightening his bowtie in the mirror.

"Pass for human."

"Just come out, Rav. We'll work on it."

The vampire gave a low growl then opened the door. He was barefoot, of course, and he had not quite managed the tie, but in the coat tails with his hair half-tamed, he looked fit for a gala. Sort of.

"What are you smiling at, conjurer?"

"Come here."

Ely unknotted the burgundy cravat and arranged it properly.

"There. Listen, Rav. You can do this. Ariel needs you."

The vampire gave a reluctant nod.

"That's it." Ely smiled and pointed to a pair of polished wingtips. "Now, put on the shoes."

The cab dropped them at the front gate to a mansion with twin flights of steps that swept up to a stately entrance. It had been difficult to convince Rav to climb into the rickety buggy that sputtered and stank of motor oil, but he had come this far already. Why stop at a car?

The doorman's eyes fell to the invitation, then flicked back to the two alleged guests.

"The Count and Countess of Belle Heights?"

"A common mistake, I fear," Ely lamented. "Even for such a modern town as South Sea, the printers are always confounded over inscribing the Count and Count of Belle Heights. You're not going to spoil our evening over it, are you?" He lowered his voice. "We were hoping to make a generous contribution."

"My apologies for the blunder, gentlemen," said the doorman, ushering them in.

"Many thanks, kind sir." He tugged Rav by the arm. "Come along, darling. Let's find you a drink."

Rav glared through his mask at the doorman and followed.

The entryway flowed down a curved staircase to a grand white ballroom with high draped windows and glittering chandeliers. Musicians played gentle music for patrons dressed in bejeweled gowns, tailored tuxedos, and of course, stunning masks with outrageous plumage.

"Not bad," Ely smirked, taking in the grandeur.

Rav grunted, flinching in the light reflecting from the blanched floors and walls.

"Now, we just have to hunt for an egg," Ely said.

A white-haired man in a gray suit positioned himself at the peak of the staircase and tapped a champagne glass with a spoon. All heads turned to answer the age-old summoning spell.

"Colleagues, esteemed guests," the gentleman drawled. "We are grateful you have all come to gather here in common interest. Before we begin tonight's proceedings, we will give you each the opportunity to view the Collection. Please refrain from touching until you've made a purchase. The Society thanks you. Now. Enjoy."

He made a sweeping arc with his arm, and in response to the gesture, three paneled doors opened in the ballroom below. The crowd dispersed between the chambers, chattering expectantly. Ely and Rav exchanged curious glances, then took the far left route, joining the smallest group of preening patrons for their tour.

Ely raised his brows as he stepped close enough to see the curiosities curated among mahogany tables and glass display cases. In the first, there were edged blades and twisted implements etched with glyphs. Vicious magic radiated from their metallic pores.

"What are they?" Ely asked, cold sweat breaking across his forehead.

"Torture," Rav murmured. Pointing to the next set, he said. "Demon hunting. Witchfinding."

They passed a case filled with thoroughly cursed shrunken heads, a coney's paw, and a wooden doll with an unsettling smile. On the wall hung skulls of beasts, each neatly labeled. Chimera, griffin, sea serpent. Minotaur horns. Dragon scales. And what appeared to be the bones of a human hand. Severed at the wrist and missing a finger.

Hand of the Necromancer.

"I think this may have been a terrible mistake," Ely breathed.

"I'm inclined to agree with you, conjurer," Rav murmured, eyes locked to a row of mirrorwood stakes.

"I think it would be best if you refrained from calling me that in the present company," Ely whispered, glancing at their white-haired host now standing a little too close to their conversation.

The old man smiled politely, and they were ushered on into the second chamber. This one held rows of cages. Horned imps and wrinkled goblins peered forlorn through metal bars. A phantom crooned a heart-wrenching lament through reinforced glass. Bottles and jars of eclectic size blinked sad, pale light.

Spirits stirred at the approach of death magic.

"Help us, conjurer," they whimpered.

"Please."

"Have mercy!"

"Kill us!"

They walked on into the third chamber. Ely's throat tightened, chest aflame as he took in the largest cage of all. Ragged Etrugan children sat among straw mounds, black-rimmed irises brightest blue with grief and fear.

"Wait here. I'll be right back," Ely whispered to Rav.

The young Etrugans huddled together in the far corner of the cage as Ely approached. He signed, "I am a friend."

The children watched him, eyes shifting between curiosity and wariness. A boy near Ariadna and Brindle's age approached the bars.

"How did you get here?" Ely asked in the Etrugan tongue.

"We were taken," the boy replied. "By the templars."

"The Canon is very far from here," Ely said.

"We were sold to these humans. They brought us to this place of nightmares."

"What's your name?" Ely asked.

"Ragnor," said the Etrugan.

"Ragnor, I am a friend of Rión Twin Axes. Do you know of her?"

Ragnor's eyes glowed bright violet with excitement. The children behind him ventured closer. "Are you here to help us?"

Ely nodded. "Yes, Ragnor, I'm going to get you home. I need you all to be brave now. I will be back for you in a little while."

He turned and scanned the room for his companion. The vampire stood near an assortment of poltergeists trapped in wooden cubes. The white-haired gentleman seemed to be asking questions while trying to catch a good look at Rav's mouth.

"There you are, my dear Count, I've been looking everywhere for you," Ely called, making jaunty strides between them and taking Rav by the arm.

"If you'll forgive me for stealing him away," he grinned at their host.

When they were safely across the room, Ely whispered, "New plan. We grab the key, rescue the children, and get out of this place as quickly as possible."

Rav frowned, glancing over Ely's shoulder. "Do you know that woman in the blue gown? No, don't look at her."

"How am I supposed to tell you whether I know her if I can't look?" Ely hissed.

"She's been watching you all night," Rav whispered. "She's turned away, look now."

Ely caught a glimpse of a royal blue dress with a hooded cape that obscured its occupant's head and shoulders.

"No idea," he said. "That gentleman, the host, he's watching us too. I think we've made an impression."

"Perhaps two Counts are more of a spectacle than you anticipated," Rav said.

"I really hope that's the reason," Ely replied. "I haven't seen anything that looks like the key. I wish we could ask our demon friend."

"There's a powder room through there," Rav pointed.

They made their way arm in arm across the room, Ely smiling, Rav scowling, and both trying not to move too quickly.

"I'll stand watch," Rav offered.

Ely stepped inside and shut the door behind him. He drew the helyx's pouch from his inner jacket pocket and unwrapped the orb from its handkerchief.

"Nix."

The helyx shuddered, golden eye opening.

"Hello, Elyssandro. You look very dashing this evening."

"Thank you. Listen. Keep your voice down. We are in a great deal of danger here. It would seem these people have a morbid fascination with the mystical. I'm rather certain they would love to have us taxidermied and set up for display, if you catch my meaning."

"Understood," came Nix's tinny whisper. "What can I do for you?"

"We haven't found the key. Can you feel it? Is it close by?"

Nix whirled and pulsed.

"She is close, but she keeps moving. She is being carried, perhaps?"

"But she's here?" Ely asked.

Nix bobbed up and down in the air. "Yes. Very close."

"Alright. I'll keep looking."

He held out the handkerchief, and the helyx floated into its folds.

"You really do look nice. I'm sorry they want to kill you."

"Thank you, Nix, please shut down now."

Nix complied, and he returned the orb and pouch to his pocket. When he stepped outside the door, Rav no longer stood at his post. Ely scanned the room, searching for a tall, pale figure in black coat tails. He was nowhere to be found. Nowhere to be felt.

His stomach dropped into his toes. Death's haze crept into his periphery.

No, he commanded.

Keep calm. Find Rav. Formulate a plan.

Ely closed his eyes. Quieting his mind, he reached out through the sea of rustling satin and cashmere. Panic, terror, and pain rushed through him. Rav. Upstairs.

Ely set out at a run, knocking aside a gloved hand that snagged at his arm as he passed. At the top of the staircase, he raced down a long corridor with checkered marble floors. A door at the end stood ajar. Ely burst through. Six men circled Rav, who knelt on the floor wrapped in chains. Glyphs glowed white hot on a collar clamped around his throat.

Death peaked their head amidst his swell of anger, but Ely bid them stand aside. He did not need their help to cry havoc now. The closest man lunged, a blunt instrument held aloft. Ely twisted his fingers. The man dropped in a heap. All that was left of him pulsed and glowed in the conjurer's hand. He crushed it to dust in his palm. There would be no ascent into the stars for him.

Death nodded their approval of the judgment, leaning back to watch his rage unfold.

Turning to snatch another soul from its shell, he hurled it like a flaming missile at an oncoming assailant who burst into violet flames. The others cried out and fled, but he caught them with ether tethers like live wires. They fell backwards, shattering into frozen ice crystals across the polished floor.

The chains disintegrated, and the restraining collar clattered to the ground the moment Ely looked at it. He held out a hand to help Rav to his feet.

"Are you alright?" Ely asked, breath still ragged.

His knees felt a little weak, but he would soon recover.

"Fine," Rav said, voice shaking. "It seems the nuisance you called a cravat has spared me the worst of the burn."

Ely turned toward the door, expecting more company at any moment. Music and laughter drifted from downstairs. The guests were none the wiser. Still enjoying their dancing, drinking, and gawking at captives safely locked behind bars and glass.

Jaw set, face grim, he turned back to Rav.

"What do you say we give this city a thirteenth of Haunts to remember?"

"My dear Count," the vampire smiled. "It would be my pleasure."

He departed in an eerie, sighing breeze. Ely followed more slowly. Calculating. He visited the central showroom first, threading death magic through keyholes, lifting latches on cages, and uncorking bottles. Shadows rushed across the walls. Red smoke swirled and vanished into cackling vapors. Claws clicked on marble floors and tinkled against chandeliers. Then the screams began.

Ely crossed into the final chamber, turning aside for a shrieking guest in a shredded gown, stepping over a murky pool of blood. Something like mottled oatmeal spattered across the wall. He flicked a speck of it from his jacket and walked on.

The young Etrugans rushed forward as he approached their cage. He directed them to stand back and froze the door from its hinges.

"Morgata says blood for blood," Ely told them.

Their eyes shifted to lethal jade, and they flashed their pointed teeth, charging off to join the mayhem. As he returned to the gore-painted ballroom, he glanced up at the bannister above. The white-haired gentleman watched from behind a heavy velvet curtain. Ely narrowed his eyes as their host receded into the shadows.

Rav materialized at his side, face a crimson mask. The cries had quieted to groans and gasps about them.

"You were right, conjurer," the vampire grinned. "I do love Haunts."

"I think the evening is coming to a close," Ely said. "Will you take the children out to the hills and hide them? I'll meet you back at the Lioncourt before sunrise."

"Where are you going?" Rav asked, elation lost to disquiet.

"I have one more interrogation to carry out. If all goes to plan, I'll be leaving with the key. But just in case."

He retrieved the helyx pouch from his pocket and set it in Rav's hand.

"For safekeeping."

"Elyssandro..."

"I'll be right behind you," Ely assured him.

Rav hesitated. Then he nodded, secured the pouch in his own pocket, and disappeared to carry out his next mission. Ely ascended the stairs once more. There was no life left in this marble tomb to disguise the old man's presence. He followed the trail back through the checkered corridor.

A silver flash blinded him. Scalding pain took his feet from beneath him. Then darkness.

When Ely came to, he sat in a dim study, hands chained to a hefty chair. Manacles singed his coat sleeves, holding death magic out of reach.

"Good. You're awake," drawled the white-haired gentleman.

He sat at an oak desk, watching Ely with hands folded in front of him. Beady eyes bright with excitement.

"You know," he remarked as though they were having a friendly chat over lunch, "I thought I had struck gold with a live vampire."

He chuckled at his joke.

"Not really *live*, is it? Pity you set it loose. But still, a necromancer?"

The gentleman sucked at the air with a most unpleasant tenor.

"I wasn't sure what you were, but I knew you were something special the moment you set foot in my house. I certainly knew you were not my dear friend the Count of Belle Heights. May his soul rest in peace, I assume. And now that I've seen you at work..."

He drummed his fingers on the desk with a gleeful grin.

"You know, just one of your hands would fetch a bounty that would let me live out the rest of my days like a king. Perhaps I will be tempted someday, but until then, I think I would prefer–"

"That's quite enough, Mr. Vesper," a light, bell-like voice rang from the shadows.

The woman in the sapphire gown emerged, face thrown into shadow under her hood. She aimed a pistol at the gentleman with a gloved finger poised on the trigger. Ely knew the voice and posture instantly.

"Miss Skylark," the old man stammered.

"It's Dr. Skylark," she corrected. "Now, if you would, the keys."

The gentleman clenched his teeth in a grimace. "You are not taking my prize from me. When your father hears—"

"Oh, he'll have my head," she said. "But he won't hear about it, will he? If I take yours first."

The pistol discharged. Mr. Vesper fell face-down onto his desk, smoke curling up from the back of his head. Leanora lowered the pistol and threw off her hood, ruby lips curved in the tiniest of smiles.

"Nice to see you again, Elyssandro," she said. "Let's get you out of here, shall we?"

Chapter Twelve

DOCTOR OF LOST LETTERS

The garden rejoiced in a chromatic explosion of blushing roses, fiery marigolds, and royal geraniums. Lea sat with eyes fixed on a single spiraling bloom whose geometry could be mapped and predicted from a series of numbers traceable back to a single origin point.

Exactly six months ago to the day, they had buried Teensy in the cemetery on Lantern Hill. It had been a closed casket, of course, her remains too gruesome for viewing on account of her tragic electrocution. Further evidence that the new electric lights were a danger to the public.

Captain Skylark had taken Stephens Electric to court over false advertisement and gross neglect. He won a handsome sum, donated in part to the Classics Academy in memory of Art Fellow Étienne "Teensy" Lavour.

It was six months also since an intriguing stranger had turned up at her door and thrown all that she knew to be ordered and right into chaos. No matter how she tried, she could not keep her mind from the amused sparkle in his dark eyes as she failed to deduce his field of study. The melodic trill when he pronounced Leanora, wrapping her name in nebulous beauty instead of the usual mousy flatness with which her mother had saddled her. The way he gazed at the stars like he knew them in a profound, intimate way that she could only dream to know them.

She could not cease thinking either of his eyes gone white as ghostly moons. His outstretched hands commanding a black event horizon that swallowed light and life. The primal fear that had overtaken her sometimes woke her from sleep, heart pounding, drenched in sweat. Yet still, she wished nothing more than to find him again and ply him with the thousand questions that rent at her thoughts. It seemed unlikely she would get the chance. The trail of blood he left on his retreat suggested her bullet had pierced the axillary artery.

A rusty squeal at the garden gate brought her back from gloomy reflection. Her gaze met blue-eyed mischief below a strawberry mop.

"Victor!" she cried.

She rushed to embrace her brother, the grayed and gloomy filter lifting from her heart for the first time in half a year.

"What are you doing here?" Lea asked, drawing back to get a look at him.

He was dressed with his usual careless disregard for the trappings of his station. It drove their father to fits, but the girls at university went weak in the knees over it. He abused that power with shameless constancy. Typical Victor.

"I came to see you," he answered.

"Why?" she frowned.

He moved to sit under the inviting branches of a shady deciduous. "Father says you've taken a leave of absence from Jade Hill."

"I needed a break from writing papers," Lea evaded.

Victor eyed her. "Lea, there is no one on this planet that takes more pleasure in writing a paper than you do."

"Surely you didn't come all the way back to Mondacca to admonish me about my studies."

"Father said you've taken what happened to Teensy very hard," Victor probed.

"I watched my friend get electrocuted. How else does one take that, Vic?"

"Was she electrocuted?" Victor questioned with a trenchant glance. "That seems rather far-fetched, considering Stephens knows wires like you know the lenses of your telescope."

"I'm not sure what you're getting at, brother."

He leaned forward, voice hushed. "I know you saw something, Lea. Something even you couldn't explain, and it's shattered your world of immutable laws and mathematical equations."

"How did you...?" she stammered.

"Because it happened to me. Something that made me ask questions of everything I knew." He took her hand, eyes alight. "Come with me to South Sea."

"What's in South Sea?" Lea asked.

"A vast and wondrous world begging you to unravel its mysteries..."

The blue-gowned figure glided toward the desk in a swish of satin. The intervening years since Ely had last set eyes on her had transformed Leanora Skylark from an elfin-faced girl to a steel-eyed woman. A doctor, to be precise. Small in stature but formidable all the same.

Leanora made first for the wall behind the desk, retrieving the bullet from a glossy wood panel. Ely watched, still unsure if he had been rescued or tossed from the frying pan into the roaring flames.

She rummaged through the dead gentleman's pockets and produced a small copper key.

"Here we are," she said.

"Is that for these?" he asked, giving his manacles a shake.

"Yes," she said, sliding the key into her own pocket. "Don't speak, Elyssandro. Best not to breathe either."

Leanora heaved the gentleman back in his seat. His mouth lolled open as if in shock, one eye lost to the projectile fired through his skull. She stepped around to the front of the desk, pausing for a moment to look at Mr. Vesper's corpse.

"I think we can be fairly certain he's dead," Ely observed dryly.

"Hush," Leonora snapped. "Hold your breath."

She took a small drawstring purse from her pocket. Instead of coins, she withdrew a bit of shimmering powder. Then she leaned over the desk and blew the sandy substance from her gloved fingertips. It scattered over the gentleman's remains in a glittering cloud. When it settled, his empty clothes slumped to the floor, spilling gray ashes from the openings.

Leanora dusted the few clinging grains from her fingers and turned back to Ely with a ruby pout.

"Alright. Where were we?" she said.

"Hopefully, not throwing any flesh-eating sand in my direction."

"It's pixie dust, Elyssandro. To be handled with great caution," she told him, returning the purse to the folds of her gown. "From the state of the ballroom downstairs, I don't think they will be inclined to investigate too deeply into one more body, but better safe, as they say."

"I take it you know about the king's ransom on my hands," Ely said as she continued to regard him with an unreadable expression.

"I do," she said, rustling closer. He flinched as she reached toward his face. She lifted the mask he had forgotten he was wearing. "You look different than I remember."

"Ten years will do that," he said.

"Fifteen," she corrected. "I was given the distinct impression you were dead."

"Sorry to disappoint," he replied.

"I think you may have misunderstood my intentions," she said, drawing the key from her pocket. "I just want to talk, Elyssandro. Will you come with me?"

"What happens if I say no?" he asked.

Leanora unlocked the manacles from his wrists and stepped back. She nodded her head toward the door.

"I can't go just yet," he said. "There's something here that I need."

"Perhaps I can be of some assistance," she offered.

Ely scrutinized her face, still uncertain. She *had* come to his rescue. That was something, wasn't it?

"I'm looking for an artifact," he said, tossing his fate into the hands of optimism. "It would probably seem unremarkable. It's black, oval shaped, very heavy."

"Does it, by any chance, resemble an egg?" Leanora asked.

"Yes! Yes! An egg!" Ely exclaimed.

Leanora inclined her head. "I think you had best come with me," she said...

A knock at the office door wrenched Lea from the volume that had swallowed her whole. She glanced at the clock ticking out the steady seconds on the wall. Somehow four hours had passed without her noticing.

"Sorry to bother you, Dr. Skylark."

Peggy Osai, her pretty, peppy new research assistant peaked an apologetic smile through the door. She still had the eager, enamored sparkle of a first week on the job. Unfortunately, assistants never lasted long in the Lost Letters department. They either grew disgruntled at the complexities of encoding glyphs, disenchanted with the tedium of long hours of research, or existentially frightened of the nature of magic.

"Not a problem. What is it, Peg?" Lea asked, removing her reading glasses.

"There's a fella out front asking to see you. He doesn't have an appointment, but he's real nice looking. Red hair, killer smile," she said with a dreamy giggle.

Lea sighed and massaged her aching temples. "That's my brother, Peg. You can show him in."

Sure enough, Victor sauntered in, looking deliberately disheveled as usual and carrying a brown paper parcel.

"Where have you been?" she asked.

It must be three months since she had seen freckled hide or ginger hair of him.

"Making the rounds," he said, setting his parcel on the guest chair and disrupting a pile of notes to sit on the edge of the desk.

"A girl in every city?" Lea glared, rescuing the rumpled sheets of paper. "Those rounds?"

Victor shrugged. "I have a reputation to uphold. Keeps Father off my back. But that's beside the point. I'm mounting an expedition. It turns out there's a great deal of interest to invest."

"Well, best of luck, then. See you in six months? A year?"

"I want you to come with me."

Lea eyed him. "My research–"

"Can come along too," Victor interjected. "We'll pack all your dusty books and scrolls. You haven't done any field work in ages. It's time you stretched your legs and got some fresh air."

"Why do you want me along?" she asked.

Victor grinned, enthusiasm contagious. "That's a boring question, Lea. I'll give you a better one. What's in the package, Vic? I'm so glad you asked."

He unwrapped the parcel to reveal a woman's coat, hooded and trimmed in white fur. Beneath it, a thick leather-bound journal overflowed with dogeared pages.

"Where exactly are you trying to spirit me off to, Victor?" Lea asked, struggling not to give in to intrigue.

"North," he declared. "Onward and upward to a Distinguished Fellowship, perhaps even a Corrigan's Prize."

Lea raised an eyebrow. "Corrigan's, really? What have you stumbled into, Victor?"

"An anomaly," he replied, pushing the journal toward her itching grasp. "I need an expert in Lost Letters and the night sky to help me unravel this discovery. Will you come?"

She gave a dramatic pause, pretending his proposal required consideration.

"When do we leave?"

"How soon can you get a passport?"

"A passport?" she frowned. "Just how far north are we going, Victor?"

He grinned. "Right off the top of the map..."

Wormwood Lane stood apart from the bustling district where raucous Haunters still roamed. It was dark, the lamps unlit. The row of townhomes looked deserted. Uninviting. Hostile, even. Leanora opened an iron gate before an unmarked address. She turned the key down a line of locks and motioned Ely inside.

A set of stairs ascended to an upper floor, but Leonora beckoned him onward down the narrow corridor to a door at the end of the hall. A young woman in a muted brown dress and apron met them.

"How is he?" Leanora asked.

"Same as always," the woman answered, looking up with sad doe eyes.

"Elyssandro, this is my assistant, Peggy. She works with me at the university."

The girl frowned at him with a spark of recognition. Her face nudged a memory too, but he could not place it. Peggy muttered a weary pleasantry, then they followed her into the darkened room. Books lay open on the table and stacked in unstable mountain ranges about the chamber. The mildewed stink of wounds unhealed dragged at the air.

Leanora approached a bed placed opposite the cinders in the fireplace. Its occupant lay on his back with eyes closed. Unruly red hair spilled over the pillow.

"Vic?" she murmured, laying a hand on the sleeping man's forehead.

He opened his eyes. They were palest blue, nearly white. Blinded.

"Lea?" he wheezed. He tensed, moving his sightless gaze toward Ely. "Who's there with you?"

"Victor, this is Elyssandro. He's an old friend. Elyssandro, this is my brother, Victor Skylark."

"Pleasure to meet you," Ely said, taking a hesitant step forward.

Something about the man's presence made him uneasy. Perhaps it was the room itself. There was a shadow. As though something unseen were listening in on their conversation.

Victor groaned, scratching at his chest while his face contorted in pain.

"Don't do that, Vic," Leonora pleaded, taking his hand gently.

"It hurts," Victor whimpered.

"I'll get you something," Peggy offered.

She fetched a glass vial from a shelf on the wall then mixed a few drops of the tincture into water poured from a ready pitcher. Leanora helped Victor lift his head while Peggy held the cup to his lips, quietly encouraging him to drink more. He fell back against the pillow, gasping for breath. Exhausted.

"Did you get it?" Victor murmured.

Leonora glanced at Ely then replied, "No. And Vesper is dead. Along with half of the Society."

Victor frowned, opening his iced white eyes once again. "Did anyone see you?"

"There's no one left to tell the tale."

"Lea, if this is traced back to us..."

"It won't be," Leonora assured him. "It was their own revolting sickness that killed them. The locks failed on Vesper's Collection. There isn't an inspector in the Free Cities that could explain the ghastly crime scene they'll find."

Victor's eyes rolled closed, his breathing slowed. Whatever drug had been administered was a potent one.

"What happened to him?" Ely asked.

Peggy flinched at his question.

"Not now," Leanora said. "Come on."

They left Victor to rest, taking the stairs up to the second floor where a kitchen, sitting room, bedroom, and lavatory lay tucked in a compact row. Leanora hung her cape over a chair.

"Why don't you go home, Peg," Leanora said. "You look exhausted."

"Will you tell me if anything...?"

"Yes, of course."

The girl left with the tired, slope-shouldered gait of the brokenhearted.

"I need to get a message to the Hotel Lioncourt," Ely said to Leanora when they were alone.

It was getting close to dawn and looking more and more like he would not make it back as he had promised.

Leanora raised an eyebrow. "Is that where you're staying? You really do have extravagant taste, sir. There's a telephone just through there. Feel free to make a call."

"A call?" Ely asked.

Leanora shook her head and ushered him into a small sitting room crowded by a cushy sofa, low desk, and line of bookshelves. On the desk sat a mahogany box with what appeared to be a black candlestick stuck in its center. Leanora lifted a tube from a hook fixed to the side. It flared out at one end like a trumpet and connected to the box with a fat copper wire.

Leanora held the trumpet to her ear and spoke into the candlestick. "Hotel Lioncourt."

She held out the trumpet to Ely, who felt nervous sweat breaking out on his palms when he raised the listening device to his ear.

"Hello?" he asked it.

"You don't have to shout, Elyssandro, I assure you they can hear you," Leanora encouraged.

A thin, polite voice tumbled from the trumpet's curve. "This is Morrison. How can I be of assistance?"

"Yes. Hello there, Morrison. I need to get a message to the executive suite."

"Certainly, sir. Just let me get ready with a pen. Alright."

"It should say, I'm fine. I'm following a lead. Don't wait up. And by all the named gods do not get in that bed without taking a shower."

"You want me to write down all of that, sir?"

"Yes, of course. Underline the part about the shower. I'm deadly serious, Morrison, I'm going to hold you responsible if the bedsheets are ruined."

"Yes, sir."

"Alright. I'm leaving now. Thank you, Morrison."

He handed the trumpet back to Leanora, and she hung it on its hook.

"Traveling with a bit of a scrub?" she asked.

"He was forced into servitude and then locked up in a cave for a thousand years," Ely said. Maybe a touch defensive.

"Shit," Leanora winced. "I apologize, Elyssandro. That was in very poor taste. Come on, I'll make it up to you."

They made their way to the kitchen. Leanora brewed chamomile tea and piled lumpy biscuits on a plate, setting them with butter and marmalade in the breakfast nook by a small window.

Though Ely felt weary and weakened after the night's activities, he could not claim to be particularly hungry. Dr. Skylark did not seem so inclined either.

Leanora fixed clear blue eyes on his face. "Alright, Elyssandro, I'll start. What do you want with the helyx?"

Ely gaped at her, not sure why he was so shocked she knew the name.

"I did my thesis on magic enhanced mechanics," Leanora explained.

"Oh," Ely said. Luckily, he had grown used to being eyed for a dunce. "I'm afraid that's not my area of expertise, so I hope you'll be patient with me."

"Not a problem," Leanora beamed, looking once again like the youthful Fellow of their first meeting. "I could talk about magical engineering all day. I wrote six hundred pages on the subject. I can fetch my dissertation, if you like."

"Maybe later," Ely said, feeling suddenly nauseous. Best to move on quickly. "I didn't know they still used Applied Magics in the Free Cities."

"It isn't widely accepted," Leanora sighed. "But there are a handful of us trying to revive the practice. Unfortunately, not everyone agrees on the ethics of its use. As you saw with Mr. Vesper and the Society."

"Ethics," Ely mused.

It never ceased to amaze how comfortably the subjects of enslavement and genocide fit into dry intellectual debate. He had left his thesis on the topic spattered across their alabaster walls.

"When last we spoke," Ely continued, "you insisted there was no such thing as magic."

"That was before I kissed a boy that could summon black holes in his hands."

Ely blushed, taking a focused interest in a dark spot in the table's wood grain.

"I'm sorry I lied to you," he said.

"I do talk an awful a lot. I don't recall giving you the opportunity to come clean," she replied, smile diffident. She continued, "I was shaken for a long time after that. I left Jade Hill. I thought I couldn't possibly be a scientist if such things could exist all this time right under my nose. Then I realized that is exactly what it means to be a scientist. You make assumptions only to set out to disprove them.

"As it turns out, Victor already had a head start. He introduced me to the writings of Dr. Ortiz. You've heard of him?" she inquired of Ely's sudden shift in expression. "He founded the Department of Lost Letters at South Sea. It's very small now, but it still has its own library and lecture hall. I transferred there. But now you've gotten me off on a monologue, I nearly forgot my question. What do you want with a helyx?"

"It's a long story," Ely began....

Lea drew her furred hood closer about her stinging cheeks. The air's frosty bite made the smile she could not seem to contain tight and painful. It was magnificent, this world of snow and ice through which their intrepid party journeyed. Fur boots crackling on crystalline tundra. Evergreens caped in dazzling white. She caught sight of an arctic fox bounding between low, needled limbs. To think she might have stayed holed up in that stuffy office.

Victor crunched over to her, broad grin a mirror of her own down to the too-light eyebrows and haughty freckled nose. His love for adventure could not be rivaled. Nor could his talent for persuading others to invest in his pursuit of it. She still could not fathom how he had pulled this one off. An expedition to Upper Pandorium would normally be met with polite dismissal at best. An expedition to Upper Pandorium to examine an astral anomaly seemed even more preposterous. Yet somehow Victor Skylark had convinced the deepest pockets in the Free Cities to open wide at the promise of a discovery the likes of which had not been seen since man tamed fire.

"We're nearly to the Fort," he said. "We can stay there for the night, enjoy a good hot meal, and head out at dawn."

"Sounds agreeable to me," Lea replied. "Why are you looking at me like there's a catch?"

"We can't bring the carts any further north, and the dogs certainly can't pull a dozen heavy trunks on a sled. They have vault safes at the Fort. You can be certain your books will be kept safe until our return."

Lea groaned in exasperation—she had been expecting some kind of dumbfuckery from her brother. She needed those books more than he needed his coat and gloves. The journal Victor had entrusted to her detailing all the data collected from the alleged astral anomaly had clearly been written by an amateur. Or by a genius that deliberately botched the process. That was the more interesting proposition.

"I've told you, Victor, I still have to work out why the measurements coming from this thing make no sense. I have six volumes of Drescher's algorithms to work through, and another trunk if those—"

"Lea, leave the books behind, and you can take your own measurements when we get to the anomaly," Victor insisted. "You'll probably figure out something infinitely more clever than your Drucker fellow."

"Drescher."

"Whatever. Leave him in the vault."

"Fine. But I'll be bringing all my sensors," she snapped.

"Of course. Those are invaluable to the expedition," Victor agreed.

They reached the Fort earlier than expected, its drab concrete a jarring eyesore amidst the scintillating landscape. It was the last point of civilization before a big blank white nothing off the edge of the charts.

The Fort seemed a little more inviting on the inside. Its drab porridge walls had been hung with bright banners belonging to the many nations from which its expeditious inhabitants hailed. Periwinkle and white for Mondacca. Black and gold for South Sea. Purple and green for Zantos. Seafoam and coral for the Barrier Keys. Even the vermillion of the Canon Protectorate kept civil discourse in the name of exploration.

Men in sealskin uniforms carried their bags and trunks to the suite of rooms reserved for their arrival. Aside from Victor and herself, their party included three geologists from the university, two wilderness survivalists who were also former South Sea Fellows, two investors itching for a hands-on experience, two guides who claimed to know the route to the anomaly, and Peggy. Sweet, bubbly Peggy with a laugh that had still not been dampened even in the face of cold and discomfort. She had hauled telescope cases, cross-referenced dense tomes, and calculated trajectories from the back of an unsteady cart all without a single complaint. It seemed the sprightly slip of a girl might turn out to be a real gem of a research assistant. She did get distracted pining over Victor, but a girl was entitled to a few faults. As the two sole female occupants of the Fort, Lea was glad the young scholar had agreed to come along.

Once settled into their close, sparsely furnished dorm, they donned their warmest evening attire and joined the already crowded dining hall. The high-ceilinged commissary contained rows of long tables. Thick, rounded windows admitted light from outside, but no view could be made through the frosted glass.

"Is that a full bar?" Peggy gasped.

"Don't drink too much, Peg. We have to leave early," Lea cautioned.

"Copy that, boss," she said over her shoulder as she skipped over to the nook where a bartender was busy pouring something tasty-looking into a martini glass. Lea turned away from the tempting little siren. She knew better than to drink on an expedition.

The next face she saw set her rethinking her commitment to sobriety. Who should be slithering past with a jack-o-lantern smile but Roman Vesper. An associate of her father's—though despised by Captain Skylark for being "new money"—Mr. Vesper and his horrific Society had been haranguing her to join their degenerate ranks for years. Lea made an attempt to sidestep his view, but he caught up to her before she could give him the old duck and weave.

"Miss Skylark," he drawled. "Yours is the last face I expected to see out here in the savage wilderness. I can't imagine your father was thrilled at the notion."

"My father wouldn't be so vulgar as to be thrilled at any notion, Mr. Vesper. And it's Dr. Skylark. Not miss," she finished with honey-coated acid.

Vesper chuckled. "What a modern world we live in. If you came up in my time, they'd have put you in a frilly skirt and taught you to keep that pretty mouth closed."

Lea met his disgusting leer with a disdainful stare. "So, what brings you out to the frozen tundra, Mr. Vesper?"

"Same thing as your brother, I expect," Vesper drawled. "There's sure to be something behind all that radioactive mumbo jumbo, and whatever all those doctors of science find, I aim to bottle and sell."

"Best of luck with that, Mr. Vesper."

"You know, it's too bad you turned down my offer. I could've made you a fortune selling lettered munitions."

"I'm afraid that's outside my area of expertise," Lea answered coolly. "I'd rather be stuffed for that Collection of yours than carve my name on a bullet."

"I'm sure that could be arranged," sneered Vesper. "Woman doctor is exactly the kind of freakish curiosity my associates like to take home to play."

"Well, I think I've impinged on your evening enough. Enjoy your brandy."

With that, Lea ducked into a passing group too distracted in their conversation to take notice of her. Where the blazes was Victor? They would need eyes on twelve and six with Roman Vesper on their scent...

Leanora leaned forward, both elbows on the table, chin resting in her palms as she listened intently to Ely's tale.

"So, each helyx node points the way to another?" she asked.

"From what I understand of it, yes," Ely nodded.

"Fascinating. I never imagined them so enmeshed. Of course, for the longest time I thought they were merely theoretical. Where's yours? Nix, you called her?"

"With Rav back at the hotel," he replied.

A wiser man might have shown more restraint in his storytelling. The old hummingbirds that had awoken in his stomach at her delighted smile had drawn out any secret he might have kept. He had already followed her to a derelict townhouse in some dark corner of the city. If those fluttering wings proved as untrustworthy as the vampire would, no doubt, declare them, a few extra details could hardly put him in a worse position.

"And she speaks to you like a person?" Leanora asked.

"She *is* a person," Ely replied.

"Was it your Dr. Faidra who placed the demon in the chassis?" Leanora asked.

"In the what?" he blinked.

"The silver ball," Leanora clarified.

"I suppose she did," Ely nodded.

"I would so like to meet her," Leanora lamented. "I bet she has answers to all the questions I've been banging my head against for the last decade."

"Yes, you she would not have poisoned," Ely muttered.

"Poisoned?" Leanora bleated.

"I'm useless at glyphs, and it drives her to madness," he replied.

"Good gods, Elyssandro. Is there anyone not trying to kill you?"

"I'm used to it," he shrugged. "You came pretty close to succeeding yourself."

Though he had meant it for a laugh, a worry line appeared between her strawberry brows. "I really am sorry about that."

She lowered her gaze, running a finger around the rim of her mug. "All this time, I've wanted so very badly to find you. To tell you I was wrong. Beg your forgiveness. I heard rumors of you the world over. I always seemed to miss you by days. Then you vanished. I heard that you had been killed. Most violently."

"Another close call," he said. "I didn't stray so far from home after that."

"Why?" she asked.

"Why don't you take a turn for a bit?" he suggested with a taut smile. "You seem to know a lot more than I do about helyxes. Helyxii?"

"Helyxia," Leanora corrected.

"Thank you, Dr. Skylark."

"It sounds so impressive when you say it that way," she purred. "Come on then. I've got a book in here you might like to take a peek at."

"Oh good, just the thing to keep me awake at four o'clock in the morning," Ely yawned.

She eyed him. "You don't like to read?"

"I love to read," Ely protested. "But sometimes the words squirm around and turn backwards, so I only do it if it's really worth the battle."

Leanora fixed him with a beguiling smile. "Well, my dapper scholar of Death, I have a feeling you're really going to like this one. Come along."

He followed her into the sitting room, marveling at how someone so short could move so quickly. In a full-sailed gown and heels, no less.

She commanded him to sit on the sofa, then drummed her fingers along the line of book spines on a shelf. Seizing a heavy volume, she set it in his lap. He squeezed his eyes shut. They already felt like they had fluid sloshing around them. This exercise was not about to help matters.

"Here," Leanora said, presenting him with a pair of rounded spectacles. Hair-fine glyphs etched the steel rims. She kicked off her shoes and settled at the opposite end of the sofa, feet tucked up under the billowing folds of her dress.

Ely opened to the first page. He read over the introduction, then read on to the next page in wonder.

"These are incredible!" he exclaimed.

With the glyph-encoded glasses perched on his nose, he could follow the words across a page without them trying to tap dance away laughing at him.

"Father used to berate Victor into the ground for not focusing on his studies, and it turns out he just needed the right pair of reading glasses." Leanora's smile faded, and she sighed. "I suppose he doesn't need them anymore."

"Are you ready to tell me what happened to your brother?" Ely asked.

The line between her brows deepened. "About six months ago, Victor put together an expedition to Upper Pandorium."

"That's north of even the Protectorate," Ely said, intrigued.

Leanora nodded. "It's north of everything. He had gotten hold of some research that suggested the stars there were not where they should be, and in fact, instead of looking at the night sky, one was peering into a hole looking out at another point in the universe. I theorized it was an optical phenomenon, some natural formation not unlike my father's observatory telescope, if you remember."

Ely nodded. "I do."

"Victor was eager to get ahead of the scientific community. I was too. There were visions of becoming the first female recipient of the Corrigan's Prize. So, we gathered a crew and made the trip. As you can imagine, the journey was a long one. I had plenty of time to analyze the research already brought back from Pandorium. None of it made sense. The frequencies, the radiation, the changing angles of the stars. It was so inconstant and volatile, not to mention defiant of mathematical sense, that it could not possibly exist."

"It was a rupture," Ely told her.

Leanora gawked, struck speechless.

"You're right they don't make sense," he added. "We'll come back to that. What happened next?"

"We got to the Fort. It's an ugly concrete waystation at the end of the map. There were all sorts of people already vying for a chance at the anomaly. What did you call it?"

"Rupture."

"Right. Rupture. But we met a man there, a friend of Victor's, who told us this thing was only a distraction from the real find."

"And did you believe him?" Ely asked.

"Absolutely," she nodded...

Lea made a hasty retreat through the crowded commissary. She found her brother in conversation with a sturdy man with long black hair, silver at the temples, beard braided with carved mirrorwood beads. He seemed tall, but since Victor was taller, she could only assume someone more vertically inclined than herself might find that assessment inaccurate. He was certainly imposing. Handsome in a regal, unapproachable way like a lion or a wolf.

Victor brightened as he caught sight of her and motioned her over. "This is my sister, Leanora Skylark. Sorry, *Doctor* Leanora Skylark. Lea, this is his majesty the King of Séocwen."

"Good gracious, how does one even address a king?" Lea stammered, bobbing an awkward curtsy.

The distinguished monarch's bearing softened with a quiet, rumbling chuckle. "There are no kings up here off the edge of the world. Kai is fine."

"Kai came along for the Demon's Crossing expedition," Victor explained.

The king crooked an eyebrow. "Came along? You mean piloted the only ship that would take you there? Fought off mutant cannibals before they made you their guest of honor?"

"Yes. Sure. And it was well worth the risk, now wasn't it, your majesty?"

"It was interesting, I'll give you that," Kai smirked.

"Are you here for the anomaly too?" Lea asked.

"No," his kingship replied. "I'll leave that battle to mainlander scientists and scholars."

The subtle amusement behind his eyes suggested he had already seen the stars at the end of the world and learned all he needed of their secrets. Before she could inquire further, she noticed her assistant across the room facing a persistent male with the wide grimace-smile of a woman cornered into an unwanted conversation.

"Excuse me, gentlemen," she said. "My assistant is in need of assistance."

She did her best to puff up to an authoritative stance. "Ms. Osai, I need you. Put that drink down at once. We have work to do."

"Oh, yes, coming, Dr. Skylark." Peggy shrugged at the obtuse lurker. "Sorry. My boss."

She scampered over to Lea and fell in step. "Thanks. That guy would not take a hint."

"Yes, this is the kind of place where we girls need to stick together," Lea nodded.

They grabbed a couple of plates and took them back to the suite to tackle some figures. After Peggy went off to bed, Lea returned to the commissary in search of her brother.

The crowd had thinned at this late hour. She noticed the Séoc king sat near a rime-crusted window. In his palm, he held a platinum print encircled by a mirrorwood frame. As Lea stepped closer, she made out a round-cheeked face with dark eyes, wild black hair, and an outrageous dimpled smile.

"Who's this little angel, then?" Lea beamed, taking the liberty of sitting beside him.

"My daughter," Kai said, a smile lifting the stone from his features. "Elyssa Morena Novara."

"Beautiful," Lea smiled. "You must miss her terribly."

Kai nodded. "She is my joy, and I think of her every moment. But it is for her that I am here."

"It's important, isn't it? What's out there in the wilds," Lea said, watching his face intently.

He replaced the photograph in his coat pocket, then looked up at her.

"Yes, Dr. Skylark," he said, voice low, almost inaudible. "This place will decide who makes the future."

"This place," Lea pressed. "But not the anomaly?"

Kai's eyes flicked to the room and then back to her face. "We cannot talk about this here, Dr. Skylark."

Lea glanced along the same trajectory to find a thin-lipped smile turned in their direction.

"Vesper?" she murmured. "Yes, he's vile."

"Not just him." Kai shifted his gaze to two other men, sitting tucked in a corner nearby. "They've hidden their crimson, but they are templars."

"So, the Canon wants a piece of it too, then," Lea mused.

"Not here," Kai repeated.

"Is there somewhere else you will talk to me openly?"

"It is as I told your brother," Kai said. "There is nothing I can tell you until you see. Leave the others behind, and I will take you both."

"I'm game. What did Victor say?"

"He said he would think about it."

"Can I bring my research assistant? I can't just leave her alone with all these strange men."

"Bring her too," the Séoc king nodded.

"Alright then. When do we leave?"

"Right now. Before the others are up, and the snow will have time to cover our tracks. You can convince your brother?"

"I'll handle Victor," she assured him. "We'll meet you in ten."

Victor had a pack ready by the time she knocked on the door to his room.

"Oh, there you are," he said. "I was just coming around to talk to you about something."

"If it's about traipsing off into the unknown with his majesty the king of Séocwen, then I'm already apprised. I just need to fetch Peggy and my day pack."

Her unflappable assistant needed no explanation. Peggy was up and ready to set off before Lea managed to figure out which field kits to carry with them. She decided on a light, portable set of sensors and her emergency encoding case that contained three styluses—one for metal, one for wood, and one for animus.

Kai met them at what appeared to be a gift shop, and they made their exit into the darkened tundra. The landscape shifted almost immediately beyond the concrete Fort. The snow deepened from ankle height to knee height, then almost thigh height, at least for Lea. Their royal guide brought them to a packed trail cut between shoulders of ice where a gentle sloping hill gradually thickened to a rocky mountainside. The terrain was treacherous here, and they stopped to outfit their boots with spiked attachments for better grip.

Lea shivered. Her fingers and toes ached despite their ample layers. Chattering teeth sounded Peggy's first complaint of the expedition. As night took its final bow, Lea made out the silhouettes of man-made statuary in the ice-layered granite. Then the geometric precision of a towering edifice. Who had built a stronghold out here in this desolate mountain?

Victor let out a low whistle. "Where did you come from, you gorgeous thing?" he asked the soaring battlements.

"The diakana built it long ago," Kai told them.

"Diakana?" Victor repeated. "Necromancers?"

"That is what the Canon named them," Kai said.

It was clear the Séoc king held a visceral dislike of the crude word. Lea didn't much like it either. Cosmologist seemed far more respectful and certainly more accurate from her brief experience.

Morning lifted its dazzling gaze as they skirted the base of the structure. It was built directly into the frozen mountainside, black turrets jutting out at sharp angles and soaring statues with hands outstretched in a posture she saw often in her dreams.

The entrance lay tucked away behind a glacial outcropping. Inside, cunning slitted windows directed lines of snow-bright light from outside. No need for artificial lighting here. Clever. High obsidian arches converged in a compass star on the ceiling.

Victor moved about the enormous antechamber, admiring the architecture in wonder. Peggy ogled and gasped and traipsed off to make notes. Lea's gaze rested with the Séoc king whose bearing had grown subdued in the brooding atmosphere. The others did not seem to notice, but she recognized it the moment they set foot inside. That same awe-inspiring vastness that enraptured her so when she looked out into the deepest heavens through the telescope.

"What happened to them?" Lea asked. "The diakana?"

Kai's expression darkened. "They were hunted and slaughtered and named abominations. I cannot say my people or yours are blameless in their persecution, but it was the Canon that drove them to all but extinction. The truth is, they knew it was the diakana alone that could throw the Canon to its knees. I have seen one man bring down a templar fleet with no weapon but his own hands."

"Where is he now?" Lea asked, breath catching as she wondered if she might again pick up the trail of her only regret.

"Dead," Kai said, voice turning hoarse. "Murdered."

Lea stepped back, wind knocked from her lungs. Perhaps it was not the same man. Still, she could not bring herself to ask his name.

Kai cleared his throat and continued. "It was my fault. I thought I could change centuries of fear in a single gesture. I was arrogant and selfish. Young. In love."

He fell silent, gaze transfixed by an onyx figure poised to take Death in hand. Lea waited, chest tight with impatient dread.

"They came while my guard was down. My mother sent them as a reminder that princes too are slaves to the law. I could do nothing to stop them. His screams still torment my dreams. The rivers of blood from spikes driven into his flesh...

"They left him there alone on the clifftop to die beneath the stars. I thought my heart died there too."

The king closed his eyes, fists clenched at his sides. Then he looked up at her again as though just recalling he had an audience.

"I hope you will forgive me for speaking so freely when we are little more than strangers."

"That's quite alright," she murmured, voice nearly lost.

"Perhaps, though, you can understand," Kai continued, "my joy and my terror when I saw the next diakana come into the world."

Lea felt chills spill down her spine, this time not from the cold. "Your daughter," she breathed.

Kai inclined his head.

"My wife, she thought it was just an ordinary birthmark. But the little white constellation was so familiar to me, so beloved, I knew the moment I saw it that the stars had entrusted me with their most beautiful gift. Even though I failed them once, I will not let it happen again. And so I have journeyed here to the ends of the earth so that maybe, this time, I can change the world for her."

"I want to help, your majesty," Lea said. "What can I do?"

Kai inclined his head. "There is something I would very much like for you to take a look at, Dr. Skylark."

"Lead the way..."

"So that's where you found the egg?" Ely asked. "In an ancient ruin in the northern wilderness that some explorer friend of Victor's happened to stumble upon?"

Leanora inclined her head. "Yes, that's the gist of it. It was still in stasis in the shell. I came across helyxia in my earlier research, but I had no idea they were possible in application. Luckily, I brought the right stylus. It's one of the few of its kind in the world."

"A spirit encoder?" Ely asked, impressed with himself for remembering.

She nodded, also impressed. "I thought I would be able to hack it in a matter of hours, but it proved a little more challenging than that..."

Lea stared in awe at the enormous tablets, rounded at the top like tombstones and inscribed with sharp, knifelike letters. Death magic. This type of glyph she had only ever seen inscribed upon a vampire hunter's stake. Mr. Vesper had given her one as a keepsake whilst trying to convince her to join his ranks. These ancient symbols before her were much more complex. Intricate. Beautiful. She could not read them, but when she stared at them long enough with thoughts suspended, they began to whisper. A low, ghostly hum at first, then the gathering roar of a multitude speaking as one.

"Lea, are you sure you don't want to take a look at this?"

Lea blinked, glaring up at her brother as his voice silenced the deathly host. Victor cradled the onyx ovoid in his arms like a small, misshapen baby.

"I'm quite sure I'm not interested in your egg rock, thank you, Vic," Lea growled for the thousandth time.

She turned back to the stone tablets laid out on the cavern floor, running her fingers again over the sharp script inscribed upon them.

"It's alright, my beauty, I know you're something special," Victor crooned to the heavy lump.

"I could take a look at it, if you'd like, Mr. Skylark," Peggy offered.

"Would you please, Ms. Osai?" he smiled. "I would be very grateful."

"Can I borrow a stylus, Dr. S?" she called.

"Yes, yes, the case is over there."

Lea waved her hand in the general vicinity, eyes locked to the tablet.

As she relaxed her mind, the ancient letters began to tremble and glow. Whispers emerged, curling secrets into her ear. Then she was no longer in the room but drifting through the infinite brilliance of space. Gaseous clouds bloomed in vivid magenta and turquoise. Violet pillars studded with tiny jeweled stars strummed the heavens like the fingers of some great celestial being plucking at the harp strings of the universe.

"Lea, look! My gods, aren't you magnificent. Lea, you have to see!"

Her brother's voice tore her from the stars' embrace.

"No!" she cried, reaching for the nebula as though she might grasp hold of it to stay.

Her plea echoed from stone walls. Deepest cold burst from the tablet and crested in a black wave through her outstretched hand. The blow struck Victor square in the chest, catapulting him across the room...

"Whatever we did, it must have triggered the device," Leanora said. "It sort of went haywire and crashed into him. He was convulsing on the ground. Screaming and clawing at himself. Then he just lay still. I thought he was dead. His eyes stood wide open, staring blind at the ceiling. And..."

She took a breath, vision swallowed in whatever horrific scene had been witnessed in the northern ruins.

"I think I had better just show you," she concluded in a whisper.

Ely set aside the book and the spectacles, following her back downstairs into the fetid infirmary. Victor lay motionless, breath shallow. Lost to soporific dreams.

Leanora gently drew down the coverlet. A bandage, ruddy where blood seeped through, swathed his hollow chest. It appeared his incessant scratching had already dislodged one side. Leanora pealed back the bandage. Ridged lacerations twisted a cyclonic spiral across his sternum. Slightly to the left side, above his heart, the rounded half-dome of a silver orb lay embedded in an inflamed cavity.

The helyx.

Chapter Thirteen
BAD BEHAVIOR

"How long has he been like this?" Ely asked, swallowing queasy repulsion.

He had seen some gruesome wounds in his time, but something about the burrowed machine evoked arachnophobic shudders.

Leanora sighed. "Months. We managed to get him back to the Fort quickly, but their physicians were baffled. They couldn't figure out how he survived, much less help him in any way."

"And the device? She can't be removed?" Ely asked, only able to draw breath again when he had turned his eyes away.

"It won't allow the doctors to touch it," Leanora replied. "Dr. Cunningham sustained some very nasty burns at the Fort. In fact, it will only allow Peggy to clean the wounds. It seems to like her."

"Interesting," Ely considered.

He ventured another look, grasping for some of the analytic detachment that decades spent around Dr. Faidra should have imparted. This time he noticed the blackened outlines that curved like shadows along the edges of the lacerations. More than that, he felt the haunted whisper dragging at his skin like the tug of a magnet.

He bent closer.

"How did you come by death magic?" he whispered to the helyx.

Pearly brume gathered beneath the protruding dome. Victor gasped softly as the machine blinked to life. At his squirming groan, the helyx sputtered and shut down again.

"Will it listen to you?" Leanora asked.

"She might if I knew her name," Ely frowned. "We need Nix."

"We could go by the hotel," Leanora suggested.

"Yes, we should go pick up Rav and Nix. Good idea." Ely thought a moment and added, "He'll be asleep by now, and we wouldn't be able to come back for a while. Maybe we should wait until a little closer to nightfall."

"Oh right. I forgot about the logistics of his condition," Leanora frowned. "Alright then. Maybe we should follow the vampire's lead and catch a nap ourselves. I know I'm exhausted."

"Sounds reasonable," Ely concurred.

Leanora fixed Victor's bandage and tucked him back under the coverlet. They returned upstairs. The sofa looked very inviting, if a bit short to accommodate him. At this point he would take a shallow grave if it meant a bit of shut eye.

"I'm going to require some assistance since Peggy's gone home," Leanora said.

"Sure," Ely yawned. "With what exactly?"

"Getting out of this dress," she replied, sashaying for the bedroom.

The saucy smirk she threw over her shoulder suggested she did not expect him to undertake the task in quite as businesslike a manner as her assistant.

Ely followed. No doubt a terrible idea. Leanora turned her back to him, sweeping aside runaway ringlets.

"What do these mean?" he asked, brushing a line of dainty glyphs tattooed along the slope of her shoulder.

"Protection," she said. "If you're curious as to how I managed to escape last night's gala unscathed, well, there you are."

"Clever," he said.

"Exceedingly," she smiled. "Buttons please."

"Yes, of course."

As much as he loved a good set of ornamental buttons, even his most complicated coat seemed economical in comparison to the pearled labyrinth trickling down her spine. No matter. He enjoyed a good challenge. Especially when rewarded with an ever-widening channel of bare skin. Here and there the swirl of a tattooed glyph emerged from beneath gossamer lace.

With his task complete, he turned to make a graceful retreat before such a thing became impossible. A silvery siren song followed him into the hall.

"Stay, Elyssandro."

He paused. Heart sinking though he could hardly breathe for want of an invitation. Nothing good ever followed this kind of longing.

"I don't know if I should, Leanora," he murmured.

"You don't want to?" she asked.

She stood framed in the door, all sinewy suggestion in the clinging slip.

"Of course I do," he said. "But it's only going to end with someone bleeding out on the floor. Probably me."

"Or," she countered, moving a step closer. "What if it just turns out to be very nice?"

Ely smiled, all too eager to give in to optimism once again. Leanora drew his face to hers and kissed him with bewitching abandon. Somewhere in the swelling overture, she relieved him of his shirt and bowtie. Her slip crumpled to the floor. Belt clicked. Pantlegs fluttered. With nothing but soft light and warm skin between them, they found their way to the little four poster bed.

Her finger traipsed over the faded bullet round indented on his shoulder.

"Mine?" she asked.

He nodded.

She pressed her lips to the scar and teased a low grunt with a strum of her wicked little fingers. "Allow me to make it up to you."

"No, please, allow me," he murmured and bent to taste a delicate glyph reposed between the luscious curves of her breasts.

His jealous hands followed suit, gentle and greedy. Thumbs brushing her sweet, scandalous nipples and raising a glorious purr as she arched against him. His lips savored the soft rise of her belly, the dangerous sweep of her hip, the opulent satin of her thigh. She cried his name as he arrived at the honeyed paradise beneath.

Yes, this was, indeed, very nice.

When none of the terrible things Ely feared came to pass, the two showered, ate breakfast, and tested fate again. Still nothing terrible. Rinse and repeat.

When lust died down to a quiet purr, they talked of their adventures. It turned out they both had a bit of a wandering streak. Leanora told him about her research expeditions to the less modern fringes of the world where Lost Letters were not so lost. He recounted his excursions into lands strange and unknown. Leanora was less interested in his destinations than the method by which he traveled. Ely did his best to recall the technicalities of ruptures, but he knew them as adversaries and friends not phenomena to be measured.

Assistant Peggy turned up at lunch time to check in on Victor. Ely learned then why she seemed so familiar. Her parents owned the Zephyr Tavern in Mondacca. Peggy, short for Wenapeg, had been a lanky little thing, all elbows and scraped knees. He remembered her running about the cookyard after her mothers. Peggy remembered him too, more especially the odd gold coins with which he paid for meals and lodgings.

"They used to tease me mercilessly at school for the holes in my shoes, for my name, for being Séoc," she said. "But it always stopped for a little while after you came around. Until my dresses wore out again."

"You're Séoc?" Ely asked with interest. "What island?"

"Seúza," she replied.

Ely inclined his head, hoping his face kept a pleasant expression. If he flinched, Peggy didn't seem to notice.

"I don't remember it at all," she continued. "My mothers left when I was a baby. There was some kind of typhoon or something that flooded our whole village. So, they came to the mainland. Fresh start, you know?"

"You never told me you were bullied," Leanora frowned.

Peggy shrugged. "At this point I could write a curse that would make their ears fall off if I had a mind."

"She really is very good," Leanora confirmed with a prideful smile.

Peggy's triumphant grin sank. "I'd trade it all in to learn how to fix Mr. Skylark."

"I know you would," Leanora commiserated, patting her shoulder with sisterly affection.

Peggy left after lunch. With dishes done and Victor looked after, they resolved to retire for that nap they still had yet to take. By the time night deepened outside the window, the pair lay tangled together much better acquainted but not in the least bit rested. Leanora lay still and quiet as she drew fingers along the pale marks arranged in a telltale pattern over his ribs.

"What are you thinking about?" Ely asked.

"Nothing," she replied. "Nothing important. I'm going to go clean up. Feel free to nod off. I'll be back shortly."

Ely rolled onto his side, out fast as a snuffed candle. A low hum, like an overlarge bumblebee buzzed near his ear. He sat up with a start to find a golden eye hovering over him.

"Hello, Elyssandro."

"Hello, Nix," he said. "What are you doing here?"

"Rescuing you," the orb replied. "You don't appear to be damaged. May I have permission to scan you?"

"That's alright. I'm fine. Where's Rav?" Ely asked, suddenly nervous to have the vampire sniffing around and jumping to conclusions before he could fully explain the situation.

"On the roof. The wards are keeping him out," Nix explained. She gave a sputtering whir that resembled a chuckle. "I could have let him in too, but I didn't want to."

"Well, let me get dressed."

"Do you have to?" Nix whined. "Your anatomy is so amusing."

"Um. Thank you?"

"You're most welcome, Elyssandro."

He found his trousers quickly, trying to ignore the gawking demon eye. Leanora returned in a slinky silk robe drying her hair with a towel.

"I was just thinking, Elyssandro..." She stopped, eyes locked to the flying machine.

"And who's this?" Nix demanded.

"I'm Leanora," she beamed. "You must be Nix. It's lovely to meet you. Elyssandro's told me so much about you."

"Is that so?" the helyx sniffed. "Funny, he hasn't mentioned a single word about *you*."

Nix drifted away toward the window.

Leanora glanced at Ely with eyebrows raised. "Did I say something wrong?" she asked.

"I don't think so. She's usually very polite," Ely frowned.

The helyx emitted a needle thin point of light that sizzled against the air. She let out a piercing whistle, then called, "Found him!"

Ely realized what she had done a split second before Rav crashed through the window in a hailstorm of glass. He lunged forward, throwing a curtain of black ether around the vampire. The trick worked well enough to throw Rav off trajectory, but the impact knocked the wind from him and rattled every bone in his body. Still, Ely locked his arms around the vampire and clung like a barnacle to a ship's hull.

"What are you doing?" Rav snarled.

"Calm down. Give me a chance to–"

Ely caught sight of Leanora edging closer. Fear rippled through him as the glint of a mirrorwood stake flashed in her hands. The cosmic bonds holding the vampire in place evaporated into violet sparks. The shift threw Ely off balance, sending both crashing to the ground.

The vampire sprang to his feet like a jaguar. In a swift, languid motion, he knocked the stake from Leanora's grasp and sank his teeth into her throat.

"Rav, no!" Ely cried.

The vampire dropped Leanora to the floor, spitting in disgust.

"A bit bitter, is it, vampire?" Leanora grunted, holding one hand to the side of her neck, the other inching toward the stake.

"You're not going to let her talk to you like that, are you, fangs?" Nix goaded.

"Everyone stop!" Ely shouted, voice echoing for a moment with Death's booming legion.

Rav and Leanora froze. Nix bobbed behind a bedpost.

"Alright," Ely snapped. "Rav, no biting. Leanora, leave the stake. Nix...come here."

He held out his hand. The helyx floated reluctantly to him like a puppy with its tail tucked.

"Shut down," he commanded sternly.

Nix sighed and plopped dormant into his palm. He tucked the immobile silver ball into his pocket.

"Now, let's start again, shall we?"

"You mind if I change into something a bit more substantial before we make introductions?" Leanora glared.

"Come on, Rav."

Ely gave the vampire a shove in the direction of the door. He bent to swipe the stake on his way past. Hopefully, this was the only death magic contraband he would need to keep eyes on.

"Are Ragnor and the other children safe?" Ely asked.

"They were when I left them," Rav replied. "I found a few abandoned farmhouses on my way into the city. No one should disturb them."

"We can go first thing in the..." Ely shut his mouth before the idiotic statement could fully escape. "I'm sure they'll be fine until we can get back."

"You said you would return before sunrise," Rav glowered as they entered the sitting room. "I thought you had been taken."

"Rav, I'm so sorry," Ely apologized. "Didn't you get my note?"

"What note?" the vampire inquired.

"Damn that Morrison," Ely growled. "He swore he'd written it down exactly."

The vampire lifted a martyred gaze. "I returned to the mansion to look for you the moment the sun went down. I scoured every room. You don't want to know what I found in the torture chambers below."

Lingering horror, fury, and relief overflowed in the currents between them.

"I was coming to get you, Rav. I didn't want to disturb you during daylight, and then..."

"You got distracted being human, as usual," Rav filled in.

"I found the key," Ely diverted, fully aware this news was not actually a victory of any kind considering the circumstances.

Rav sensed his apprehension. "What is it you don't want me to know, conjurer?"

Ely's brow furrowed, and he hesitated, trying to take a delicate approach. "Rav, I need you to go through the remainder of this evening without behaving like a..."

"Vampire?"

"Yes," Ely sighed, rubbing his swollen eyes.

Rav looked irritable for a moment, then he turned to Ely with a contrite expression. "I should not have bit your paramour. I misjudged the situation. I could not be more mortified."

"Our demon friend was a little misleading about the whole thing," Ely offered. "It was an honest mistake, and you were very heroic crashing through the window to rescue me."

"I will admit that our Haunts outing has left me out of sorts."

"Do you have a hangover, Rav?" Ely asked.

"Worse," he winced. "I'm probably going to be ill for some time."

Ely set a reassuring hand on his shoulder. "That's alright. We'll get through it."

"Please don't touch me, conjurer. The smell of blood is nauseating."

"Sorry."

Ely stepped back, happy to offer moral support from a distance.

"I'm going to go look in on Leanora. You can sit down if you like. We'll talk about the key when I get back, I promise."

Rav nodded, face even more pallid than usual. Ely knocked at the bedroom door, feeling, once again, like a stranger in her house.

"Come in," came a shaky reply.

Leanora had managed to change into a smart pantsuit, very doctorly, but now she sat on the edge of the bed, leaning forward on her knees, head in her hands.

"Are you alright?" Ely asked.

"A little woozy," she told him. "It burns worse than the snake bite from the South Napor expedition."

"May I see?" Ely asked.

She lowered the crimson charmeuse wrapped around the twin punctures in her neck. They didn't appear too deep, but the skin flared angry red.

"I'm surprised he managed to get a fang in. Brahm's sigil isn't as effective as studies suggest," she said.

"Rav feels awful about the whole thing. He thought I was being held hostage."

"By a woman in a silk bathrobe?" Leanora asked with a sardonic side eye.

"I don't believe Rav gives a great deal of thought to human attire," Ely justified. "And he never got my note. If anyone is to blame, it's that careless bastard Morrison."

"Damn him," Leanora groaned. He wasn't sure if she meant Morrison or the vampire. Maybe all men in general.

"Do you want me to clean up this glass?" Ely offered, glancing at the explosion of shards on the floor.

"Just leave me for now," Leanora instructed as she crawled to her pillows. "I think I'm going to have to sleep this off. You and your toothy friend can share the sofa."

Ely nodded. Gutted somehow. He had known from the first unclasped pearl that this was a doomed affair. The messenger between his head and his heart appeared to be about as reliable as Mr. Morrison at the Lioncourt.

"Call if you need anything," Ely murmured on his way out the door.

Rav sat engrossed in the book left behind by the sofa's previous occupants. He held a finger to a passage about limitations in a helyx's parameter programming and something, something, something rerouting circuitry. It had been absolute gibberish to Ely, but Rav appeared captivated.

"Is she alright?" Rav asked, looking up with a note of remorseful concern.

"She's resting," Ely replied. Of course, the vampire caught the melancholy undertone.

"I'm sorry to have spoiled your evening."

"You didn't," Ely assured him. "I should have come back sooner to tell you what I had learned."

"Tell me now, conjurer."

Ely nodded. "Follow me."

The two descended to the musty study where Victor lay sleeping off the effects of his latest draught.

"Is something rotting?" Rav grimaced.

"Victor?" Ely tested.

Victor remained as a statue, fluttering eyelids the only sign of life.

"This is Leanora's brother, Victor Skylark. He was with her on the expedition that discovered the second helyx."

Ely gently drew back the coverlet and bandage, exposing the lacerated spiral that surrounded the silver orb nearly buried in his chest. Rav did not speak, but his alarm raised the hair on the back of Ely's neck.

"What did this?" Rav asked.

"Leanora told me it was the helyx. Something went wrong when she used the spirit encoder," Ely said.

"The helyx could not have done this." Rav extended a hand toward the black-tinged wounds then dropped it back at his side. He turned to Ely, asking in a low whisper, "Do you trust her?"

"Leanora?" Ely frowned.

"Is there any reason to think she might not have told you the whole story?" Rav clarified.

"Why would she lie about it?" Ely asked.

Rav blinked at him. "Wouldn't it be nice if we could ask someone who knows her intimately?"

Ely blushed, avoiding his gaze. "I can't make promises about her good intentions. This is the first time I've spoken to her in fifteen years. Last time we met, she called me a monster and shot me with a pistol."

"Damn it all, Elyssandro," the vampire hissed.

"I know, I know. You don't have to tell me."

"Well," Rav sighed, "the fact that I am looking at death magic etched into her brother's rib cage suggests that there is a layer missing from the story."

"I was hoping Nix could help," Ely said.

His pocket bumped at the sound of her name. Nix wriggled free.

"Oh my," she gasped, taking in the gruesome sight before her. "Sweet sister, what have they done to you?"

She turned back to Ely.

"May I speak with her, Elyssandro?"

"Will it cause Victor discomfort?" he asked.

"I'll use a low frequency protocol. It won't disturb him, I promise."

Ely nodded. The helyx hovered above the sleeping man's ruined chest. Her clouds swirled speckled gray, the golden eye blinking amber.

"She says she is damaged," Nix told them. "No wonder I had such trouble finding her. The human is sustaining her for now, and she is doing what she can to keep him functioning. She says he is badly damaged too, and that if she leaves him now, they both will die. If you don't mind, Elyssandro, I would like to run some tests."

"Sure," Ely frowned. "Whatever you need to do, just don't hurt Victor, understand?"

"Yes, Elyssandro. I understand."

The helyx flashed steady pale light once again. Rav groaned.

"Are you alright?" Ely asked, turning to the vampire.

"No," Rav gasped. Ghastly green tinged his stark cheeks.

"The bathroom's upstairs, last door down the hall," Ely told him.

The vampire swept off like a sickly tornado.

"Nix, how's it going over there?"

"Please try to keep quiet, Elyssandro," the helyx modulated. "I'm running diagnostics."

"Right. Apologies."

Ely left her to her work. Upstairs, he gave a light tap on the bathroom door.

"Need anything, Rav?"

He was answered by sounds of retching followed with a snarled, "Leave me be, conjurer."

Feeling useless, not to mention on the brink of death by sleep deprivation, he settled down on the sofa to wait.

"Elyssandro."

"Hello, Ariel," he grumbled, sitting up, resigned that he was never to sleep again.

The phantom appeared almost solid. He could make out features in the light. Wide eyes under serious brows, aquiline nose, downturned mouth.

"Nice to finally see you," he said. "You're looking substantial this evening."

"You damaged the Hollow when you fell into it," she said. "It's weakened slowly."

"Glad to hear it. We've found the second key, but it's come with a bit of a catch."

"You're in danger, Elyssandro," she interrupted. "There's an Apostle in the city. I can only assume he also is looking for the key."

"Does he know where to find it?" Ely asked, spine prickling.

Death too listened intently.

"It is only a matter of time."

"Can't you look in on him?" Ely suggested. "Get a little insight into his plans?"

"It doesn't work that way, Elyssandro."

"Well, how does it work? Is that why you're talking to me and not Rav? You're stuck wherever you fall?"

"It's complicated."

"Well, just stay there a moment, let me call him in here, and you can explain—"

"I don't have time for this, Elyssandro."

"Why not?" Ely demanded. "You can't take five minutes to tell the man who's endured a thousand years of hell for you that you're not angry with him?"

"The Ravan Aurelio I knew is dead," Ariel snapped. "I am not responsible for the monstrosity that wears his face."

"He's not—"

Ariel vanished. Ely gaped at the air, now empty of her presence.

"She's right, conjurer," the quiet voice startled him from the doorway.

Ely turned to Rav, utterly gobsmacked. The vampire showed such unbending devotion to Ariel, it never occurred to him that the feeling might not be mutual.

"I didn't mean to..." he stammered. "I didn't know."

"It's alright," the vampire intoned. "I did."

Rav dropped onto the sofa opposite him, hands folded in his lap. His face betrayed no expression, and for once Ely could not get a grasp on what the vampire was feeling.

"I told you, Elyssandro," he continued. "What is dead doesn't always come back as expected. After my resurrection, I could only wonder why, when everything else had been erased, her face remained etched upon my heart. When it was revealed to her what they had done, she looked on me with such disgust, I thought I might die again under that gaze."

"So, what about your proposition of setting her free so that we would no longer be lonely agents of Death?" Ely asked.

"You. Not me," Rav replied. "The two of you will have someone of your own kind with which to brave this world. And I will get to marvel at one last sunrise."

Ely leaped to his feet.

"No!" he exclaimed. "This whole business cannot be just some tragic suicide mission. I won't have it! I thought we were friends."

"Friends?" Rav blinked.

"I will not take one step further on this quest if you're just waiting to die."

Rav watched his face, looking amused despite his agitation. "Isn't that all life is, conjurer? Waiting for death. The only difference is that you are guaranteed yours. I must orchestrate mine."

"How old were you when you died?" Ely inquired.

"I've been in this vampiric shell for centuries," Rav spat.

"Asleep in a box," Ely countered. "You were what, thirty-five? Forty at best?"

Rav shrugged. "No idea. Get to the point."

"Listen, Rav, you didn't even live half a lifetime, and you only remember the world at its worst."

"Are you offering to take me sightseeing, conjurer?" Rav asked with a dry smirk.

"Why not?" Ely shrugged. "I'm homeless for the foreseeable future. Your one true love isn't talking to you. Let's finish this jailbreaking business, of course—I wouldn't just leave her in the Hollow—but afterward let's you and me go out and see what else this world has to offer. Then if you still want to leave it, we'll hike to some remote, breathtaking mountaintop, and I'll play you a magnificent funeral march as you greet the sun."

Rav regarded him with surprise and the smallest hint of a smile. "Do you promise?"

Ely nodded. "I promise."

Rav's smile vanished. His face snapped toward the window. He overturned the sofa, throwing himself over Ely as the wall exploded in a disc of blinding alabaster light. Air crushed from his lungs, ears ringing, Ely blinked through a haze decidedly not cast by Death coming to his aid. Rav groaned, shaking a snapped beam from across his shoulders.

"Are you alright?" Rav asked.

"Fine," Ely choked through the dust. "It's an Apostle. He's come for the key. Can you carry Victor?"

Rav nodded.

"Get him. You and Nix meet me at the Lioncourt."

The vampire tore away through the wreckage. Ely regained his shaky feet, only just sidestepping an avalanche of plaster and wood.

"Leanora!" he called, limping as best he could down the hall.

"Elyssandro!"

The desperate cry brought a wave of relief. She had survived the explosion, but the bed where she had been sleeping now lay a heap of matchsticks. She had managed to squeeze into a tiny unburied pocket that threatened to collapse at the slightest shift in the air.

"Hold very still, Leanora," Ely instructed.

He wove blackened coils through pinpoint openings between the rubble, shaping them into a shell-like a cocoon around Leanora's refuge. With the sides reinforced, he dislodged the splintered bedposts. She crouched inside. He reached for her hand and helped her to climb free. Plaster dusted her hair, but she appeared otherwise unharmed.

"This is shaping up to be a real humdinger of a night," she said.

"I did warn you," Ely replied with an apologetic smile as he stabilized her route to the door.

"Victor!" she cried.

"Rav is taking him to safety. We're meeting them at the hotel," Ely explained quickly. "We have to go. There's an Apostle hunting us."

They picked their way through the wreckage. Fire had ignited in the kitchen, flames spreading noxious fumes. They reached the street outside panting and singed. A white-robed figure stood waiting beneath a rippling lantern, eye and blade talismans dangling from a thin chain draped around his waist.

Ely pulled Leanora behind him, armor already rolling into place. The Apostle regarded them with his eerily pleasant smile. Though he had the white hair of an older man, his face seemed ageless, as if he carried at once all the tenacity of youth and the wisdom of eons. If there was a soul beneath the grinning mask, Ely could not feel it.

"Did you think that you could just vanish? That I wouldn't find you behind a simple witch's wards?" the Apostle asked, voice light. Cordial.

"I didn't know you were looking for me," Ely said. "To be honest, I thought you were at the bottom of the ocean."

The Apostle chuckled, hollow and mirthless. "I wasn't speaking to you, necromancer." His gaze moved past Ely. He folded his fingers before him in a prim, menacing triangle. "Did you not understand the terms of our deal?"

Ely looked to Leanora, heart turning somersaults. She stood her ground, jaw set in a hard line, eyes fixed with perfect recognition on the Apostle.

"Vesper lied," she said, voice tense but unwavering. "He didn't have what you were looking for."

"You made a deal with the Canon?" Ely asked through clenched teeth.

"I'm sorry, Elyssandro," she breathed. "I had no choice."

Pale plumes dimmed his sight. He resisted, though he longed for the release of the darkened void. The Apostle raised two fingers to the heavens. An alabaster halo gathered about the index.

This is our fight, Death pressed.

"Run, Leanora," Ely said.

His warning delivered, he closed his eyes and let the silent, peaceful veil close about him.

Chapter Fourteen
Woman in White

Rav stalked the boards of the executive suite, already wearing an ellipse in the glossy finish with his bare feet.

The convalescent lay on the bed, clinging to life by a Fate's thread. He had begun to cry and squirm on the journey over, but it took only the lightest brush of a temple to send Victor Skylark back to his dreams. It never seemed particularly useful, the paltry magic left to his hands. Least of all the lullaby touch that sent mortals into sleep like death. He was grateful for it now. Perhaps the unfortunate soul would keep long enough to nurse the helyx back to health. The less he moved the better.

Rav, on the other hand, could not keep still. The clock on the wall read the wrong time, but he felt the sun readying in the wings for its entrance. It had been too long already. Even for a human on foot, Elyssandro should have returned by now.

He will come, Rav told himself.

Perhaps he had been injured in the blast more than either of them realized. Perhaps he had met with difficulty extracting the witch. He was alive. Of that Rav was certain. Where and in what condition had yet to be seen.

Rav threw open the curtains, fully expecting to catch sight of a gaunt figure wending his slow, maddening plod toward the Hotel Lioncourt. No doubt getting distracted by a butterfly or a ham croissant on his way. The clouds that rolled in black and ominous from the sea augured nothing good. There was magic in the fog and the wind. More than usual.

A knock at the door made him jump high as a spooked cat.

"Rav!"

The desperate voice belonged to the witch. Elyssandro was not with her, or if he was, he had not come upstairs.

Rav unbolted the door. Leanora appeared singed and bedraggled. Wild eyed.

"What happened?" he demanded.

Stay calm.

"The Apostle," she panted.

Calm.

"Where are they?"

"I don't know," she breathed. "Elyssandro told me to run."

Rav returned his gaze out the window. The sky lay black as a mountain cavern. South Sea would have no sunrise today. Not with Death at large.

"You have to help him," Leanora insisted.

"I am," Rav told her. "Ms. Skylark, was it?"

"Dr. Skylark," she corrected.

"Of course, another scholar," Rav shook his head. "Damn you, conjurer."

"Is there a problem?" Leanora demanded.

"Yes. We're too high up here. I need to get you and your brother to safety."

She scowled at him, tiny body aquiver with fragile human rage.

"What are you talking about? You're the only one that can help Elyssandro. Go after him at once!"

"Give me one more order, Dr. Skylark!" Rav snarled, flashing fangs.

Leanora shrank back, behaving, at last, like the mouse she resembled. Not that he would ever bite her again. She tasted like raw sewage left to stew in summer heat. He should have known a witch scholar would have Brahm's sigil marked somewhere on her person.

Calm.

"Perhaps you don't know him well enough to realize this," he continued, once again in command of his tone, "but the friendly, mercurial smile is merely a defense intended to put you fickle, intolerant humans at ease in the presence of Death. Elyssandro is safer now than we are by far. We have to get to shelter. Preferably underground."

"Peggy has a cellar," Leanora suggested.

"Who's Peggy?"

"My assistant. She already knows about Victor's condition. In fact, she's the only one the helyx will allow near his wounds."

"Where do we find her?"

"Number twelve Seabreak Drive. It's down in the Lower Ward. By the docks."

"I know it," Rav replied.

That was the exact borough he had been sent to destroy a thousand years ago.

It was common practice in the Tower to hire vampires out for various tasks. Military operations. Governments. The wealthy for their estates. A vampire could carry more timber and rocks than seventy men combined, and some were skilled at trades like carpentry or shipwrighting. Rav had presented a more unique value to the Cosmologists. When he awoke to a second life, it seemed the name Ravan Aurelio was known to all but himself.

The searing lamplight stung his eyes with vicious fury. Cacophony plagued his ears. The deafening thunder of heartbeats. The rattling of lungs drawing breath. The grating itch of voices whispering. Next came the smells. Acrid sweat. Mildewed damp. Hot, salted blood wrapped in sweet fleshy capillaries.

All of these things too he knew by name. Only his own eluded him.

"He's awake. Hold him, please."

The voice scratched at his memory. It belonged to a man with sandy hair and serious brows. A Cosmologist. Dr. Brahm.

He tried to throw a hand up against the light but found his wrists shackled at his sides. Something heavy dragged at his throat. Burning.

"Ravan."

He blinked through the blinding light to find that the face belonging to the voice matched his memory, though not exactly. The mouth was thinner than he remembered. Twisted at one corner. Eyes wider and more blue than gray.

"Ravan, can you understand me?" Dr. Brahm asked.

"Is...is that my name?" he asked. His tongue fell leaden against his teeth. A razor tip drew blood.

"Yes. Ravan Aurelio. That is your name. You will learn quickly to answer to it."

Dr. Brahm nodded to the others standing at the ready. They hauled him to his feet. He was naked but for restraining iron. The doctor shone a light in his eyes and dragged back his lips with white-gloved fingers. Peered into his ears, tugged his hair, prodded his flesh.

Something hot and vicious awoke in his chest. It wanted to tear the doctor's arms from their sockets and sink teeth into his exposed throat. He could not move to answer the impulse. He could not even raise a plea to stop.

"The subject seems to have taken well to the process," the doctor declared. "He should be conditioned for the next few weeks, but I think we can report this a success."

"What's wrong with me?" Rav asked. "Why is everything so loud? Why can't I remember anything?"

One of his captors thrust a thin baton into his side. It bit like an avenging hornet. The doctor halted the tormentor with a raised hand.

"Your condition will be made clear to you shortly," he said. "All you need to know at this moment is that you are not alive. You are not a person. You are a tool. Carry out your functions, and your existence will continue. Do you understand, Ravan?"

He stared at the doctor, unmoving. Unblinking. The vicious impulse seethed to wreak bloody havoc. He could not make a move even when the guard pressed the stinging rod into his side.

"Answer him," the guard hissed.

"I heard you," he said.

The hornet stung again.

"*Yes, dominus,*" the doctor pronounced. "Those are the only words that should pass your lips unless otherwise required."

Sting. Silence. Another sting. Another silence.

Dr. Brahm intercepted the next blow and stepped closer, setting a hand lightly on his shoulder. His skin crawled as though wriggling worms escaped from the Cosmologist's grasp.

"I am prepared for you, Ravan," Dr. Brahm said. "Your defiance. Your pride. Your persistent belief that rules and laws are beneath you. These traits have already earned you an execution. Until you are broken of them, finally and completely, death will be the kindest part of your sentence. Do you understand me?"

Silence.

"Yes, dominus," the doctor corrected.

Silence.

Dr. Brahm's eyes narrowed, fury channeled into a thin smile. "As you wish."

He nodded to the guards. They seized his chains and dragged him from the chamber...

Rav alighted in the Lower Ward with Victor cradled sleeping in his arms. The quaint little seaside village had made a complete metamorphosis from the shacks and lean-tos he and his fellow monsters had been sent to devastate.

He had left Leanora on the front steps of a well-framed cabin. It was built of sturdy logs and low to the ground. Certainly better suited to wait out Death's fury. He told her, along with the rumpled young woman who had answered the door, to draw all the curtains and stay back from the windows.

The second journey from the Hotel Lioncourt proved far more harrowing. Lightning crackled through the clouds, and the wind lashed at him, trying to tear the invalid from his grasp.

By the time he reached Peggy's cabin, dawn had arrived with no trace of sun to drive him underground.

Leanora and her assistant met him upstairs. The two women had already dragged a bed down a set of narrow steps into the cellar for

Victor. Rav laid the groaning man down, fever sheen on his forehead. His pale, blind eyes opened, straining. He clawed at his chest in panic.

"It's alright, Vic," Leanora soothed. "There was a storm. We had to evacuate. We're at Peggy's place. You're safe."

Victor moaned, face contorted in pain. The assistant brought a wetted cloth and laid it over his forehead. Then she drew back the soaked bandage. The wounds had burst open on the journey.

Peggy set to cleaning them, murmuring soothing intonations in what sounded like Séoc. Victor did not appear to be lucid, but after a moment, Rav realized that it was the helyx to which the girl ministered.

He noticed also that as she worked, she moved her fingers in familiar patterns, drawing invisible glyphs around the outer edges of the curving lacerations. As she did so, the oozing blood congealed, and the raw edges calmed. This was no mere assistant.

"You've studied healing?" Rav asked.

Peggy looked up at him, eyes bruised with the tired shadows of extended months with little sleep. "Some. Only since Victor...Mr. Skylark had his accident."

"There aren't many texts on the subject of healing," Leanora added.

"No, there wouldn't be," Rav mused.

He left them to finish dressing Victor's injuries, returning upstairs to take measure of the storm through the dining room window. The pale shocks of lightning did not move like natural forked currents but instead in widening discs that knifed through the ether clouds. The Apostle.

"How long will this go on?" Leanora's nasal scritch startled him.

"I don't know," Rav answered.

He closed his eyes, searching for the familiar presence in the midst of the tumult. Where are you?

"Will he be alright?" Leanora pressed.

"I don't know," Rav whispered. He cleared his throat and drew the curtain closed.

"I had no idea a Cosmologist could even do something like this," Leanora puzzled.

"That isn't him making the storm," Rav told her. "It's what he holds back from swallowing the world."

His eyes narrowed.

"And Elyssandro is a conjurer not a Cosmologist," he added.

"Is there a distinction?" Leanora frowned.

Rav inclined his head.

"The Cosmologists stole their magic, transcribing from the stars that which was never meant for them. They needed tablets and scrolls and muttered words to wield death magic. They were conniving and vicious. He is nothing like them."

"They really did a number on you," Leanora observed.

"I am one of their bastardized conjurings," he said, setting a hand on his chest where the death magic sigil lay inscribed over his heart. "Ripped from the cosmos for nefarious purposes."

Leanora lowered her gaze, freckled brow furrowed.

"Surely they weren't all terrible. Surely some of them were just trying to learn. Who doesn't look at the stars and want to unravel their mysteries?"

"Curious and cruel often go hand in hand," Rav replied, training a hard gaze on her face.

"Is it intellectuals you don't like or just women?" the mousy doctor snapped.

Her thumbs were tapping nervously against her sides. He could smell the flared nerves. She was hiding something. Something for which she felt guilty and frightened.

"I couldn't care less about what sits between your ears or your legs. You've been lying to him since the moment he set foot in your house," Rav accused.

Leanora glared, shoulders rigid. No defense.

Rav took a step toward her. He could move unnervingly slow when he wanted to, and since he towered above her as it was, the effect held her paralyzed.

He spoke in low, lethal tones. "It is not the helyx lodged in his chest that is killing your brother. His wounds are poisoned with death magic. Your whole story reeks of treachery and deceit."

She gasped for breath through her fright. Tears filled her eyes. "I didn't know how to tell him," she whispered.

"You're going to tell *me* now," Rav intoned. "If you're lying, I'll smell it. And all the sigils in the world won't save you."

"I'm not sure, in this case, that the truth will set me free," she said. "Try me..."

It was blessedly cold and dark in the catacombs. Rav huddled in a damp corner, wedged between a stalagmite and a rough wall. One hand he held cradled against his chest, blackened, peeling. Knuckle bones peeking through charred skin. It stank like a forest set ablaze.

"You're only hurting yourself, Ravan," Dr. Brahm's quiet voice haunted his thoughts. *"Two words, and all will be forgiven."*

He had kept silent. Always. Even as the glaring sun melted flesh from bone, he held her face before his mind's eye. He remembered how that same light caught the hidden auburn in her hair and shimmered on her warm olive skin. When he could not hold onto her smile any longer, he remembered the sea green of her eyes lost to white as she molded Death between her fingers. That was how she would come for him, with vengeance that would erase them all from existence.

Rav tensed as a figure approached. It moved with inherent grace and inhuman speed. His eyes could still make out the other vampire's features despite the near absence of light. Narrow, crooked nose, thin lips, and wide cat eyes. He recognized her, but he did not know her name.

"Stay back," he spat.

The vampire stopped, regarding him with calm, knowing eyes. "Sunburn?" she asked.

He made no reply, instead withdrawing deeper into the cubbyhole he occupied. She sat cross-legged near the wall, still leaving him room to escape should he wish.

"I'm Astrik. You can call me Riki," she said. When he did not return the introduction, she continued, "You're Ravan Aurelio. Dr. Brahm's favorite corpse to kick. You're becoming a bit of a legend among the locals."

"What an honor."

"It's not easy, getting respect in these parts. You could probably use a friend or two."

"Is there something you want from me, Astrik?"

"Nothing at all, sweetie. I just don't think it's very nice leaving people to sit all alone in dark corners."

"I prefer to be alone," he said. "And I'm not a person. Haven't you heard?"

Riki shrugged. "They've been telling me that since I was alive. Hanged for whoring. Woken up again for whoring. I think maybe they just got tired of paying."

"So they gave you fangs? That doesn't seem very bright."

"It's part of the thrill for them," Riki shrugged. "All that power caught in a chokehold. I'm sure the psychologists have a name for it. Good on me, I didn't forget how to turn a trick. Yes, dominus. Whatever pleases you, dominus. Gets them so hard, they can't remember their own names, much less how they planned to hurt you. Your way is very noble, though."

"I'm not being noble. I won't be in this place much longer," he said. "When she learns what happened to me, she will come for me and punish them all for what they've done."

"I sure hope so, sugar," Riki commiserated. "Who is she then? Your savior."

"Ariel Marcellus."

"Ooh. Very impressive."

"You've heard of her?"

"Lady Death? Who hasn't heard of her in this place?" Riki smiled. "Hope she rains holy hell down on all their heads."

Rav drew his knees closer to his chest. He didn't realize he had been whimpering until Riki scooted closer.

"Let me take a look, honey," she offered.

Despite his reluctance, Rav crouched near the entrance to his sanctuary. Riki squinted at his hand, nodded her head, and disappeared in a languid leap. Before he could wonder where she had gone, she had returned, starlight trickling between her fingers.

"Here," she said, holding it out to him.

When he had consumed the first handful, she burst off again, returning shortly with more of the sky's lifeblood clutched in her fist. When dawn neared, new sinew protected the bones, and the blackened burns had eased. Still raw but on the way to healing.

"Alright, love," Riki smiled "Rest up."
She gave him a kindly pat on the shoulder and disappeared.

Rav didn't catch sight of that homely smile again in the nights that followed. By week's end, even the scar had disappeared. Rav had made up his mind to seek Riki out to offer gratitude. Perhaps it would be wise to try to make an ally.

He found his plans interrupted as Dr. Brahm descended into the catacombs with two attendants. Three Cosmologists against a hive of razor-fanged monsters, all cowering in the darkest of corners.

"Ravan Aurelio."

Rav made no answering call, but the metal circlet around his throat would not allow him to remain hidden in the shadows. They marched him out to be scrubbed, his rags exchanged for clean linens. Shackles were fitted. Collar polished. They placed him in a windowless coach drawn by horses black as the surrounding night.

When they unloaded him at their destination, he recognized the imperious walls from a deluge of fractal memories. All he gleaned from them was that the University of Dianessa held some significance to the life of Ravan Aurelio.

They marched him through a small side entrance, down a narrow hall to a plunging staircase. This dungeon-like space felt much like the Tower catacombs, dark and sheltered, but constructed of vaulted brick instead of skull-studded rock.

Dr. Brahm placed him near the brightest available lantern.

"Wait here," he commanded.

A woman with steel gray eyes and flaxen hair caught in a militant bun strode into the dungeon. A pair of spectacles hung on a thin chain around her neck.

"Why is Fiona White and her pack of hyenas waiting in my office?" she demanded. The woman's eyes fell on Rav, and her face drained of color. "What have you done?"

"I was going to tell you," Dr. Brahm replied, a cautious fly eying a spider, "but since I knew this would be your response, I prepared my apology for today."

"You fucking fool," she breathed.

She approached Rav with the wary movements of an experienced lion tamer.

"Ravan?" she said, voice low, fear rising in a caustic perfume.

"Dr. Faidra," he responded. He had not realized that he knew her name until it left his lips.

"How long have you been awake?" she asked.

"Six months," Dr. Brahm replied over her shoulder. "Ample time for proper conditioning."

"Is your memory intact?" Dr. Faidra continued.

"He knows some names and faces. Nothing more," Dr. Brahm interjected.

"I am speaking to Ravan, you delusional excuse for a scholar," she snarled.

"We've guests waiting, Selene," droned Dr. Brahm.

She rounded on him. "Surely you're not planning to hand him over to White?"

"It's a standard loan. Dean Hallicus approved it. Even you won't find fault in the paperwork," Dr. Brahm replied.

"Do you even fathom what you've done?" she hissed to Dr. Brahm. "If she learns of this—"

"That is precisely my intention, Selene," Dr. Brahm smirked.

"If you are so eager to taste her vengeance, Harald, enjoy. I will have no part in this," Dr. Faidra spat.

She shoved her way past him, throwing a last look at Rav before she made her exit.

Dr. Brahm let out his breath, straightened his tie, and strode after her. He returned with a small group dressed in refined attire. They appeared sorely out of place in the sinister light of the dungeon. The entire party stopped frozen in their tracks as though the sight of him cast a spell to turn them to stone.

A woman clad all in white was first to break free. She approached Rav, gaze running the length of him with invasive audacity. Golden hair swept high off her forehead, full lips, amethyst eyes. Most would have called her a supreme beauty, but something in his shattered memory cautioned that appearances ran only skin deep.

She ventured closer, circling like a vulture. The citrine sweetness of her perfume sent prickling alarm down the back of his neck.

"I was certain I had seen the last of your smug pout," she leered. "How positively euphoric to be so wrong."

Rav remained silent, eyes fixed on a fingerprint pressed deep in one of the bricks in the wall.

The woman called back to Dr. Brahm, not taking her eyes from Rav's face. "Can he speak?"

"I assure you, Lady White, he understands."

The woman reached toward him. Rav's mind flinched, but his body remained still as carved marble. The quiet fizzle of restraining glyphs served as the only evidence of his inner conflict. Lady White caressed the metal circlet around his throat.

"Oh, I truly thought it was enough," she purred. "Knowing you lost it all. Your hallowed halls. Your stolen name. An empire built so foolishly upon the sand. There is not a man in our esteemed circle that wouldn't give his firstborn to see you down on your knees."

She seized his chin, polished nails digging into his jaw.

"But lucky for me, it's ladies first."

"I will remind you, he is University property, Lady White," Dr. Brahm coughed politely. "But so long as he is returned in mendable condition, I don't see why anything else must be noted in the final report."

She smiled. A mask of exquisite treachery. "Thank you, Dr. Brahm."

Lady White motioned to her men with a lazy flick of the wrist. They checked Rav's manacles and tied a blindfold over his eyes for good measure. Then they ushered him from the chamber to yet another transport. This time the journey seemed to rattle on for ages. He felt night making its retreat as the coach jolted to a halt. Still blind, he followed them across yielding earth. His ears picked up the titter of awakening birds, lowing cattle, and the ruffled grousing of hens. The scent of perfumed blossoms, sap-veined trees, and pungent herbs mapped a garden in his mind's eye.

His tension eased a little as they entered a building's shelter. He smelled straw and the stale scent of livestock. A barn perhaps. One of the men fitted a chain through his manacles. A heavy door rolled closed. More chains rattled. Padlocks clunked. He was left alone still blindfolded.

Rav lay down on the cool earth floor. The day passed in fitful sleep. Footsteps sounded outside. He climbed to his feet, a fettered statue awaiting whatever fresh devilry this night intended. His guards fumbled with the chain and shoved him forward.

They entered another building. A domicile by the human scents. At last, they stopped and removed the blindfold. Rav blinked, eyes dazzled by dozens of winking candles that illuminated an elegant drawing room. Lady White graced an ornamented settee. Full lace skirts cascaded down in a dramatic train that curled around her feet like a feline's tail. Her bone corset cinched impossibly tight around her waist, hoisting her bosom high like a threatening pirate's flag.

"Good evening, Ravan," she greeted lightly. "Those won't be necessary, will they?"

She crooked a finger, and her man unlocked the manacles. Rav massaged his wrists, skin rubbed raw.

"Do you know where you are?" Lady White inquired.

Rav glanced around the room. Save for the candles, every detail lay exactly as he expected. The polished furniture, the woven Marikej rug, the piano with mirrorwood keys. A portrait smirked down at him from above the mantle. The face was his own.

"This was my house," he said.

Lady White smiled. "Well deduced."

She rose, frosted diamonds capturing the light at her throat.

"Dr. Brahm said that you have been a stubborn case. That his efforts to coerce you into cooperation have been less satisfying than he had hoped."

She chuckled.

"All those Cosmologists think they're blessed with such divine brilliance, yet they are so dismal at understanding the mind. We mustn't blame the poor doctor though, must we? He simply doesn't know you quite like I do."

She snapped her fingers. The men at arms hauled in a feebly struggling girl. No more than twenty at most. Wide-eyed, innocent, reeking of terror.

"This is Laurel Delaney," Lady White introduced, gracious as a host at a party. "She studies natural magics at the University. Honor student. Talented pianist. I heard her play just last week. It was transcendent. Sit here, my dear."

She directed the girl to the piano.

"Let us hear that charming piece you played at Selmar Hall."

Laurel whimpered. She raised shaky fingers over the keys and began to play a bright, laughing melody entirely at odds with her tear-mottled face.

"Let her go," Rav growled.

Glyphs hissed against his throat.

Lady White turned an exquisite, soulless smile toward him. "That's all in your hands, Ravan."

"Please, Milady," Laurel sobbed. "I'm sorry. Whatever I did, I'm sorry."

"Oh, dear heart, you didn't do anything," Lady White crooned. "Isn't that so like a woman? Apologizing for the faults of a man. Now, my sweet little lamb, this creature before you has caused unspeakable harm without apology or remorse. He is a bloodthirsty demon. What befalls you today is entirely up to him."

Rav stared at her, heart galloping, restraining glyphs aflame. She snapped her fingers, and the man at arms seized the girl's hand, forcing it open over the keys with a discordant jangle. Another handed a mallet to Lady White.

"Wait," Rav burst. "What do you want from me?"

Lady White stopped. Triumph glowed on her fair brow. She flicked her hand at the guard who released Laurel's wrist.

"Place your hand on the piano, Ravan," Lady White directed.

He stepped forward, not waiting for a kindled glyph to compel compliance. The mallet stroke fell without pause. Rav tasted blood on his tongue, cry throttled in his throat.

"There," she beamed, caressing the blunt instrument in her hand. "So, you see now how this works. I want you to know, you may refuse anything requested of you. You may choose respite. You may choose your pride. It will be at the expense of our lovely musician. Do you understand?"

"Yes."

"Good. Then let us begin."

Rav lay wedged beneath rugged eaves of gray rock, one eye beaten shut. Crooked ribs stabbed at his lungs. Broken lips parched for starlight that would not come for long hours. For months on end this cycle continued. They threw his battered body into the catacombs to lick his wounds. Then, just when they were on the brink of healing, Lady White would send for him again. If he just inched forward far enough, the sunrise would set him free. The collar sizzled on his throat, holding him hostage in this loathsome shell.

"I thought I might find you here." Riki squeezed through a narrow chasm in the granite and sat on the ledge beside him, joining him to watch the morning bleed along the cavern opening.

"What is it, Astrik?" he groaned.

"Just checking up on you, love. From what I'm hearing, you've funded a whole new observatory all by your lonesome."

Rav closed his one good eye.

"Do you think I find that amusing, Astrik?" he murmured.

"No, sugar. I just figure, if you've got enemies shitting gold to get a piece of you, then surely you must have friends in high places too."

"I doubt it," he said. "Whoever Ravan Aurelio was...whatever he did, he could not have had many friends if he deserved this."

"Sweetie, I been here seventy years. Seen some bottom feeding, lowlife scum in my time. Ain't nobody deserves this."

"Seventy years?" he wheezed.

"I'm one of the longer-lived inmates," Riki smiled. "I think the record is eighty-seven."

"I have no interest in dragging on for decades, Astrik. Can you push me just over there where the sunlight will reach?"

"Sorry, sugarplum, I can't," she said with a condolatory smile. "Used to just get you thrown in a sarcophagus, you know. Mercy killing. Then they started scratching a preventative into the collar. Don't nothing say I can't carry a message to somebody in my free time though. Where do I find her? Your Lady Death."

"She was only a fever dream, Astrik," Rav murmured.

Riki watched him, shadowed eyes thoughtful.

"There are better ways to do this, you know," she said. "Insatiable as pigs they are, but they gorge themselves on more than violence."

She stretched out beside him, blocking out the morning's glare with her crooked-fanged face.

"Just tell them what they want to hear. Smile. They love a good smile. Make them forget they're fragile, petty little parasites. And just remember they'll be rotting in the ground in two shakes of a lamb's tail."

She gave his hand a gentle squeeze, then slipped back into the safety of the dark cavern...

Rav stared at Elyssandro's witch familiar, the implications of her words rushing over him in waves. "So, you stole death magic from an ancient tablet, and your brother paid the price."

Leanora lowered her eyes, hiding not remorse but defiance.

"I didn't know," she said. "I didn't know it was even possible for me to channel death magic."

"Why lie about it then? Why lie to the one person who might actually be of help to Victor?"

"Do you want to hear the rest of this story or not?" she snapped.

"Go on," Rav nodded.

"We returned to civilization in hopes of figuring out a way to help Victor. Our guide escorted us back to the coast. We took a Séoc ship to South Sea, but the king returned north. I heard nothing more until a few weeks ago. I got a letter from his majesty asking me to meet him. But it was not the king that arrived that day. He calls himself Titus. Apostle Titus."

"You knew about the Apostle?" Rav frowned.

"Why do you think we were hiding in that dump of an apartment?" Leanora retorted. "Your helyx destroyed my wards. I swear to you I had no idea they had ever met before. I didn't even know Elyssandro was still alive until I saw him at Vesper's party."

"The woman in the blue dress," Rav realized. "So, what were you doing there?"

"I'm getting to that. The Apostle promised that Victor could be healed, but he needed something to extract the death magic from his wounds. Vesper was supposed to have an artifact. I have no idea what it was. *Aplora di ciarra.* It's Paxat, but I don't know what that means."

"Elyssandro could have told you, considering it's his native tongue," Rav pointed out.

"Well, Vesper didn't have it," she continued, looking more distressed by the second. "He laughed in my face and said if I did find it, he would trade me his whole collection for it. I was supposed to meet Titus yesterday morning. Obviously I missed the appointment."

"I still fail to understand why you didn't tell Elyssandro any of this."

Leanora sighed. Her speckled brows drew together. "I've been looking for him for years. He is the reason I even know that magic exists at all. He started my whole life. It was selfish. I know it. But the moment I told him the truth, he would be out the door again in a second."

"If you believe that, then you don't know him very well, Dr. Skylark," Rav said.

Leanora shook her head. "I haven't finished yet. The hope of a cure for Victor was not the only leverage Titus brought to me. His majesty never reached the northern fortress. He was taken hostage by the Canon. I don't know where, but he had very convincing proof."

"If there's a hidden meaning in your tale, please get to the point of it," Rav growled, patience a fraying thread.

"Has Elyssandro never mentioned Kai Novara to you?" Leanora asked.

Rav shook his head.

"I suppose he wouldn't tell that story. It certainly doesn't have a happy ending. They were in love. I'm told it was very serious. So serious, in fact, that Kai's mother conspired to have Elyssandro murdered rather than allow them to be together. His majesty thinks that the plot succeeded."

"And the Apostle holds this man captive?" Rav asked.

Leanora inclined her head. "If Elyssandro knew—"

"You're right. That was selfish," Rav glared at her.

"This will cost you your quest too," she shot at him. "What would you do?"

Rav frowned. She wasn't wrong. The conjurer was distractible on a good day. What would he do when he learned that someone he loved stood at the mercy of the Canon?

"Not so noble now, are we?" Leanora scoffed.

Rav's eyes flicked to her face. Fierce cold spread from the seal on his chest through the ends of his fingers.

"You mortals are so alike. Even after a thousand years, all you want is for me to look into your eyes and tell you that I am as despicable as you are."

He stood, drawing back a sliver of curtain. The storm churned black overhead, still blotting out the sun. Elyssandro was out there, lost somewhere in the tempest. Would he drift all the way to the stars with no one to tether him back to the earth?

Rav tugged open the window. The wind tore at the curtains and blasted a pile of overdue bills from the table.

"You can't be seriously thinking of going out there now," Leanora squeaked.

Ignoring the duplicitous mouse, he rolled back his sleeve and extended a hand outside the window. No rebuke from the sun. Not even a hint of a sting.

"Nix," Rav said.

The helyx rose from his pocket, bleary demon eye blinking.

"What is it, fangs? I was having such a nice a dream."

"I think our conjurer has gotten himself in above his head," he said. "I'm going to fetch him. Would you be so kind as to keep an eye on the witch for me?"

"Gladly." Nix bobbed, then turned to glare at Leanora.

"Many thanks."

Rav balanced on the windowsill, taking a reflexive breath to settle his nerves. It was refreshing this feeling. Wanting to live.

He tensed, then launched into the furious storm...

Rav reclined between opulent sheets, surrounded by gold and mahogany trappings. He remembered once liking the feel of satin, the plush comfort of a mattress. Just as he remembered liking the electric friction of skin against skin and its accompanying feast of sights, sounds, and scents. How easily such pleasures turned torturous.

"Smile. They love a good smile." Riki's voice played a mantra in his mind. Surely this was better than nursing broken bones in a dripping cavern. Wasn't it?

Lady White stalked from behind the curtains, thin slip of pearled silk plunging like a waterfall over her treacherous curves. She wore a satisfied smile as though she had read some favorable portent in the wind.

"Tell me again, pet," she said.

"I'm yours, domina," he replied.

She laughed. The declaration never ceased to delight her.

"Get dressed. We have guests this evening."

"Yes, domina."

Lady White swept off for her dressing room. She spent half her life haunting closets hung floor to ceiling with silks, furs, leather, and lace. It would be a good hour before he had to endure her poisonous beauty again.

Rav dressed quickly when she had gone. He slipped behind the curtains, reaching for silver light with famished desperation. They fed him whatever blood happened to be on hand. Human, pig, chicken, rat. It made little difference. Breadcrumbs in a duck pond. He starved for a clear night sky.

Something in the air shifted. The voice that called his name sent his heart soaring to the heavens on angel's wings.

Ariel.

When he turned, he found her face exactly as he remembered. She flickered, then solidified again. This was a casting only. No matter. She had found him at last. It would not be long before she followed in person.

Ariel took him in, a look to sink a ship on her face.

"You're not him," she declared.

I am.

He tried to say the words, to move nearer to her projected figure, but the glyphs sang at his throat. Holding him still. Silent. A voice from the doorway answered for him.

"I assure you it is," Lady White crowed. "What's left of him, anyway."

Please.

His silent entreaty echoed in the sealed cavern of his mind. All these months obeying with no resistance had strengthened the magic that clasped metal fingers around his throat. He could not fight it anymore.

"Tell her to whom you belong, pet," Lady White commanded.

Don't leave me here.

Save me.

I love you.

A frigid tear made his sole rebellion.

"I am yours, domina," he breathed.

Ariel eyed him with stone-faced disdain, then turned back to Lady White.

"Do you think you can rattle me with some grotesque puppet?" she spat. "Keep it. I'll have your corpse soon enough, Fiona."

The casting blinked out, leaving him alone with the cackling woman in white...

Rav fought against the driving storm. He felt the conjurer wrapped up at the epicenter, only the barest spark beneath the legion's tempest. There was no more sign of the Apostle. The fight was long since over, but Death remained unsatisfied. It would use Elyssandro into ashes and dust if he could not be found soon.

Where are you?

He saw the shadow in the clouds cast by the shuttered sun. Like an arrow from a bow, he plunged into the abyss. An ice shard sliced across his cheek. Voices wailed in the wind. His arms closed about the suspended figure. The conjurer made no resistance, but the storm dragged at his fragile body. So weakened, he could fracture like glass at any moment.

Rav carried him back to solid ground, setting him gently on a grassy hillock. They were somewhere in the empty meadows outside the city. Elyssandro convulsed. Black ether trickled like tears from the corners of his eyes.

"Release him," Rav shouted to the bleak wind. "Your enemy is gone. Your fight is done. Let him go."

"You give us orders now, abomination?" the furious multitudes howled.

"Only a humble prayer," he called. "Please. Let him go. Before it is too late and you lose a foothold in this world."

The winds slowed. The clouds dispersed. Elyssandro sighed, limbs falling slack, head lolled. The volcanic sun, newly released from the storm's veil, cast down its murderous glare. Rav growled. With no other shelter to be had, he dug into the earth, throwing cool sod over himself until the searing light could no longer reach him.

There he waited. Impatient. Terrified. He could sense the conjurer's feeble presence lingering above ground. He dreaded feeling it blink to nothing.

The moment the pressing heat lifted, he burst from his haven. Elyssandro lay exactly as he'd left him. Rav touched his forehead. It was frigid as the grave.

"Wake up, conjurer," he entreated.

Rav searched for a pulse. So faint a rhythm. Hardly even a nudge. Snatching up light from the barely wakened stars, he lifted the conjurer's head.

"Drink, Elyssandro. Please. Just a little."

His heart pommeled against its death magic seal. The breath he did not need tore at his lungs in panicked gasps.

Calm. Think.

A face came to mind, smiling despite seventy years of tortured hell. What had Astrik done when his wounds left him so weak he could not stir?

Rav drank in the light, holding its frozen elixir on his tongue. Then he turned down Elyssandro's shirt collar and bent to his throat, fangs sinking deep enough to feel the weakened heartbeat thrum. The trapped light flowed into the artery. Mingling. Spreading. Rav drew back, pressing another handful of starlight against the conjurer's neck to seal the wound.

Elyssandro sat up coughing and blinking, dashing ether from his eyes. He took in heaving breaths, struggling to gain his bearings.

"I don't think that was sanitary, Rav," he rasped at last.

Rav breathed an ecstatic sigh, blinking back tears which the conjurer kindly pretended not to notice.

"Did we win?" he asked.

"I believe the Apostle fled," Rav replied.

Elyssandro nodded. "Let's call it a win then."

Rav resisted the human urge to throw his arms around the beaming fool before him. Crushing the life out of one another seemed such an irrational way to express relief.

"The helyx is safe," he recounted. "And your witch. I took them away from the storm. Then came back for you."

"That was reckless," Elyssandro chided. "I could have killed you."

"That seemed a trivial concern when I am already dead."

"You're not," Elyssandro told him. "I know exactly what death feels like. You're not dead. Or undead, for that matter. You're..."

He frowned, searching.

"An abomination," Rav supplied.

Elyssandro shot him an incredulous look. "What? No, Rav. We really need to work on your self-esteem." He snapped his fingers. "Timeless! That's the word I was looking for. You're timeless."

The conjurer climbed to his feet, wobbling dangerously. Rav steadied him, wondering why his peculiar mania felt so soothing.

"Many thanks. Still a little lightheaded. There was something important I needed to tell you. What was it?"

Elyssandro's smile fell, replaced with the hardened edge that emerged whenever he lowered his guard enough to let Death's shadow show in his face.

"You were right about Leanora," he said. "She lied to me. She made a deal with the Apostle. And Vesper too."

"She told me," Rav replied.

Elyssandro looked up at him, waiting.

"He promised her a Miracle that could save her brother. People are not themselves when they're afraid, Elyssandro," Rav told him, not sure why he suddenly felt compassion for the witch. Perhaps it was the fear now creeping into his own stomach. The one that told him not to speak of the secret with which Dr. Skylark had burdened him.

Elyssandro lifted a curious half-smile to his face. "I didn't think you liked her."

Rav shrugged. "I don't. She tastes like a rotten corpse, and I deplore scholars. But I cannot say I would have behaved any differently in her shoes."

"You don't wear shoes," Elyssandro pointed out with a smile.

Rav tried to muster some sign of mirthful appreciation. He failed.

"That's not the part she was afraid to tell you," Rav continued. He despised the way his heart was throbbing.

You'll be left behind again, it said. *Abandoned. Forgotten. Waiting to die.*

The fear held him frozen as surely as a collar about the neck.

Elyssandro watched him with bristling alarm. "What is it, Rav? Are you still blood sick?"

"No," Rav replied, voice steady.

He would be damned if he let anything hold him captive again. Least of all the voices in his head.

"Walk with me, Elyssandro. We have more to talk about."

Chapter Fifteen

Ad Astra

Ely stared up at the night sky. Dazed. Tired. A thousand years older than yesterday. Any rage that might have overtaken him had already been expended. Rav had withdrawn anyway. Offering space for shock to make its transformation through all the dimensions of grief.

His eyes felt like stones, but when he closed them, all he could see was Kai in an iron gag. Searching for a single captive in the Canon Protectorate would be like trying to find a diamond lost among the sands of a vast desert. If he lived.

Is he with you? Ely asked, seeking inward for the presence, so distant and faint after the day's tempest.

Not us, the legion whispered. *He's your charge. You would know if we took him back.*

How do I find him?

Pregnant pause.

Do you think you're equal to the challenge?

Show me.

The hillside rumbled. Shadows like the empty depths of the universe spiraled from his feet. Then the ground dropped from beneath him, and he plunged into darkness.

Nothing broke his fall. Weightless nothing. He drifted, limbs, clothes, and hair afloat as if underwater. There was no air to draw breath.

Yet he felt no panic or fear. He was not alone in this void. He was part of it. And it of him.

Follow.

He felt as ripples in a pond. Moving. Expanding. Seeking. Then the void pushed him out like a daisy atop a grave. He found himself in bleached sunlight. Dry, dusted air smelled of pure heat.

When he recovered his sight, he found he was, in fact, standing on someone's remains. Inanimate, he was relieved to note. Might have been awkward otherwise.

Ely stooped to look at the corpse. It was only beginning to show signs of spoilage despite the tremendous heat, so the poor fellow could not have been dead for long. No, not poor fellow. He flicked aside a layer of grainy powder from the man's shirt to reveal the eye and blade insignia. Canon.

Ely straightened up, taking in his surroundings with trepidation. Wherever he was, it was all grimy, naked slopes. Where had Death lured him?

"Show me your hands," a voice at his back commanded in Paxat.

Ely raised his hands, proving them empty of weapons. At least the kind suspected by an ordinary human.

"Turn around."

Ely faced his would-be captor. A young man with green eyes made striking against dark hair and olive skin. He wore white linen pants and tunic. His belt bore tasseled talismans of the eye and blade. Another Apostle? If he was, Death did not seem so displeased to see him.

The youthful Apostle stared at Ely as if trying to draw a murky memory from his face. "Who are you?" he asked.

"A traveler," Ely replied. "I'm looking for someone."

"There is no one out here to find," the Apostle replied. "Unless you seek the dead."

"I'm looking for Kailari Novara. He's been taken captive by your brother at arms," Ely said. His native tongue felt like such a stranger after all this time.

"Never heard of him," the Apostle frowned.

"He is the king of Séocwen," Ely told him.

"Diego Sorach is the king of Séocwen."

"You must have your enemies confused, Apostle."

A familiar shadow crept into the boy's emerald eyes. "You will come with me," he commanded.

Ely flexed toward Death, but they did not yield their power.

Follow, they prompted.

The baby Apostle?

Follow.

The Apostle raised two benedictive fingers, and opal light slithered around Ely's wrists, tethering him back to the youth with a shimmering alabaster rope. Ely's heart quickened. Was this really the plan? Get captured to find a captive? Perhaps not the most reckless thing he had ever done. But close.

They set out across the wastes. More bodies littered the slopes, pinioned with arrow shafts. This did not appear to be a very welcoming corner of the world in any capacity.

"You seem rather young for an Apostle," Ely observed.

"You're not the first to say it," the Apostle replied.

"I've only met one," Ely shrugged. "And to be honest, I couldn't tell you if he was young or old. Do you know the Apostle Titus?"

"If you're fishing for something, traveler, you will catch nothing from me. There is no Apostle by that name."

"Do *you* have a name, then?" Ely asked.

"You first," the Apostle prompted over his shoulder.

The truth, Death instructed.

"Elyssandro Santara Ruadan," he replied.

"Where are you from, Elyssandro Santara Ruadan?"

"Saint Lucio."

"Never heard of it," the Apostle answered.

Ely tilted his head to the side. What kind of Apostle didn't know the capital city of the most expansive occupied territory in the Protectorate?

"You would not have won your foothold in Marikej without Saint Lucio's army," Ely reminded him.

"Does it look like we have a foothold in Marikej?" the Apostle frowned, casting a glance at the templar bodies strewn about them.

So, that's where they were. He did not recall Marikej looking quite like this. Though the dry heat felt familiar.

"Elyssandro, you are either very confused or a very convincing liar," the Apostle concluded.

"I *am* a convincing liar," Ely said. "But I'm afraid I've been refreshingly truthful today. You still haven't told me your name."

The Apostle jerked on the luminous tether, and they continued their miserable trek. For a bright, shimmery Miracle, the rope sure bit something fierce.

How long do I put up with the dragging about? Ely wondered.

Silence from the hecklers' balcony.

"So, nameless Apostle of the equally nameless god," he called to his captor, "what brings you out into this wilderness where so many of your brethren have perished?"

"Counting sins," droned the reply.

Ely rolled his eyes. He could slip this rope and have the Apostle in a chokehold, if only Death would permit it.

You spout a hurricane for Titus, but for this little weasel you won't let me lift a finger?

You said you were up to a challenge.

Are you toying with me? Where the fuck is Kai?

Such language, Death smoldered. *We're bending the rules for you.*

The Apostle paused, looking back at Ely with questioning surprise. Could he sense the unspoken argument?

An arrow tufted with striped feathers buried itself in the dust by their feet. The Apostle scanned the waste for their attackers, but the hills remained motionless. Ely felt life slithering closer on the barren slopes. The shadow warriors of Marikej that crept unseen to slaughter their foes were storied throughout the world. And extinct for centuries.

"I count five," Ely whispered.

"There's more behind us," the Apostle murmured.

The whistling twang of arrows loosed sent them diving onto the ground. Ely sheared through his luminous restraints, summoning his armor. A bronze-headed arrow made a hollow *thunk* against his shoulder and bounced away. That was going to leave a bruise.

Ely sank his fingertips into the powdered earth, injecting death magic through rock and root. Corpses jerked to their feet from the hillsides, dragging weapons from the dust. The living shadows sprang from their hiding places, screams of terror mingling with the mindless moans of the raised effigies.

The Apostle crouched like a stalking cat, then sprang into the air, outstretched arms catching the wind just as they fanned into feathered wings. Now a shrieking falcon, he sailed toward the panicking assassins, then dove into their midst, emerging again as a mist-shrouded figure with slender hands lifted. Bright souls rushed to answer the command. The encircling warriors fell, their empty shells left behind.

Ely strode toward the conjurer masquerading as an Apostle. The templar effigies snapped to attention as he passed. He left them at watch in case they received any other unwelcome visitors.

The figure that met him was not the same as the one that had sprouted wings and taken flight. She resembled the boy Apostle like a sibling. Same dark hair, olive skin, and vivid seafoam eyes. The rest of her features were her own, and this face he recognized. Younger. But just as fierce.

How is this possible? he demanded of his smug passenger.

Time is a mortal illusion.

"So, that's why the records say you don't exist," Ely said. "The Protectorate only knew you as Petros."

"But you know *me*?" she asked, hope igniting in her eyes. "The real me?"

Ely inclined his head. "Ariel Marcellus. Legendary conjurer. Beloved by some, feared by others, but certainly known by her proper name."

"How far ahead are you?" she asked.

Death sent a restraining pulse.

"I'm not to tell you," he said. "But they wanted you to know my name."

"I'll remember," she said.

Ariel frowned, gaze unfocused as though turning her sight inward. She blinked, then unhooked the eye and blade talisman from her belt. "You're going to need this."

"What for?" Ely asked.

He didn't like the radiation leaking from the dreaded symbols of apostolic office.

"Do you know the Iron Cathedral?" Ariel asked.

"I've heard of it," Ely said. In nightmare tales of Canon atrocity whispered by his heathen mother.

"Your king is there," she replied. "This will get you inside."

She placed the talisman in Ely's hand. He half-expected his skin to sizzle at the touch. No burn. Just strained energy. Stripped of soul and trapped in iron. A little nauseating to handle.

"You'll get used to it," Ariel told him.

"Won't they wonder what you've done with it?" Ely asked.

"I lost it in the desert when I was attacked," Ariel shrugged. "An easy mistake for a rash, inexperienced boy, don't you think?"

Ely tucked the Apostle's talisman in his pocket. "It's going to be quite some time before I repay you, but I will."

"What's a favor between new old friends?" Ariel grinned.

Ely smiled. He didn't have the heart to tell her they weren't on the best of terms in his moment in time. It was quite a different vantage point seeing her as a lonely-eyed kid longing for the world while hiding from it. He knew how walking in those shoes blistered. Imagining this girl trapped inside the monstrous tree made his insides squirm.

"Ariel," he started.

Caution, the passenger hissed.

"You're going to have to watch your back. Friends aren't always friends. You must be wary of–"

Enough out of you.

He fell through the earth into empty air. A dizzying drop broke on uneven cobblestone. His leg twisted, bones shifting along their recent fault lines. Ely staggered, gasping for breath. His stomach had nothing to heave, but it tried nonetheless.

Have you learned?

Yes. No spoilers.

Ely took in his surroundings through a pain-clouded haze. A row of high, balconied townhomes lined each side of the street, bricks painted in cheerful hues. The architecture struck a familiar chord.

"Dianessa," he determined aloud.

But when?

"What the hell are you doing? Trying to get yourself killed?" a familiar baritone barked.

"Rav! Thank the named gods."

Rav stopped, fixing him with a quizzical stare. His face appeared as though it had emerged from a black and white photograph into living color.

Ely froze. It was still full daylight. And this Rav was wearing shoes.

"You're human."

"How astute," Rav observed. "Did you mean to jump off the roof?"

"No. Complete accident," he groaned.

"We'd better get you inside," Rav said, casting a glance down the row of townhouses. "Can you stand?"

Ely took his proffered hand, managing to regain an upright orientation with much gnashing of teeth. Rav draped Ely's arm across his neck and braced him around the waist, letting him keep most of his weight off the injured leg.

"The real devil of it all is that I just recovered from a nasty break. Same leg," Ely grumbled.

"Not to worry...what was your name?"

"Ely," he replied. No breath to spare for a formal second first introduction.

"Not to worry, Ely. We'll set you right."

They hobbled toward the front stoop of a coral brick townhome with cobalt storm shutters. The inside was more economical than the charming exterior. Spare furnishings. Bare walls.

Rav set him on a sturdy chair then rummaged in a cabinet. "It's lucky you caught me today. I was headed out of town tomorrow. There you are, you little scoundrel."

He set a slender paper roll between his lips, then struck a match. When the fragrant ganja smoked sufficiently, he passed it to Ely, who imbibed with gratitude.

"That should take the edge off until we know what we're dealing with," Rav said.

"Many thanks, my friend," Ely sighed.

Rav scrutinized his face. "Remind me again how we know each other? I'll apologize now if we met at any kind of social event. I tend to get nerves and overdo it."

"Yes, I seem to recall you ending up in the lavatory," Ely smiled.

"Excellent," his host coughed. "Love it when I make a good impression."

Ely laughed. Damn this Rav. He was too disarming for his own good.

"Let's have a look at your leg, shall we?" Rav suggested, offering a crystal ashtray for the smoking bundle.

Ely rolled up his pant leg.

"That's where you broke it before?" Rav asked, probing the scar where bone had pierced the skin after his tumble into the roots of the Hollow. Ely nodded, wincing even at the slight pressure.

"It's clean, at least, no need to reset it," Rav assessed.

He moved his fingers in a slow pattern, two short swirls and a longer curve. Ely had no idea what they meant, but he knew the pinch of healing glyphs.

"Are you a doctor?" he asked.

"Certainly not," Rav replied with disdain. "I can fix the fracture. That won't be a problem. I just don't have the blessing of the almighty scholars to do it."

Ely watched him work, fascinated. Did his Rav have any idea he had been a healer? The vampire had set his leg and cleared the fluid from his lungs in a "most professional manner" according to Quinn. No mention of magic though.

"Where did you learn this?" Ely asked.

"I was a medical student at the University," Rav replied, continuing his ministrations without missing a beat. "Never finished. The academic circle can be unsavory at best. I enlisted as a medic after the Canon attack on Lower Usher. Thought I could make some kind of a difference."

"I'm sure you made all the difference to the wounded," Ely said.

"Sometimes," replied Rav with a veteran's quiet regret. Dismissing his ghosts, he continued, "I had the honor of observing Etrugan healers. Their methods can be quite unconventional but very effective used alongside modern human magic. I've been writing a book, but I think I'll be old and gray before I finish it."

Ely smiled, trying to ignore the saddened pang knowing his friend would never see a grizzled age. Nor would he remember his life's work.

"So, now that I've bored you with the story of my education," Rav said. "What has you leaping from buildings?"

"If you must know, I was running from trouble," Ely replied. He was used to concocting backstory on the fly, but it stung lying to Rav.

"What kind of trouble?" Rav asked.

"The kind where men with pointy weapons say I don't like the way you talk, why don't you go back to where you came from? Well, sir, I'll be clapped in irons and burned at the stake for a heretic, thank you for asking."

"You're here for asylum?" Rav asked.

"More or less," Ely replied.

"Unofficially, am I right to assume?"

Ely nodded. "Sorry if that puts you in an awkward position."

"Not at all," Rav answered with a reassuring glance. "Alright, you can get up. Give that leg a test."

Ely rotated his knee, walked a few steps, stood on one leg. Hopped. Not only had the fresh fracture healed, the old stiffness from his accident had gone with it.

"Better than new," he grinned.

"Glad we could get that sorted out," Rav nodded. He frowned, looking more than ever like his future self as he observed, "This, however, is an infection waiting to happen."

Ely had forgotten about the reviving throat chomp until Rav's nosy fingers made it burn again.

"I told you it wasn't sanitary," Ely rejoined before he remembered. "Him! I told him. My friend. That doesn't make it sound any better, does it?"

Vampire Rav would have blinked at him in glowering annoyance. Human Rav also blinked at him but with a hint of subtle amusement.

"How about I just fix it for you?" he suggested.

"Thanks, Rav. You're a true gem."

Rav drew a rhythmic kata around the fang marks he would not inflict for another millennium. The burn soothed, itched, then stilled.

"Do you spend a lot of time around vampires?" Rav asked.

Ely gaped at him, unsure why this question took him by surprise.

"It's not my first time curing a fang puncture. Not in these parts," Rav added, expression darkening.

"I only know you...you...Ewan," Ely recovered. "Good old Ewan. He gets a little salty sometimes. You have something against vampires?"

"Not personally," Rav replied. "Slavery, on the other hand, I am wholeheartedly and outspokenly against."

"I couldn't agree more," Ely said. "We're staunch abolitionists, Ewan and I."

"And where is good old Ewan?" Rav asked.

"Laying low," Ely replied. "We recently liberated a substantial collection of souls held captive."

"You're freedom fighters?" Rav asked, regarding him with peaked admiration.

"I suppose so," Ely replied.

"I'd love to hear more," Rav declared. "What do you say we discuss it over dinner?"

"Dinner?" Ely repeated, again taken by surprise.

Rav eyed him. "You do eat, don't you?"

"Of course. Yes. I'm famished," Ely said with an emphatic nod.

Rav smiled. A rare occurrence it seemed even for human Rav. Akin to catching sight of a fire rainbow or a unicorn.

"They set a good board at the Blue Elephant up the road," he said. "My treat."

"That's a very generous offer," Ely replied. "I accept."

"Good man," Rav nodded. "Let's find you a change of clothes."

Ely beamed. "Many thanks. Yet again."

Upstairs in the bedroom, loose pages lay draped over the furniture like fallen autumn leaves inked with careful handwriting and detailed sketches.

"Excuse the mess," Rav apologized, collecting sheets from the walkway.

Ely bent to get a closer look at a diagram. Muscle, valve, and ventricle annotated with glyphs.

"Cure for a broken heart?" Ely asked.

"Yes, as a matter of fact," Rav smiled. His second in five minutes. Unprecedented.

Ely turned his gaze back to the page, goosebumps prickling his arms. Had Rav unknowingly composed the answer to saving Victor Skylark? Was that why Death tossed him here?

Rav set out a pair of trousers, a white shirt, and a magnificent leather jacket that looked soft as butter and smelled as divine.

"You can't lend me this," Ely swooned.

"No? Keep it then," Rav smirked, tossing a pair of clean socks on the bed. "Those are the real find. Enjoy."

When he had gone, Ely dressed and folded the remains of his singed, desert-dusted suit neatly on a chair. He placed the Apostle's eye and blade talisman in his pocket along with the few coins left over from the Haunts outing. Finally, he drew the supple leather jacket over his shoulders. A perfect fit. Damn this Rav.

Focus. You're not here to play dress up.

Sure thing, Ely nodded to the voices in his head.

He located the healing spell that had drawn him into this century. Lying to Rav stung but stealing felt much worse.

"You'll thank me later," he murmured, folding the page and tucking it in his pocket.

He joined Rav downstairs. His friend had donned a dashing long-coat, a sword belt hung with a silver-hilted rapier, and most delightful of all, a cavalier hat with an alabaster plume.

"Is there something amusing?" Rav frowned.

"No. Nothing," Ely beamed.

Rav shook his head.

They set off just as the lamp lighters began their work. Ely looked around in fascination at streets he knew only under a decayed patina. Scrubbed clean, no doors askew off hinges or shattered glass. Skeletons all housed properly in sinew and skin. He wondered if he knew any of the hurried passersby. Popping in to pay a visit to Sir Quinn, he assumed, lay strictly outside the rules.

The Blue Elephant stood a cockeyed little tavern with red brick peaking through ashy plaster. Pale blue storm shutters flared like pachyderm ears astride each of the windows and doors. Ely had never seen it before, though he knew the street. Must have been flattened sometime in the intervening centuries. A pity.

Rav elbowed past a group of rowdy characters hovering at the door. Patrons packed every corner. Rav spotted a table and steered Ely to claim it, but a balding man with close-set eyes and fleshy jowls blocked their path.

"Well, well. If it isn't the high and mighty bastard himself," he sneered. "You've some stones on you, showing your face about town tonight."

He made an exaggerated *tsk* with his tongue.

"You'd best keep a lookout over your shoulder, Aurelio," he added with a patronizing pat on the arm before taking his exit.

Rav brushed off his sleeve. Where his vampire self would have torn the leering man's throat out, the human just looked miffed and queasy at the unwelcome contact.

"Why don't I get us drinks?" Ely offered.

Rav nodded, swallowing his disquiet as best he could. Ely pushed his way to the bar and ordered two pints of Dianessa's finest. While he waited, the barkeep, Geoff, regaled him with tales of the city's thriving craft beer community.

"We put on a festival every fall. Nothing grand, mind you, but we're growing. We'll have a brewers guild by year's end."

"How exciting!" Ely exclaimed, wondering if there was still an undead brewers guild in this corner of the city.

He set a gold coin on the counter in payment, and Geoff's eyes grew round.

"I don't have change for that," he said.

"Oh. Don't worry about it. I would've left a tip," Ely replied.

"That's...very generous. Thank you, sir." Geoff cocked his head to the side, strumming a different tune. "You know, my shift ends at ten. If you'd like to come see what's brewing in the basement."

It seemed death magic still kept its potency even out of time. Or maybe it was the gold.

"Tempting," Ely said, "but I didn't order both of those drinks for myself, if you follow my meaning."

"Ah, yes." Geoff shot a displeased squint across the crowded tavern. "I saw you came in with Lord Aurelio."

"Lord?" Ely mused. Interesting detail.

"You should be careful going about with him," Geoff said in a hushed tone. "Might end up caught in the crossfire. If you follow my meaning."

"Many thanks for the warning, Geoff," Ely said. "Where are those pints, then?"

The barkeep located the glasses that had migrated to the other end of the counter in the midst of their conversation.

Ely thanked him and set off with drinks at last procured. Out of habit, he sent a ripple of death magic through the bubbling libations as he walked. On most occasions, the probing pulse just disappeared beneath the surface. Tonight it swirled about the tops, forming misty black skulls among the foam.

"Shit," Ely muttered, glancing about the busy pub in search of an assassin.

Rav relieved him of a glass, but Ely dashed it from his hand. He sent his own glass after it to shatter on the floor.

"Sorry about that, how clumsy of me," he blustered with a jolly laugh. He leaned close to Rav's ear, whispering, "Poisoned. Someone wants you dead."

Rav glanced around the room and nodded, less than surprised that someone planned to murder him.

"We need to leave without signaling that we know there are games afoot," Rav murmured.

"Right," Ely nodded.

He slapped Rav across the mouth. A little harder than he meant to, but the stunned look certainly sold the scene.

"How dare you!" Ely cried with resonance enough to reach the cheapest balcony seats. "This is the last time you crush my heart, you bootless swag-tongued coxcomb."

He turned on his heel and stormed off.

"Come on, kitten, can't we at least talk about this?" Rav called after him.

"Save it for some other fool!" Ely shot over his shoulder as he exited stage left.

He committed to swift, angry strides until he turned the corner onto Hotspur Lane, then waited by the barber's shop until Rav finally caught up.

"Bootless coxcomb?"

Ely crooked an eyebrow. "Kitten?"

Rav winced. "You made an uncanny impression of my ex-wife."

"Deepest apologies. You never told me you were married."

"I'm not anymore," Rav shrugged. "Another boring story."

"Why don't we skip to the one where you're not surprised when someone tries to poison you?"

"Ah, yes. Probably more relevant," Rav said with an apologetic turn of the lips. "I'm sorry you got caught in the middle of it. How did you know?"

"Old habit," Ely replied. "I once spent a very unpleasant night after taking a tainted cup from a stranger. Never doing that again. So, my friend, who's trying to kill you? Surely not Kitten?"

"No," Rav dismissed with a bitter chuckle. "She would look me in eyes whilst twisting the knife,"

"Unpopular politics, then?" Ely deduced.

Rav nodded. "I'm only in town for the hearing. I plan to leave right after I cast a vote tomorrow, but I think someone means to stop me."

"What hearing?" Ely asked.

"We're putting an end to the exploitation of the dead," Rav replied. "We have the votes. All that's left is the hearing."

"You're trying to help the vampires?" Ely realized.

"For a start," Rav said.

Ely glanced behind them. It was difficult to read the masses of living souls that congested Dianessa's streets in this era. However, it seemed some of them moved too purposefully in time with their steps.

"Rav," he whispered.

"I know," Rav replied, hand poised on his rapier hilt. "This way."

Rav ducked into an open grate. Ely followed. He knew this tunnel well. It led to the old amphitheater where he used to smoke Etrugan hash with Rión. Except it wasn't old at all. Now it stood a magnificent arena with towering tiers of wooden benches and pristine boxes. An elaborate set stood upon a rounded platform. It appeared to belong to a play involving some fantastical woodland scene.

Their pursuers emerged from all four stage entrances, fanning to surround them. They wore peaked black hoods with flowing capes made all the more eerie by the papier-mâché forest. Rav drew his sword, but from the look on his face, he merely intended to die fighting.

The black hoods began to chant in unison. Their dreadful dirge tugged at Ely's guts like tiny barbed hooks. Death magic?

The passenger prickled with indignation.

Amateurs. Put them in their place.

Ely teased an ether ribbon between his fingers, but triple the effort yielded a quarter of the expected result.

What's the matter with you? he demanded.

The enraged legion hissed like a volcanic vent. All bark. No bite. Was the coven of Cosmologists choking death magic from the very air?

Shadows shivered and elongated from the chanters' feet, void lurching into tall, faceless forms, black blades in their hands. Rav met the first of the shades with a skillful swipe of his rapier. It parried with a ringing swish. Rav's sword split it in twain, and it evaporated into wisps of violet embers. He turned to meet two more.

Ely reached toward the onrushing ether swordsmen sinking invisible claws into their shadow shoulders. They jerked backward like fish caught on a line. Rav sheared through them. Four more lunged in their place.

Ely raised his hands ad astra, silver light seeping from the glowering dome overhead into his skin. Yawning, all-consuming gravity seethed from the wellspring within, forming as black holes in his hands. The shades stopped, turning toward him, stretching and distorting in his orbit. Their limbs fused into shadow.

Ely took in a breath. With its release, he threw the Cosmologists' own witless conjury back at the circle. The smoky wall of death magic crashed like an avalanche down an alpine slope, toppling the hooded figures. Ely lowered his hands, breath heavy. He stepped forward as the stunned Cosmologists stirred, moaning. Their sorcery rang too hollow to kill them.

Ely spoke, and Death's multitudes echoed in booming warning, "Tell the crooks and charlatans at the Tower their days are numbered."

He turned to Rav who regarded him with an intent, undecipherable expression.

"Shall we?" Ely smiled.

Rav sheathed his blade and followed in a trance. Ely navigated the tunnels with practiced ease past set changes, chariots, and stables filled with live animals. All the way back to Guildenstern Grove at the aft of the amphitheatre.

"I hope you know your way home from here," Ely piped. He noticed his voice slipping into the overly congenial tone he used to soothe spooked humans back to ease.

"It's not far," Rav intoned, face expressionless.

He started down the empty boulevard. Ely hung back. Rav stopped and turned back to him.

"Aren't you coming?"

"I haven't frightened you off?" Ely asked.

"Frightened?"

He strode back to Ely, face lighting with excitement.

"That was the most incredible thing I have ever witnessed!" he exclaimed. "We've been fighting the Tower with protests and injunctions. But a real conjurer? You could change everything."

Ely took in his enraptured smile, chest tight. Aching for the suffering his friend had yet to endure.

Can't I help him?

You already did, the passenger whispered.

"What's wrong, Ely?"

"I can't stay," he said. "I wish I could. I'd tear the Tower to pieces brick by brick..."

He lowered his gaze. Black currents coiled beneath his feet. Ready to spirit him away again.

"Keep fighting, Rav," he said. "I'll meet you in the next act."

The earth yawned to swallow him. He drifted in weightless suspension, slipping through wrinkled folds of time and space. The void ejected him into briny waves. He flailed for the surface, but the water slurped at his clothes. He never had learned to swim.

A meaty hand seized him by the collar, hauling him dripping onto a boat's deck.

"God's tits! What are you doing in the middle of the ocean, starshine?"

Rión stared at him, eyes gilded with curiosity.

"Riri!" he coughed.

Make it quick, the passenger advised.

"I don't have much time," he sputtered. "When are we?"

"I just saw you a few days ago. You kicked over a ten thousand year old temple."

"Ah. Nearly caught up then," he nodded.

"The fuck's going on?"

"Kai's been captured by an Apostle. Morgata's taking me to find him. We've made a few detours along the way," he explained with haste. "What are you doing out here?"

"Tracking child thieves," she replied.

Ely snapped his fingers. "Ragnor! That's why they dropped me here. I have the children you're searching for. Or I will in a few days. Meet me in South Sea."

"For fuck's sake, Ruadan, I can't wander around South Sea like some shiteating human tourist."

"It's Haunts. You'll blend right in. Meet me at the Hotel Lioncourt, and tell Morrison at the front desk I'm expecting you. Don't let him give you the runaround. He's shifty, that Morrison."

Time's up.

"See you soon, Riri."

Blackness swallowed him up and spat him back out in a gray drizzle. Ely hoisted himself to his feet. The last stop had already drenched him, but now he found his knees and hands embedded with rough gravel.

A road slunk like a sidewinder across heathered hills. A fortress on the far bluff raised sharp gunmetal spires to the bleak sky. An ominous briar crowned in thorns.

"Iron Cathedral?" he asked aloud.

An invisible host nodded as one.

He reached in his pocket for the Apostle's talisman, breathing a sigh of relief when he found it undisturbed by his journey. Its dull radiation still set his teeth on edge, but his stomach had grown accustomed to the discomfort.

He set off at a brisk trot toward his destination. A triad of pointed arches marked the cathedral entrance. Gargantuan winged figures in gray robes barred passage with greatswords crossed. Strips of cloth bandaged the top half of their heads, rendering them blind. Ely's insides dropped. These were no mere statues. They emanated living spirit. Or something like it. Ely remembered his mother's voice narrating a bedtime horror story that had sent him nestling deep into her arms with prickled gooseflesh from head to toe.

"*Seraphim guard the Iron Cathedral, their eyes bound. One glance from their holy gaze would melt your flesh and bones to a puddle at their feet.*"

The dread of her tale held not even a flickering candle to the truth.

You're sure he's in there? Ely asked.

Yes.

No turning back, then.

Ely wrapped the talisman's chain around his hand, holding the eye and blade aloft in hopes that it might keep the sentinels at bay. The metal illuminated, casting a shimmering halo about him. The seraphim's feathered wings ruffled. Breath like thundering gales huffed from their nostrils. Yet they remained in place.

Ely's heart careened as he passed beneath the hallowed blades. They creaked. No death knell. He reached the door unscathed.

Many thanks, Ariel, he thought.

It seemed he had been in her debt all along.

The cathedral doors stood open, offering ingress to any the sentinels deemed worthy. He found himself in a vast hall, vaulted and ridged as though he had been swallowed by some great beast. Arches upon arches. How their nameless god loved his arches. Chandeliers dangled from iron chains, bristling with dripping candles. Somewhere in the echoing chamber, an organ droned.

Ely pressed close to an indented pillar. He closed his eyes, taking in the breadth of the sanctuary, the winding passageways, the vaults below. Whoever lit the candles and played the hair-raising music, he couldn't feel them at all. Did the Apostles really have no souls under their empty smiles? He looked down at the eye and blade clutched in his hand. Of course. They were still human. The apostolic talismans masked them.

He expanded his search, mind tiring at the exploration. There it was. Buried deep in the iron belly. Life. Faint and waning. Ely followed the beckoning spark down a gradient of staircases into tangled corridors lined with cells.

Footsteps echoed. He drew back into the shadows, a flash of crimson catching his eye. Templars. Ely crept behind the patrol line, unwinding the talisman chain from his hand. Swift as a shadow, he flipped the chain across the trailing templar's throat and pulled it tight, dragging him out of sight around a bend in the corridor.

"Not a sound," he hissed in Paxat.

The templar nodded, shaking. He was young. Probably conscripted from some territory whose name and heritage had been wiped away by the Canon.

"I'm looking for Kailari Novara. Take me to him, and I will let you live."

"They'll kill me if I let you take him," the boy whispered.

"Show me to his cell and shut me inside. You can't very well get in trouble for locking up an intruder, can you?"

"No," the boy puzzled. "I don't think so."

Ely relaxed the chain. He hoped inexperience, confusion, and curiosity would render the boy honest. The confounded young templar escorted him through the snaking cell blocks, each more damp and stale than the last.

The boy stopped at an unmarked door and unlocked the cell. Ely stepped inside, and the templar shut the door behind him, key rattling the bolt.

His heart rejoiced one beat and broke the next at the sight of the ragged figure chained to the wall. The pirate king leaned his head against the stones. Eyes closed. Breath shallow. He did not stir as Ely rushed to his side.

"Kai?"

His eyelids fluttered. Blood matted his hair and violet bruises ringed one eye. Ely unlocked the irons with little difficulty. No enchantment to these. Only cold, vicious metal. They stood no chance against death magic.

Ely knelt close to Kai and brought a gentle hand to his face. The pirate king groaned, at last opening his eyes.

"*Che'miora?*" Kai breathed, reaching for him like a drowning man to shore. "They told me you were dead."

Ely gathered him close to his heart. He seemed so thin and frail.

"I'm sorry," Kai whispered. "I'm so sorry."

Ely pressed his lips to Kai's temple. "Everything will be alright. Let's get you home."

Needing no further prompting, Death ferried them into the dark. On the other side of weightless nothing lay sun-warmed sand and gentle lapping surf shaded in twilight hues. Kai blinked up at the thatched peak of a bungalow. He sighed. His eyes slipped closed, lost to the world.

Ely lifted the pirate king with a grunt, setting out across the shifting sand. Three figures bounded out to meet them, faces shocked and overjoyed. Yamon and Mirit took Kai and carried him toward the bungalow. Ely began to follow, but Salía planted herself in his path. Arms crossed. Scowl stern. She didn't mean to let him pass.

"We are grateful to you," she said.

"Salía, *na lora,*" Ely pleaded.

"His wife and daughter are inside," she whispered. "We will look after him, diakana. I promise."

"At least send word that he is well," Ely pressed, floundering to keep his heart above the waves of despair.

"I'll relay news to Rión Twin Axes," she promised. "Go now."

Ely nodded. He stole a last look at the bungalow, then returned in the direction from which he had come.

I'm ready.

Rippling void encompassed him. He emerged on a grassy knoll under the stars. Not a second past the moment of his departure.

Thank you.

You owe a debt, chorused the reply.

Understood.

Rav alighted at his side. Ely's heart danced a doublestep seeing that his excursion to the past had not erased his friend from this century.

"Nice jacket," the vampire frowned. Rav bent closer, inhaling his travels. "You set it right, then?"

Ely nodded. "He's safe with his family. All thanks to you."

The vampire ducked his head, radiating pleased discomfort. Ely wished his stoic, anxious friend still remembered the little adventure they shared a thousand years ago.

"I think we found the answer to our quest too," Ely said, retrieving the manuscript page tucked away in a pocket. It was a little smudged from his plunge into the ocean but mostly decipherable.

Rav took it from him, walking away a few paces to dispel his shock.

"You got this from me?" he asked.

Ely nodded. "The outfit too. It turns out you were a healer. And an activist. A bit of a flirt, now that I think back on it. Very handy with a sword–"

"Don't tell me any more," Rav cut him off.

"Why? You're a real diamond in the rough, Rav."

"I said enough!" Rav bared his fangs. He slapped the page back into Ely's hand. "That man is dead. I don't want to hear about the pleasure of his company."

The vampire swooped away, melding with the midnight shadows. Ely called after him to no avail. He was gone.

Chapter Sixteen

ROAD TO RUIN

Memory gathered and climbed, a tidal wave disturbed into existence by a tectonic tremor. Rav tore through the night in reckless haste to outrun the cresting breaker. Faster. Fly faster.

He discerned no direction until he had plunged through a tremulous seam in the sky. The rupture burrowed between stars and spit him out above skeletal bluffs. A narrow gap in the stone admitted him to the damp womb of the earth. Deep into the roots of the Spine.

Rav collapsed beside a weeping stream. He needed no lantern or torch to make out the cavern's crenelated corners and creeping tentacles of living rock. If he followed the water, it would lead him to the rubbled basin where lay the remnants of the box that entombed him for centuries. Why had he fled here of all places?

His head pulsed like it meant to detonate under the unbearable pressure. Images flashed before him in rapid succession. Voices roared in his ears. Tides of emotion eddied about him. Transcendent joy. Aching sorrow. Crushing terror. Love. Loathing. Desire. Despair. He clamped his hands to his temples and gritted his teeth.

When at last the tsunami's cataclysm came to rest, he lay quivering in the mineral dust. The onslaught had honed to a single point. A fossil unearthed from the depths of his mind.

He stood at attention before a disapproving woman in a lumpy mustard sweater. Her bullfrog chin bloated and contracted while she fussed over his unruly hair.

When was this? It was a birthday. His tenth. But there was something else. Something more important. A grave mound still fresh in the village cemetery.

"How've you gotten smudged already?" the bullfrog inspecting him croaked. His aunt. That's right. "Named gods, you must be the filthiest boy that ever lived."

She swiped her tongue across her thumb and scrubbed at his cheek.

"You've got to be on your best behavior, Ravan. Do you understand me?"

He remained frozen, hypnotized by the wobbling dewlap.

"Are you listening, boy?"

"Yes, ma'am."

"Your whole life depends on today. Don't disgrace your poor mother's memory."

Rav lowered his gaze to his choked toes trying to burst their way to freedom from within ragged shoes.

"Ravan! Are you deaf?"

"Yes, ma'am. I...I mean no, ma'am."

The aunt loosed a growl like gargling gravel. "Sometimes I think you've nothing but cotton stuffed under your skull. Don't slouch. His lordship won't take one glance at a grubby little hunchback."

With a sigh of resigned disapproval, she loaded him up into a sagging cart behind a tired donkey. The journey lay an obscured haze. Trees and meadows all ran together. Meaningless gray drained of life and color by the absence of the bright, warm sun now set forever beneath the earth. Cordelia Lovelace. "Cordy" to friends. "Ma" to one quiet little boy.

The road flowed past a high stone wall divided by a wrought iron gate which parted in the center of an elaborate *A*. Pastures dotted with fruit trees rolled to dense pine forest on either side. Dappled horses grazed, tails flicking lazily in the afternoon sun. The winding road carried them onward toward a craggy mountain. No. Not a mountain, as it turned out. A house with gables like lofty peaks and walls inlaid with rhombus rows of reflective mirrorwood. Multitudes of windows peered out like insectile eyes, fringed with preening ivy. The sprawling manor lay in the contoured arms of a garden, meticulously arranged in an interlacing mural of blooms.

The aunt goggled up at the formidable fortress. Her chin constricted in a nervous swallow.

"Out. Out. Quickly!" she hissed at Rav.

A silver-haired man in coat tails waited at the front steps, one hand resting behind his back. His blank expression flickered curious for a moment as he looked Rav over.

"I've...I've brought the boy," the aunt stammered. "We're to meet his lordship at two."

The man inclined his head. "If you'll follow me, madam."

They ascended to sloped, cherry-colored doors and into a high, empty foyer. A glittering chandelier cast faceted light upon paneled archways that guarded inlets to either side of a carpeted staircase. Rav craned his neck to where the steps disappeared into lands unknown.

The silver-haired butler escorted them down the right side hallway into a spacious drawing room. An emerald green settee with matching chairs assembled in a half circle around a relief-etched mantle. Above it, a man with dark hair and eyes like a midnight sky peered with disdain from an oil portrait that dominated the wall. A grand auburn piano made the room's only saving grace. His mother kept a much smaller instrument, teaching him to play in the late hours of the night. Rav reached out to stroke the shining mirrorwood keys. Such a magnificent piano would surely hold magic in its notes. The aunt slapped his hand, shaking her head in aggravated warning.

A chill entered the room along with the master of the house. Tall. Imperious. A deep green cape swirled about his shoulders held in place by a gold chain across his chest. His hair appeared much longer than in the portrait, brushing his shoulders, and he now sported a meticulous mustache above a thin, dark triangle in the center of his chin. Rather like a villain from the melodramas the village players put on at festivals.

"Mrs. Regan, Milord," the butler announced. "And her nephew."

"Ravan Lovelace, your lordship," the aunt filled in, voice a half octave higher than usual. "Mother is...was Cordelia Lovelace. She was buried in the Maribone cemetery three days ago. The fever took her."

Lord Aurelio's eyes flicked over him, mouth a melting red grimace. Rav felt his cheeks flush hot. He studied his jailbreaking toes harder.

"That is most unfortunate, Mrs. Regan," Lord Aurelio stated without a trace of accompanying feeling. "My condolences for your loss."

"Thank you kindly, your lordship. I'll be relieved when we're finished with this last bit of business."

Lord Aurelio's eyes narrowed like a sleek tom sizing up a dingy rat. "I assume, Mrs. Regan, that you have a particular sum in mind that will put this matter to rest."

"Sum?" the aunt spat. "No, I want you to take him. She worked for you until she was busting out of her aprons. And look at him. He's your spitting image. Bastard or not, a man's got to provide for his child."

"Are you suggesting I ask my wife to take him under her wing?" Lord Aurelio sneered.

"Where you put him is your business. I've brought him. I've done my duty to my poor departed sister. He's your problem now."

Rav reached for the aunt's sleeve as she keeled for the door. She might be a snide bullfrog, but she still cried for sweet little Cordy. That had to count for something, didn't it? The aunt jerked her arm from his grasp without a backward glance.

Rav stiffened as Lord Aurelio's boots thumped the boards. He towered like a great oak, eyes a looming thunderstorm as he lifted Rav's chin. Lord Aurelio tutted his tongue and released his grip.

"It's a pity you haven't your mother's looks. You might have been worth something."

Rav fidgeted with the hem of his jacket. Tears prickled the corners of his eyes, but he managed to hold them at bay.

"Can you read and write?" Lord Aurelio continued.

"Yes, Milord."

"I'll send word to the Corps. They'll make a place for you. In the meantime, there's a cot in the attic loft." Lord Aurelio gestured to the silver-haired man hovering like a phantom in the doorway. "Dougray will show you to your quarters."

Rav followed the scowling butler through a maze of hallways to a dim set of stairs hidden away like a secret artery at the back of the house. At the top floor, the opulent grandeur gave way to practicality along a row of sparse rooms. A servants' dormitory. Dougray opened a cupboard at the end of the corridor. Instead of shelves with linens or boxes, a narrow ladder ascended into a gloomy hole high above.

"Go on up, lad," Dougray instructed. "I'll send someone to fetch you at supper."

Rav nodded, shoulders shaky as he climbed up into the dim, drafty space. A diamond patterned window emitted paltry light through grimy glass. As evidenced by the dust, this room saw few visitors. A cot took up one corner and a scuffed writing desk another. The final dregs of a candle sat on the desk with a matchbox beside it. He opted to conserve the stub of a taper until after dark. Instead, he unlatched the window.

The view brought him to a halt. Sprawling meadows and stately trees rolled among craggy emerald hills. The expanse seemed to croon a mournful ode to loneliness. Its song lured free the tears that threatened since they lowered Cordelia Lovelace's coffin into the earth...

Rav blinked as two cold droplets kissed his cheeks. He lay trembling on the cavern floor. His mind felt as if it bent and folded around the emergent memory like hands clutching a fresh wound. He brushed his face, frowning at the tear that beaded his fingertip.

What did you do to me, conjurer?

It was dawn when Ely emerged from cow-spangled meadows into what should have been civilization. With Rav flown off and Leanora sheltering somewhere unknown, the only sensible destination seemed to be the Hotel Lioncourt.

He found South Sea in battered chaos. Debris littered the streets. Windows brandished glass poniards. Buggies lay capsized. The city's inhabitants wandered the rubble masked in Haunts makeup and their own caked blood. The names of the missing rang out in forlorn cries.

Ely walked among them. Cold. Numb. Guilt readying in the wings. A woman stumbled in front of him, death still fresh upon the motionless bundle in her arms. More bodies lay entombed beneath collapsed buildings. It would take weeks for the people of South Sea to uncover them. He felt them all. Addled spirits still reeling from sudden, unexpected release.

The Hotel Lioncourt appeared to have held up better than the surrounding buildings. Rafters peeked like vulture-picked ribs between the surviving clay roof tiles.

A familiar bark echoed from the street, "Put your fucking backs into it!"

One gray-cheeked Etrugan warrior strained with a group of Haunts-painted humans to lift a fallen section of wall from a man pinned underneath. It appeared the pitstop to Rión's ship had paid off.

Rescue complete, Ely approached, smile lifted in a half-hearted toast. Rión strode to greet him, unruffled by the mayhem visited upon the city.

"Zygos' cock, it's about time!" she boomed. "I came just like you asked. The little shit at the front desk wouldn't give me your room number. Had to drag him into the boiler room and threaten to tear his limbs off."

"Is that why he never delivered my note?" Ely wondered aloud.

Rión ignored his aside, continuing, "Then you set a hurricane loose on the city. Morrison had a key to the cellar, at least. We had a good heart-to-heart during the storm. And some bottles of wine. A little too sweet for me. You'd have liked it, though."

"There was an Apostle," Ely explained. "It's been a very eventful three days."

"So it would seem," she eyed him. "You said you have the missing children?"

Ely nodded. "Yes. They're safe in an old farmhouse outside the city. Rav knows precisely where, but he's a little out of pocket at the moment."

"Rav?" Rión growled, eyes irritable lime green. "You're running around with that shiteating vampire that destroyed Kristor's distillery?"

"We all just got off on the wrong foot," Ely assured her. "He's a good egg."

Rión fixed stern cobalt eyes on him. "I love you, little brother, but your judgement of eggs has always been fucking atrocious. Come on, then. It appears we've got some tracking to do."

"We should wait until nightfall," Ely suggested. "I'm sure Rav will be back after dark."

"I see from your stupid face that you haven't the tiniest baby bastard of an idea where he is."

"No. I don't," Ely sighed. "I think I offended him."

"Of course," Rión rolled her eyes.

Ely looked up at the suffering chalet. He half-hoped to see Rav glowering through a crack in the top-floor curtain. No such luck. Maybe he was sleeping?

"Alright. At least let me go up and check...out. Yes. Check out. I left my violin upstairs."

Rión eyed him skeptically. "Five minutes."

Ely nodded and loped off for the Lioncourt. The elevator was out of service, so he took the stairs two at a time all the way to the top floor. Since he had dropped the room key somewhere in the past, he jimmied the lock with a little death magic trick and slipped inside.

"Rav?" he called.

No response. No turbulent presence lurking in the dark.

Ely found his belongings strewn exactly as he had left them the night of the Haunts gala. That seemed lifetimes ago now. He packed up his threadbare clothes, his spell-ringed water flask, his violin. His eyes crossed paths with the mirrorwood stake left on the bedside table. Reluctant to leave such implements lying about, he packed it too. He planned to destroy it, but something told him it would not be as simple as throwing it in a fire.

"Damn it all, Rav. Where are you?"

Rav gritted his teeth against the burn that had dragged him from the yawning pit of memory. A pinpoint of sunlight pursued him down into the crevice, burrowing into the back of his hand. He crawled toward the gurgling underground stream and doused the blaze in the chilled water.

The pressure behind his eyes began to throb. More memories drumming to escape.

"Go away," he snarled aloud. "I don't want your life."

Something tittered in the gloom. Rav tensed. He was not alone in this cavern. Long, slender fingers slithered across his throat. Visions shuddered before his eyes. Filling his senses. Spewing sight and sound.

"Look at you, fighting like a red-eyed savage. You must be more demon than boy."

"You are not a person. You are a tool."

"I know you. You're Wulfric Aurelio's bastard."

"You're a disgrace to this chamber. I'll see you drawn and quartered by winter's end, mark me."

"Tell me again, pet."

"Let it be, Aurelio. You can't heal dead."

"This court finds you guilty of sedition and high treason against the state of Dianessa. The penalty for your crimes shall be death."

A breathy voice like night wind rustling across the cavern egress sighed, "Hell's bells. What's wrong with your head?"

The fingers clamped harder around his throat. A rusted chuckle cracked in his ear. "You've been all scrambled up inside. What else have you got for me?"

Leering childish faces surrounded him, cackling like crows, taloned fingers grasping. Rav ducked, letting his arms slide from his jacket sleeves. He crouched, snatching up a handful of dirt and flinging it into the nearest boy's eyes. The boy shrieked, pawing at his face. Rav drove a shoulder into an exposed stomach, bowling over the front line of the blockade. He sprinted for the gap, throwing fists into faces made ghoulish under the bloated moon. Arms closed around him, holding him pinned. He bit a hand that tried to stifle his shouts.

Crack!

A colorless flood overtook him. He felt himself being lifted. Dragged. Hefted. Rough wood scraped against his arms. Something closed above his nose. He screamed, struggling in the confined space.

Rap! Rap! Rap!

His teeth rattled together. It was not until the banging ceased that he understood the sound. Nails pounded into a coffin. He was trapped.

"You're taking it too far," a shaky brogue piped.

"He's just a bastard, Whitey. You want to go in with him?"

His prison jerked. They were carrying him off again, the cackling crows. When the box thudded to solid ground, deafening silence fell for a moment. Then a patter like rain tinkled against the lid of the box.

"No!" he shrieked, scrabbling in vain to escape before his schoolmates buried him alive...

The memory snuffed out. In the fleeting moment of clarity, Rav recognized the shriveled little beast that latched onto his throat. It went by many names. Succubus. Algos. Memory demon. They infested dark places, feeding on troubled minds. The Cosmologists used to set traps for them like rodents in the catacombs.

Recollections bubbled and burst, a river rushing from a broken dam. Littered with debris, no rhyme or reason to their flooding.

"Mmm, is that war I smell?" the creature creaked. "Let's stop here for a while."

Dusk shadows draped the countryside as Ely once again found himself making the trek back to South Sea alone. Rión had sniffed out the dilapidated farmhouse where Rav stashed the kidnapped children. The Etrugan warrior had already departed with them, anxious to return to her ship moored somewhere down the coast away from meddlesome humans.

She offered Ely a ride back to their side of the world, but he declined. He still had a stolen spell to deliver. Surely Leanora could make sense of it. If he could find her again. Or Rav. Even Ariel seemed to have written him off.

The events of the past few days crashed in on him one breaker after another. No pause for reflection. Now, with nothing but time on his hands, he was free to spiral around the same sequence.

Friends gone.

South Sea destroyed.

Danger to humanity.

Apostle on the loose.

Cosmologist fortress in the snow.

Kai.

Kai.

More Kai.

Wife and daughter inside.

Stay away.

"Kai Novara has done nothing but shake your heart around like a child with a fucking ragdoll," Rión had snarled on their stroll.

Ely had recounted the tale of his tumble through time in colorful detail that waxed wistful at the finish.

"What happened to me wasn't his fault," Ely bit back.

"Of course it was!" Rión exclaimed, eyes reeling between enraged emerald and impelling gold. "You can't possibly be so blind stupid as to think he believed you could be together. You couldn't play your fiddle better than he played you."

"It's a violin," Ely muttered.

"Who sat with you through the nights when you were burning up with fever? Fed you like an infant when you couldn't even close your fingers around a spoon? It sure as hell wasn't Kailari fucking Novara."

"I know what you did for me," Ely murmured.

"That isn't the point, Ruadan."

"What is the point?"

"The moment you finally let go of the one man on this shitblistered earth you can't have, you'll meet someone who actually deserves your beautiful, cockbrained heart."

"I did meet someone," Ely started.

Rión lowered hostile lemon eyes in his direction. "If you say the vampire, I'm going to break my boot off in your ass."

"She's human."

"Thank the named gods," Rión sighed.

"Buuut," Ely drew out the word until the Etrugan warrior shut her toothy trap and let him to continue. "She was so afraid of me, that she lied to me on several very important topics, and we got blown up by an Apostle. And now all of South Sea is in shambles. So, I hope you see the fallacy of your point."

Rión shook her head. "Well, maybe this quest you're on will be good for you. You'll have another of Morgata's chosen at your side."

"Ariel? Why is everyone trying to paint us together? One macabre trait in common and it must be written in the stars. It's maddening."

"If you say so, starshine," Rión nudged him with a jostling elbow. His arm went dead...

A whirring drone like a large, lazy insect drew Ely's gaze from the descent into madness to the disembodied amber eye approaching.

"Nix!" Ely called with a relieved grin.

"Hello, Elyssandro," she modulated.

"Did Rav send you?" he asked.

"No, he told me to stay with the witch, but the probability that you were damaged or terminated exceeded my control threshold. So, I overrode the directive and followed your signal."

"I have a signal?" Ely asked.

"Yes. I have scanned you many times," she purred.

Ely shifted his feet, exceedingly uncomfortable all of the sudden. "Can you take me to Leanora?"

"Yes, I can take you to the witch," Nix replied with a sour edge. "Follow me."

He hastened after the darting orb. She paused every now and again to look back at him. In the distance, Ely caught a glimpse of the city's namesake. The South Sea lay a dark, murky expanse on the horizon. His heart surged at the sight of it. Not the pristine waters of Séocwen but next of kin. Enough to raise a homesick ache in a wound that would never heal right.

They had returned again to human habitation. It appeared Death's tantrum had mostly spared this corner of the city. Palm tree limbs and mailboxes seemed to be the worst casualties.

Nix glided up the front steps of a log cabin with a green tin roof. A wicker rocking chair relaxed on the porch. He recognized it from the tavern in Mondacca. Esperanza Osai wove chairs, tables, baskets, and planting pots in the Zephyr's back courtyard. This must be Peggy's place.

Ely knocked at the door. Sure enough, Peggy Osai answered with a shadow-eyed smile.

"Hi there, Mr. Ruadan. Come on in."

Ely followed her inside, peering about the shadows in the house. None of them tall, pale, and fanged. It wasn't until disappointment sank a fist in his stomach that he realized he'd been holding out hope that Rav was just cooling off. Waiting for him to catch up.

No such luck.

Blackness lifted as a stage curtain, plunging Rav back into the dreary mist and sedge of Lower Usher. His blistered feet and chafing armor set the scene in excruciating detail. Soldiers in Dianessa navy and gold marched across the wooded lowlands. Their burdens swayed on the backs of squinting, wooly-headed llamas, nimble footed on the difficult terrain. Smoke brewed in the distance accompanied by the cloying stink of human flesh commended to flame.

A commotion ahead brought his sword to hand, body crouching low, eyes scanning for danger. His comrades surrounded a figure in a black mantle, face blood-streaked from a slash across her forehead.

She raised her hands in surrender. Desperation and pain shone vivid in her sea green eyes.

"Asylum!" she shouted in heavily accented Lanica. "Asylum! Asylum!"

Her limbs betrayed her, and she dropped to her knees.

"Lower your weapons!" Rav barked, sheathing his blade and shoving through the bristling throng. He thrust aside the nearest sword trained at her throat. Then he turned back to her, showing both hands empty of weapons.

"It's alright," he soothed, unsure if she understood. "I'm a medic. I can help you."

The woman met his gaze, focusing all her failing senses on forming a single word. "Asylum."

Rav nodded. He considered a moment. "*Te cura*," he pronounced in careful Paxat. "You are safe."

She let out her breath. Then her eyes rolled closed. He caught her before she dove face first into the mud.

The scene melded and skipped. He ducked through the entrance of a spacious tent lined with cots and racks of medical equipment. Gentle lantern light flickered from canvas walls. The green-eyed woman sat up on her cot, looking about with a keen, anxious gaze. A bandage bound her head. He didn't recall tending to her wound, but he knew, nonetheless, that he had done so with care.

Her face relaxed as she caught sight of him. She spoke in quiet, urgent tones. He shook his head with an apologetic look. Lifting a finger in the universal gesture of "hold on for a second," he took a small book from his pocket and thumbed through the thin, crinkled pages until he found the phrase he sought.

"My name is Rav. What is your name?"

"Ariel," she replied.

"Well met, Ariel," he replied in Paxat.

She laughed. Rav smiled, encouraged by her amusement. His pronunciation was sure to be all wrong.

"How is your...?" he searched through the book, grew impatient, then touched his own forehead to convey the rest of the question.

She answered. He consulted the pocket dictionary, then nodded. Sore.

"Permit me?" he asked, gesturing to her forehead.

She nodded. He unknotted the bandage, gently inspecting the wound. Fearing he might cause her pain, his fingers shifted in a simple but powerful pattern of numbing glyphs. She inhaled in surprise.

"Hurt?" he managed.

"No."

She took his hand, examining his fingers between her own.

"Witch?" she asked.

That word he recognized. It rang similar in both languages, but the connotation could not be more opposite.

"*Te cura*," he assured her. "You are safe."

She turned his hand over and pressed her fingers to his palm. When she lifted them again, an obsidian five-pointed star glittered like dark, polished glass. Rav traced the star's angles with fascination.

"Witch," she said, pointing to herself. "Asylum."

He lifted his gaze to meet hers and repeated, "You are safe..."

"Ugh, too sweet," the gusty voice hissed at his ear.

Rav lifted heavy eyelids to the darkened cave.

"I smell something mouthwatering," it whined. "Where is it? Wait. What's that?"

A wolf snarled, lips curled back over fearsome teeth. Blood glistened on her coat. Rav knew the sea green eyes, wild with desperation.

"Ariel?" he murmured in low warning.

The wolf whined softly. He lifted a hesitant hand toward her muzzle. She sniffed, red tongue swiping her jaws.

"Easy. Let me help you."

The wolf collapsed, rusty flanks heaving. Her eyes closed and her body shrank, fur melting into the remnants of a tattered black dress. The wounds, gruesome enough inflicted in a wolf's hide, scourged her from the nape of her neck to the bottom of her spine.

Rav tugged his jacket from his shoulders and draped it over her.

"I'm sorry," she shivered. "I didn't know where else to go."

"You did the right thing. Let's get you inside," Rav said.

He lifted her against his chest, careful not to jar her as he ferried her up the darkened path toward the manor. The grizzled groundskeeper, a self-taught scholar who defied the tyrants of academia longer than Rav had been alive, peered out the carriage house door.

"Double the wards, Mr. Harris," Rav instructed. "We're sure to have company on the way."

"Yes, Milord."

A weather-beaten woman with a scar hooked in a permanent question across one cheek met them at the door, crossbow clutched in her gnarled hands.

"Hot water, if you please, Mrs. Winchester."

"Sir."

She paused, taking a closer look at the invalid in his arms.

"Is that who I think it is?"

"Quickly, Mrs. Winchester," he asserted.

She hurried off, shaking her head and cursing in a low hiss. Queen of the kitchen by day, guerrilla insurgent by night, his head chef could whip up a Wintertide cake or a landmine with equal speed and skill.

He cleared one end of the immense dining table with an arm and laid Ariel down, setting to work drawing glyphs to slow the bleeding. The rest of the house had woken, gathering to whisper in the doorway. Mrs. Winchester barked at them to get out of her way as she hefted a basin of water. A boy at her heels carried an armload of rags.

"That's her?" the boy piped. "Lady Death?"

"Quiet, you," Mrs. Winchester snapped. "Really, Milord? My good tablecloth? How do you expect me to get all that blood out?"

"I'll get you a new one, Mrs. Winchester, I promise. Send them out of here."

The cook bellowed at the gathered spectators, herding them out and closing the doors. She returned to the makeshift operating table, watching him work with a seething scowl.

"I already know what you're going to say," Rav murmured.

"Would it have been so hard just to let her bleed out where you found her?" the old woman growled.

"She needs our help," Rav insisted. "We're not going to turn her away."

"Are we to forget, Milord, that she tried to kill you?"

"That was a misunderstanding," Rav answered.

"You're not invincible," Mrs. Winchester scolded. "That wicked worm of a notion that's burrowed into your head has made you more reckless than ever. Whatever you think, you can still bleed. Still die."

"One day, yes, but not today, Mrs. Winchester, and until that day, this house will remain open to anyone in need of sanctuary." He met her steel gaze with metal of his own. "Whether you approve or not. Now, will you please go see about a bed and clean clothes?"

The seething cook growled incomprehensible frustration and left him to his work. He had managed to quell the worst of the bleeding. The jagged punctures, too precise for animal teeth, spoke of some wicked piece of machinery.

"You were right about the Cosmologists," Ariel's quiet admission startled him. He hadn't realized she was awake. "And she is right about me. I am a danger to you all."

"They won't get past the wards," Rav assured her. "Mr. Harris is very good at his job."

"That isn't what I meant."

"Everyone under this roof is dangerous, Ariel. That's the reason we're all gathered here. Just lie still."

When muscle and skin had been knitted in fresh layers, Rav cleaned away the last of the blood. Some scarring remained, but it might fade given time. Mrs. Winchester returned with garments scavenged from among the manor's more generous inhabitants. The cook pulled him aside while their controversial guest changed.

"The attic loft is made up," she informed him.

"You're not putting her up there," Rav protested.

"We're full to the brim. You want someone to give up their bed? Ask them yourself."

"She can have mine. I'll take the loft."

"You're impossible!" Mrs. Winchester hissed. "I will not have the staff know you're sleeping in the attic."

"Is there a window up there?" Ariel interrupted, joining them.

Rav nodded. His pulse tripled as she neared. From the scathing glare, his cook also noticed the way the newcomer turned his head.

"Then let me have the loft," Ariel insisted. "Please."

"Of course," Rav breathed.

Mrs. Winchester grunted and turned on her heel. Cursing yet again as she made her exit.

"She'll come around," Rav apologized. "And you don't have to stay in the attic."

"I'm not robbing you of your bed," Ariel said.

"You're not. It's freely offered."

Ariel smiled. "Is it? I'll remember that, Rav..."

"Ack! Disgusting! Curse you!"

The throttling fingers gouged deep.

"I smell it! The horror. Where is it? Give it to me!"

Victor Skylark's condition had taken a steep downhill plunge. His face paled to a waxen corpse pallor. Shallow gasps struggled to raise his sunken chest. His spirit clung to its sinking ship with wavering tenacity.

Ely stood at the foot of the bed, Leanora and Peggy poised at the dying man's shoulders. There would be no healing without first lifting the curse inadvertently flung at his heart. Ely lifted his hands, a maestro conducting the death magic embedded in the winding lacerations. Victor gasped. His milky eyes opened. Leanora and Peggy pinned him down.

Ely arched his fingers, and fine black particles spilled from the wounds, compassing his outstretched palms. Whispers echoed in his ears and raised gooseflesh on his neck. This was not everyday death magic, channeled and filtered through his own veins. This was something ancient. Primal. Ripped from the depths of the universe.

When the last of the death magic lifted, Victor released a gasp of relief and sank back into unconsciousness. Ely drew the swirling matter together between his palms, fusing and shaping it until it compacted and hardened. When he opened his hands again, he held an iridescent black butterfly. Ely slipped it into his pocket for later study.

Leanora selected a smooth indigo stylus from among a selection laid in a row. Her workstation consisted of two wicker card tables wedged along the wall. One for her implements and another with a contraption fitted with a light and a magnifying glass.

Peggy placed her fingertips along the outer edges of Victor's wound. Leanora stepped forward, taking a steadying breath. The helyx trembled as she pressed the stylus to its base, crackling and clicking. Emitting warning jolts of pale electricity.

Ely withdrew the helyx that reposed in his own pocket, whispering, "Nix, we need your help to calm her. Please."

Nix whirred to her sister, hovering above her. "She does not like analog glyphs," Nix informed them.

"If I use the spirit encoder now, it could kill Victor," Leanora explained. "Please tell her we can save them both if she will let us."

Nix hummed softly. The angry electricity ceased. Cautiously, Leanora applied the stone stylus, etching a delicate row along the rim. Ely marveled at her astonishing speed as she transcribed the arrangement of characters from rote memory. She worked with the same intensity of concentration as Dr. Faidra, though Leanora rendered the exercise exquisite rather than formidable.

Peggy worked in tandem with her employer, fingers shifting healing patterns. The pilfered manuscript leaf lay on a stool at her side for reference. Neither Peggy nor human Rav seemed to need the aid of soul to mend flesh and bone. Perhaps, then, true healing was a trait inborn. Like death magic.

The helyx vibrated. Victor groaned, and his milky eyes sprang wide. Peggy moved her ministrations to his temples to sooth him back to merciful stasis. Leanora coaxed the machine free. The doctor carried her burden to the makeshift workstation. Nix hovered over her shoulder.

Victor gasped again but now lay too feeble to stir. Ely felt spirit seeping from the battered husk. He raised his hand, pressing back against the runaway soul. Dark blood seeped from the cavity, but Peggy's fingers raged against the flood. Fighting nature's brutal course. Peggy paused to peer at Rav's page, then renewed her efforts. Forging a dam of raw fibers to curb the blood.

At last, the gruesome crater disappeared. A spiral of fresh pink skin left the only remembrance of injury. Victor's chest rose and fell in a gentle rhythm. His life force settled back into reforged veins. His eyes opened, and he raised a hand to his heart.

"It's gone," he breathed. "The pain. It's gone."

Peggy uttered a quiet gasp. Tears glistened in her eyes.

"Is that you, Ms. Osai?" Victor asked.

"Yes, Mr. Skylark," she choked, taking his outstretched hand.

Ely glanced at Leanora who stood at her workstation, staring at her brother with a ghost white cheek. Hand pressed to mouth, she fled for the cellar stairs.

Victor strained to sit upright. Months of prolonged illness left him weak. Ely helped brace him while Peggy propped pillows behind his back.

"Where's Lea?" Victor asked.

"She stepped out for a moment," Ely said. "I'll go find her."

He found her outside leaning on the landing. Tiny frame quaking. Ely set a gentle hand on her shoulder. She collapsed in his arms with a sob.

"It was all my fault," she whispered.

Ely stroked comforting fingers through her strawberry waves. "What happened to your brother was an accident. The magic you stumbled upon at that fortress is something that no human was meant to touch. Whatever Kai was doing, it was dangerous. Believe me, he knew better. He should not have brought you there."

The words tumbled from his lips with vehemence that took him by surprise. After that dizzying merry-go-round of contemplation. How had he only just realized he was furious at Kai?

When her tears ran to salt, Leanora drew back. Eyes blazing red. Ely searched his pockets for a handkerchief. He found one folded neatly, R.L.A. stitched in gold at a corner.

Many thanks, Rav, he toasted in silence to the absent hero of the hour.

Dawn had arrived in a rosy concerto. Another night gone with no sign of the vampire. It seemed his friend really wasn't coming back.

Leanora dabbed her face dry, and they made their way to the cellar. Peggy sat at the bedside, Victor's hand still clutched in hers. They spoke in low tones, smiles aglow on both their faces. Victor turned his head toward the entrance. His heart had been repaired, but his eyes remained pale and blind.

"Lea?" he asked.

Leanora approached, still unsure for a moment. Then she rushed forward and wrapped her arms around her brother's neck. Victor smiled, embracing her with enthusiasm.

"So," a tinny voice interjected, "we're just going to leave the device to suffer now?"

Nix floated by Leanora's work table where the other helyx lay secured beneath the magnifying glass.

"You're right, Nix," Leanora apologized, straightening up.

She returned to her table and selected a crystal clear stylus like the one Dr. Faidra used to wake Nix. Light pulsed from the conical tip.

The helyx vibrated. Flashes of fevered color burst along fine fractures in the ball's surface. Muffled static crackled from beneath.

"She is trying to communicate," Nix explained.

"Do you understand her?" Ely asked.

"The audio input is too distorted," the helyx replied.

Nix focused a pulse of white light toward her ailing sister's surface. The other helyx droned and shivered. It answered with a weak stream of light that separated into chromatic bands.

"She said she wants to see Victor," Nix replied.

Leanora looked uncomfortable with this request, but Victor directed, "Bring her here, Lea."

She loosened the clamp from the helyx. It drifted in a wobbly, uncertain pattern into Victor's waiting hands.

"Hello, my beauty," he smiled, leaning her gently against his cheek. She made soft crepitations. Then she fell dark.

"Mel?" Victor murmured.

The helyx shuddered back to life.

"You have to let my sister help you. She's brilliant with circuitry. She's your best chance to get well. Alright?"

The helyx—Mel?—blinked. Victor held her out to Leanora. The doctor took the demon artifice back to her workstation. Nix droned just above her shoulder.

"Nix," Ely called, gesturing her to follow him upstairs.

Safely out of earshot, he asked in a hushed voice, "Will she make it?"

"She has a fractured harmonic transformer," Nix informed him.

"I don't know what that means," Ely said.

"They are similar to your amygdalae," Nix explained.

"My what?"

"The regulatory organs in your brain that moderate emotion and memory."

"Oh. That's not a good thing to fracture then, I take it?" Ely asked.

"It is not ideal," Nix confirmed.

"Do you think she will be able to tell us where to find the next sister node?" Ely asked.

"He's a brother node, actually," Nix corrected.

"Oh. Sorry."

"That's alright, Elyssandro. He is called Prometheus. He..." Nix emitted a stannic chortle. "He's very humorous. You'll like him. I already extracted his location. Back when I first ran diagnostics on Melandromache."

"Why didn't you say so, Nix?" Ely exclaimed.

Nix wobbled. A shrug, perhaps?

"The probability that we would continue on our journey without helping my sister exceeded a comfortable threshold."

"I'm sure I can't argue with your math. Will you tell me now?"

"Of course. He is in the valley of eternal smoke. I have reconstructed the map."

Light spun in gridlines from the center of her eye, forming a basin between tree-ridged bluffs.

"Can you give a broader view?" Ely asked.

"Certainly."

The map shifted, drawing out a continental shape with a small circle marking Prometheus's whereabouts.

Ely frowned, tracing the latitudes with a finger. "That's in the Protectorate."

"It is a disputed territory according to the metadata," Nix said.

"Rav would know exactly where this is," Ely pined.

"He does seem to be proficient in geography," Nix bobbed. "Let me cross reference with my geospatial systems. Ah. Yes. That appears to match the territory of Usher. Specifically the lowland region known for volatile organic compounds which interact with atmospheric substances to produce perpetual vapors."

"Valley of eternal smoke?" Ely asked.

"That would be the logical conclusion," Nix agreed.

"Usher...Usher. Why does that sound familiar?" Ely wondered. "Well, this is going to be quite a trek, isn't it? And we still have to scour South Sea to find wherever Rav's holed up."

"He's not in South Sea anymore," Nix informed him.

"You know where he is?" Ely demanded.

The demon eye curtseyed in the air. "I scanned him too. You know, just to keep tabs on him."

"Damn it all, Nix! Why didn't you say so before?"

"Hmmm. This looks promising," the airy hiss commented.

Rav plunged into a sea of jeering visages. Manacles weighed down his wrists. Blood flumed in channels past his eyes. The crowd swarmed like frenzied apes, lips peeled back in grimaces. Spitting, howling, tearing at his clothes. His captors shouted at the crowd, forcing them back so they could haul him to the platform in the center of the square where the hooded executioner loomed.

He scanned the sky. It stood a bright crystal dome. No clouds. No birds. No sign of rescue. Was this really the end? It couldn't be. Not yet.

"Keep fighting, Rav."

The mantra rang in his thoughts as it had every day since he met the time traveling conjurer. Ely was supposed to come back. They were friends somewhere in the future. So, his death could not be today.

"Keep fighting, Rav."

He lunged at the executioner, striking out with the irons that gouged his wrists. Ducking swords and grasping hands, he charged for the back of the platform where chestnut horses shifted nervous hooves. A running leap landed him a mount. The horse bellowed and galloped for the gap in the square. If he could lose them in the Etrugan Channel, he could make it to...

Thunk.

The whistling bolt drove him face down against the horse's neck.

Thunk. Thunk.

He tumbled from the saddle, cobblestones rattling his bones and snapping one of the crossbow shafts lodged in his back.

"Keep fighting, Rav."

He dragged his limbs from the ground. Looking down, he found a metal barb protruded from his chest. Painted black with his heart's blood. Someone grabbed him as he sank, but his eyes had gone dark. He tried to speak, to draw breath. His pulse floundered.

How? It wasn't time yet.

Agony ebbed numb...

"Wake up, Rav!"

The conjurer's voice roused him from the precipice of long ago death. He tried to stir but found himself still mired.

"What did you do to him?" Elyssandro growled.

The creaky voice shrieked, "I finally dug it up! It's mine! Delicious despair!"

Rav opened his bleary eyes, blinded for a moment by flickering lavender light that spilled from a wrought ether lantern nestled between two stones. The shriveled succubus scrabbled for his neck with long, hooked fingers. It squeaked with dismay as Elyssandro gripped it by the shoulders and hefted it into a delicate grove of stalagmites.

Black magic spilled from the conjurer's hands, coiling about the creature's limbs to drag it back to his clutches.

"You like despair?" the harrowing legion overlaid his voice, booming from the cavern walls. He clapped the creature's bulbous head between his hands. Fingers sank indentions in its pale skin. "We remember every death that ever was. Gorge."

The monster gasped and wailed. Its eyes bulged from its skull. It convulsed, skin crackling and curling like burnt paper. Then it crumpled into ash at the conjurer's feet.

Elyssandro lowered his hands. Death receded from his eyes. When he regained his equilibrium, he rushed to Rav's side, helping him sit up.

"She left you some nasty bruises, that little goblin thing," Elyssandro said.

"I heal quickly. No need to fuss, conjurer," Rav grunted, smothering an outpouring of gratitude and relief. "How did you find me?"

"Apparently," Elyssandro smiled, settling himself on a smooth stone with a shoe propped on the opposite knee, "N-I-X keeps track of our whereabouts. Which is either sweet or concerning. Or both. I haven't decided yet, but it's certainly been useful thus far."

Rav watched him, perplexed by all the conjurer contained behind his friendly cast. Plumes of feeling, too frazzled together to name, spilled into the eternal tide between them. He wondered if his own emanations felt as bewildering.

"Victor Skylark is on the mend," Elyssandro continued. "He may not see again, but he'll live. Thanks to...you know why."

"Yes, I understand the gallant and indomitable Lord Aurelio had a magnificent gift. Named gods rest his soul," Rav dismissed with a scornful flash of fang. "You know, I sometimes still feel the phantom itch of magic. Like a lopped off limb. He would have been a lot more use after your wrestle with the Hollow."

"You taught me how to help myself," the conjurer countered. "Besides, olden days you couldn't have saved my life with nothing but his teeth."

Rav hissed at him and turned his back, drawing his knees to his chest.

"We have our next destination," Elyssandro ventured on.

"Where?" Rav sat up straight.

"It's called Crucible Valley now," Elyssandro said. "In your time it was—"

"Lower Usher," Rav finished.

Elyssandro caught his arm, apprehension amplified through contact. "Can I say something before you fly off?"

Rav paused, only just realizing that he had, in fact, been gathering momentum to launch through the crevice in the cavern ceiling.

"I'm sorry to have offended you. I was a leaf on the wind, and Death dashed me right on your front stoop. I never meant to trespass."

Rav found himself staring at his companion as he calculated the illogical journey back to the Spine. A ship from South Sea would have reached West Usher in no time at all. From there it was only a short hike to the valley. Why come all this way just to apologize?

Elyssandro frowned, worrying through his words for a moment. "I know that I fray your nerves. But so far, we've only succeeded together."

The conjurer paused, waiting for something. A response, perhaps? Yes, Rav considered, he should probably speak or nod. Show signs of life. When he did not, Elyssandro pressed on.

"We could travel after dark. Maybe I could get a horse."

He shook his head.

"No, that would be a disaster. I'm not good with living animals. I'll walk fast. I can keep up a very brisk gait when I–"

"Conjurer, are you under the impression that it's *your* company that is unsavory?" Rav interjected.

"Isn't it?"

Rav's laughter volleyed between the dripping rock formations. "My mind has been carved up and cauterized into oblivion. Now, I get the distinct pleasure of that ill-fated buffoon's memories hemorrhaging in my head. I don't have the barest clue what I might do next. I'm not holding the reins at present."

"But that's exactly my point!" Elyssandro exclaimed. "We're walking acts of god, you and I. One wrong turn, and we're liable to wipe a city off the map. But you seem to be able to steer me off the road to ruin. And I think I could do the same for you."

Rav eyed him, straining to surmise what possessed this fool of a conjurer. He laughed to himself again. The answer to that question had just disintegrated a succubus with visions of a thousand deaths. Perhaps they were kindred terrors after all.

"Alright, conjurer," he said. "If you fancy a walk with a mad monster, be my guest. I hope you still have a stake on hand."

MOVEMENT 3
Winter's Bones

Chattan

Chapter Seventeen

The Coming of Night

Breathless cold. Dancing silhouettes. Fluid, untenable vibrations rose and crested like ocean cathedrals. Form and figure did not exist here. Only timeless void. A space behind matter where the unseen drifted listlessly beyond the reach of mortal perception.

Ariel coursed through the shadow planes with practiced haste. There was far to travel and little time. All too soon a distant rumble would drag her back into haunted dreams. At least as a wandering shade she might peer out on the world that had left her behind. A spectral spectator.

She found them as she left them. Ambling over mossy hills between endless moon-drenched pines. The whirring sphere buoyed ahead, spreading warm light over an overgrown forest path. The beaming conjurer loped just behind, excitable curls unable to keep pace with his swiveling head as he took in his surroundings with evident delight. A dark, sullen figure stalked at the rear, sharp eyes darting between shadows. Brahm's monster. Unholy desecration of the best of men.

She had followed them from the skeletal ridges of the Spine through the weirded wastes of Dianessa to the empty wilderness they now trod. They traveled under cover of darkness, subsisting on handfuls of starlight. Sometimes they tracked the miles in silence. Sometimes conversation took flight, leading them on through the dark, fevered hours past midnight.

"I've been thinking, Rav. The fortress to the north. If the Canon gets its hands on death magic..."

"An unspeakable disaster, yes."

"Will they be able to use it?"

"Maybe. Even channeled clumsily like your Dr. Skylark's unfortunate incident presents a hazard. The more time they have with the relics left behind, the greater the peril..."

"What does the L stand for?"

"What L?"

"Your initials. I know the R and the A. What's the L?"

"Lovelace."

"Lovelace?"

"No. Stop it, conjurer. I forbid you to be charmed."

"I thought it would be solemn. Lovelace. How delightful..."

"Oh, you can thank Riri for that little gem. And any other colorful language in my arsenal."

"She's your Etrugan friend that detests me?"

"Detests is a strong word. But yes. Rión Twin Axes. She used to visit the University with her mother when we were young. And I would spend summers in Fjarat. We got into a lot of trouble together."

"Why did you stop?"

"She found a mate. Had children. War with the Canon. No, I'm lying. It was me that drifted away. I left everything."

"After they hurt you?"

"I wanted so badly to live like an ordinary man. Home. Family. I thought somehow because Death gave Kai back to me, that we were fated to be."

"You brought him back too?"

"I killed him first. It was an accident, but that makes no difference in the end."

"Is that what brought him to the northern wilds in search of a Cosmologists' fortress?"

"I've wondered a great deal about that..."

"What are you talking about a hideous monster? Sure, it's hard to tell when you're covered in dirt, but splash a little starlight on your face and you clean up very handsome."

"Don't take this the wrong way, conjurer, but most of your associates are missing their skin. I'm not sure I trust your aesthetic discernment."

"That's ridiculous."

"And you're sleeping with that mousy little academic."

"What's wrong with Leanora? She's got eyes like an alpine lake and hair like...like...lustrous carrots. And she's brilliant."

"She shot you."

"Water under the bridge, my dear Lovelace."

"Please answer me this, conjurer. Do you think Sir Quinn handsome?"

"Exceedingly. Ah. Alright, yes, now I see what you meant..."

Sometimes they stopped in a moonlit meadow or at the summit of a sweeping vista before sunrise drove the monster underground. Often during these pre-dawn interludes, Elyssandro uncased his violin and played soaring melodies that nearly lured Ariel out of concealment with their soul-stirring vivacity.

The monster too sat spellbound. It was only in these moments, when the firelight lent warmth back to his skin and the music humanity to his expression, that Ariel could bear to look at him. Was he really so different from the gifted healer and renegade lord she had loved so fiercely? There was the same lean, hollow look to his face. Dark, serious brows. Eyes like the sea at twilight. Same voice. Same bearing. Was it fair to revile him so?

Then the moonlight would catch the pale, bloodless cheek or glint from a vicious fang, causing her to withdraw into the darkened void with shuddering disgust.

When she happened to come upon them during daylight hours, she often found Elyssandro sitting on a fallen log, deep in contemplation as he stared at a fragment of death magic resting in his palm. It was shaped like a delicate butterfly, but even in her present ethereal state she felt its gravitational force. Immense as a supernova. Ariel longed to assume a more corporeal form and ask about this strange amulet. She did not dare disrupt his contemplation. Instead, she observed her fellow conjurer, fascinated by the weighted stillness that came over him in solitude.

Then the monster emerged from soil and root, a dead thing clawing from the grave. Elyssandro always sprang up to greet his loathsome companion like a dignified hound whose exuberant tail insisted upon making a fool of him.

The filthy monster met his enthusiasm with a disdainful sigh and a muttered, "Good evening, conjurer."

It was not until Elyssandro turned away that the faintest ghost of a smile visited the monster's lips.

On this particular night, she caught up with them mid-journey. Elyssandro appeared in a transcendent mood having discovered a snowy, nocturnal queen of the sky. The monster seemed more out of sorts than usual. His fingers agitating his uncouth hair. Eyes wild.

"If you utter another word about that mangy owl, I'm going to fly after it and wring its neck," he snarled.

Elyssandro turned to look at him, brows raised in concern. "Are you having headaches again?"

"It's nothing," the monster muttered.

"Maybe we should rest," Elyssandro prodded.

"Just keep walking. We're bound to find an end to this godforsaken forest soon."

The monster winced and unsheathed his horrible teeth. He pressed his hands to his temples, unleashing a hair-raising howl. The helyx darted into the conjurer's coat pocket. With unearthly speed, the monster charged the stoutest tree in the vicinity and dashed his forehead against the trunk.

"Rav!" Elyssandro exclaimed, sprinting to restrain him.

The monster tossed him keel over deck. Elyssandro scrambled to his feet again, brushing leaves from his clothes and limping doggedly back up the incline to where the monster knelt. Brave? Stupid? Certainly stubborn.

The monster stared straight ahead, looking dazed but subdued. He accepted the helping hand to regain his feet.

"It looks like you've hurt the tree more than your head," Elyssandro observed.

"He is concussed," the helyx diagnosed, bubbling from its hiding place.

"Stop scanning me, demon," the monster hissed.

"We'll rest here awhile," Elyssandro insisted.

They settled in the crooked roots of a monolithic tree. Elyssandro built a fire pit while the monster hunched in a secluded corner.

"You should eat something," Elyssandro prompted.

The monster huffed and snatched a handful of starlight that tumbled between the autumn bare branches.

"Do you want to talk about it?"

"There's nothing to talk about, conjurer. Just another of his unsolicited memories detonating in my head."

"Well, tell me about it. It'll make you feel better."

The monster exhaled. He stretched out long legs, digging bare toes into the soil as if he might plant himself there.

"He stands at the forefront of a wide chamber. All eyes are fixed on him. It is freezing cold but the vile vipers that watch him are sweating. Oh, I recognize every single face in this room. He knows they hate him, but he can't even fathom the deranged fantasies they harbor when they look at him. But I digress.

"Our hero is in a righteous passion. There's a man with him. Young. Mid-twenties. Missing an arm. He's in a ragged coat. Hair matted. No doubt *you'd* insist he's handsome. He does have skin.

"The noble Lord Aurelio addresses the chamber, 'This is August Vane. He survived three years among the vaporous killing fields of Lower Usher only to spend another three as a prisoner of war to the Canon.'

"Oh, I see where this is going. I won't bore you with it. He continues on in a speech about the man's sacrifice and suffering only to be cast aside upon his return. He says there are many such men left in ruins by the war but denied proper treatment for their ills. Named gods, what an insufferable bore he was. He might have saved his breath if he knew what reprehensible reptiles he appealed to."

"That's really no reason to try and brain yourself, Rav," Elyssandro admonished.

"It wasn't the speech. It was the hell fiend watching from the second riser. I nearly got my teeth into her throat."

"Who?"

"I'm going to be sick."

The monster disappeared into the darkness, his whereabouts projected only in the sounds of retching.

"Rav?"

"Vomiting is to be expected of a concussion," the helyx droned.

Ariel watched confounded as Elyssandro fretted at the fire with a poker stick, gaze locked in the direction the monster had fled. The scene reminded her of an old folk tale she once heard of a beautiful princess whose betrothed had fallen under a terrible curse. While the princess stayed faithful to her beastly love, the bloom faded from her cheek and her comely frame twisted and bent with careworn age. She died a withered crone, desolate and alone. It was not until the beast wept on her grave that his spell was broken. Too late.

Presently, the monster slunk back into the firelight.

"That fatuous lunatic was truly the author of his own destruction," he spat.

With that, the monster curled into the crook of a tree root, sinking into its shadows like a demented ghoul.

"Sweet dreams, Rav," the conjurer called.

Silence.

Elyssandro sighed. Then he retrieved his violin from his pack and set bow to strings as though he might himself weave those sweet dreams into the gloom.

Rhythmic pulsing disturbed the shadow planes. No. Please not yet. *Return.*

"Elyssandro!" Ariel called through the thickening veil.

He stopped playing and turned his head toward her plea.

Return.

The Hollow wrenched her back to her faraway body. Deep into a waiting nightmare.

Chapter Eighteen

BALLAD OF THE DAUGHTERS OF PARRIS

Winter stirred its chilled, long-slumbering limbs. The fallen leaves lost their autumnal fire to brown, brittle decay. The evergreens kept their frosty crust long after the sun arose.

Ely had lost count of the nights they had traveled in the magnificent wildlands of Usher. Vast and unspoiled by humans, he had fallen madly in love with the way the light sifted through the branches. The birdsong. The thump and flutter of fur and feathers. Many of the forest's occupants had settled into hibernation, leaving only the dry rustle of the wind for company. And occasionally a phantom presence that lingered just out of view.

Ariel had been following along since they departed the Spine. As she never seemed inclined to make herself known, he pretended not to notice when she joined them on their journey. It had been some days since he felt her. Perhaps she didn't like the cold. Perhaps the Hollow was regaining strength.

As the last lingering daylight dripped along diamond-tipped pines, Ely threw the rest of his kindling on the fire, attempting to melt the chill from his bones before Rav joined him for the nighttime tour. He felt the vampire's presence beneath the frozen earth a few paces away. Muted with sleep but ever present at the periphery.

Staring into the flushed flames, Ely's thoughts tread back to his final hours in South Sea. Leanora had promised to tune Melandromache into working order before his return.

"You *are* coming back, aren't you?" she asked, sky crystal eyes fixed on his face. Just the right way to make a heartbeat quicken.

"Yes, Leanora. I'm coming back," he promised.

"For the helyx?" she clarified.

"That would probably be the right reason," Ely answered, brushing a strawberry curl from her cheek.

"Probably," she nodded, gaze straying to his lips...

The snap of a twig drew him back from sweet mistakes. Something approached. He focused a moment to take in the shape of it. Man-sized. Slight limp to the right foot. Definitely living. Definitely human.

The stranger strode from the trees. He carried a heavy pack with a bedroll strapped to the pinnacle. A cloak lined in peppered fur draped his shoulders, a black cap with a silver buckle covered his pate, and thick white whiskers weatherproofed his folded cheeks.

"Spare a seat at the fire for a peaceful traveler?" the man asked. He spoke in a strange, rustic dialect of Paxat.

"Of course. You're welcome to it," Ely replied in his native tongue.

Alarm rippled from underground. Ely sent a warning tremor in response, entreating his newly awakened companion to stay hidden.

The stranger hefted his pack to the crunching leaves along with a slender crossbow. A flutter of the cloak revealed numerous glints of metal. It appeared the peaceful traveler was heavily armed.

"Gratitude," the stranger rasped. "I took a turn betwixt the wrong trees."

"Where are you headed?" Ely asked.

"Crucible Valley," the stranger replied. "I hath business in the township of Parris. And thyself?"

"Just passing through," Ely answered. "Do you have a name?"

"Forgive me. I am Father Meritus Hale."

"You're a priest then?" Ely asked.

"Witch hunter," the man responded.

"Ah, of course," Ely nodded with a pleasant smile. "Are there many in these parts? Witches, I mean."

"Oh, yes. Wherever there be men to waylay. Though the terrain be difficult and the elements unforgiving, the witch doth always find a way in."

"Yes, yes," Ely nodded in solemn agreement. "Bolt the door and they doth find a window or some such. What sort of witch are you looking for? Troth tell."

"A necromancer," Father Hale glowered.

"Oh, terrifying."

"Abominable. It hath murdered young maidens and possessed their corpses."

"That doesn't sound good," Ely commented. "Parris, you said? Is that far? Prithee."

"Just over yon rise," Father Hale pointed.

"Thank the named...erm all praise to the One."

Father Hale grunted as he strained to his feet. "Well, I thank thee for thy gracious hospitality. I must be on my way."

He tottered and pitched toward the fire. As Ely reached to steady him, the witch hunter sprang back like a wiry jackrabbit, flicking a thin chain against Ely's hand. The stark white metal seared where it touched his skin. His pained cry fell short as he peered up the long snout of a pistol.

"I knew thou hadst a touch of devil about thee," Father Hale growled. "Tell me, necromancer, what evil hast thou visited upon the good citizens of Parris?"

"None yet, but now I just might be tempted," Ely snapped, clutching his singed hand.

"Thou shalt tell me how to unravel thy mischief so I may speed thee to a merciful end. Speak not, and I shall prolong thy suffering tenfold."

An explosion of rocky soil and splinters threw the witch hunter from his feet. The gun made a sharp retort. Ely clapped his hands to his ears, head ringing.

Father Hale rose, attempting to free another of his weapons. Shadowed arms snaked around him and carried him screaming into the newly starred skies high above the treetops. The body crashed to the foliage, neck wrung, throat punctured.

Rav dropped at Ely's side, Father Hale's blood curling over his chin. "Are you injured?" the vampire demanded.

"Not mortally, but that damned trinket burned like the dickens," Ely hissed. "Look, there's already a blister coming up. What is that?"

Rav knelt to examine the alabaster chain. He jerked back his fingers with a curse.

"I just told you it burns, Rav. Weren't you listening? Nix, will you scan this bit of wicked jewelry, please?"

Nix bobbled from Ely's pocket. "This is a strange alloy," she mused. "It does not match anything stored in my archives."

"It's a Covenant Lash."

The ethereal voice startled all the gathered company. Its owner followed, shimmering to near solidity in their midst.

"Ariel. Just in time," Ely half-grinned, half-grimaced. The burn was growing decidedly worse. "A covenant what now?"

"Covenant Lash. It reacts to death magic. That's why you can't touch it," Ariel explained. "You're going to need a hamamelis salve."

"Please use real words," Ely grumbled.

Rav, who had frozen into a grimy, bloodstained statue, reanimated to interject, "I can find it."

He disappeared into the darkened undergrowth. Ariel visibly relaxed when he had gone.

"How ever did you avoid getting caught with angry old friars running about lashing everyone?" Ely groaned.

"That is not a time I like to remember," she replied. "But it was you, Elyssandro, that gave me the courage to leave."

"Glad I could help. I never did get a chance to thank you for your assistance with the talisman. You have my eternal gratitude for that."

"Set me free. We'll call it fair," Ariel replied.

She fell silent as Rav made his return. The vampire held what appeared to be a handful of hairy yellow spiders.

"Witch hazel," he explained.

Rav popped the tentacled winter blossoms in his mouth. Then he wound a trickle of starlight around his fingers and mixed it with the mashed flora.

"Hand."

Ely held out his welted palm, and Rav applied the slapdash salve. The instant relief excused the crudeness of its manufacture. Rav tore the already ragged hem from his shirt to mummify the dressed wound.

"Many thanks, Rav. That's much better."

Ely glanced back at their visitor, but she had vanished. No lingering apparition. Rav also seemed to have noted her departure. Melancholy torrents coursed from him.

A distraction. Create a distraction.

"We're very near a town called Parris," Ely said. "Father Hale here was on his way to hunt a necromancer."

"Perhaps, then, we should search for a way around," Rav suggested.

"Or, hear me out, we go to this town and find an inn. Shower. Eat a hot meal. Then find out who's possessing corpses."

Rav's eyes narrowed. "We haven't time for your games, conjurer."

Ely countered his glower with a smile. "There's a method to my madness, my dear Lovelace. Who in this valley is more likely to know the whereabouts of our demonic device than the local witch?"

"I can't think of a better way to get burnt at the stake than to plant yourself in the middle of a town that's already employed a witch hunter to sniff out undesirables," Rav spat.

Ely picked up Father Hale's peaked cap from where it toppled, shining the silver buckle with a sleeve. "Not if we're the ones doing the witch hunting."

"Are you suggesting...?"

"A disguise," Ely nodded. "You can have the cape. You'll look dashing in a cape."

Rav eyed him doubtfully. "Might I call to your recollection the last bit of play acting we attempted?"

"These are simple country folk, Rav," Ely replied as he relieved the dead man of his implements of trade. "We have quite a convincing display of props to choose from. What could go wrong?"

The township of Parris comprised a collection of rough timber cabins surrounding a single thoroughfare. Post office, cobbler's shop, and tanner's warehouse. Blacksmith. Baker. General store. Everyday needs and nothing more. Gossamer mist rose in ghostly wisps. The famed eternal smoke.

On a high hill overlooking the town resided a rustic but sizable chapel, Canon blade crowning its brow. Ely felt his skin crawl at the sight of it. Disguised as he was in the witch hunter's cap and collar, he still blanched under the dead-eyed gaze of stained glass glinting in the moonlight.

Rav walked a solemn caped shadow at his side. He wore also Father Hale's boots and rapier. Having paused at a stream to clean away the blood and the most conspicuous of soil patches, he resembled his former self more than Ely planned to tell him.

"It's late in the season for roses," Rav murmured.

Ely followed his eyeline to the chapel on the hill. It was difficult to make out, but he assumed the vampire's keen eyes could better discern the patchy shadows interlaced around the structure.

It was still early evening, though the sun had been sinking earlier every day. The villagers had not yet retired indoors for the night. They found the postmaster still at his post.

"An inn? Crucible Station be just at the end of the row. Thou wouldst find a welcoming fire and a hearty meal. Goodwife Simple usually hath many choice rooms."

"Crucible Station. Ask for Simple?"

"Yes. It be the noble establishment adjacent to the mill."

"Many thanks."

They found the noble establishment by a gurgling brook that rolled an ancient-looking mill wheel. Oversized barn might better describe the structure, but since it overflowed with men in peaked caps and rugged travel cloaks, Ely assumed this must be the place.

The interior stood a hot, smoky den overtaken by tired furniture and lit with reeking tallow lamps. A fire roared in the hearth, adding a layer of dry heat to the sweat of too many men in cold-weather dress.

Ely hailed the lone woman running about with a rag and a duster. She wore a blue potato sack of a frock with a draping white collar and a white hood to match. Despite the unflattering costume, she possessed a pretty face with rosy cheeks, warm brown eyes, and rosebud lips.

"Are you Goodwife Simple?" Ely asked. "We're looking for a room."

"I am she, but I fear I hath no rooms to spare this night," she said.

"Yes, I see you're very busy," Ely nodded, hopping out of the way of two men comparing daggers with wild gesticulations.

Goodwife Simple's eyes darted past him to Rav then dropped anchor there. "Thou art here to join the hunt?"

"Yes," Ely nodded. "I am Father Santara. This is my associate, Father Lovelace."

"Blessed to make thy acquaintances, Fathers Santara and Lovelace. On second ponderance, I do hath one chamber left vacant, though there be but a single mattress."

"Not a problem, we'll take it," Ely said.

"A moment, then, to fetch the key. Make thyselves comfortable."

She offered Rav a smile most unbefitting of a good wife, then rustled off, skirts swishing. In the meanwhile, Ely lent an ear to some of the pastoral looking patrons convened in conversation.

"Giles Proctor's daughter be the last taken by the fiend. Yesterday morn."

"Not young Annabel. She carried such a healthy bloom."

"Aye, she did at that. A rare and enticing beauty. It be propitious you should mention her bloom. She was last seen at the doors of the sanctuary wrapped in the devil's blossoms with blasphemy upon her fair lips."

"Is it true the fiend hath o'er taken the holy house?"

"Aye, its hallowed ground hath been befouled of sorcery. Four maidens now it hath gathered in its thorns. It is said Judge Proctor along with Bertrand Winthrop, Milton Thomas, and Samuel Farrow went up the hill and ne'er returned."

"I see why such a company hath been summoned."

"What are they saying?" Rav whispered.

Ely glanced up at him. He had forgotten his companion didn't speak the language. "The girls are at the church. It seems our friend has set up shop there. You were right. Those roses aren't natural."

Catching sight of Goodwife Simple scanning the jammed commons, Ely squeezed past a couple of stout, white-haired men to meet her. She presented him with an iron key, a bit rusted at the ring.

"Up the stairs thou canst turn the lock on the last room to the left," she said. "Frivolities commence at half past eight."

"Frivolities?" Ely asked.

"Aye. To celebrate the great and goodly men who challenge the minions of evil without fear," Goodwife Simple replied. "Tonight we shall eat and drink and be merry. For tomorrow dawns a black day wherein thou shalt all band together to exorcize the terrible scourge that seeketh to cast our dead to damnation."

"So," Ely recapitulated, "am I to understand that every witch hunter in Crucible Valley is here now?"

"Aye and its surrounding territories," the innkeeper chimed. "We have yet to receive word of good Father Hale, but otherwise, there be thirty-four present. Thrice a dozen with thee and thine most winsome companion."

"Oh, rapture," Ely choked on his benevolent expression. "I will tell Father Lovelace at once of these joyous tidings."

Ely made a gently alarmed beeline to where Rav stood absorbed in a painted landscape framed on the wall.

"Rav, don't panic, but there's an army of witch hunters here to catch the necromancer. Three dozen counting us."

Rav nodded, countenance unchanged. "Naturally."

"The goodwife is throwing a party in their honor tonight. *Our* honor, I should say."

"Thou shalt join us tonight, wilt thou not?"

The innkeeper approached, batting long doe eyelashes at Rav.

"Of course, Goodwife Simple," Ely replied.

"Oh, please, callest me Abigail, kind Fathers," she sang, mostly to Rav, who had twisted away as far as he might without actually turning his back.

"We will be at thy shindig, Abigail," Ely assured her politely. "Now, if thee'll excuse us. We must doff our travel attire."

He seized Rav's arm and steered him toward the stairs.

"What does she want with me?" Rav frowned. "Have I given us away already?"

"No. No. She'd like you to call her Abigail. And she'd very much like to call you Father. I think the cape has done its job too well."

The room proved little more than a converted stall with a lumpy bed on a rattletrap frame and a bucket tub with a pump spout.

"Still think this is better than the woods?" Rav droned.

Ely sighed. "It's a bit more rustic than I anticipated."

Rav kicked off the dead man's boots and tested the mattress. Ely lifted the handle on the spout. Russet water gushed into the tub.

"So much for cleaning up."

"By all appearances, you'll blend in better down there with a healthy layer of topsoil," Rav said.

"Was it this primitive when you were here?" Ely asked.

"We were further west. There was a decent port city, but I don't know if it survived. I was already interred whenever Usher finally fell. From what I've seen today, the Canon sent them back to the Twilight Ages."

"They did the same to Saint Lucio," Ely said, taking occupancy of a worn chair. "Named gods, I was so stunned when I arrived at Dianessa to discover lights without fire, respite from the elements, and a bathhouse full of hot water. Even under the Curse that city is a marvel."

"As it ever was," Rav said. "A marvel with a rotten underbelly."

"You despised it, then?" Ely asked.

"No. I must have loved it. *He* must have. Why else would he have fought so hard to save it? Died for it."

Rav lifted a burning gaze. The smoky lamp caught the hidden blue in his dark eyes.

"Did I tell you he was thinking of you when he died?"

"You didn't," Ely murmured, heartbeat suddenly solemn.

Rav nodded, a wild, fevered look stealing over his face. "They marched him up to the gallows to answer for his defiance. You told him to keep fighting. So he did. You were the one thing he believed in to the last beat of his heart."

"I'm sorry, Rav."

"Why would you say sorry? You've given me all of this," he gestured to the room with a laugh. The pillow spit a puff of dust as the vampire collapsed back.

Ely watched him for a moment, unable to bring himself to ask the questions that breached his mind. Instead, he returned to the pump and splashed icy rust water on his face.

He unwound the bandage from his blistered hand. The welts had faded to a faint line. No pain. As vehemently as Rav rejected his past self, Ely wondered if his friend even realized how alike they remained. Perhaps he didn't want to see.

"Move over, Father Lovelace. I need a little shuteye before we go down to the witch hunter soiree."

Rav eyed him, making room on the bed. "We're not seriously going, are we?"

"Of course we are. A party is the best place for reconnaissance," Ely said, determined to ignore the stains on the quilt as he slid underneath. "But I'm still tired. It's been far too cold for a good rest."

"You're not going to get any warmer sleeping next to me," Rav said.

"Just keep your feet on that side. Oh! Do your trick."

The vampire swept two fingers to Ely's temple. Sleep descended in a blissful curtain. Rav's voice followed him as he drifted off.

"Sweet dreams, Elyssandro."

The party rolled at high tide when the Fathers Santara and Lovelace made their entrance. The cramped commons now filled to bursting with townsfolk gathered to join in the festivities. A red-bearded fellow plucked a lively banjo accompanied by a buxom lady with a trilling harmonica. Mead and wine circulated in plentiful supply. It seemed the township of Parris had clung to something of a lively spirit despite the long arm of the Canon.

Ely fetched two glasses of mead. Rav sniffed the honeyed concoction with unfiltered disgust.

"It's just a prop," Ely said. "You don't have to drink it. Enjoy the music. I'm going to perambulate. See what I can find out."

The great and goodly Fathers appeared more interested in reliving their previous glories than discussing the details of the hunt at hand. Ely sipped his mead, wading through tales of pyres built, heads spiked, and hands severed. From talk of the bounties collected, witch hunting made a lucrative profession. Particularly if one could bag a necromancer.

"Thou shalt never get close to yon church, Father Warren. Not with those puny instruments of salvation," boomed a bear-broad man with his head bound in a linen bandage.

"Thy formidable claymore made no better case, Father John," sputtered a wire-thin witch hunter with a stringy yellow mane.

"I at least passed the threshold, a feat no man among thee can claim."

Father Warren shot a daggered look and stamped off. Ely filled in the gap left behind.

"Did I hear you say you've been to the church, Father John?" Ely asked, refreshing the rosy-nosed rector's glass.

"I have, aye," he said with a nod. "Remind me of thy name, my young confederate."

"Father Santara."

"Santara? I do not recall thee from our last full congregation."

"I'm not surprised. Thou wast hitting the wine cask rather hard wasn't thee, Father John?" Ely said with a nudging elbow.

Father John erupted in guttural laughter, raising his cup and draining it to the dregs.

"Now," Ely continued, setting an encouraging hand on his jolly round shoulder, "what's the word on the church? Did you speak to the necromancer?"

Father John shook his head. "I saw not the witch, only the defiled daughters of Parris. I charged in head on but found myself battoned back through a window. I was rendered then unconscious and woke in the care of Goodwife Simple."

"What can you tell me about the victims? Is there anything that connects them?"

"They all hail from fine, upstanding families. Strong in conviction. Their paters hath served the Canon for generations. It be a cruel and deliberate blow taking pure and innocent maids to stain with sin upon the grave."

"What sin?" Ely frowned.

"They walk as unholy sirens, profaning the church of the One with wicked tongues," Father John replied in a low, graveled voice.

"So, what are they saying?" Ely asked.

"Wicked things."

"Right. Such as?"

"I darest not repeat."

Ely stifled a groan. "Nice catching up, Father John. I see you needest a refill, and so doth I."

As he set off in search of his fellow charlatan curate, he felt an inaudible yelp of distress emanate from across the commons. Rav stood trapped in a corner behind the skirts of the not-so-goodwife. The vampire seemed to be trying to evanesce through the wall, a look of panic on his pallid face. Ely elbowed past a reeling witch hunter, narrowly avoiding a waterfall of mead.

When Abigail made her proposition with all the subtlety of a sonic blast, Rav bolted past her, knocking the wind from her sails and smashing into a table on his way to the door. To his credit, the vampire did not run much faster than could be attributed to everyday adrenaline. The table, however, met a bitter end.

Ely held out a hand to the stunned Abigail. "What were thoust thinking throwing thyself upon a man of god?" he scolded. "Are thee ...thine...thou badly bruised?"

"Forgive me, Father," she whined. "The spirits hath addled my head."

"You can say that again. Go find some other occupation for thy wicked hands."

Ely kicked aside the smithereens of the table and headed out into the eerie mist.

"Rav?" he called.

The vampire did not reply, but the wave of revulsion, shame, and confusion laid a clear trail to a coven of trees near the creek. He found Rav crouched high in the branches of a sturdy oak.

"I hope I didn't cause too much of a scene," his voice descended as Ely approached.

"Nothing to worry about. You reacted remarkably well, all things considered. She should not have laid hands on you without your consent."

"I can't play at being human," Rav murmured. "I'm sorry."

"Don't be," Ely said. "People get very discourteous when they've written you into a fantasy. But you know that all too well, I've gathered."

"I don't want to talk about it, Elyssandro."

"You don't have to," Ely said. "But it might help to—"

"It won't. Whatever was left of desire or passion, it was strangled with a collar and made obscene. His enemies paid fortunes for the chance to possess him body and soul. But he was gone. I bore the brunt of their violence and lust. They sent me back to the Tower a used and broken thing not worthy even of the merciful kindness of death. I don't want to remember, and you don't want to know."

Ely sat down in the elbow of a limb outstretched near the ground and leaned his head against the oak's bearded trunk. It felt like resting under a weeping thunder cloud. He closed his eyes and pictured the gentle solitude of a sandy shore, waves lapping about his feet. The scent of woodfire smoke under simmering food. The caress of a salty breeze. Peace. Safety. Home.

Rav released a quiet sigh. Silence settled. The branches rustled above, and the vampire returned to solid ground. He allowed himself a breath and pushed his hair out of his eyes.

"Shall we go investigate those misbehaving corpses?" Ely asked. "Get your mind off it?"

"Yes, I'd like that, conjurer."

The pale mist thickened to revenant clouds as the ministerial imposters took the steep path to the church. Thorny creepers ensnared the outer walls and knotted above the roof slats. Their roses lifted voluptuous petals in praise to the full moon.

The front door dangled off its hinges. Inside, effulgent flowers shed uncanny light on a sanctuary lost to primeval wiles. Ely drew in an awed breath as he crossed the threshold. He felt like he stood in the presence of something fathomless.

Death gave an amused nudge and directed his attention to the pit that swallowed the center of the floor before he stumbled over the edge. Deep in the jungled abyss, he made out thick, tangled roots. An arm, a leg, and the crown of a head jutted out from between them. Perhaps the remains of the villagers that had climbed the hill never to be heard from again.

Rav sprang into the air, disappearing into the overgrown rafters above. Ely tread carefully over the vegetated boards. Four dainty figures stood at the foot of the altar, their girlish frames wound around with delicate, flower-studded vines.

"Hello?" Ely called.

A miniature figure clad in green moss emerged from the shadow of the eye and blade. Dark cherub cheeks, wide button nose, and black coils, she appeared a child no more than five at most. Lambent golden eyes marked her true nature.

"Hello, Morgata," said the girl.

Death bent their head in acknowledgement. This was no mere child. She was something ancient. Powerful.

"I am Nemesis," the being declared. "Spirit of divine vengeance."

"Pleasure to meet you," Ely said. "I'm–"

"I know you, Elyssandro Santara Ruadan."

"Great. Excellent. No introductions then," Ely said, palms breaking out in a cold sweat. "So, what brings a named god back to Canon territories?"

"Their blood summoned me with cries for justice." The grave little goddess motioned to the flowered quartet assembled behind her.

"Why? What happened to them?"

"Sit, Elyssandro," Nemesis bade.

Ely settled in the silhouette of the pulpit. A shadow dropped at his side, tensed in a defensive posture.

The goddess inclined her head to the vampire. "You also are welcome, Ravan Lovelace Aurelio."

She lifted her hand and blew a gentle gust. Glowing spores danced from her fingertips and burst in sparkling golden embers against Rav's face. He sneezed.

"Now the dead may speak to you both," Nemesis explained.

She motioned to the first girl. Sixteen perhaps with hair like straw, wide blue eyes, and a heart-shaped face.

"I am Lilabet Farrow," she said. "My father be Samuel Farrow, keeper of tomes and talismans. He holdest a respected position, and is renowned throughout the territory for his wisdom in matters of doctrine.

"Every fortnight since I can remember, we traveled o'er the far hill to Saint Pomona to visit mine aunt at her orchards whilst he traveled abroad in consultation with great and goodly men. In my sojourns there, I become bosom companion to the servant's daughter, Giselle. We played such riotous games as children, and as we grew toward womanhood, we found a common love for lyrical poetry. When we met in the orchards, we read aloud our verses and commended them to song.

"I thought I had entered the realms of Heaven when first she kissed me under the blossoming apple tree. Our songs ever after spake of forbidden delights and secret longings. It were mine aunt that discovered us. I begged her to tell not my father of our trespass. She would not listen. He took in her words in silence and spoke not at all on our journey home.

"When we reached Parris, he took me inside and locked the door. He took a belt to me. And when that did not cool his anger, he put his hands to my neck."

Lilabet lifted her chin, and the vines that covered her parted to reveal the black fingerbone bruises that marred her tender throat.

"Named gods," Ely murmured.

Rav rippled unspoken dismay.

The second girl stepped forward. Full-cheeked and black haired. All of thirteen.

"I am Mary Thomas. My father be passed on from this world, and it be left to my uncle, Milton Thomas, to look after our home. By custom, he should marry my mother, but he say she be plain and he hath not yet decided if he shall take her to wife. Myself, though, he found most winsome. He took to visiting me in the dark of night. He told me also that were I to uncork my lips and speak the truth, he would break my pretty neck and leave me in the woods.

"It took six long months to garner courage enough to tell my mother. She slapped my cheek and called me liar. Wench. Harlot. She bid me be silent. I begged her to plead my case to the judge. She dripped poison in my cup and set me abed as though I slipped away in the night."

Mary Thomas stepped back. Nemesis touched her cheek gently, then held out a hand to the next girl in line. She was no taller than the golden-eyed goddess. Narrow gray eyes. Cheek painted with a spectacular purple birthmark.

She lifted her hands and signed, "I am Madeleine Winthrop. My father be Bertrand Winthrop. He aspires to one day serve as minister of Parris. He saith I look not as a proper minister's daughter. When I spoke not either, he saith I hath the mark of a witch and must be locked away. For my own salvation.

"I have not seen the sunlight since my last birthday. It be close and damp in the cupboard under the stairs. I fell sick. My father saith it be for my own good that I take no more bread or water. I fell asleep some days past and never woke."

Nemesis nodded and patted the girl on the hand in gentle encouragement. The last of the fallen maidens stepped forward. Long chestnut hair, deep brown eyes, and a dimpled chin.

"I am Annabel Proctor. My father be Judge Giles Proctor. He presideth over the court of Parris. He is known well in these parts, and his name doth mean all to him.

"In the bloom and flower of springtime, I made sweet acquaintance with a young prosecutor that took residence for a season in our fair township. Many an afternoon we spent in heavenly fellowship. We whispered of all things beautiful, forlorn, and forbidden. He departed with the fall of autumn leaves. I discovered soon after I was to be left with more of him than memories."

The flowered vines uncurled at her waist, outlining the gentle slope of her belly.

"When I told my father the tidings, he tore at his hair and cursed me for befouling the name Proctor. He struck me and pressed the pillow over my face until I moved no longer. The babe lived on within me for hours before her heart too stilled."

Ely wiped a tear from his cheek, looking between the fresh, unlined faces. Blossoms crushed underfoot.

Nemesis approached. "Their tormentors lie now beneath my vengeful roots," she declared, gesturing to the pit. "Their price is paid. But the wrongs done these innocents have trapped them here. Me with them. They need your help."

"My help?" Ely echoed.

"To move on," the goddess canted. "You have born witness to their stories. Will Death be kind and grant them peaceful passage?"

Ely glanced at Rav then back to the childlike deity. "You want me to kill them?"

"Free them," she corrected.

"They're so young," Ely lamented. "Wouldn't it be better to try to restore them? I don't really know how, but maybe with some godly advice I could...?"

"Were you not listening, Elyssandro?" Nemesis reproved. "In their short years, they have suffered. Would you deliver them to more suffering? You have the power to return them to the sublime stardust from whence they sprang."

Ely stared at the floor. Truth sprouted ugly thorns in her words. He could not deny them. A cool hand descended on his shoulder.

"She's right, conjurer," Rav murmured in his ear.

Ely nodded. He stood, chest constricted as if his heart gasped in a python's coils.

"This is what you want?" he asked, eyes moving one girl to the next.

Lilabet. Mary. Madeleine. Annabel. Each in turn inclined her head.

Ely took a breath and held out a hand. One by one, the troubled souls loosed their earthly bonds. Death greeted them with the softest of songs.

The creeping vines lifted their charges and laid them gingerly in a row. Then Nemesis raised her hand, and the vines evaporated, covering the avenged daughters of Parris in a shroud of vibrant blooms.

The goddess turned back to Ely, eyes aglow.

"You have aided me in my mission, and I do not leave debts unpaid," she said. "You are here for a purpose, are you not?"

Ely nodded. "We're looking for something. A device. It might look like a stone egg or a silver ball."

"The helyx known as Prometheus," Nemesis stated.

"Yes!" Ely exclaimed.

Nemesis inclined her head, expression too sober for her youthful features. "I fear you still have far to travel. While you have tarried here, another seeker has plundered the tomb in which the demon artifice rested."

"What? Who?" Ely cried in alarm.

"An Apostle."

"Titus," Ely growled. "Damn him. Do you know where he's taken it?"

"He is still on the move," the golden-eyed goddess replied. "Traveling north. Your demon familiar should be able to follow."

She took his hand and deposited a gilded teardrop in his palm, small but weighted.

"I leave you with the seed of vengeance," she said. "May it come of aid to you in your quest."

"Thank you," Ely said.

The goddess inclined her head. Then she crossed her hands before her chest and dissolved in a flurry of golden spores.

Midnight descended on the vaporous forest. Once again, the stately wooden soldiers of Usher surrounded the intrepid travelers. Nix paused in her navigation to pulse and buzz in search of her missing brother. She adjusted their direction by a few degrees, and they strode on.

Parris lay three days behind them, but the ballad of its lost daughters underscored their steps. The townsfolk hailed them heroes having driven the evil necromancer from the chapel. Fathers Santara and Lovelace were to be immortalized as the most exalted of witch hunters. None would ever care that the true villains lay digesting in the roots of an enchanted thorn bush.

Night or day, Ely found his mind returning to the florid sanctuary. At first, it was the spiritual sepsis of his part in the curtain call of four young lives. Then existential exposition subsided to the low echo ever eating away at his consciousness.

"She's right, conjurer."

Three words. Endless torture. Repeated over and again, mile after mile. Rav too seemed lost in rumination. Perhaps the words of the goddess shed a light for him that Ely still feared to look upon.

"Do you think I did the wrong thing?" he asked abruptly.

Rav eyed him sideways, startled from his thoughts. "You sent them to their rest. That's all you could be asked to do. You can't go resurrecting everyone that meets an untimely demise."

"I'm not talking about the girls," Ely said.

"What then?"

Ely stole a shaking breath. "I had the opportunity to tell you everything. To warn you. Maybe I could have spared you all of your suffering. I didn't want to return to a future without you in it. But I didn't ask what you'd want."

Rav considered in excruciating silence.

"It all comes back to the parable about the merchant," he said at last. "Have you heard that one? No? It blasted into my memory last week. Made my nose bleed. So glad it can be of use.

"A merchant goes traveling abroad and meets a mysterious woman all in black with a crow perched upon her shoulder. Or maybe it was a raven. She's mystically macabre. I'm sure you can picture the scene. She tells the merchant he will die in a fire, and he becomes so obsessed with avoiding his fate that he goes mad. He loses his home. His livelihood. His family. Everything that makes life worth living. Until at last, he sets himself ablaze."

"So you're saying it was all inevitable?" Ely asked.

"I don't think his fate would have changed," Rav concluded. "You may absolve yourself of whatever guilt you've latched onto."

"What if you didn't take the fatalistic view?" Ely pressed. "Did I make the right choice?"

"I would rather not be dead or cursed," the vampire said.

Ely trudged onward, still dissatisfied. Rav stopped and took hold of his arm.

"Alright, Elyssandro, I'll say it aloud and not just leave it to weight the air between us. I am astonished and deeply moved that you cared enough for me to leave him to his fate. Whatever acid spills from my tongue at times, I'm here with you because I want to be. My plans for greeting the sunrise have been postponed indefinitely."

"That's very good news," Ely grinned.

"Put your smile away and listen. If there comes a day that I am lost to madness and you must choose between us, have no doubt that I want you to put an end to me."

"Rav..."

"If you can't promise me that you have the strength to use the stake, then I will go far away somewhere the demon can't track me and you can't follow. Do you understand?"

Ely met his somber eyes and answered, "I do. And I promise. But you have to make one too."

"What is that, conjurer?"

"That you will be kind to yourself. Past and present. You can't heal if you're forever tearing yourself apart, and I want to go on adventuring with you for a good long time. If that sounds agreeable."

Ely held out his hand. Rav gave it a shake. Then they resumed their quiet, moon-soaked stroll. Hounding the heels of an Apostle.

Chapter Nineteen

Miracle Aligner

Ariel woke to golden dusk descending on neat trellis rows. Delicate vines laden with clusters of plump violet grapes swept over hillsides beyond view. The apricot stucco and clay tile of a titanic villa crowned a distant knoll.

"Welcome home."

The voice, expected but startling nonetheless, murmured at her shoulder. She turned. Rav leaned against a post, clad in the stern navy and gold of a Dianessa soldier.

"I know it's you," Ariel said. "Why bother with the disguise?"

The Hollow smiled. Rav's smile from the day they met on the misty sedge of Lower Usher. Almost. An echo.

"He's on your mind," it replied. "And you keep running off to see him. Naughty girl."

Ariel eyed it with cool disinterest. "A thousand years and you don't know me at all."

Hollow Rav gave a chuckle that frayed mechanical. "You think not?"

It slithered to her side, leaning close with lips that did not belong to it.

"I know all the secrets that creep and fester behind that mask you've fashioned for yourself," the Hollow whispered. It sucked in a sharp, vicious breath. "Oh, it's so ugly underneath, isn't it?"

Ariel turned away. Hollow Rav caught her by the throat. The figure blurred and transfigured. Complexion darkened. Hair curled.

"Do you think I would cross woods and wastes for you if I knew the crooked villainy that stains your soul?" asked the echo of Elyssandro.

The Hollow rippled again, waning to a willowy figure with the same warm brown eyes that arrested her from the conjurer's face. Ariel's heart gave a sharp retort.

"You earned yourself this prison in the candlelight of the Marble Keep," the phantom murmured in a soft, sweet tone. "Didn't you, Apostle Petros?"

The sky bled gray, and ominous thunder set the vineyard hills undulating.

"No, don't take me there," Ariel breathed.

Pulsing. Pulsing.

She swayed to the rhythm, eyes growing heavy...

"Petros? Petros, wake up, son."

Ariel opened her eyes with a gasp. Cold, stale air lodged in her lungs like barbed fish hooks. A worn face squinted down at her, crinkled brow unfurling with relief seeing her eyes opened again.

"There you are, boy. I wondered if you'd crossed over for good."

"How long have I been gone?" she asked. The voice that issued from her lips rasped lower than her proper tone.

"Six hours," Apostle Prosperus intoned with reverent awe.

"Strange," she murmured. "It felt like eons to me."

He reached out to help her sit up. She had been lying on the floor of a bare vestibule. Dripping tapers housed in gold held vigil around her. Their shadows marched a solemn procession about the bloody curves of a sigil imbrued on the floor.

Death gnashed fretful teeth from outside the circle, separate and shaken. She felt their fears dispel beyond the barrier. Wrath remained. Betrayal.

A warm trickle brought her hand to her cheek, staining her fingers crimson with sanguine tears. Her stomach felt knotted and cramped. Her chest rattled and parched.

"Did you reach it, Petros?"

Ariel shook her head. "We sailed over troubled black waters and treacherous cataracts. There were strange spires and ancient lava beds. Peaceful green shores with joyous music. No sign of the Bone City."

"No matter, son," Apostle Prosperus said with a pat on her shoulder. "We must get you to rest before the day commences."

Death approached like a wary animal as she left the circle. Sniffing at her essence. Curling proverbial lips in distaste.

I have a reason, she insisted.

So you always say, they replied.

Apostle Prosperus unchained the door to the Keep. A dim hallway made thoroughfare back to the many colonnades and alabaster domes of the seaside temple tucked away on the rugged isle of Calurion.

Ariel's suite lay in the shadow of the lighthouse beacon in the eastern terrace overlooking a gray, thrashing ocean.

Apostle Prosperus set a hand on her shoulder. "Get some sleep, young Petros. I will attend you after your session with Father Antonio."

With the door at last bolted behind, she released her breath with a weary sigh. She ached like a ship run aground, mast splintered and sails rent. She drew a chair to the window, collapsing into it and leaning her head against the paned glass. Outside, the gloomy waves writhed. Pulsing. Throbbing. Was this really today?

A soft knock at the door and a voice like a gentle prayer roused her from unsettling questions.

"Petros?"

Ariel rose and stumbled to the door. Sister Miranda Santara regarded her with concern as she entered with a clay stew pot. She had eyes of smoky jasper and black curls that escaped her veil at the forehead and temples. A Watcher's habit could not conceal her divine beauty.

"Petros, what happened to you?" she exclaimed, rushing to lay aside her burden.

"It's nothing," Ariel replied, wiping at her cheek with a sleeve.

"Sit," Miranda instructed.

Ariel did as she was told. The room was spinning, and she felt a fever sweat break on her forehead.

"He took you to the Keep again," Miranda accused the absent Apostle.

"He truly believes I can bring back a new Revelation," Ariel murmured through shaking breaths.

Miranda wet a cloth and bent to clean the bloody tears from Ariel's face.

"He is not keeping count of the cost," the Watcher told her.

"Nor am I," Ariel replied.

"You should be," Miranda reproved. Her voice softened, expression turning earnest. "Someone should. They know how gifted you are. They'll lose no chance to use you down to cracked sinews."

Ariel lifted her gaze sharply to the sister's face. "You should have a care how you speak."

"Am I not safe with you?" Miranda asked, meeting her eyes with a penetrating stare.

"Of course you are," Ariel said. "I only meant they have ears everywhere."

"You think I don't know that?" Miranda laughed. "Or do you forget who you're talking to?"

"Never," Ariel murmured with a weighted edge.

Ariel had come to the Temple at Calurion from the deserts of Marikej. Of the devastating ambush from which Petros Marcellus returned as sole survivor, the scribes recorded that the young Apostle battled a necromancer that had raised the bodies of his fallen comrades in unhallowed battle against him. Only Ariel knew the truth. And Elyssandro, whenever he might be. She had thought she only dreamed him. Until, that was, she spied Sister Miranda Santara planting the terrace garden.

The Watcher, too, was young for her calling. Seventeen at the time of their meeting. Five years at Calurion had forged the most sacred of bonds between Apostle and Watcher. The Canon named such attachments *anselis apostolis*. A familial servitude. Dutiful. Devout. And above all pure. To unwind a Watcher's virgin knot was to sow discord to her power. Choke her visions with loathsome weeds. Ariel didn't know if there was truth to the superstition, but the pyre built by devout hands would burn hot, nonetheless, for a fallen sister. It was as good a hindrance as might be contrived. The more complicated truth need not show her face. Not yet.

"Are you alright, Petros?"

Ariel blinked. She had nodded off with her eyes still peeled. Miranda watched her with distress and set a gentle hand on her brow.

"Should I fetch Father Francisco?"

Ariel shook her head. "I am well. I just need to rest."

Miranda crossed the cell to a small cot cluttered with cast off clothing. She gathered the laundry into a pile and set about righting the sheets that had been twisted in the course of a nightmare.

"Miranda, stop," Ariel pleaded. "You're not a slave to my neglect. I'll set the room in order."

She caught the Watcher by the hand. Miranda halted, straightening slowly. Breath arrested. Ariel lost her own under the Watcher's gaze.

"I am forbidden to give you what I want to give," Miranda said, "much less take what I am dying to demand. So, I will perish as your *anselis apostolis*. The best that ever served."

"You are so much more than that," Ariel insisted. "You should be pedestaled in a temple spiced with incense. Served cake and wine on gilded finery. I should be washing your feet with perfumed oils. Don't cry, my angel."

Ariel brushed the dew from her satin cheek.

The Watcher made a quiet, bitter laugh. "How can I not? You set me afire with your silver tongue and send me back to my desolate bower to burn."

"You think you are alone in the flames?"

"I don't know, Petros. Sometimes you look at me like you yearn for me. But your eyes are so rarely fixed on this world."

Ariel caressed her face. "Don't you see? I'm trying to save it."

"What am I to do if your purpose destroys you?" Miranda asked, gaze intent.

Ariel turned away from the blazing beacons that seemed to puncture her soul.

"It won't."

Miranda sighed. Ariel called after her as she turned for the door.

"I can't be the cause of your undoing."

The Watcher stopped, hand resting gently on the latch. "You undo me every time you open your lips and paint me some golden sunset I'll never behold."

"I love you, Miranda. I would pluck the moon from the sky for a jewel if it pleased you and string the stars beside it."

"Yes," Miranda nodded. "Exactly like that. Good night, Petros."

Ariel let out a slow breath when she found herself alone once more. She sat by the window, eyes cast down to the sea. Its unnatural pulse disquieted her still. Perhaps it was not the sea at all. They said the crossing to the Undying Lands changed a man. Shifted his soul. Crooked his vision in the mortal world.

But I am not a man, she reminded herself.

Before the downbeat of the sea could disturb her eye again, she hoisted herself onto unsteady legs. Cast a nauseated glance at the stew pot. Donned loose fitting sparring linens.

The temple lay in predawn contemplation as Ariel wound her way through the empty corridors to a pagoda at the crest of a high garden terrace.

A gargantuan bell cast in bronze hung from the interlaced rafters. Ariel heaved on the rope. The bell swung a rhythmic pendulum, mallet tolling at either end of its journey. Ariel took up her stance in the center of the platform. At each sonorous strike, she shifted through the motions of a martial pattern. The templar's war dance. Her feet whispered against the boards, and her arms dragged heavy. Poor form. All her lambasted limbs would yield.

"You're unfocused."

The bark arose from the pagoda steps.

Father Antonio, steel-eyed master of metal, advanced with lips downturned in rebuke. "They call you the next in line for the Ascended Throne, but I don't see it."

"Nor do I, Father Antonio," Ariel replied.

"False humility may get you far, but lazy footwork?"

He tutted his teeth.

The sword swept from beneath a disguising fold of his homespun robe. Blade aflame in the morning light. Ariel dove to the dusty ground. A clumsy dodge to his elegant arc. The weapon sang after her, driving her through each motion of her kata. Demanding perfection or death.

A dizzying blow loosened her grip on the wrathful observer that lingered at the periphery. Her vision wavered white. When she blinked back to consciousness, the sword master lay on his back, hand clutching his chest.

Ariel extended a hand. He slapped it aside.

"Apologies, Father," she said.

"Apologize to yourself, boy," Father Antonio grunted, breath short. "Miracles are just that. Fantastic and fickle. What will you do when your prayer goes unanswered and you are left with only your own wanting skill?"

Ariel lowered her head in weary agreement.

Father Antonio waved a dismissive hand. "We're done here. Tell good Prosper he is bound to kill his own prodigy if he presses on like this."

"It's not his–"

Father Antonio laughed and bent to retrieve his blade. "You would not be the first to die for his obsession. Only the youngest."

The disgruntled priest returned his sword to its hidden scabbard. He stumped away, a new hitch in his step.

Ariel sighed, gaze returning to the sea. She had forgotten the strangeness of the waves.

Pulsing.

Pulsing...

"Are you well, Petros?"

Ariel blinked.

She stood in the gilded candlelight of the Keep. Apostle Prosperus leaned close, white beard brushing her shoulder.

"I am well, your eminence," she echoed.

How did she get here? Where had the day gone? The week?

Ariel forgot her confusion as the door to the Keep opened, and a cavalcade of white robed figures drifted into the chamber. They guided a captive with hands chained. A slender slip of a woman. Face obscured beneath a heavy veil.

So it was time, then, to cross over once again. Of course it was. How had she forgotten?

The acolytes pressed the trembling figure to her knees on the stones, hands clasped together in prayer. Apostle Prosperus placed a long-bladed knife in Ariel's hand. It was cast in bronze and etched with sacred sigils. She took her position behind the sacrifice, drawing the knife in a swift, fatal line across the unknown throat. An acolyte took the blooded blade and handed Ariel a golden chalice. She held the cup to the crimson fount and brought it to her lips. Death gnashed their teeth, enraged by the ritual disrespect.

Tongue ringing metallic, Ariel took the chalice to the faded sigil on the floor. Death separated from her as she stepped inside its faded bounds. Their terror echoed after. Pleading her to turn back.

I have a purpose.

Ariel knelt at the watchful eye drawn in the center. From her belt, she took a tapered crystal shaped like a pinion. *Aplora di ciarra.* Feather of Heaven. It was an ancient relic, passed down from the first Apostles.

She dipped the chiseled end like a quill in the blood of the sacrifice and renewed the symbols around the circle's perimeter. Then she sat with legs crossed, arms outstretched, breath rhythmic as, one by one, she tapped her thumbs to each finger.

Otherworldly wind crept up behind, whispering through taper flames and wrapping her in misted tendrils. She breathed in the vapors and in a gasp, found herself alone on a stone pedestal under a fuchsia sky. Below, a calm bay sheltered a gleaming white ship with full sails. A lion's head roared upon the prow.

Ariel descended the stone steps and swiftly trod the familiar path to the solitary dock. The captain with his grizzled beard and empty eye sockets waited aboard the ship amidst a crew of silent, solemn souls. Seekers of immortality indentured for eternity before the mast.

"You return," the blind captain intoned in a lilting language Ariel knew without knowing.

"I seek the Bone City," she replied, the same tongue rolling fluent from her lips.

"I advise you, as always, to return to the domain of mortal Death."

"And, as always, I decline."

The captain nodded his gray head. "Then let us depart."

The damned crew went about their work, and the ship set forth on uncharted tides.

Weeks.

Months.

Years.

Time marched to an unsteady beat in the Undying Lands, purpose lost where Death held no sway. They sailed past lush islands where ethereal songs lured from verdant shores. Ariel had made the mistake before of setting foot in Paradise. She nearly forgot herself. A nameless immortal lost to mindless pleasure. Such existence turned to madness.

They sailed past strange cities and haunting jungles. Blackened ruins of ancient lava flows. White mists beneath a bloody disc of a moon.

Decades.

Ages.

The blind captain and his muted crew pressed on into dark and dangerous waters where monsters wide as cities lurked at unfathomable depths.

Ariel had never seen this stretch of ocean before. They were close this time. She felt the presence she sought growing nearer. Drawing her in.

Then came the tempest.

The iron sky poured torrents like steaming pitch, and the waves roared mountainous.

"Yare! Yare!" the captain bellowed. "Bring in the topsail. Devil plague this howling wind!"

Ariel rushed to join the crew in battle against the storm.

"Lay a hold!"

Water crashed upon the deck, sweeping men out into the thrashing sea. The mast groaned, and the hull begged aloud for mercy.

As they rose on the back of a towering wave, Ariel peered into the valley that yawned below. A flash of blistered lightning outlined ephemeral walls and towers.

"We've split! All is lost!"

Ariel woke in the Keep, water erupting from her mouth. Apostle Prosperus thumped her back while she wretched out the salted ocean.

"No!" she cried, striking her fist against the marble floor. "It was there. I saw it just below. We were right there!"

"No matter," Apostle Prosperus soothed. "No matter, son. You'll get there."

Ariel looked up trembling. Tears heavy with blood.

"You don't understand," she whispered. "We were a thousand years at sea. We've never been so close."

"Come. Rest. We'll try again when you've recovered."

She left the sigil's boundary, but Death stayed at a wary distance. Ariel stumbled on, too weary to care they regarded her like a stranger. She hardly reached her apartment before her bones failed. Blissful nothing descended.

When she opened her eyes, she found herself tucked into bed. Miranda sat on a chair, an open book unattended in her lap. The Watcher leaped to her feet, a smile more radiant than Heaven upon her lips.

"I feared you'd never wake," she cried, reaching to steady Ariel as she rose.

"How long have I slept?"

"Days," Miranda sighed.

"I saw it, Miranda. The Bone City. It hides in the midst of a furious tempest. I felt him there. Like he's waiting for me. Testing me."

"And what Revelation could you possibly receive that's worth your life? " she demanded.

"There are many ways to suffer across that threshold, but dying is not one of them."

"You are mortal the moment you open your eyes to *this* world," Miranda rebutted. "Whatever dark and terrible plan possesses you to return again and again to the Undying Lands, abandon it. Come away with me. We'll seek asylum in the Free Cities."

"Lower your voice," Ariel hissed. "We can't speak like this here."

"Then let us go to where we can speak freely."

"Please, Miranda. I beg you, be silent."

Miranda clasped her hands, voice tremulous with passion. "I can't any longer, Petros. I can't help them shape this world to their crooked will. With or without you, I will renounce the veil. Let them drag me before tribunal. Let them light the pyre. Let them—"

Ariel interrupted the rest of the declaration with divine blasphemy. Miranda melted into her arms, drinking in her kiss like a desert flower in summer rain.

Ariel drew back, stroking the Watcher's face between her hands. "Speak no more of deadly things," she beseeched. "Until I have fulfilled my purpose, I must stay here at Calurion. I need you safe at my side. I beg you to trust what I cannot speak aloud."

Miranda's face distorted, and for a moment she appeared as a rotted corpse. Ariel leaped back, knocking Miranda off balance and nearly losing her own feet.

"What's wrong?"

The gruesome vision passed, and she beheld the Watcher's flawless face regarding her with alarm.

"Nothing," Ariel choked. "A moment. I need a moment."

The room swayed. This wasn't right.

That wasn't how tonight ended.

The walls assumed a heartbeat, palpitating in and out. Then she stood again in the Keep, ceremonial knife in her hand. Hooded victim held before her with wrists chained.

Ariel attended the ritual in a delirium. Sweat-drenched. Frayed of breath. Her hollow chest rattled as the creeping mist transported her to the Undying Lands.

She was greeted in the throes of the tempest. It caught her up and hurled her from peak to valley. Salinated water filled her lungs. The violent sea crushed her in its folds and spit her forth again in torment so fierce she yearned for beneficent Death.

Weeks.

Months.

Years.

A groaning monster snapped her up in its jaws, and she spent an eon in its slow digestive tract. Then back to the swelling waves.

When the mollified waters at last set her ashore, the Bone City loomed before her. Its gate stood open. Unguarded.

Ariel rose on feet stripped to bare bone. As she hobbled down streets paved with broken teeth, the city lay still. Deserted. Curved ribs stacked together into rows of high rises with spinal column colonnades. Skulls grinned down from the bulwarks. It appeared the god of eternal life built his kingdom in grotesque tribute to Death.

The path came to rest at a palace built within the ribcage of a primordial beast. Figures towering fifty feet high flanked the gargantuan doorway. Crystalline plumes shimmered on their folded skeletal wings. Chains girthy as tree trunks held them fast by bolts screwed into their translucent white chests. They peered down at her through mottled, bloodshot eyes and made no move as she passed.

He waited in the deepest chamber. Bodiless. Blazing. Pure light collected in the vague shape of a man.

"You come at last," he said with a voice like a fiery chromosphere.

"You know me?" she asked.

"I called you," he replied. "Amidst the maze of temptation I have tested you. Astride the raging tempests I have tempered you. There is nothing precious that you have not sacrificed to reach this the holy of holies. You are the champion for which I have waited."

"For what does the lord of light and life need a champion?"

"Come."

She approached the altar. The nameless god fell in step beside her. The walls of his sanctuary melted away, and they joined the traffic of a human city.

"You see here the frantic currents of life ever rushing toward the precipice of oblivion. Mortals must toil and scrape in haste for they know the scythe comes to reap all in paltry years."

"Isn't that what it means to live?" Ariel questioned.

"Mortals know nothing of living," the light being declared. "They know only what it means to die. You who have tasted the vastness of eternity, do you not see the difference?"

Ariel pondered the question with eyes fixed on her exposed foot bones. She recalled the long agony of her immortal journey through the unforgiving tides.

Around her, the faces of the throng began to corrode, the skin flaking and peeling to raw sinew, then naked bone.

"Together we shall banish Death," the nameless god intoned.

Eyes tumbled from shrunken sockets to dangle on fleshy cords. A man in a silk vest caught his moldering head as it toppled from his shoulders. He walked on, unhindered by the inconvenience.

"And bring forth life eternal to all."

Ariel gasped. Apostle Prosperus pounded her on the back while coughing spasms tried to split her spine. Back again in the dim candlelight of the Keep.

"Well, my son?" the Apostle pressed.

She wiped blood from her lips. "I saw him. He showed me...his design."

Ariel shuddered, failing to find words for the horror she had witnessed.

"As my soul prompted, so it goes," Apostle Prosperus crowed, brimstone in his eyes. "I knew it was your earthly ties that hindered you."

"My earthly ties?" Ariel repeated, hoarfrost stealing through her chest.

Apostle Prosperus set a heavy hand on her shoulder.

"Have courage and keep faith, my son. It takes a pure sacrifice to receive a Revelation."

Ariel heard none of the Apostle's next words. She lurched to her feet, stumbling from the circle. Dodging Prosperus' warning grasp, she cast herself to the cold marble floor where the sacrificial victim lay. Her blood still clung acrid to Ariel's tongue. Stained her fingers.

Her hands trembled as she drew back the hood. Even with the iron gag clamped viciously over her mouth and chin, Ariel knew the curve of her nose and the lilt of her brow.

"Miranda," she choked.

Her fingers found the hidden latch under the Watcher's chin and sprang the mechanism. The cruel ore had broken her lips and grooved indentions in her cheeks. Ariel searched in vain for a pulse, hidden breath. Death scoffed at her efforts.

You already know what you've done, they accused.

A knotted hand fell on her shoulder. "It is a difficult path, my son, but you will see one day it was worth–"

Ariel twisted away from the Apostle's grip.

"Do not touch me," she snarled. The vengeful host underscored her voice, setting Prosperus a step back.

Ariel lifted Miranda and carried her down the steps of the Keep. Past the domed pagodas and terraced gardens. Down a steep, slippery path to the rocky shore. After she lay her beautiful burden beneath the wide gaze of the moon, she cast off the Apostle's treacherous form. Cheeks wet, she loosed a wailing cry that drowned in the ocean's roar.

Death took solemn watch, unstirred by her tears.

"Please," Ariel implored. "Give her back."

That is not our nature, the host replied.

"I'll do anything you want. Anything. Don't take her from me."

You want a Miracle? Get down on your knees, Apostle. Beg your nameless idol.

"I am still *your* servant. I haven't betrayed you!" Ariel insisted as Death turned their back on her.

She knelt beside the Watcher's still form and pressed her forehead to Miranda's waxen brow.

"Forgive me, my love," she whispered.

A trilling laugh sounded beside her. Waning mechanical. She sat up to find Miranda gazing down at her with empty eyes.

"Still think I don't know you?" the Hollow asked. "You are the great and terrible failure that destroyed me."

The Hollow shifted back to Rav.

"And me."

A host of familiar figures rose from the shifting ground, pressing in about her.

"And all of us."

"Let me go!" Ariel shrieked.

Surging rage snuffed out the accusing faces like wisps of smoke. The sky fractured. The Hollow groaned and shuddered. Then all fell to black. Ariel found herself back in her body. Her real body, held fast within the heart of the living prison. Wasting no time, she cast her mind free, escaping into the effervescent folds of the shadow planes.

Elyssandro sat beside his fire, violin leaned against his chin. His companion had already disappeared into the depths. He played a melancholy melody with tones that ached and rent. As if he channeled the pain of his slain kin and her loving murderer.

He paused his playing and turned his gaze to where she wavered. "You can go on as a ghost if you like, or you can come sit," he offered, smile ringing all too familiar with memories refreshed.

Ariel strained against her faraway tether until she felt the cold kiss of a breeze on her cheek and the crunch of solid ground underfoot. She took a seat beside the crimping fire.

"Our guide says we're closing ground," Elyssandro told her. "It won't be long now."

"Do you know what you're up against?" Ariel asked.

"Titus?" the conjurer shrugged. "He's a tough old cockroach. That's for certain."

"Not the Apostle," Ariel spat. "He's a puppet. I'm talking about what he serves."

"The nameless god?" Elyssandro asked. "I always thought he was more a metaphor."

"He's real," Ariel said. "Real and dangerous."

Elyssandro considered, brow pensive. "What does he want with a helyx?"

"Nothing good for any of us."

Hypnotic pulsing plucked at her tether.

"Elyssandro," she whispered as the woods faded.

Ariel opened her eyes again to golden dusk on the vineyard. Her father's villa peered down from its high vantage.

"Welcome home."

Chapter Twenty

THE SEPTUS SEAL

Winter winds bit bone-deep on the arid tundra. The shaggy rainbow grasses had not yet donned their raiment of snow. Solid permafrost layered beneath the ground rendered burrowing an impossible feat even for a vampire. A week had elapsed since that terror-drenched discovery.

As a seam of light tossed pale rays in an arc on the horizon, Rav had found that only a shallow layer of topsoil furnished the grass with its roost.

"Ely," he murmured. "I can't get underground."

The tension in his voice shuddered in fearful plumes that stopped them both in their tracks. What few trees braved the arctic chill stooped low to the ground and offered no cover.

Already the sun crowned the distant hills. Ely turned to the vampire, finding him a frozen statue, transfixed by the omen of doom rising into the heavens. Steam billowed from his pale skin like overnight frost evaporating into vapors.

"Rav, snap out of it!" he cried.

Shield. Make a shield.

With a running leap, Ely seized the vampire by the shoulders, tackling him to the uneven ground. He threw ether over the top of them like liquid metal in a mould. If death magic could protect against the violent folds of a rupture, then surely it would save Rav from the sun's wrath.

"Are you alright?" Ely asked.

"Fine," Rav's reply rumbled in his ear.

Ely shifted in attempt to give the vampire a little breathing room, but the hastily constructed shell made maneuvering tricky.

"You didn't think through this configuration, did you, conjurer?"

"No. I saw you smoking and panicked," Ely said. "Are you comfortable?"

"No."

"I can try to rearrange it," Ely offered.

"I'd rather not be roasted while you play architect," Rav grunted.

"Alright. So, we've what? Ten hours until sunset? Give or take?"

"Will it hold that long?" Rav asked. His voice remained steady, but dread seeped from him in pooling waves.

"It'll hold, I promise. Now, I think if we sort of ease over to one side we can make this not so unbearable. Big spoon or little spoon, Rav?"

"What?"

"Roll to the left. I'll slip right here in front of you. Named gods these rocks are horrible. And there we are. Spoons in a very cramped drawer."

Rav yielded the smallest of chuckles as the simile finally struck.

Lesson embedded in stiff joints, Ely spent his next days perfecting the art of the death magic yurt. Its central firepit warmed the shelter and vented smoke. Rav slept in his own sculpted compartment that blockaded any stray sunlight. Ely enjoyed a pliant ether mattress and drifted off marveling at how cunning his conjury had grown.

When they set off into bitter nights, Ely donned his armor, finding its cosmic contours an excellent protection against frostbite. He fashioned a smaller casing for Nix, whose instruments misbehaved in plummeting temperatures.

Rav remained unaffected by the hostile elements. He had already discarded Father Hale's cumbersome cape somewhere in the woods. Barefoot. Face to the howling wind. He appeared nigh on cheerful.

As the polar stars thinned to ice-blue morning, they made camp on the edge of a petrified lake. Ely conjured their lucifugous shelter, as usual, while Rav harvested fuel for the fire from the hardy shrubs and peat-like groundcover. Ely coaxed them to conflagration, burning first violet then ochre as death magic abated and chemistry took its shift.

Ely sat up while the yurt gradually warmed. His thoughts, as they did of late, turned over Ariel's parting words. The Apostle they pursued was, like himself, a conduit. Not to a metaphor. Not to an idea. To an entity. As real and palpable as Death.

The more he pondered Titus's vacant smile, the strange nothingness that emanated where his soul should be, the more he realized the truth he had known all along. The battles he had already fought were but paltry skirmishes in a war begun long before his time. Perhaps before time itself.

He wished he could ask Ariel any of the thousand questions her opaque comments unleashed. There was not even a fleeting prickle of her presence in the weeks since.

Faint whimpering escaped the vampire's vestibule.

"Rav?" Ely called.

No audible answer. Only nauseating dread. Ely peeked through the curtain that shrouded his friend's refuge.

"Rav?"

He found the vampire in a tremulous heap, hands threatening to crush his own skull between them. Ely knelt beside him. Rav made no response to his name. When Ely reached to touch his shoulder, the vampire pounced like a startled tiger, pinning him to the ground with fangs extended.

White haze frosted Ely's vision. The waiting legion itched for an excuse to rain punishment. Ely channeled their fury into just enough barrier to give his throat a thin harbor.

"Rav," he gasped. "Wake up. You're safe."

The vampire blinked. Feral flame receded. Confusion followed. Dismay. Rav shrank back, folding into the shadows.

"I...I'm sorry," he stammered.

Ely followed him deeper into the sunless alcove. The vampire sat with his back braced on the ether wall and his knees drawn up against his chest.

"Did I hurt you?" Rav asked as Ely dropped cross-legged beside him.

"Nothing to worry yourself about," Ely assured him. "I've a hard head, as you know."

The vampire closed his eyes. Tension sculpted pained lines across his alabaster brow.

"I thought I'd reach the end of the flood," he said. "But I fear a tide's been thrown in motion that will never come to rest."

Ely set a hand on his arm. "We just have to ride it out, Rav. Eventually you'll run out of jarring memories."

"How long before I wake from his life to find your blood screaming on my lips?"

"It won't come to that," Ely promised.

"It could have just now."

"I could have stopped you just now," Ely insisted. "Had words failed to wake your reason, I could have stopped you."

Rav watched him with gaze unbroken. Conflicted undercurrents. Hope.

Ely resumed, "I am more intimately acquainted with your fears than you will ever know. But you won't have to live them, Rav. Not with Death at the helm. You're safe with me."

"*I'm* safe?" Rav echoed in astonishment.

Ely nodded, wrapping a reassuring arm about his shoulders. "Always, my dear Lovelace."

Ely's breath steamed white under a half mad moon. Snow fell in feathered wisps. Nix's gentle purr led the slow train. Her warm amber light melted a thin track through the misty darkness. It would be morning soon by the proverbial clock but not dawn. The sunlight hours had dwindled over a week until, at last, the days ran their course with eyes closed.

"So, remind me again, who is Lord Winestone?" Ely asked over the muffling press of his protective mask. Nothing thawed the winter cold like a splash of hot thousand-year-old gossip.

"Lord Winestone was the Speaker of the Council," Rav replied.

"And Freddie is...?"

"His wife. Winnifred."

"That's right." Ely cleared the irritating tickle he had been trying to ignore at the back of the larynx. "She's the one that he sent to orchestrate strategic scandals."

"Correct."

"But she failed to seduce you."

"Him."

"Him. Right. Yes," Ely corrected, dodging an iced bramble. "So, Lord Winestone and his solicitous wife, Freddie, threw their annual Wintertide party and invited you...*him* out into the shark infested waters and you...*he* accepted. Why?"

"Because his cook and various other members of his household were laying explosives at a military foundry, and he needed an alibi."

"Of course he did," Ely interjected, another cough interrupting his delight.

Over their nightly jaunts, Ely had garnered a narrow window into the crocodile-laden swamp that muddied Dianessa's politisphere. The players thus far:

LORD RAVAN LOVELACE AURELIO, the most dashing of healers, soldiers, cavaliers, and rebels

ARIEL MARCELLUS, Lady Death, shapeshifting conjurer, adversary, lover, it's complicated

LORD DORLEUS WINESTONE, the Speaker of the Council of Dianessa, a war-mongering snake in the stateroom

WINNIFRED (FREDDIE) WINESTONE, the elder statesman's young wife whose tiptoes on tabletops launched a thousand blackmails

DR. HARALD BRAHM, the head Cosmologist of the Tower, evil scientist extraordinaire

DR. SELENE FAIDRA, a professor of applied magics, two-faced, back-stabbing technomancer, nauseating even to think about her stupid, deceitful face, sorry what were we talking about?

MRS. WINCHESTER, a cook and guerrilla insurgent, hard-nosed, loyal to a fault

AUGUST VANE, a former soldier turned renegade, one-armed, possibly handsome

KITTEN, the malicious ex-wife who...sorry, sorry, I was just trying to sort it out...

How it all added up to apocalypse? Neither conjurer nor vampire could guess.

Ely freed his face only to smother a cough in the crook of his arm.

"Do you need to rest?" Rav demanded.

"I'm fine," Ely managed through a paroxysm. "We've only been out a few hours. I don't want to lose ground."

Nix puttered a little too close to his head for comfort. "Fangs is right. You have inflammation of the lung tissue."

"It'll work itself out in a few days," Ely gargled.

"Ely..."

"Rav."

The vampire narrowed his eyes but paused mid-rebuttal to ask, "Do you smell that?"

"Smell what?"

"Fire."

Ely detected nothing burning except his lungs.

"There is an excess of carbon dioxide in the atmosphere," Nix informed them. "It appears to be most concentrated in our direction of travel."

They continued their journey in vigilant silence. A line of blazing signals flickered on the horizon. Ely raised a full ether helmet, but even layered death magic failed to filter out the cloying stink.

The inferno simmered to a ruddy glow as they approached what must have been a village or outpost making a brave stand against the brutal elements. Only smoldering walls and blackened posts marked human habitation. Nothing stirred among the ruined buildings.

"What happened here?" Rav wondered aloud.

The overwhelming vacuum of fresh death drew Ely's attention toward the largest of the abandoned town's structures—a church in the midst of devouring flames. A dripping warning marked the padlocked door.

SEPAGARO

"Plague," Ely translated.

They put the town quickly to heel, but the sea of smoke rolled on. The next outpost lay engulfed in a hazy shroud. And the next.

Another night's journey brought them to a larger settlement tucked away in a valley basin guarded by snow-cloaked mountains. A lone sentinel kept watch atop a ramshackle tower where a regiment of purring braziers fought the wintry gloom. He held a crossbow over one shoulder and a flint lock on his hip.

Nix dove into Ely's hands as the lookout called in Paxat, "Fair night to you."

"Fair night," Ely echoed, assuming this to be the regional address. He let his helm dissipate and rearranged his armor enough to slip Nix into his coat pocket before stepping into the light.

"Have you business in Septus or are you passing through?" the sentinel inquired.

"We're meeting someone," Ely replied. "Do you know, sir, what's happened in the hamlets outlying yours?"

The man nodded a somber flaxen head. "I've heard news. Never you worry, good travelers. We don't play Caj with Death here in Septus. We've taken our precautions."

Ely nodded, though the cryptic colloquialism escaped understanding. "We'll be on our way then."

The watchman waved them on. They followed the flow of foot traffic down a thoroughfare lined with lantern posts. Though it was no true metropolis, the streets seemed almost congested after weeks of frozen nothing.

"Why are you so disturbed?" Rav whispered.

"Something he said about playing Caj with Death. I'm not sure what we're walking into here, Rav. Keep both eyes open."

As if to punctuate his point, a harrowing scream rent the night. Ely and Rav exchanged glances. The other pedestrians hardly waved an eyelash.

The progression swept into the nexus of town where another conflagration licked the poles and rigging of a pyre. The shrieks rose from amidst the flames. A teenage girl lashed to the stake. The wooden sign hung by a chain around her neck read: *Eztriga*.

Witch.

"Heaven knows my name!" she cried through the billowing smoke. "Heaven knows my name!"

Ely froze, rooted to the street, eyes caught on the fire-framed countenance. Rav bumped his side like a circling shark, trapping his hand just before it lifted to free the girl's soul from her tormented body.

"Don't," the vampire hissed. "Let Death do their own work."

Rav clamped his arm in an iron grip and propelled him away from the pyre. The closest inn overlooked the square. Near enough that the stink of burnt hair followed them into the lobby.

"Terrible shame," the fur-clad crone at the counter shook her head. "None of us reckoned poor Klara for a witch, but thinking back on it, well, it does make sense."

"What did she do?" Ely asked.

"Do?" the innkeeper frowned. "Nothing. Not that I ken. But this ain't a season for gentle deeds what with us being the last station. We don't play Caj with Death here in Septus."

"So I hear," Ely nodded.

The woman handed him the key to room twenty-nine. He made it up the stairs and down the hall before the smoke that had taken residence in his throat tried to double him over.

His bones blazed, and his head throbbed as he unlocked the door to their suite. A sitting room with a settee and a well-kindled wood stove opened into a narrow bedchamber. The suffocating armor shell that encased him contracted as he collapsed on the log-framed bed.

Rav laid a merciful cool hand against Ely's forehead and made a low rumble of displeasure. His fingers shifted in a purposeful pattern that trailed from Ely's temples along his jaw, down either side of his neck, coming to rest on his wheezing chest. Then back again from the top. The look of determination in the vampire's eye sparked to frustration as he passed through the motions of healing once, twice, thrice more to no avail.

Ely took hold of his hands. "I'm fine."

Rav shook his head. "You're not."

"Your bedside manner needs some work." Ely's wry chuckle turned to a sputter.

"I should be able to set you right," Rav seethed.

The vampire unlatched the window and returned with a fistful of starlight, thin and anemic from the cloud cover. Ely managed a sip, then lay back with eyes closed. Exhausted.

He didn't remember falling asleep. And he certainly didn't remember wandering into the woods where sunlight gamboled between leafy summer branches.

Ely came upon a stump sawed flat across where a Caj board anticipated an opening set. A white-robed figure sat on a fallen log considering his tiles. He looked up with an empty smile. Titus.

The Apostle gestured to the vacant log opposite. Ely sat and began arranging his hand as though he had expected this match all along.

"So, your weary miles have dragged you all the way to Septus. I am impressed with your tenacity."

"I'm nothing if not tenacious," Ely said, laying down his overture.

He looked up to find the Apostle watching him. Never blinking. The textureless blue of his eyes gave him the appearance of a clay model. A façade.

"You're not Titus," Ely stated.

"No, But it makes it simpler for you, does it not?"

"Sure. Since you refuse to give a name."

"Why should I need a name?" not Titus asked. "I am."

He laid out his tiles and claimed two of Ely's from the board.

"Are you going to tell me why you've invaded my dreams?" Ely asked.

"Don't you know where you are, necromancer?"

"Pretty positive I'm in my own head," Ely replied.

"Seven seals peer from the Undying Lands into the realm of mortal Death," the nameless god declared. "One holds my betrayer in its breast. One sleeps beneath the frozen stars. Four belch poison and writhe in turbulent trembling. And the last rests in the silence of the Septus."

"Is there something I'm supposed to take away from this word salad you've tossed in my lap?" Ely asked, laying his counter and collecting a tidy pile of tiles.

The blue clay eyes narrowed on the Caj board, then back to Ely.

"I'm told you have a gift," the entity continued in Titus's gentle voice. As creeping smooth as his eyes.

"That's not what your people call it," Ely answered.

"I don't mean common conjury."

"You'll have to enlighten me then. I'm not following."

"Resurrection," the nameless god intoned.

"Oh, that," Ely dismissed. "I really had nothing to do with it."

"By whose will did the prince of Séocwen breathe again to take his throne? Or Terésa Santara walk fresh from the tomb?"

"And where did you hear such fantastic tales, might I ask?" Ely inquired.

The being in Apostle's guise folded soft fingers and tilted his head. "You are wasted in service to Death."

"If you knew me at all, you'd know how I adore being wasted."

The clay Apostle scowled. Entendre lost in translation.

Ely straightened his pieces. "We passed through towns torched to the ground. Bodies piled inside your churches. There's a young girl burning outside my window, presumably a precaution against the pestilence. For all your gnashing of teeth about Death, you sure like to call down the reaper's scythe."

His opponent rearranged his hand and laid down a pair of tiles aligned in a classic Hellman's Feint. Clever. For an amateur.

Ely laid a quartet of tiles arranged as though he had swallowed the Hellman. Risky, but if patient, it staged the Jester's Coup.

"What do you say we make this a bit more spicy?" he asked. "Play for stakes?"

The loamy smile widened. "Name your terms."

"I win, you hand over Prometheus. Then you and your zealots will leave me and my friends to go on our merry way."

"Agreed. If I win, you will cross the Septus Seal into the Undying Lands and teach me the secrets of pure resurrection."

"Done."

The nameless god slid a pair of red-painted kings into play.

"Hm," Ely mused.

He added an emerald star, a silver knife, and a black raven. He claimed a golden goblet off his opponent.

"What do you need a helyx for, anyway?"

"It's mine to begin with," answered the earthen smile. "Or did you think the scholars of old outwitted Death on their own?"

"To be perfectly honest, it's been difficult to get to the bottom of everything that happened of old," Ely said. "So, the Canon and the Tower formed a cautious alliance against a common enemy. Is that it?"

The clay Apostle chuckled and swept half Ely's tiles with his next move.

"I'll forgive your mortal mind for its inability to grasp the scope of time. You'll see it more clearly in the Undying. The Tower and the Canon are different means to the same end. Whatever wars and intrigues played out upon this world's stage, my servants have always joined hands beneath the table."

"Titillating," Ely smirked as he mounted a new defense upon the board. "So, on the one hand you had the Canon to put Death in a chokehold, and on the other the Cosmologists to dissect it. What's the endgame?"

"The scope of my desires is beyond your comprehension," the nameless god sniffed.

"Fine," Ely shrugged. "Your predilections make little difference to me. How does my knack for the odd resurrection fit in with your grand plans?"

"To defeat Death finally and completely, I must know how to unknot their power."

The masquerading Apostle gritted his teeth and slammed fresh tiles on the board, vexation indenting his waxy brow as he continued, "I know what it takes to bring back a soul that's been loosed from its mortal coil. I can bind it to bones and putrid flesh. I can freeze it in a monstrous perversion of human form."

"So, Dr. Brahm's work with vampires?" Ely interjected. "That was for you?"

The nameless god scoffed, poking at his unlaid tiles with a fitful finger. "Brahm was too consumed with petty revenge and self-serving schemes to achieve true greatness. But I don't have to tell you. You're well acquainted with his cheap craftsmanship."

Ely lined up a pair of sapphire knights. "I'm exceedingly fond of his work myself. But they say art is subjective."

The nameless god sucked his teeth in contempt. He flanked the knights, shattering their formation. Ely gazed down at the board, jaw flexed, final tile pinched between his fingers.

"I'll see you in the Undying," the clay grin declared.

Ely set the little ivory square in the newly empty hollow at the center of the board. A silver Jester's bell.

The imitation Apostle gaped at the configuration. Clay eyes darting. "No," he howled. "You've cheated me!"

Ely sat back with a smile. "Didn't the watchman tell you? Never play Caj with Death."

The nameless god looked up, a glow like pale fire melting through his veneer.

"You owe me a helyx," Ely said.

"Meet us at the cathedral beyond the square," the nameless god snarled, voice distorting. "Come alone."

Ely woke to cold, endless night. Blankets swaddled him. His jacket and shoes had been removed. Rav lay asleep across the pillow, one arm propped beneath his head, the other draped lightly over his ailing bedfellow. Ely lifted a fevered smile. The vampire stirred as though he felt the fond gaze brush his face, but he didn't wake.

No doubt Rav would fight day's leaden weight to accompany him on his errand. Still, Ely hesitated to rouse him. Something sinister lurked in the smooth voice and earthen glance when the nameless god spoke of Dr. Brahm's brand of resurrection. Subtextual threat coupled with the vampire's recent episodes pleaded a convincing case for keeping Rav far from the Apostle and his master.

Ely eased from the nest of bedclothes. His chest blazed. His bones throbbed. He recognized this burn now. Somewhere along their journey he had breathed in the fumes of an unstable rupture. One that had poisoned the outlying towns. The answer to the riddle of the Septus Seal lay in silent wait for him in the cathedral. Of that he was certain. If only he could be so certain he'd manage to stay upright long enough to walk inside.

You may have to take the lead on this one, he told the onlooking legion.

Obviously.

Any chance you could clear up this little cough?

We could kill you, if you like.

Ely rolled his eyes as he knotted his bootlaces. Nix lay nested in his coat pocket, her silk handkerchief wrapped with delicate precision. Ely left her at rest as he donned his jacket and raised ether armor over them both.

He cast another glance at Rav who lay boulder-still. They would be back well before evening roused the vampire from his rest. Surely the third helyx would suffice as an apology.

Locking the door behind him, Ely passed through the empty lobby and out into the winter darkness. The pyre glowed in bitter embers. A steaming skeleton all that remained of the youth offered up in sacrifice.

Is she with you now? Ely asked.

The passenger rippled grim denial. No explanation, but he knew the answer all the same. The dead of Septus knew no eternal peace among the stars. The rupture sluiced newly discharged souls into its vortex. What became of them? The nameless god only knew.

She will be the last, Death vowed.

Beyond the square, Ely found a post office, a manufactory, a lumberyard with rows upon rows of logs quilted in snow. No sign of a cathedral.

"Where do you commune for worship?" he asked a passerby.

"We live our worship," the muffled voice emerged from bundled furs.

"So, there's no cathedral here?" Ely frowned.

Perhaps his little foray into the woods had been a fever dream after all.

"There's the old confessional," the helpful Septan suggested. "They haven't used it in a decade. Bedrock's unstable."

"Will you point me in that direction?"

"Behind the sawmill."

"Many thanks."

Ely skirted the log mounds and found a concrete outbuilding making derelict exile among the shadows. A stamp in midnight indigo marked the door with the eye and blade.

His knees jellied. Stomach wambled. The abandoned church grew misty before his eyes.

Your turn, he surrendered. *See you on the other side.*

Tranquil stillness fled as he crossed the threshold. A hissing shriek like a hurricane gale echoed through the frozen black. Ely dropped to his hands and knees. His armor writhed and disintegrated. His entire being felt emptied. Void gaped where Death should be. His swimming eyes found the curves of a sigil painted in mottled gore on the stone slab beneath him.

Laughter oozed through the grille upon the door to the booth beside the altar. A figure in white furs bespeckled in blood emerged from the confessional. Soulless grin curled victorious on his lips.

"And now," the Apostle chanted. "Our game shall end."

Chapter Twenty-One

FALLOUT

Rav woke with a hollow in his chest like someone slipped a scalpel beneath the tattooed seal and carved out a corner of his heart. For a millennium of a moment, he feared the conjurer had succumbed to illness. When he opened his eyes, he found the bed empty. And the suite.

Don't panic. Stay calm.

Perhaps Ely had simply gone in search of supper. His indignant human stomach often disturbed the quiet with piteous pleading, and even starlight had grown scarce of late. Rav followed the conjurer's fading scent downstairs.

No sign of him in the tavern. Had delirious wandering drawn him out into the clutches of winter? This raging chill could claim a fragile life in half a blink.

Focus. Calm.

Rav hastened to the emptied streets. If any of the prints stamped in the sooty snow outside had a deeper instep on the left foot, they had long since been trampled away. Rav clung to the shadows, sniffing the air like a bloodhound. There it was. A hint of Death and starlight.

The faint trail rounded the deserted square and meandered past shops boarded up for the night. As he neared less traversed drifts, his keen eyes picked out a familiar set of footprints. Blurred and stumbling. A battle with unconsciousness circumnavigating the lumberyard.

No sign of a body. More troubling, no echoes of manic curiosity and idiot optimism intruded on his thoughts. What once felt like an alien invasion had grown so habitual. The absence left him anxious and nauseated.

Something shuddered on his periphery. His hand moved of its own accord, snatching the shadow from the air.

"Fangs!" the metallic squeak emerged from between his fingers.

"Nix. Where's Elyssandro?"

"In trouble," the helyx replied.

The light in her amber eye stuttered. Static shivered between her words.

"He was...waiting...church...on the floor...blood...b-b-blood..."

Her voice smeared. Glitched. Vanished.

"What are you saying, demon?"

Rav shook the infernal contraption. She rattled and sputtered. He turned the helyx over with his thumb to find a spider web of hair fine cracks fractured her smooth surface.

"Who did this to you?"

"The...Apostle...is not..."

Her eye rolled toward her topmost pole. The clouds under her surface evaporated, and Rav saw only his own face incurving the chrome.

"Nix?"

No response. He pressed the unconscious orb into his pocket.

Don't panic. Stay—

Calm burst like an overburdened dam.

"Elyssandro!" he shouted, tearing across the lumberyard. Scattering logs in thundering avalanches.

Vision swallowed in scarlet, ears drowned by a roaring electric hum, Rav turned back toward Septus. He caught the wind, whipping it around him in a shrieking tornado. Concrete and wood exploded into splinters. Rooftops shattered. Septans charged screaming from their beds out into the slick snow.

Rav collapsed somewhere on the outskirts of town. A warehouse with an unexpected steel frame had crippled his left shoulder. A slivered femur speared his thigh. Cold blood leaked from nicks, gashes, and splinters that rent his skin from head to toe.

"Are we finished with our little tantrum?" a feathered voice inquired.

He lifted his head, searching for the intruder through dim eyes. A woman watched him from the shadows. She wore a shapeless shift lined in white fur, a heavy veil wound around her head.

Rav bared his teeth with a warning hiss. The woman smiled. A thin, menacing smile.

"Your friend can't answer you at present."

She giggled and tutted her tongue.

"All that shouting and banging about for nothing."

Rav gathered strength for one last charge. The woman stood planted before him, unflinching. Time seemed to slow to a snail's crawl. He moved as though mired in a vat of glue. The woman shifted lightly, feet barely brushing the snow. Laugh tinkling like Wintertide bells around him. Then she stood behind him, a chain in her hand connected to an iron noose circling his neck. Burning. Subduing. Wrapping his muscles and heart and brain with choking weeds.

No. No. No.

Not again.

He halted. Standing at stiff, broken-limbed attention.

"Good boy," the woman crooned.

Silence throbbed as heavy as an ocean's depths. The rupture shivered in the darkened pit. A rippling curtain blasting voltaic fuchsia light and the aching antithesis of sound. Its jarring magnetic field spurred an already pounding headache toward hallucination.

"Not that I don't enjoy a good healthy silence," Ely called, "but what is it we're doing here?"

Sigils painted in blood on the foundation slab kept Death at bay. The ropes knotted about his wrists and ankles galled him. Such a simple, insulting restraint had no right to hold him helpless in this damned uncomfortable chair. Rión had always berated him for his refusal to waste time learning proper warcraft.

"If you were a weak human with no Morgata to drag your sorry sack out of trouble, you'd be fucked."

"If I were a weak human with no Morgata to drag me into trouble in the first place, I'd find a big strong warrior to protect me so I could spend my days cooking cassoulet and baking bread."

"You can't cook for shit, Ruadan. You'd just be fucked."

She was right. She was always right. He had never learned to properly cook or fight, so now here he was in an underground bunker tied to a chair.

"Titus? Hello? Are you awake?" Ely called to relieve his ears of the maddening lull.

The Apostle made no reply. He stood like a statue. Hands clasped behind his back, gazing into the warped neon blemish.

"How do you do it?" Titus asked. "Cross through unscathed?"

"Stick your head in. Find out," Ely muttered.

The Apostle grunted and returned to his ruminations. Ely tugged at his bindings again. The cords bit deeper into his wrists with every twist and jangle. Something gouged into his leg. His breath caught. The point of a petrified ether wing. The butterfly! If only he could reach his pocket.

Keep talking. Distract him.

"What do you want to cross through for anyway?" Ely asked.

Titus raised his hands in a gesture of praise. "An eternity at the feet of the one true god. What could be greater?"

"A pastrami sandwich. With sauerkraut and mustard," Ely suggested. "Some pickles on the side. Dill, obviously. None of those bread and butter atrocities."

"I wouldn't expect you to understand," Titus flouted. "You who commune with Death."

"You're right, I don't," Ely said, lifting his toes a hair to give his wrist some wiggle room. "Have you met your god? He's terrible at Caj. All around bad sport. What're you going to do with him for a whole eternity?"

A grating rumble disturbed the room's hermetic seal, relieving the pressure for a moment as the door opened and closed. A slender figure in a winterproof Watcher's habit descended the high stone steps that led from the sanctuary above. After her limped a tall, pale shadow tethered by a length of chain attached to a metal collar clamped around his neck.

"Rav!"

Ely fought his restraints, heart a rampaging beast.

Rav's shoulder hunched at an unnatural angle, battered face barely recognizable. The glyph-etched collar glowed as smelted iron followed by the sizzled fetor of burnt flesh.

Ely searched for the vampire's presence. Nothing. Whether it was the collar or the sigils or the silence of the Septus, Rav stood beyond reach.

"My goodness, Sister Ignatius. What have you done to that fell beast?" Titus asked.

The Watcher's giggle bubbled like acid. "He did it to himself. Flying around like a bat out of hell, looking for the necromancer."

Sister Ignatius secured the chain through a ring set in the wall. Titus strode toward the newcomers, hands still clasped behind his back.

"He's brought you a gift, your eminence," Sister Ignatius beamed. She turned to Rav. "Go on, puppy. Give it to him."

Rav rumbled a pained growl. The glyphs crackled around his throat. He reached a hand in his pocket, movements stiff and jerking as though he fought a possessing spirit. Ely strained against the ropes, rage knocking his plan from between his temples.

Rav held out the helyx. Titus took the silver sphere, examining her a moment. Just a glinting lump of metal at present. He nodded and passed Nix to Sister Ignatius.

"Put it with the others," he directed.

Sister Ignatius nodded, tugging loose a sharpened stake from a scabbard at her waist and handing it to the Apostle before making her departure.

Titus held up the smooth shaft between his fingers so the death magic inscription caught the rupture's flushed light. "You recognize this, yes?"

"Yes," Ely hissed, reaching for the hole where Death should be to wipe the sneer from his crooked lips.

Pocket. Get to the pocket.

"What do you want from me?" Ely asked. "And I mean *you*, Titus. I already know what old Anonymous wants. But once he's figured out how to banish Death and swallow the world, or whatever boring schemes these gods get up to when they've too much time on their hands, what then? I don't see where you fit into that picture."

Titus glared at him, rigid and still as an adder readying for the strike. His babbling had poked a tender nerve, it seemed.

"Why?" Titus snarled. "Why does he speak to you? You deviant. You unclean abomination. Why does he summon you to his kingdom?"

Ely regarded the Apostle with a smug smile. "So that's it then? You're jealous because Daddy's not giving you attention when you've been such a good little boy?"

Titus rushed at him. He seized Ely by the hair and wrenched his head back. Rav's chain rattled, and the wall splintered before the collar drove him into a heap on the floor.

The Apostle's jaundiced blue eyes blazed, bloodshot at the corners. He breathed out a sweet, putrid odor. Unpleasant but familiar. Like he slowly rotted from the inside. Like one undead.

"You are not worthy of his presence," the Apostle declared.

"Who are you to decide who is worthy?" a voice boomed from the walls.

Titus leaped back, whirling around to face his accuser. The phantom hovered in front of the rupture. Translucent and imbued with otherworldly light, it appeared to emerge from the shimmering veil, but Ely recognized the thin, contemptuous face from the desert of Marikej. Ariel's holy warrior guise.

The Apostle Titus fell to his knees.

Not one to waste a good diversion, Ely angled again for his pocket. The ropes nipped. Burned. Drew blood. The tip of one finger brushed the bulbous end of an antenna. His entire being flexed toward the tiny object, and the ether butterfly flitted into his hand.

The interstellar death magic liquified. It flowed into his pores like water into sand. Spilling through his blood in a rushing tide stronger than an elixir of a thousand stars. An infinite universe. Combusting. Spinning. Expanding.

The ropes that bound him exploded into violet flames. Titus sprang to his feet, astonished. He raised two fingers to summon a hasty Miracle. Ely waved a hand, and a black spiral torpedoed the Apostle into the wall. He raised the other, and the collar around Rav's neck crumbled into shards on the ground.

"Elyssandro, the rupture!" Ariel called with Petros's commanding baritone.

Ely gathered the remaining cosmic force into a compacted disc between his hands and directed it hurtling into the rupture. The silence burst, unleashing sound and fury that rattled the bedrock. Threw him from his feet.

Rav whooshed to his side, hoisting him upright with one good arm. Before them, the Septus Seal bellowed and choked. The walls and floor seemed to be crumbling inward toward a ravenous supernova.

"Hold on," Rav rasped.

The vampire careened toward a widening hole in the ceiling. Debris pommeled from above. They cleared the church and rushed through open air. Faster. Faster. Ely felt consciousness slipping in the howling wind tunnel. Then they were tumbling, leveling out, dipping again. Falling.

Rav managed to slow their descent before making impact on solid ice. Ely rolled like a runaway boulder then lay breathless. His cells felt charred and trembling in the wake of empyrean death magic. The deep and ancient wellspring from which it had been inadvertently tapped was not meant for human hands. Not even a conjurer's.

"Are you alright?" Rav grimaced as he crawled to Ely's side and collapsed.

"A little worse for wear, I think," Ely gasped. "You?"

"I'll heal," the vampire managed.

Ely gazed up at the scintillating realms that arched in a fond Reaper's smile. The stars pulsed and danced to joyous celestial harmonies. Beckoning. As their silver light trickled over his face, soaked into his skin, pain grew distant. Breath slow. Heart quiet.

The heavenly voices shaped images before his eyes. His older brothers chasing after an ox hide ball down a stone corridor. Uncle Misha brandishing his cane as a sword in the thrust of a fireside tale. His mother positioning his fingers on the violin. Hm. Probably not a good sign, this.

"Rav," he murmured. "Not to alarm you, but I'm seeing some very vivid flashes of my childhood."

An arm wrapped around him, scooping him from the ice to rest against a steady heartbeat. In the arctic cold, the vampire's embrace felt living warm.

"Don't go to sleep," Rav said. "Talk to me. Tell me what you see."

"There's the courtyard below my window at the University. Black dahlias in bloom around the fountain. Dr. F in her workshop glaring up over her glasses while I pester her. I'm probably lucky she didn't kill me back then. I'm just going to rest my eyes for a second."

"No, focus." Rav shook him gently. "What else do you remember?"

"The floating stones at Fjarat stacked with snow like old white-haired men. A huge Wintertide feast table overflows with smoked hogs and winter squash and braided loaves of bread. Xaris the Hammer laughs like an earthquake. Riri passes another mug of beer while I pretend I'm not hopelessly drunk."

"Keep talking."

"Kai's bungalow on the beach. A sky so blue your heart bursts to look at it. The light doesn't seem real. It looks like someone else's life. And now it's you and me. Walking in the forest. Under a grinning moon."

Rav's fingers outlined his face.

"Stay with me, Ely."

"Always, dearest Lovelace," he whispered as his eyes drifted closed.

Chapter Twenty-Two

Meanwhile

It was a glorious fucking morning. Skies blue as a tanuba egg. Brined mist spraying from sidewinder waves. Throaty voices humming Leif's Shanty to the dip and splash of oars. By the named gods, a glorious fucking day to be at sea.

Rión strode the deck from stem to stern and back again. She paused and growled from time to time, as was expected of a shrewd and taciturn commander.

Brindle leaned on the starboard rail. The spitting image of her father with her sweet round cheeks and emotive face. Almost human in its expression. What that beautiful child saw out on the ocean tides, Rión would give ten years and a finger to view for herself. Since toddling around in diaper cloths, Brin reported seeing plants breathing and electric currents flowing through animal cells. The sort of magical shit anyone else would have to eat fistfuls of poison fungus to experience.

It was the first trip at sea for the twins. Jorig had begged to keep them home for another year, but after recovering Ragnor and the other children from captivity, Rión could not grant her beloved his wish. Whether hunted by the Canon or kept as pets in the Free Cities, the human threat to Etrugan kind grew by the day. This was no time for lingering youth. Not even for softhearted Brin. They would need her healer's spirit just as they needed their warriors. Maybe more.

Feeling eyes on the back of her neck, Brin looked over her shoulder. Her irises gleamed purple with excitement.

"Flying fish!" she signed.

Rión threw a glance over the railing and nodded at the leaping school. Their fibrous red fins caught the breeze like wings, sending them sailing in graceful arcs over the water.

"The god of the depths favors us," she signed to her daughter.

"Mother!" Ariadna bellowed as she dropped to the deck from the rigging above.

"What now?" Rión asked. "I already know all the ropes are frayed to shit up there. We'll lose that sail next time the wind picks up."

"There's a ship on the horizon," Ari growled. "Séoc, I think. Moving this way on the tide."

"Colors?" Rión asked.

Ari shook her head. "Little bastard's almost invisible. I only saw it by a lucky trick of the light."

By the time Rión found her spyglass in the chaos of her cabin, she no longer needed it. There was no mistaking the sleek mirrorwood vessel with its cloudlike sails and serpent's maw.

Kailari fucking Novara.

Rión commanded the oars to halt. As their momentum slowed, the lighter Séoc ship would catch them within the hour.

Where Etrugan warships were built solid to withstand Canon artillery, the mirrorwood vessels of the islands were meant for gliding in undetected and riding away swift as lightning on the wind. As much as she despised this particular ship's sovereign, she watched the Marisola approach with admiration.

The Séoc crew raised the teal and coral emblem of the Barrier Keys followed by a flag of parlay. Rión responded with consenting colors. For all their shitbrained behavior, she at least appreciated the humans' chromatic communication ship to ship.

The two hulls drew parallel, fenders placed and mooring ropes exchanged. Kai stood perched on the railing clad in the purple and ochre of an island monarch. Black hair and beard plaited with shells and feathers like the old sea wolves of the heroic age.

He had not been long on the throne, and already he stood among the most storied of Séoc kings. His ruthless quelling of the Seúza separatists followed by the public execution of their king impressed even the seasoned warriors at Xaris' table. The raids he led along the Protectorate's coastline became instant legends.

"I am Kailari Novara, King of Séocwen addressing Rión Twin Axes," he called in terrible Etrugan. Like most humans, he failed to grasp the proper placement of growls and flashed teeth. "I request permission to board."

Kai unsheathed his cutlass and laid it down on the deck along with a pistol and a curved dagger. The customary submission of weapons.

"Granted," Rión replied.

Kai crossed a rope suspended between the ships with acrobatic ease.

"I humbly request a private audience," he said.

"Acceded," Rión replied.

Kai followed her to the commander's quarters at the rear of the vessel. She kicked aside a heap of charts and dulled blades as they entered.

When the door shut out subordinate eyes and ears, she turned to him. "We can drop the cock tickling now. What do you want, Novara?"

The pirate king met her eyes. She knew the hue meant nothing on a human apart from their ancestors' climate. Still, the jet black stare postured like a declaration of war.

"Tell me where to find Elyssandro. And don't lie to me. I already know he's alive."

A growl boiled low in her chest, exploding at him along with her steel-shod foot. The pirate king toppled to the floorboards, and she weighted his sternum with her knee.

"Why the fuck should I tell you?" she snarled. "After all he did for you, for your people, where were you when he needed you most? Suckling at your mother's tit to win back your crown."

"You're not wrong," Kai wheezed, unable to budge her. "You'll hate me more when you hear what I have to say. It doesn't matter. Ely's in danger, and I need to find him before it's too late."

Rión eased off the pirate king's chest and held out a hand. He accepted the boost. By the reeling look in his eyes, he had no choice.

"Come sit," she commanded. "I need a fucking drink."

Lea paused to adjust the light over the little silver sphere gently secured in the tinkering harness. She lifted the thin glass stylus in her hand, drawing flashes of light in glyph patterns over the helyx's ailing ulterior circuit.

A blue pinpoint flashed near the top curve just below the pole.

"Does that hurt?" Lea asked.

Fleeting lights flickered across Melandromache's outer chrome, repeating a pattern of short and long bursts. Lea had yet to decipher the nuances encoded in color, but the flashes played out in simple binary. At last her mercilessly mocked childhood obsession with coding messages in zeroes and ones paid off. Choke on that, Griselda Alderman. Old cow.

"Tensor input duct jammed," the helyx said.

"Can you open up for me?" Lea asked.

The helyx shuddered. She uttered a mechanical hiss like a sigh.

"I can't reach the tensors from outside, Mel. You know that," Lea insisted.

The reluctant machine whined. Her smooth surface segmented into a geometrical grid. A cluster of hexagons near the back northern hemisphere peeled outward, revealing the intricate world of circuits, coils, and tubes within.

Lea selected a pair of pincers and a copper stylus, long and thin like a needle. She repositioned the light, then gently moved aside a bundle of wires with the pincers. The tensor units, stacked in neat layers outside the helyx's main power source, lay positioned out of reach of a spirit encoder. A precaution against unwanted hacking as much as protection from friction or moisture.

The copper encoder—meant for manipulating the helyx's hardware components—etched the finest of glyphs that glowed white then faded. The procession of light resumed within the delicate tubes.

In the first week after Elyssandro's departure, she did her work at Peggy's dining room table. She could accomplish a great deal with nothing more than her wits and a field kit. The effects of death magic and extended months trapped in a human chest cavity necessitated better gear. So, she returned to her post at South Sea University. It was nice to have the distraction of teaching again along with access to her lab. Less time for worry or wistful thinking.

When she did find a moment to herself, usually between the hours of three and four in the morning, she spent it thinking about how she had to take the long way around Center Street since the damage from the Haunts hurricane made driving the main concourse hazardous. They were still uncovering bodies from the wreckage. Her fault. Just like Teensy.

And just like all those years ago in her father's house, she had underestimated the force of nature that disarmed her with an attentive smile. For all her scholarly endeavors, despite having touched the stars with her own hands and unleashed their wrath, she could not seem to wrap her hubristic skull around the notion that maybe, just maybe she was out of her depth palling around with Death.

Inevitably, her mind found its way back to the fortress in the snow. Its stone tablets a gateway to the constellations that called to her for as long as she could remember. The light and harmony glimpsed in her fleeting journey through the cosmos left cravings that woke her from dreams like a haunting. She could taste traces of it on Elyssandro's lips. Making love brought on echoes of that faraway nebula. The lingering yen frightened her.

Were he a charming, dyslexic vagabond and nothing more, would she spend every undistracted moment sweating for his return? Rather doubtful. Men didn't tend to stick in her head. Not even after months of cohabitation. Of course, *those* men didn't do that little twist of the tongue that made her toes curl up and her legs melt like butter.

Damn it, Lea, pay attention. You're a doctor for gods' sakes!

"Is that better?" Lea asked, withdrawing her instruments.

Melandromache shuttered closed, seams disappearing into a flawless sphere. A band of green lights blinked.

"It appears to have improved."

"Glad to hear it," Lea nodded.

After running through the standard system checks, she unstrapped the helyx from the harness. Mel floated in an unsteady oblong orbit while Lea put away her tools.

"Alright, finished," she said, holding out her hands.

The helyx dropped between her palms with an exhausted sputter.

"Work on thrusters next," Mel signaled.

"The moment I get my hands on dragon ore," Lea promised.

"Dragons do not exist."

"It's just a name, Mel. You know, some people say helyxia don't exist either."

"Some people are stupid."

A knock rapped at the door. The handle rattled, but Lea always locked up her lab when tuning Mel.

"Victor is here," Mel announced. Her bands of light flushed ebullient pink. As usual when she spoke of Victor.

"Lea?" Her brother's voice from the hallway confirmed the helyx's assessment.

"Coming," she called.

Lea tucked Mel gently into a pocket specially sown into her lab coat for the little machine's comfort and concealment. The helyx tickled her ribs with excited quivering.

Her brother had come alone, dark round glasses over his scarred eyes, mobility cane in hand. He didn't need the probe to get around. While the accident on their northern expedition had left him blind, he remained perfectly capable of navigating an unfamiliar space or reading facial expressions. Almost as if he had absorbed some of the helyx's scanning capabilities during their entanglement. He wore the glasses and carried the cane mostly to avoid more complicated explanations. A little for the dramatic effect. Typical Victor.

With the door safely locked once again, Mel burst from her hiding place, leaping into Victor's waiting hands like an eager labrador.

"Hello, my beauty," he crooned, pressing her to his cheek.

She jittered and flashed.

"I've missed you too," he replied. "Of course I haven't. How could I forget you?"

Lea knew full well her brother, even with functional eyes, couldn't have read binary if he sat with pen and paper for a month. Yet he understood Mel with perfect clarity. Another side effect of their signal transference.

"No, no, kid. It's just business."

"Not to interrupt, but I have a class in fifteen minutes," Lea said, a touch irritable.

After all the sliced fingers and electric shocks she sustained to nurse that ungrateful gadget back to health, the best she ever got was robotic apathy.

"Cancel it," Victor declared.

"What? I can't do that. We're introducing Cobb's differential transformations today."

"As gripping as that sounds," Victor droned, "I think you'd best call in Dr. Gunderson for the rest of the week."

"Good gods, Victor, can you stop with the theatrical suspense? Tell me what's going on."

"Kai Novara is on the way to South Sea," Victor announced. "We're meeting him in the Bywater in an hour."

"Blast it, Victor. I'm not dressed to meet with royalty," Lea glared through sudden panic.

How like Victor to spring a visit with her fall fling's illustrious ex while she was in her lab scrubs. Hair a mess. Hadn't even bothered with lipstick this morning.

"Better to keep it low key," Victor replied with a vexatious smirk.

While Lea locked up her lab, secured a substitute, and gathered her belongings, Victor hailed a cab. Mel chose to ride in Victor's pocket, to no one's surprise.

It was a thirty minute journey from the University District to the Bywater on a good day. In afternoon traffic, Lea found plenty of time to overthink everything from her hat to her lab clogs. Of all the days to choose comfort over style.

The Bywater lay past the calm waters of the bay where less reputable vessels made berth to deliver illicit cargo and partake in illicit vices. It was also an excellent place to catch more lively music performances than might be found at the concert hall. Victor had dragged her to a few, which she enjoyed after a few drinks took the edge off her terror of being mugged or kidnapped.

The cab left them at the last respectable street where the houses still had all their window glass. As they made the two mile walk to the tavern set for their meeting, Lea reconsidered her earlier misapprehension, thankful now for her clogs and loose trousers.

Victor led the way without the pretense of his cane. The buildings sagged. The streets grew grimier and dingier, as did the characters loitering on them. They dipped inside the Rat and Parrot whose entrance lay hidden down an especially ominous alleyway behind piled rubbish.

Kai waited for them in a corner booth accompanied by a stone gray Etrugan. Both wore cloaks with hoods raised. All indications of rank and place of origin obscured or removed.

"Victor, my friend. Glad to see you're on the mend," his majesty rumbled, extending a hand. Victor grasped it as though he had seen the action.

"Dr. Skylark," Kai nodded with his usual gruff but amiable manner.

"Your majesty," Lea replied, returning the nod and stilling her nervous foot tapping under the table.

The Etrugan eyed her, irises shifting from blood red to pale blue. Lea had never seen one of the demons of the western bluffs in person. The changing eyes, so casually described in literature, raised the hair on the back of her neck and stuttered her breath.

"This is Rión Twin Axes," Kai introduced the Etrugan.

"Twin Axes?" Lea interrupted. "You're Elyssandro's friend. He told me all about you and your adventures."

"Did he?" Rión asked, heliotrope rivers in her eyes. "He told me about you too, tiny human doctor. You got him blown up by an Apostle."

"Um. Yes. Well..."

Lea stared hard at the table, knowing and hating the shade of scarlet she had turned.

"Let's talk about why we're here, shall we?" Victor redirected.

"That *is* why we're here," the Etrugan stated, moss green tongue flicking her pointed, shark-like teeth.

"We were hoping he might still be here," Kai said.

"He's been gone for almost a month now," Lea replied. She glanced over her shoulder and lowered her voice. "Looking for another helyx. Somewhere in the former Usher territory."

"He went into the Protectorate?" Kai exclaimed.

Lea inclined her head.

"Alone?"

"Well, Nix was with him," Lea said.

"Zygos' cock!" the Etrugan snarled, granite fist rattling the table. Acidic lime spilled into her gaze. "What happened to the shiteating vampire?"

Lea shook her head. "I don't know. He went out into the hurricane and disappeared, thank goodness. That bite still itches."

"And you don't know where Ely went precisely?" Kai asked, gaze as frightening intense as that of the monster at his elbow.

"No, but we might be able to assist with locating him," Lea replied, glancing at Victor.

Her brother made no response, instead sitting stock still as if he had frozen in place. Then he nodded. He had been engaged in a private conversation.

"Yes, we can help," Victor confirmed.

A drunken smile of a moon shivered in the arctic waters. As the Marisola drifted between frozen islands and white mountains of petrified ice, Kai kept eyes on the black water, seeking out dangers lurking beneath the surface. Wreckage from old voyages or hidden glacier roots would rend their hull like a blade across the ribs. Rión Twin Axes' stout, hardy ship rode his wake. The Etrugan vessel would shatter any ice that dared hinder its passage. In fact, both parties would have preferred Rión take the lead to deal with any obstacles by blunt force, but Kai had sailed the northern wildlands before. He knew better how to navigate this treacherous corner of the world.

What Ely was doing all the way up here in the long winter night with a demon ball as a guide...well, what else might be expected of Elyssandro Santara Ruadan? Of course, his beloved knew nothing of the ravenous foe that now hunted him. The unintended betrayal that ate at Kai's thoughts. No matter how he tried to distract himself with the positioning of the stars and the angle of the wind, the eerie voice and malignant smile from that evil prison penetrated his memory.

Their rescue party too followed a mechanical spirit guide, with Victor Skylark serving as interpreter for the silver sphere. Dr. Skylark also traveled with them to tend the machine and assist her blind brother. So she claimed. Kai recognized the look of one captured by the stars.

He had observed her on the journey back from Pandorium. Her ashen face and solemn silence could easily be explained away by devastation over her brother's condition. Kai would know no better had he not endured the weeks of sleepless nights sweating poison after his return from the stars. It felt as though his soul rebelled against his flesh, fighting to ascend heavenward. The violent tremors passed in time, but the restless urgency remained. With so much more to existence than could be fathomed, why was mankind so consumed with violence and hatred? Why did they waste their time persecuting each other for every little difference?

At first his rage had focused on the Canon. An easy target considering their relentless assault. It was not until Ely's murder that the fury turned inward. His people were no better than the Canon. His own mother.

With bruises still fresh, he rallied a small fleet of fighters, bent on putting a swift end to the rebellion brewing in Seúza. Not many knew what had happened in the Council. Nor even that a diakana had set foot on the island. They saw an assault on their prince, a challenge to the supremacy of Séocwen.

"Do you think this is what he would want?" Salía questioned as they departed the bay with forty ships in formation behind.

"This isn't about him," Kai insisted. "Morag laid a challenge to the sacred order. He spoke it in Council when he demanded *Sémar Esanto*, and he made it clear with his actions against me."

Salía blocked his path as he made to turn away. "I will follow you to Hell and back, cousin, for no reason more than that you wanted to spit in the Red Serpent's face. But they..." She gestured to the ships that accompanied them. "They believe honor demands this bloodshed of them."

Kai kept eyes fixed on the unwavering horizon. "It does."

Salía's hard stare made his heart flinch, but he would not relent. She left him alone at the helm.

Morag anticipated their attack and met them at sea with a force of his own. The battle raged swift and brutal. In the end, Séocwen retreated, unable to hold advantage against Seúza's reinforced ships and rabid currents.

King Tennoc—Kai no longer thought of her as Mother—issued a stern rebuke on his return. He made a case for the danger Morag posed to their position.

"How am I to believe you give a thought to the Novara name, to the sovereignty of Séocwen when you so eagerly tried to set them both aflame?" Tennoc demanded.

Kai humbled his head. "I was a fool, *che'alta*. I have learned the lesson."

"Have you? So, the son I knew, the boy who sailed off to the ends of the earth to escape his duty? The boy who defied his king and nearly toppled a dynasty of ten generations? That boy has learned the lesson?"

Kai gazed at the dappled leopard pelt that lay prostrate under the monarch's feet. Its curved teeth petrified in final defiance.

"That boy is dead."

Tennoc eyed him, shrewd and calculating. A king. Never a mother.

"Seúza must be brought to heel," she said. "For that reason alone, you will have retribution, Kailari. But you must follow my word to the letter. No more running. No more resistance."

"Yes, *che'alta*."

Promise kept, he strengthened the Séocwen alliance with Lilipon, marrying a niece of King Jian. Tala was quiet and duteous. Delicate featured. Golden haired.

"The most rare and exquisite flower on the islands," Jian boasted.

"Will she bear strong offspring?" Tennoc demanded.

"She will."

Tala arrived on a barge with a throng of admiring sisters and cousins. Flowers shone in her hair, and she peered out at her new shores with frightened gray eyes.

The high priest married them on the beach before they ever spoke a word to one another. Tala kept her gaze on the sand, now and again darting a shy, curious glance at him. He could not summon a smile. Not even a nod. Any motion at all might let spill tears.

They feasted at the palace. Three days of revelry that Kai remembered through a haze of laythan smoke and zaqual.

When they returned to the quiet bungalow on the beach, he gave Tala his bedroom, taking up residence on the balcony where he spent long, sleepless hours gazing at the stars. He never saw her cry, but Tala's eyes bore signs of nights spent weeping. He should not be so cold and distant. So silent and sullen. Was she not the one forced to leave home and family for a prince with no heart?

When Tennoc learned from his wife of three weeks that the marriage had yet to be consummated, the king sent for him. She received him in her private chambers along with the palace chamadara. A wisened woman with puckered eyelids and buckled fingers. The crone examined him, sucking at teeth dyed russet from corra root tea. He endured the indignity in silence. Then he set out for home with a packet of pungent herbs.

"This will overcome his...condition," the old hag pronounced.

Kai veered from the trail to the bungalow, setting off over low dunes curdled with plump succulents. He wandered to the grave of a long ago eruption whose corpse made a black bridge into the ocean. The hypnotic waters foamed and curled about his feet as he sat at the end of the basalt jetty. There he stayed as the sky thinned to reveal its hoarded treasure trove of stars.

His mind escaped to a day in his wandering youth when he visited Norrholdt at the summer equinox. He arrived just as the Etrugans lit their first bonfires on the bluffs that overlooked the foreboding sea below. He had hardly taken a sip of the fuming goblet thrust in his hands when he heard the voice he prayed would call his name every time he set foot on foreign shores.

"It *is* you!" Ely beamed. "I knew I spied your ship."

He wore Etrugan-tanned leather, face streaked with red and black paint. Smile radiant as the sun god they exalted in their revelry. Kai embraced him, the rough exuberance of friendship disguising the tender beat of his heart. He remembered a thousand such moments of that night. Firelit glances lingered. Hands and knees found reasons to rest together. Laughter overflowed around thoughts mangled in translation.

When Ely fell asleep beside scintillating embers, Kai watched him until his own eyes grew heavy.

"Sa'miora," he had whispered.

Even if his beautiful friend happened to hear the confession in his dreams, he would not know its meaning.

"I love you."

Now, sitting on the rough lava rock, Kai repeated the same words to the stars where his diakana had disappeared. Then he dusted the sand from his clothes and made the journey home to see his duty fulfilled.

Some weeks later, Tala gave him the news in her tremulous voice that she was with child. The chamadara confirmed. Feasts were held. The strength of Séocwen renewed for another generation.

Kai turned his full attention to gathering favor among the inner islands and reinforcing ships for battle. King Tennoc offered him steadfast support. For the first time in living memory, his mother seemed to gaze upon him with respect.

Then she appeared. Perfect and beautiful. Her mother's nose, her father's smile, and three white stars emblazoned on her tiny brown shoulder.

"Elyssa?" King Tennoc spat with disapproval when she learned the name on which he had insisted. "Have you lost your mind, Kailari? Is it not bad enough she has the mark?"

"She is his daughter as much as mine. You don't have to like it, *che'alta*, but she is your blood."

How his mother glared! Lethal daggers that choked his breath and knotted his stomach.

"What do you do, Kailari, with blood that is poisoned by snake venom?"

"She is a gift, *che'alta*. She will be King after me."

"The islands will never accept a diakana on the throne. They will say our line is tainted. No. No. Better they think she died at birth."

As he left the palace with Tala and the baby, he met his cousins in the garden. Salía read the conversation on his face, though it was many hours before he recounted the scene to her on a remote cliffside. The roar of the sea drowned words forced out through hopeless tears.

"She will never be safe so long as Tennoc rules."

"No, cousin. She won't," Salía agreed...

Kai adjusted course in narrow time to stay within a tightening channel between ice sheets. What was that strange light on the glacier ahead? The golden glimmer had roused him from his trance at the helm.

Ethereal flickering concentrated into a vague form, splashing gilded light over the ice. When his eyes focused on the radiation, he made out human features. A woman, he thought, staring directly at him with eyes like galaxies. She held out a hand. A gesture of urgent beckoning.

Kai called his first mate, Ak'hila Novara, to the helm. He wished, as he did every day, that Salía remained at his side, but he could not leave his daughter in any other hands. Ak'hila was young but loyal and skilled at navigation.

"Get me as close to the ice as you can," he commanded.

Kai sent up a hissing flare to alert the Etrugan ship of his plans to venture ashore. When they neared the tiered shelf, he seized a climbing hook from the row along the side of the ship.

"Steady, Ak'hila! Keep her steady."

With a quick breath, he flung himself overboard, driving the hook in front of him. Praying it would catch something. The hook chunked into ice with a dull thud, anchoring him in place. Cold bit through his winter clothes, throbbing into his bones.

By the time he found his feet, the phantom already swept up the glacial slopes ahead, an impatient guide over the treacherous terrain. Kai heard the Etrugans shouting as they joined him on the ice, but he scrambled onward, never losing sight of the golden spirit.

At last she came to a stop, then evaporated in a shower of sparks. Under the glare of the swollen moon, he picked out a shape ahead. A body lay on the glacier, strangely contorted. No, not a single body. Two. A pair of men huddled together. One a woefully underdressed stranger. The other a profile he knew even in silhouette.

"Here!" Kai called to the Etrugans behind him.

At his shout, the stranger's eyes startled open. He snarled at Kai, lips sliding back over fearsome fangs. He moved with the lithe speed of a panther, carrying Ely thirty feet across the ice in less than a blink. The creature collapsed on his knees, struggling to hold onto his burden. He was injured. Badly so.

Kai pursued them only to find himself sprawling on his back, breath knocked loose.

"Rav!" Rión Twin Axes' growl boomed at his shoulder. "We didn't sail up the world's icy rectum to chase you through the fucking snow!"

"Rión?" the creature panted.

Relief kindled in his eyes. Only for a fleeting moment.

"He's fading," the creature told them. Desperation lined his battered face.

"We can help," Rión made gruff assurance. "Let me take him."

Rión lifted Ely as though handling a fragile child. She lumbered off, surefooted on the slick surface. Rav slumped forward, bracing his fists on the ice. His leg looked unnaturally twisted, and one shoulder bowed far too high.

Kai offered a helping hand. The creature cast a wary eye that prickled his spine. The look reminded him of a wounded tiger he rescued from a poacher's trap in the high mountains of Tenegal. Proud and distrustful. All the more volatile in vulnerability. Kai kept his hand extended, unmoving despite the fear that groaned in his chest. And like the great beast, Rav too, at last, gave in to the instinct for survival.

Kai hauled him to his feet and served as a human crutch while they plotted a slow course back toward the waiting ships.

Chapter Twenty-Three

The Trick of Kindness

A ching. Burning. Throbbing. Don't leave, Ely. Don't fade away. Stay upright. Take another step.

"Do you need to rest?"

The black-bearded man paused to adjust his bracing grip. Rav shook his head and gritted his teeth through the deluge of pain and fear and guilt.

Faster. Move faster. He's fading.

"We can rest, *che'oma*. I can't carry you on this ice."

"I don't need to rest."

Rav grunted and ground out another step.

Wrenching. Piercing. Can't feel him. Too far behind. Falling.

Black beard steadied him long enough to make a chair of a patch of grim stone that jutted from the ice.

"The Etrugans have a healer. She will help him. You and I would only be in the way. Sit a moment."

Rav growled in frustration but leaned against the outcropping. Will smothered. Escaped the collar only to be enslaved by his own exhausted body.

My fault. Lost control. Lost Nix. Lost Ely. Weak. Pet. Don't go, conjurer.

"He's in good hands, my friend," black beard soothed.

Rav glanced at the stranger, taking him in for the first time. He wore a brown coat made from sleek animal skin that smelled of tallow and ocean. Seal perhaps? Hair littered with shells and feathers. Appraising black eyes. High cheekbones. Broad shoulders. A figure familiar from a thousand anecdotes. Beyond a passing resemblance to starry-eyed descriptions from the most sanguine of observers, Rav sensed the thumbprint of the cosmos left on an unsettled soul. No mistaking that.

"You are Kai Novara," he stated.

The stranger blinked in surprise. He made no move to confirm, as though he feared claiming his name might provoke an attack.

"How did you find us?" Rav asked.

"We followed a demon just as I am told you did."

Rav stared at his bloodied knuckles gripping the granite. Demon. Have to find the demon. Lost her. Gave her away. Good boy. Good boy. Good boy.

The voices mutated from the Watcher to Harald Brahm to Fiona White. Rav drove his forehead into the stone. Only when they fell silent did he hear Kai Novara making exclamations of alarm from a safe distance.

Rav sat upright. Blinking blood from his eyes. The Séoc stared at him, hand on a pistol resting at his side.

"A bullet won't stop me," Rav hissed. "Your sword would be better, but you'll need a clean swipe at my neck. Don't miss."

"I have no wish to hurt you," the pirate king said.

"Nor I you, Kai Novara. Leave me here. Go to Ely."

"You'll freeze."

Rav laughed. The demented echo startled them both.

"Go."

Kai paid him a last uncertain glance, then departed. Rav sank against the stone. Pain sang along the fresh wounds on his forehead. Better than the voices. Better than the guilt.

His fingers scratched at his throat where the latest glyph burns stung. Raw and sticky. Pet. Good boy. You're not him. Pet. Good boy.

"Ravan."

A brisk, no nonsense voice emerged from torturous tumult. Cold vanished. In its place dank dungeon heat. He blinked in the dim lamplight. Smoke tickled his nostrils. Scents of scalded metal and mildew.

Dr. Selene Faidra peered over half-moon spectacles with sharp blue eyes. Face ageless. Unlined. Perhaps from never permitting a smile. It was her pale hair pinned tight at attention that lent an illusion of age.

"I was told they were squandering you on common violence," Dr. Faidra said.

His eyes narrowed on her face. "You would prefer me squandered on *un*common violence?"

Dr. Faidra smirked. "So you are still in there. Good. Come here, Ravan."

She beckoned him to a work bench cluttered with books and scraps of parchment. Unrolling a hefty bundle of draft papers, she invited him to examine the anatomical drawings and scribbled glyphs. His eyes swept over the pages, mind making sense of them in a dizzying cloud of automated knowledge. Absent context or continuity.

"Do you understand these?" she asked.

"I can read them," he replied.

Again that smirking twitch at the corners of her mouth. "But you disagree with them?"

"Is the intent to kill the subject?" Rav questioned.

"Sedate," she clarified. "Suspend animation. Preserve function. Indefinitely, if possible."

"Is the subject human?"

"Yes."

"This will kill them."

"Can you revise it?" Dr. Faidra asked, an eager glint in her eye. The spark reminded him in what beastly institutional belly he stood. Trust no one.

"To what end?" Rav questioned.

"Consider it your salvation, Ravan."

"How so?"

"Should you accept my offer, you will no longer stay in those festering catacombs. You'll live here. It is impervious to sunlight. You will have access to any materials, books, and instruments you need. You will have no shortage of volunteer subjects for trials."

"I can't do magic anymore," Rav told her.

"I know," Dr. Faidra replied with a bitter edge. "I am quite familiar with Harald's savagery. You need only commit your visions to paper. I'll bring you the hands you need to test and refine. Apart from occasional direction from myself, you will have complete autonomy."

"You'll remove the collar?" he asked, mouth suddenly dry. Heart pounding.

"They wouldn't agree to that," Dr. Faidra said, a sour downturn to her lips. "But that doesn't mean I can't implement a few modifications. More importantly, Ravan, while you are in my employ, no one will lay so much as a finger on you without your consent. That I promise you."

Rav fixed suspicious eyes on her smirk. "And what kind of favors do *you* expect in repayment for this protection?"

Dr. Faidra let out a rusty laugh. "I find male anatomy nearly as off putting as fangs, Ravan. You having nothing to fear from me on that account."

Rav clenched and unclenched his hands. He wanted to weep for relief. Why did this smell like a trap?

Dr. Faidra watched him with her pale, probing gaze. "It is your choice. I will not have you here against your will. Do you need time to think it over?"

"No. I'll do it..."

Black-rimmed eyes and piked teeth roused Rav back to the ice. Rión Twin Axes righted him, easy as a child with a scraped knee.

"The fuck are you lying here for, vampire? Kailari said you tried to crack your head like an egg."

"It was too loud in my head," he explained.

"You frightened the little pirate king," chuckled Rión.

"Is Elyssandro alive?" Rav demanded.

"Of course he's alive. He's back on my ship. Can you walk?"

Rav hauled himself to his feet.

Stay upright. Take another step. Have to find the demon. Betrayed her again. Never forgive me.

Didn't know. Didn't know. Didn't know.

He fought the rising memory, but it found him in the chaotic cadence of his thoughts. A man laid out on the table. Veins like blue meridians underneath translucent skin. Rav could trace them in his mind from the temple to the heart, branching out through the body. A delicate sapling, the human circulatory system.

A pale, thin boy at his side held his stylus in an unsteady hand. Gael. The promising young scholar engaged to spend his summer internship on an exciting project with Dr. Faidra and the fanged researcher now haunting the dungeon lab.

"He can't hurt you, Gael," Dr. Faidra told the downy-faced intern as he gaped slack-jawed and goggle-eyed at the vampire. "Unless you do something stupid. Then he has my permission to drain your blood to the last drop and lay you out on the slab."

The boy consulted the notes on the table, ink still drying. Blotted in haste at places.

"Who was he?" Gael asked. No doubt procrastinating making his first glyph stroke.

Rav flashed a contemptuous fang. "Was? Already decided to kill him, have we?"

"N-n-no, sir. Of course not, sir. I've just never..." He twiddled the stylus with a nervous giggle. "Not on a real human."

"I thought you were a medical student," Rav glowered.

"We don't take Applied Healing until third year," the simpering child stammered.

"Damn it all."

Gael flinched, raising his shoulders just slightly. As if that would shield his jugular. "Sorry, sir. That's why I was asking..."

"I'm sure Dr. Faidra will tell you he's a volunteer," Rav answered sardonically.

Dr. Faidra's oxidized voice emerged from her work station where she hunched over a metal ball overflowing with wires like tiny copper intestines. A passion project of hers in Demonic Intelligence. "Paperwork's filed with the Dean's office. Waiver signed for accidental death or dismemberment."

Gael took a dry gulp.

"Well, go on then," Rav prompted.

Gael lowered the stylus, outlining a tentative loop on the subject's inner wrist. When the inert man did not suddenly convulse or burst into conflagration, the boy let out his breath and drew the next glyph.

His confidence caught, gears clicking into place across his brow. It was not until they reached the delicate operations along the sternum that the experiment took a turn. The subject's breath grew shallow. Sweat slickened his skin.

"You're channeling too much. Narrow the stream," Rav instructed.

"I can't reach the heart if I pull back," Gael argued.

"You're going to send him into cardiac arrest. Put down the stylus. You don't need it. Use your hands instead."

"My hands?"

"Yes. The phalanged slabs of meat at the ends of your wrists. That way you can feel arrhythmia and correct yourself before you stop his heart."

"But how am I to channel without a...?" Gael blinked.

Rav snatched the stylus and snapped it in two. "It's a fucking metal twig. Do you think I would need your staggering incompetence if it were imbued with its own magic?"

The boy cowered, eyes popping from his head like a gawping fish. Terror stench engulfed him.

"That will be all for today, Gael," Dr. Faidra called, this time raising her head.

"Y-yes, Dr. Faidra."

The piss poor excuse for a medical student scrambled for the door. His panicked footsteps pattered on the stairs.

Dr. Faidra sighed and set down her instruments. She pushed up her magnifier goggles onto her forehead and crossed the room with a stern look.

"He's the top of his class," she stated, cocking her head and crossing her arms.

"We need a healer, Selene," Rav entreated. "A true healer."

"Unfortunately, Ravan, the only true healer I've ever encountered got himself executed for a traitor."

Rav glared at her, ignoring the barbs sinking into his chest. "Don't bring me any more of your lobotomized scholars."

He tossed the broken ends of the stylus across the floor stones in a chorus of tinny pings...

"Good gods, what happened to you?"

The mouse squeak burst his recollections. Rav found wide blue eyes watching him from behind wisping red curls that had broken loose from captivity. He had hardly noticed the boat ride that had carried them to the great gray island adrift in the center of the arctic channel. Now he stood on a low deck swarming with Etrugans. And Skylarks, apparently.

"He needs a couple of bones set. Can you help, tiny doctor?" Rión asked.

"I'm not that kind of doctor," Leanora apologized.

Rión shook her head and turned an annoyed tangerine glance to Rav. "Fucking humans."

Rav flashed disdainful teeth in agreement. Rión laughed.

"I like you, vampire. Let's get you cleaned up. You look like you got mauled by a rabid firewolf."

Rav shook his head. "Take me to Ely."

"He's already in the infirmary. Come."

As they walked, he caught darting minnows of conversation swirling about him.

"Cold as mammoth balls out here..."

"You know what those feel like, do you, Heimrik?"

"Keep your shiteating claws off my grog..."

"Shifty as a fucking roach on feast day..."

Good to know the Etrugan language had yet to rust in the addled cauldron he called a mind. He had known their vivid, bellicose tongue when he woke from death's embrace. It was not until Dr. Faidra led a hulking, shackled figure into the Oubliette that he rediscovered this latent knowledge passed down from his former life.

"Here you are, Ravan. A true healer," Dr. Faidra smirked. "Fresh from the Iron Dunes."

"I didn't ask for a slave," Rav glared.

Dr. Faidra raised rancorous eyes over her spectacles. "I find it doubtful that either of you wants to go back to the stinking pits from whence you've been plucked. Take what you can get."

The Etrugan watched her return to her tools and scraps of metal. He stood a full head taller than Rav, complexion a delicate shade of periwinkle made fierce by his mountainous stature and black-rimmed irises.

Rav met his gaze. "What is your name?"

He found the growled utterance formed easily in a fanged mouth already inclined to make a toothsome point. The Etrugan betrayed surprise only in the gilded ring that brightened the muddy gray of his eyes.

"I am Fraynulf Light Touch."

"I am Ravan Aurelio."

"You are not human," Fraynulf observed, curiosity growing monochrome in his eyes.

"I am not."

"Are you a captive too?"

"I am."

Rav noticed Dr. Faidra casting furtive glances from her cobwebbed corner. He continued, "Did Dr. Faidra explain to you our task?"

"She said you need my healing hands. The purpose was not revealed to me."

"There is no need to know the purpose, only to succeed," Dr. Faidra called in Lanica. A deliberate reminder she understood their conversation even if she did not deign to speak the tongue of the western highlands.

Fraynulf signaled his next message with his hands. This too Rav followed with hitherto unrealized fluency. "What of the doctor?"

"Not evil like the others," Rav returned. "Not to be trusted."

"Are you to be trusted?" Fraynulf signed.

Rav shook his head and adjusted his jacket collar to reveal the glyph-ridden metal encircling his throat. He signed, "My will is not my own."

The Etrugan's eyes made contemplative patterns.

Aloud, Rav continued, "Shall we begin?"

Fraynulf lifted a page of notes and sketches from Rav's drafting table, curiosity already bright-kindled in his eyes. His claws drifted over the annotations, then moved to the next page.

At last, he looked up at Rav, eyes vacillating between radiant golden calculation and frozen blue dread.

"What is the point of living forever if you are asleep?" the Etrugan asked.

"I don't know," Rav replied.

"You wrote all this?" Fraynulf gestured to the messy manuscript.

Rav inclined his head.

"You are clearly a master healer. This would impress even the Circle of Shaman. Why do you need me?"

Rav lowered his gaze to his inkwell, nearly bled dry in the thrust of manic invention.

"They destroyed my magic," he said.

"Magic is woven into the soul," Fraynulf growled. "How can it be destroyed?"

"Maybe my soul is gone too," Rav signed...

"Watch your step, vampire."

Rión lent a meaty hand as they descended a set of stairs leading below deck. The infirmary lay a dim, tidy compartment beyond barrack rows where long bunks stacked one atop the other in shallow indentations along the wall. A furnace blasted dry heat against the winter freeze.

Ely slept the sole occupant of the sick bay cots bolted to the floor. A small, round-cheeked Etrugan leaned over him, deep gray fingers extended above his chest. Golden light spilled from her hands, dancing over the conjurer like sunbeams filtered through soft woodland boughs. Rav searched for any strained notes radiating from the limp figure. There. A faint shimmer. Like a feeble reflex squeeze from a coma patient's hand.

"Come," Rión prodded his elbow.

Rav limped onward. Rión guided him to a large wash basin. He collapsed on the half-barrel seat adjacent. Rión wetted a cloth and sat opposite him, raising the sturdy cotton to his brow.

"I don't need coddling," he hissed.

"I only coddle my beloved's cock," the Etrugan snarled. "Now hold still. There's a hole like a hellmouth in your forehead."

Rav grunted resignation, sitting a disgruntled statue while Rión mopped the blood from his face. His gaze crossed the sick bay, drawn to the aureate light spilling from the young healer's palms. His imagination rendered its luminous journey through the conjurer's pores to the vessels of his heart. Inside its struggling chambers. Soothing. Fortifying. Flowing into his veins.

Wake up. Grin. Make a stupid joke. Right the world.

"Shoulder next, vampire. Do you want a drink first?"

Rav shook his head. "Just do it."

Pop! Flames crackled a gunpowder trail along his nerves. Then relief.

"Not so easy, this next part," Rión warned.

When he still refused the bottle, she took a gulp for herself. Three thick-muscled Etrugans hefted him onto a cot and held him in place while Rión set his leg. He howled. Retched. Sank teeth into a mossy green forearm.

The wronged Etrugan shook him loose with profanities, and he spat out thick, tar-like blood. Bitter and salinated as seawater. A terrible mistake, biting Etrugans.

Rav lay back, drained. Spinning. A handful of starlight would quench the residual ache, but he could not move to return to the deck above. No matter. With bones back in place, the healing process would take over quickly. Faster by leagues than a human.

"Rest, vampire," Rión commanded.

Rav lifted his eyelids only as she walked away. Rión stopped at the foot of Ely's bed. The young healer had lowered her hands and sat back. Slate face pinched with exhaustion. Eyes palest blue. She lifted her stony hands with their curled claws and signed, "I've done all I can."

"You've done good work, daughter," Rión signed back. "You must rest yourself."

"He can't die, Mother."

"It is for Morgata to decide. Come eat, Brin. You must keep your strength."

The healer lowered her face, laying her hand over Ely's with familial tenderness. Brin heeded her mother's gentle prompting tap and scampered off.

Rión laid an enormous paw over Ely's forehead. Then she bent close to his ear. Rav heard the low, guttural whisper clear as if he knelt beside her.

"Come on, starshine. This world is too fucking dark without your light."

Then she straightened and followed her daughter from the infirmary.

Rav tried to connect electricity to his impulses. Just a few paces to the bedside. Might as well be a galaxy to cross.

Wake up, conjurer. Why won't you wake?

Presently, he noticed Kai Novara peering in from the dim corridor. His face remained unreadable, but Rav recognized the look of a silent war waged within. Finally, the pirate king released a heavy breath and retreated. Coward. Come back. Tell him to wake up. He'd listen to you.

The ginger scholar ventured down next. She hovered at the end of Ely's cot. Paced. Flexed her devious little hands. Then she sat down and kept vigil.

Rav closed his eyes, drifting on a tide of lingering pain and itching bones fusing back together. His mind returned again to the sepulchral gloom of the Oubliette where Fraynulf wove his spells through organ and vein and musculature. When he completed the task on one immobilized patient, Dr. Faidra bid them removed to an alcove in the neighboring dungeon. Then she brought in another. If one subject was large, virile, and male, the next was a petite pubescent female or an elderly intersex paraplegic.

With each new case, they recorded meticulous observations. Diet. Magical affinities. Defects. Then Rav adjusted the parameters of their experiments on paper, and Fraynulf administered the enchantments.

At first, their subjects woke within hours or days. But as weeks passed into months, they accumulated a collection of bodies lying in stasis without need for food or water or air. No changes in vitals or body composition. No organ failure or excrement. No bed sores. Just living sculptures embalmed in serene rest.

"Do they dream?" Fraynulf wondered.

Rav shook his head. "They shouldn't be dreaming, Fray. Not if their brains are to remain properly preserved."

It was the Etrugan healer that thrashed about with night terrors. His hands grew hesitant. His handwriting weary. Daily observations illegible.

"Gods' balls, how long must we continue?" he demanded.

"Until Dr. Faidra is satisfied," Rav replied.

"Then what?" he signed. "What will become of us?"

Rav studied his ink-gored quill. He should lie. Spin rose-tinted fantasies to keep the hope alive. Such fairytales were better left to humans.

"Death if they are kind," Rav signed back.

"When are they ever kind?"

"Never. But I will be. I swear a blood oath, brother in chains, you will not live in dreamless sleep nor return to the mines."

This seemed a comfort to Fraynulf. More than any fragile hope. The strength returned to the healer's hands, and he woke trembling and screeching no more.

One night, while the Etrugan slept, Rav made his usual rounds. The "pickle jar" Fraynulf called this room with its rows of brined humans lying in padded crates. He walked to each, lifting a chart fixed to the end of the box and marking in vital signs. Unchanged. Unchanged. Blood pressure elevated. Bring Fray in to take a look.

As he passed into the dungeon corridor, locking the door behind him, he caught a scent that raised the hackles on his neck.

Rav slithered into the shadows outside the laboratory door which stood open a crack. Just wide enough to see Dr. Faidra standing with arms crossed opposite Dr. Brahm, his hair oiled back and lab coat exchanged for a slick three-piece suit.

"Everything is going to plan, Harald. There is no reason to change course now when we're so close."

"I don't think you understand the nature of ingress, Selene."

"Of course I understand. I'm not a simpleton," Dr. Faidra snapped.

"No, you're a genius when it comes to your contraptions. But this is outside your realm of expertise, and you know it. I am beginning to doubt that we can control the ingress long enough to safely open the Hollow, much less secure her inside."

"Is it your own skill you doubt, Harald, or mine?" Dr. Faidra inquired, tone dripping arsenic.

"Both, if I'm being honest," Dr. Brahm replied, massaging his temples.

"Come look at this, Harald," she directed.

Rav edged closer to observe the sheaf of papers that Dr. Faidra lifted from the junk heap of her desk. Dr. Brahm leafed through them, brow ruffling as he read over their contents.

"So, you think the keys will be able to control the ingress?" he asked.

"Correct."

"I'll need to review the equations," Dr. Brahm murmured.

"Take your time, Harald. I leave tomorrow, as you know. I won't need those back for a few weeks."

Dr. Brahm raised an eyebrow. "Demon hunting?"

"Just an observational expedition this time. Nothing to get excited over. I still have a few modifications to make before we're ready."

"Well, be careful out there. Those elemental bastards are tricky."

"Touching, your concern," Dr. Faidra droned.

"I just need you in one piece until this is all over and done with."

As Dr. Brahm turned for the exit, Rav retreated to the cramped cell where Fraynulf snored.

"Fray," he whispered. "Fray, wake up."

The Etrugan snorted and swiped a groggy claw across the air.

"She's working with him. Selene and Dr. Brahm. They're planning something together."

"Of course they are. Did you think this was all just an experiment for the sake of science?" Fraynulf scoffed.

"No," Rav glowered. "But I was under the impression that Selene was at odds with the Tower. With Brahm."

"What gave you that idea?"

"They hate each other. He's a conniving, vicious monster."

"And?" Fraynulf blinked at him.

"Why would she do it?"

"Ah..." Fraynulf nodded, shaking an epiphanous digit. "We Etrugans call this Aethelstock's Affliction. To find affection for your captor because they show a trace of kindness."

"I hold no affection for Dr. Faidra," Rav spat.

"It is clear, brother in chains, that you are hurt by her allegiance to the Cosmologist that maimed your soul."

Rav clenched molten-raged fists. He could deny nothing.

Fraynulf bobbed his head. "Classic Aethelstock."

"I need to find out what they're planning," Rav hissed.

"Naturally. And yes, I will help you."

"Selene is leaving on her expedition tomorrow. We can search for answers then."

"At last, something to look forward to in this dusty shithole."

Dr. Faidra left them under the supervision of a fleshy, bald-crowned Cosmologist armed with a stake and a crossbow. Their monstersitter disappeared for hours at a time, then returned to sip mead from a green glass bottle until he rattled the stones with apneic snuffling.

After a few days' observation confirmed this routine, the two prisoners awaited the witching hour when the mead completed its spell. The drunken Cosmologist slumped over in his chair. The vampire searched among the papers left on Dr. Faidra's desk, and the Etrugan picked the lock on the filing cabinet.

After combing through stacks of scrawled notes, Rav reached for a desk drawer handle only to come to a halt in a crackle of burning glyphs.

"Fray," he called. "I can't open this drawer. There must be something in here."

The drawer slid open easily for the Etrugan. Not even a lock to spring. Fraynulf lifted a bundle of scrolled draft papers. The glyphs sizzled when Rav reached for them.

"I can't touch them," Rav whispered. "This is it "

Fraynulf unrolled them carefully. The first depicted a thick-limbed oak with mechanical roots. The following page diagrammed an angle of the machine's geared bowels, meticulously shaded and labeled to the smallest bolt and nut.

"Do you understand it?" Fraynulf asked.

Rav strained to focus. The glyphs sang on his neck every time he cast his eyes upon the page.

"I can't look long enough," he grunted through gritted teeth. "Can you make anything of it?"

Fraynulf shook his head.

"I'm no engineer. This is all fucking Grognik to me."

"Damn it all," Rav snarled.

Fraynulf raised a claw. "This one is of interest. It shows a figure, human I assume, bound inside a chamber in the false tree's trunk. Dr. Faidra has copied some of your notes here, Rav. Whatever devil fuckery this is, our work is part of it. And the witch doesn't want you to understand how the pieces fit together."

"Why should it matter to me?" Rav asked, dread kindling as he, once again, pondered where lay the trap.

"Hm," Fraynulf mused.

"What is it?"

"She's specified some of our parameters. This is intended for an adult human female. Mid-sized, if I were to compare to our sleeping beauties. Considerable magical orientation. Named gods, we've never tried to pickle magic like this."

Rav snatched the page out of the Etrugan's hand, every muscle trembling as the glyphs raised black smoke and a stench like a hog on a spit. A name stood emblazoned in beautiful calligraphy beneath the figure.

Ariel.

So that was why the good doctor kept him in the dark...

Rav opened his eyes, tears raised with the memory newly bloodied in his mind.

Betrayed. Betrayed. Traitor.

He pressed his fists to the sides of his skull, ready to fracture the bones to block out the flooding voices. His knees cracked against the floor as he thrashed from the cot.

Monster. Evil. Abomination.

Hands grasped his shoulders. Someone shouted his name from across a canyon. Hard limbs twisted around him, holding him immobile.

Weak. Pet. Good boy. Good boy.

Then suddenly a sliver of peace. Like the eye of the storm come to shield him from chaos.

Hush. Calm. You are safe.

Lost Nix. Lost Ely. Lost Ariel. Forever. Forever. Forever.

Safe. You are safe.

Breath poured into his dormant lungs. His vision cleared. His thoughts eased their cramped knots. The young Etrugan healer crouched before him, clasping his face between warm, glowing fingers.

"Are you with us again, vampire?" Rión's growl rumbled in his ear.

"Yes," he rasped.

When Rión released her python's grip from around him, he signed to his cherubic rescuer, "Thank you, Brin."

Her eyes beamed delighted gold. In a most un-Etruganish gesture, her lips curved into a smile made all the more precious by the myriad pointed teeth that protruded from beneath her granite lips.

"You're welcome," she signed. "It must hurt to have thorns inside your head."

Rav nodded. A smile bloomed on his own lips. It wilted as his gaze spilled over to the conjurer still motionless on his cot.

Despite his violent fit, Rav found his injuries had already healed enough that he could walk without too pronounced a limp. He touched Ely's waxen brow, the skin cold and moist.

Brin tugged at his sleeve. He turned to her, and she signed, "You can help."

Rav shook his head. She took his hands and squeezed them once in pointed indication. Then she added, "Touch the stars."

Rav's heart fluttered. The conjurer lay immobile like this before in South Sea when Death had nearly burned him through.

"Rión, can you carry him outside?" Rav asked.

The Etrugan warrior eyed him. "You want to take him back out into that cold?"

Brin signed, "Please, Mother."

Rión's eyes warmed at her daughter's entreaty. She lifted Ely, bundling his blankets around him to buffer against the frigid night. Brin looped her arm through Rav's as they ventured above deck.

Rav breathed a sigh as he beheld a cloudless sky abundant with stars. Rión led them to a clear space on the topmost of three layered decks. She laid her burden on the floor and stepped back. Brin joined her mother leaning against the iron railing.

Rav knelt beside the conjurer and lifted his hand skyward, winding a ribbon of starlight about his fingers. He sipped the first draught himself, letting the nutrient elixir warm his stomach and frolic through his veins. The second he let rest on his tongue.

He wasn't quite sure how the Etrugans would take him sinking his teeth into the conjurer's neck. Mortifying, the notion of attempting such a thing under their watch. He bent to Ely's mouth as he would to resuscitate one drowned. Instead of breath, he delivered light. Paused. Siphoned more.

The conjurer stirred. *Yes, stay with me. Don't fade again.*

Ely curled gentle fingers around his wrist. The conjurer's presence revived in a sudden burst, a fading sun combusted back to brilliance. Rav wished to bask in that warmth and light forever.

Evil. Traitor. Pet.

Rav drew back. Ely gazed up at his face with concern, sensing the discord that rippled from the bleak pool of his thoughts.

"Rav? What's wrong?"

"Rest, conjurer," Rav replied, brushing his fingers along Ely's temples. Sending him off to sleep. Like a bone set back in place, healing could begin with death magic's rhythm restored.

Rav sat up and signaled to Rión. "Get him inside. He just needs time now."

Rión breathed a hefty sigh and squeezed Rav's shoulder in gratitude before scooping up the conjurer and carrying him back to the furnace warmth below deck.

Rav climbed onto legs as unsteady as his insides. The dark stretch of fjord and glacier that surrounded them reminded him of the ghostly Spine under the spell of the moon. He could disappear into the frozen labyrinth. Never to face the disdain or disappointment that would surely follow for a scarred, dead thing with half a mind and a hollowed out soul. Lost Nix. Gave her away. Pet. Good boy.

He had fought it, hadn't he? Just as he fought then. When he discovered the true purpose of his occupation all those months, when he discovered the cost behind the trick of kindness, he never wondered what should be done next. The only question was how. He could not destroy his work. The collar wracked him with such spasms for tearing a single page that their guard grew suspicious and sent him out for the day.

When the Cosmologist slept, Rav pored over the doctor's plans, memorizing their wicked workings to the reek of melting flesh. Fraynulf treated his glyph burns as best he could with a metal barrier concealing the worst of the damage.

Though the lengthy proofs and mathematical jargon escaped him, Rav gleaned enough to understand the insidious nature of the biomechanical prison.

Then one night, he waited for the Cosmologist's telltale snores and set off. Down the hall. Up the stairs. No one had specified how far he might stray from the subterranean vault. So long as he kept no ill intentions in his thoughts, he violated none of the directives etched about his throat. Just going for a walk.

The midnight campus stood deserted. Here and there a studious lamp flickered in a window, but the rest slept on in shadowed silence.

One step beyond the eastern fountain bowled him backward into the water. White steam poured a ghoulish haze over the courtyard. He clawed a showering escape from the fountain and hurled himself into an arching updraft. For a moment the wind's cackle drowned out the shrieking of glyphs. He had grown used to their seething and simmering.

Something twinged in his side. Then wrenching agony consumed him as his ribs imploded. Legs and arms twisted as if in the clutches an invisible assailant. His back arched, spine cracked with a retort like a canon. The collar gave a final shriek and crumbled from his neck.

He careened in a plummeting spiral and slammed into the earth with meteoric force.

He lay motionless. Blind. Paralyzed. Mercifully numb.

The collar was gone. His body would soon repair itself enough to crawl into some hole to wait out the day. Then he would find Ariel. Warn her.

Voices made garbled syllables in his ears. He felt himself lifted and transported. He still could not see, but he recognized the smell in a wave of futile panic. The Tower.

His eyes began to make out shapes and shadows as the rough hands that bore him heaved him down. Close walls on all sides. Toes scraping tapered iron. Glyphs rang and ignited around the perimeter. Even when his bones mended he would not be able to escape the sarcophagus.

A face appeared above the opening.

"Most impressive, Ravan," Dr. Brahm sneered. "I've never tested the collar to such a limit. Selene will be disappointed you won't be there to see your work completed. But we have what we need. Be a good boy, and maybe you'll get to come out and play again in a decade or two."

Rav uttered a choked plea that died in his crumpled larynx. Dr. Brahm gestured with his hand, and the heavy lid groaned into place, trapping him in stifling darkness...

A soft, leathery paw patted his elbow. Rav took a stunted breath, returning to the cool open air of the Etrugan ship.

"Are you okay?" Brin signed.

He managed a brittle grimace. "Don't worry about me."

"Why not?"

"Waste of magic."

Brin shook her head. Her jagged grin melted the iceberg throbbing in his chest. "You're funny, Uncle Rav. Now come inside. I'm cold."

Chapter Twenty-Four

Midnight Sun

Ely woke to find a cheery gray face peering down at him through lustrous amethyst eyes.

"Hello, Uncle Ely," Brindle signed.

"Hello, sunshine! Nice to see your face."

His hands talked a little lopsided, but not too bad considering it came as a delightful surprise to be alive at all.

"You healed me?" Ely realized with a gentle smile.

Brin shook her head, eyes glowing shy lemon. "I tried, but I couldn't fix you. Uncle Rav star kissed you and brought you back to life."

Ely blinked at her. Perhaps he was still a bit slow. A stone sank in his stomach. He seemed to recall a hazy memory of his friend in abject distress.

"Where is he?" Ely asked, searching reflexively for the vampire's presence. His bated breath returned as his consciousness brushed against tumultuous darkness. Rav lingered somewhere close by.

"He's with Mother," Brin reassured him.

Ely sat up slowly, a freight train roaring in his ears. The swollen cacophony passed, but he still felt the whole room bobbing like a harvest apple in a barrel. They were in a dim, lamplit space with two rows of cots bolted to the floor. Tables and shelves housed linens, bandages, and surgical implements. Ah. He knew this place well. They were aboard the Ulvebrand, named for the firewolves that trotted as cinderous shadows beside their Etrugan familiars. *"Because just like Siggy and her brothers, this beast should not be trusted at sea,"* Rión liked to chuckle.

His old friend had last brought him down to this infirmary to dig a rogue fish hook out of his shoulder after a little incident involving a bet and half a bottle of zaqual.

Ely kicked his way from the nest of blankets. With the blaring furnace belching hellish fury in the corner, sweat puddled between his shoulder blades. His stomach growled like a bear waking from hibernation.

"Is the kitchen still open? I'm starving. I haven't eaten in..." He thought a moment. "Months now."

Brin gasped, stark white horror in her eyes. "Follow me."

A gusty tornado admitted a rush of fanged emotion. Anxiety. Assessment. Relief. All in such rapid succession, Ely found himself shocked that the vampire had not, in fact, bowled him over but merely blocked his path with a neutral expression. Rav appeared to be entirely recovered from the savage beating he endured in Septus. He even sported a new Etrugan longcoat to thoroughly debonair effect.

"He's fine," the round-cheeked Etrugan signed.

"I see that," Rav's long fingers returned. "Thank you."

"You know Etrugan signs?" Ely asked, astonished. "Since when?"

"Since always."

"Of course. You worked with Etrugan healers," Ely recalled, then quickly corrected, "*He* did."

"Starshine!"

Rión thumped into the infirmary, her embrace an affectionate avalanche.

"How are you feeling?" she asked.

"Good as new thanks to Brin," Ely smiled. He glanced at Rav. "And you, apparently?"

Rión laughed like a seism. "Ah, yes, the kiss of life wakes a sleeping beauty."

Though no blood stirred in his cheeks, the vampire's aura blushed.

"Our friend here was just trying to explain what brought you to this night-locked shithole."

Rión's fist cudgeled Rav's shoulder for emphasis. He blinked twice, and his mouth twitched. But he held his footing.

"We're still hunting down the keys to Ariel's prison," Ely said.

Another heavy brick sank in his gut as he met Rav's eyes and found the same thought reflected back. Nix.

Rav dropped his gaze, awash with guilt and shame.

"Can we have a moment, Riri?" Ely asked.

"Of course, little brother. I'll meet you in the mess."

The two Etrugans left them in semi-privacy, though Ely suspected he heard snores from the bunks down the hall.

Rav's hands trembled at his sides. He balled them into fists. They trembled still. Fear spilled in an unfiltered deluge. The tears that glinted in his ocean dark eyes sank a switchblade straight to the heart.

"It was my fault," Ely blurted. "Everything that went wrong in Septus. I hope you can forgive me."

"Forgive...*you*?"

Ely inclined his head. "It was vanity and recklessness and I'll admit a bit of delirium. I dreamed I played the nameless god at Caj for Prometheus. I won. Not surprising. He plays like he learned from a children's picture book. Anyway, I'll explain all that later. The point is, I should never have left you. I'm sorry."

Rav stood motionless, eyes riveted to his face. His presence felt more raw and frazzled than ever. It crackled like a live wire severed in two and sparking at both ends. Though his visible wounds had vanished, Septus left a mark not easily erased. Ely's blood cooled serpentine. When he got his hands on that Watcher...

White haze trembled at the edge of his vision. *There you are. Welcome back.*

Ely felt Rav's questioning hand on his arm.

"I'm fine," he said. "Back to cosmic equilibrium, it would seem. But you know that, don't you? Are you ever going to tell me about this kiss of life that's taken over the scandal sheets?"

Rav sighed. "You were burnt out. I resuscitated you. There was nothing untoward about it."

"I've never known you to be untoward, my darling Lovelace," Ely grinned.

"Tell that to your sister in arms," Rav smirked.

"She likes you," Ely said as they set out for the stairs.

"I can't imagine why."

"You speak beautiful Etrugan. You cut a rugged, swashbuckling figure in her clothes. And you make her daughter smile."

"I bit one of her crew," Rav admitted.

"Yet another reason she'd find you endearing," Ely shrugged.

He paused as his gaze alighted upon an enchanting and most unexpected face.

"Nice to see you up and about," Leanora lilted.

Ely beamed, the usual butterflies scattering across his chest as she peered up at him through a fringe of auburn lashes. "Don't tell me you came all this way just to rescue me, Dr. Skylark."

"Not to worry, dear man," she breezed. "I'm here to look after the machines. And my brother who seems to have disappeared."

"Ah, Victor's here too? This is turning out to be quite the expedition."

"You only know the half of it, Elyssandro," she said with a wry curl of the lips.

"Well, we were just headed to the galley to find something to eat, if you'd like to join."

"You two go ahead," Rav interjected.

Ely caught his arm. "What's the matter?"

"Nothing, conjurer," he said. "I can't stomach the cooking smells. You go. I'll be close by."

The vampire sprang away into the rigging, a great dark bird. Ely's gaze followed him, tracing his presence when he melded into shadows. Perhaps it was months of constant proximity. Perhaps it was the close call at Septus that latched fitful talons in his chest.

He found Leanora watching him with a curious expression.

"Shall we?" Ely asked, fitting a smile in place.

The mess hall lay within the Ulvebrand's mid-level forecastle and thrived, as ever, the heart of ship life. Smoke and charcoal working sorcery on savory delights revived his long-reposed humanity. Ely's stomach bleated a pitiful reminder of its long months with only starlight for sustenance.

Rión banged on a table to summon him over to her. She had already piled him a colossal wooden board with chunks of peppered meat speared on kebabs, marinated tanuba eggs with electric blue yolks, fire-blackened root vegetables, and hunks of crusty bread.

"I didn't know you were coming, tiny human doctor," Rión grunted.

"I'm fine, thank you," Leanora replied with a polite shake of her strawberry mane.

"Share with me, Lea," Ely offered, sitting down on a rough bench opposite Rión. "I'll explode if I try to eat all this,"

"Well, maybe pass me one of those herby potatoes, Elyssandro."

"Certainly. Have a skewer too. And you must try the mushrooms."

"I'm deathly allergic to mushrooms, Elyssandro."

"Oh, shit. Sorry. Have an egg then."

Victor Skylark approached their table balancing a bowl of stew and two frothed-over mugs of beer. A sturdy, handsome figure in a hooded anorak lined with tawny fur, he appeared to be restored to full vigor. Ruddy life returned to his freckled cheeks. Red hair neatly trimmed. Only his moon-pale eyes recalled his accident.

Blindness did not seem to deter his mobility. He plotted a direct course between the tables without a single misstep and greeted Rión by name before sitting down in the vacant space on the Etrugan's bench.

"Mr. Ruadan. Good to see you," Victor said.

"Likewise," Ely replied, reining in his tongue before he questioned the use of the word *see*. He diverted, "You're looking much more energetic than last I saw you."

"Nothing like a good expedition to regain the old fighting spirit," Victor answered, smile a square-jawed echo of his sister's.

"Yes, the expedition," Ely said. "Perhaps someone might finally explain what you all are doing up here and how you found us?"

Silence volleyed between the Etrugan and the Skylarks. Something they hesitated to share with the class, it seemed.

"We tracked you," Leanora explained. "More precisely, we used Melandromache to track Nix. We followed the signal all the way from South Sea to whatever godforsaken place this must be."

Ely's eyes shifted to Victor, who had grown unnaturally still, like a watch ground to a stop mid-tick. He shuddered free from his petrifaction and asked, "Where's Nix? She's not with you."

"She was captured," Ely replied.

"She's been sending out distress signals since yesterday," Victor said.

"What?" Leonora exclaimed. "Why didn't you say something?"

"Can someone please take me back to chapter one of this story?" Ely interjected. "I seem to be missing some key details. Are you psychic now, Victor?"

"Sort of," Victor chuckled. "No, I can't read your mind."

"How did you know I was thinking that?" Ely asked with narrow-eyed suspicion.

"Easy guess. No, I can't read minds, but for whatever reason, I can still talk to Mel. She just passed along that little morsel about Nix a moment ago."

"Fascinating," Ely chimed. "That still doesn't explain what you're doing here. Unless Nix asked you to come. Doubtful. We were having a merry old time of it until Septus. You couldn't have sailed that fast."

Ely turned to Rión.

"You're being awfully quiet, Riri. What aren't you telling me?"

"It was Kailari Novara that warned me you were walking into trouble," she grumbled with reluctance.

Ely frowned. "Kai? Why would he think that?"

Rión's eyes fumed poison green. "Because he tossed your name to the Apostle like a fucking scrap of bacon."

"He didn't mean to," Leonora jumped in. "He didn't even know Elyssandro was alive."

"Why are you defending that arrogant island shit bird?" Rión spat.

"He's my friend," Leonora replied, nostrils flaring, blue eyes defiant in the face of the razor-toothed monolith glaring down at her.

Rión laughed. "Kailari is no one's friend, tiny doctor. He is a king first, a selfish bastard second."

"Enough!" Ely snapped, voice charged with the legion's distorted fury. Death magic dispelled in a blackened spiral around his clenched fist.

Rión stared at him. Eyes obsidian from wall to wall, their expression obscured as with armor. Ready for battle.

"My children are aboard this ship, little brother," the Etrugan intoned in a lethal, warning growl.

Ely took a shaking breath and concealed his hand beneath the table. The escaped ether spiral remained embedded in the wood grain.

"I'm sorry," he murmured.

"No, *we're* sorry, Elyssandro," Leanora insisted. "We wanted you to have a moment's recovery before we started pestering you with all the circumstantial details. That's why his majesty returned to his ship. So you could speak to him in your own time."

"Returned to his ship?" Ely repeated, that dull, swimming ache bewailing his temples again. "He's here?"

"He was the one that found you out there on the ice," Leanora told him.

Ely rose from his seat, suddenly woozy and stifled by the packed, smoky room. He left the galley without offering an explanation, relieved to breathe in the arctic chill.

Climbing the narrow stairs to the topmost deck, he walked the length of the railing. He saw nothing apart from night sky reflected on black water, but as he turned starboard, he found the hint of distortion in the gleaming pelt. Mirrorwood.

"Do you want me to take you across?"

Tangled tightness unsnarled in his chest as the vampire descended at his side.

"I don't know," Ely murmured, turning his gaze once again out to the channel. His throat turned to viper's coils and his tongue to sand. "Maybe we should just go. Return to Septus and track down Nix."

"We could," Rav nodded. "But I suspect, conjurer, that your thoughts will stay behind on that ship. It never turns out well. You trying to accomplish anything at all while distracted."

Ely sighed. His fingers rapped out a staccato rhythm on the railing.

"It's more difficult than usual, Rav, holding it in," he confided.

"Give it some time," Rav advised. "I'm sure you'll be back to sugarplums and daffodils soon enough."

Ely looked up at the silver-flecked shadow of the Marisola, then back to the vampire.

"What would you do?" he asked.

Rav's jaw tightened, unrest boiling once again beneath the surface. "Don't leave it to regret, Elyssandro. Believe me."

Ely watched him a moment. Imbibed the essence of the pain his friend kept locked inside his death-sealed chest.

"Alright," he said. "Let's go."

The vampire hooked an arm around his waist, and they catapulted from the high Etrugan deck to the sleek Séoc vessel. Ely's heart thundered as his feet touched down on mirrorwood. A silhouette straightened at the helm, face patterned in shadows and moonlight. The start to a thousand yearning dreams.

Rav disappeared before Ely could entreat him to stay. Any traces of cool, collected ease departed with him.

The pirate king descended from the quarterdeck, spry as ever. They stood at a respectful distance, gazes reacquainting, adjusting to harsh angles and foreign lines wrought by the years.

Kai cleared his throat. "You are well, diakana?" he asked.

"Well enough," Ely answered.

Why did words loll so heavy? He had lived and relived this moment. What happened to all the eloquent speeches planned in such meticulous detail?

Kai stared at his face, agony afire in his eyes.

"*Che'miora,*" he whispered.

The word seemed to lend the pirate king courage enough to approach. To reach out and touch Ely's face with fingers weathered by sail and sword.

"*Che'miora,*" he repeated. "My love."

Ely lost the breath trapped in his chest. Tears broke loose to douse those tender, stroking fingertips. Kai bent closer, pressing his mouth to the salted flood.

"Damn you, Kai Novara," Ely breathed.

Kai entrapped the curses between his lips. Ely devoured his kiss with violent hunger. Describing the long, lonely years with tongue and teeth.

Kai welcomed his despair, arms crushed around him, fingers curling in his hair.

"They told me you were dead," the pirate king managed at last.

"Why did you believe them?" Ely demanded.

"I'm only a man, diakana," Kai answered when a moment's breath allowed. "I couldn't scour the stars to learn their lies. Why didn't you come back to me? Write to me. Anything!"

"You were married!" Ely growled.

"What could that matter?" Kai exclaimed.

Ely broke away, driving the pirate king back a step. "I would have died for that place at your side, and you gave it away. How could that not matter?"

"It meant nothing without you," Kai replied. Voice hoarse. Eyes glistening. "I was yours, *che'miora*. You wrote your name on my soul when you stole me back from Death. I would have forsaken any vow. I would have run away with you to live in your beautiful world of ghosts and talking bones. But now..."

He lowered his head, voice lost to grief a moment.

"Will you come inside with me, Ely?" he murmured. "Just to talk."

Ely followed him to the captain's cabin. The small, cold room with its single porthole gazing out at the sea looked so bare and colorless. He remembered the decadent flare of patterned fabrics hung from the ceiling. Floor and walls made spectacular with animal pelts and iridescent feathers. All barren now save for a white flag stitched with a single black sun. Its wavering corona arched and folded around itself. A death magic spiral.

Kai lit a lamp on the scuffed desk. Ely glanced at the paint flaking from the wall. The faint scent of decaying wood, preserved only by the sudden freeze without. How had he let his beloved Marisola fall into such disrepair?

"Nothing is as you remember," Kai said, following the path of his eyes. "Enemies and allies alike run for cover when the shadow of my fleet spills across their horizon. They call me *Ne'mori Raka*."

"Midnight Sun," Ely translated with a glance at the death magic ensign hung on the wall.

"Seúza will never crawl from beneath the blistered black skies of my vengeance. I rule with iron that would turn even Tennoc's heart cold if it still beat in her breast. That it does not is also my doing."

Ely turned over this revelation in silence. Kai pressed on.

"My hands are forever stained with the toil of making Novara a name to fear. I will do it a thousand times over again so that when I pass it down to my daughter, she will be as the kings of the ancient days. Divine. Unquestioned."

"Is that what you were doing in the Cosmologist fortress?" Ely asked softly.

Kai inclined his head.

"You can't trifle with death magic, Kai. It will destroy you."

"It's not for me," the pirate king replied.

He sprang a hidden compartment in the desk and retrieved a photograph from inside, holding it out to Ely. The dimpled grin captured in gray and black was the mirror of the mischievous boy he had met on the beach so long ago. Before life's crucible fires transmuted him to brutal steel.

"She has your hands," Kai said. "Elyssa Morena Novara."

Ely tried to draw breath but found it caught like a knife between the ribs.

"At night she sits upon the beach, listening to the stars. I have seen her thread silver light between her hands and play with it like any other child might shape clay."

"How? How can that be?" Ely asked, voice a strangled whisper.

Kai turned his harrowed smile toward him. "I told you, *che'miora*, you claimed my soul when you brought me back. And all my line with me."

Ely looked down again at the exuberant grin. Restless fireworks crackled and hissed within him. *You stole from us. Did you think it would come without a price?*

Would she be cursed to live as he did? Hated. Hunted. Damned to a life among cobwebs and wraiths.

Ely set down the photograph. Heartbeat crooked.

"I didn't tell you this to burden you," Kai soldiered on. "I needed you to understand why I betrayed you."

"Are you talking about the Apostle?" Ely asked, turning to face the pirate king.

"When I was captured by the Canon, I thought it was a simple act of war. They know my name. I have raided their shores. Sunk their ships. Piked templar heads on mothers' doorsteps. But they didn't bring me to that prison because of my name or deeds."

"Titus wanted to know how you came back from the dead," Ely said.

Kai confirmed with gaze averted. "The smiling Apostle learned quickly he could not break me with mere torture. But his woman."

"The Watcher? Sister Ignatius?"

"Yes, that was her name," Kai shuddered. "She is a thief of the mind. She made time stop. She sniffed out my terrors and brought them to life."

Kai let his eyelids drop, swallowing the poisoned draught of a memory. He inhaled slowly.

"I could not allow them to learn the truth about Elyssa. I gave them your name. I told them it was you that brought me back. That you had also resurrected your mother. I didn't know then that you had survived Morag. But..."

"It wouldn't have made a difference," Ely finished.

Kai's cheek bled sallow, but resolve flinted his eyes. "No."

"How can you imagine that I would see protecting your daughter as a betrayal?" Ely enjoined.

No defense parried.

"Don't you know that I would trade my life for hers in an instant? What in this world could be more precious? I would tear the soul out of anything that threatened her harm."

"*Che'miora*," Kai murmured. A frail plea.

"Didn't you ever wonder what kind of father I would be?" Ely asked, only just discovering the thorn lodged in his heart as the words tumbled from his lips.

Maybe it was unfair, such a question. Who was he but a lurking specter haunting a past that never truly belonged to him?

"It doesn't matter," Ely said, fury punctured. "I will take care of the Watcher. Believe me, she will answer for all she has done. And when I accomplish what I have set out to accomplish, I will have freed the most powerful diakana ever to live. Elyssa will be safe. And she will not be alone."

Kai gasped a sharp exhale. Like the world's weight budged just a fraction from atop his shoulders. As silence divided them into their own thoughts, Ely took his leave. Weariness stooped his spine. He wanted to crawl into a hole to sleep or cry for the next decade.

Out on the solitary deck, he took a deep breath of frosted winter midnight. The cool draft cleared his head a touch.

"Are you there?" he whispered. No more than a prayer.

Something stirred from the side of a nearby glacier. Then a tall, soothing shadow spirited him away on a gale.

"How much did you hear?"

"I can sit on the ice and hear that your pirate king suffers from severe hypertension."

"So you heard..."

"About the girl? Yes."

Ely pressed his hands to his aching head. His eyes felt like waterlogged grapes about to burst.

He had raised the old shelter out on the ice. A bit more compact. Sloppy at the corners. A conjured stove leeched heat thanks to petrified tanuba guano burgled from the Ulvebrand, long burning and near odorless. Well, tolerable, at least. Rav lay stretched out on a death magic cushion beside him, pectinated fingers resting on his chest.

"What am I supposed to make of it all?" Ely lamented.

"The circumstances are...unique," Rav mused. "But you're hardly the first man taken by surprise at having played a role in the existence of a child."

Ely sat up, regretting his dramatic change of position as the blood drained from his head.

"Role? What role?" he seethed. "Mother. Father. Oh, yes, how could we forget the grinning Reaper?"

"This is a brutal world no matter how you enter it," Rav countered. "Better to be born a dragon than a lamb."

"They're both slaughtered just the same," Ely spat.

He lay back with a groan. Rav lent icy fingers to tame the wildfire rampaging behind his eyes.

Ely continued, "When I spoke with the nameless god—and I know in my marrow that it was not a fever dream—he wanted me to tell him how I did it. Raised the dead without consequence. But there is always consequence."

Rav took back his hand to prop himself up on one side. Observant. Hesitant?

"What happened to your mother, Ely?" Rav asked, voice a volcanic purr.

Ely choked through a breath. That place in his mind seeped like an abscess, neglected and putrid. His whole being flinched away from the rot.

"I can't, Rav," he whispered.

The vampire nodded with a wince and a shudder.

An intruding presence ruffled their shelter like a moist, hot breath on the back of the neck. Rav went rigid at his side.

"Hello, Sister Ignatius," Ely said in sharp Paxat. "Are you lonely out there without your master?"

No answer. Pressing animosity.

"Happy to come keep you company," he said. "Why don't you meet me back in Septus?"

The muggy, malignant presence diffused.

"Challenge accepted, I think," Ely said, slipping back to Lanica.

"You mean to go after the Watcher?" Rav asked.

"I do," Ely answered. "Now, Rav, you don't have to come if you—"

The vampire flicked stone-solid fingers upside Ely's head with a *thunk* like a ripe melon.

"Ow! Fuck me! Why?"

"To stop something idiotic about running off alone from dribbling out of your mouth," Rav replied, climbing to his ever-bare feet. "I'm done basking in bird shit. I want to taste blood."

Ely rubbed his stinging skull. "So do I, dearest Lovelace. So do I."

Silence once again ruled in Septus.

Heaps of smoldering rubble and bone were all that remained of the rustic depot tucked away in the frozen wilderness. Ely had seen the shape of the destruction from above as Rav ferried them to their destination. Tentacles of obsidian death magic radiated a spiral from the murky socket where the church once stood. A midnight sun.

His fault, of course, but every time he reached for guilt, he remembered the girl screaming from the stake as these same flesh-plump bones strode past unmoved by her pleas. The heavens did know your name, poor child. All of Septus burns with you.

Ely planted himself in the town's ruined central hub. Armor raised to the neck. A thin ether mask sheltered his nose and mouth. No helm. He meant to look his opponent in the eye as he plucked out her soul.

Kneeling into ashes, he sank his fingers down to the frozen earth below. Fresh death sang along his knuckles. Carnage reigned to the leveled watchtower at the outpost threshold. Not a single ray of life.

Where are you hiding, Sister?

A slender forked tongue slithered along his cheek at the mask's ridge.

"There you are," he murmured.

The presence bubbled. A mocking giggle just beyond hearing.

Ely spread his fingers wider, injecting ether into ossified earth. A corpse at his side twitched. Across the charred remnants of Septus, effigies groaned to their feet, the tatters of hair and clothing and mollified flesh clinging to blackened skeletons.

He straightened and tugged at the delicate spider silk woven through his newly raised horde. As one, they turned to face him and stamped their feet.

"I like games too, Sister," Ely called, the legion's voices intertwined. His skin vibrated with their impatient seething. "Come play with me."

Rav dropped from the furrowed clouds above. He shook ice crystals from his hair and flourished fangs with a low grunt. Nothing. Still toying.

"I'm getting bored, Sister. Do you have a move or not?"

"Do you think it a good idea to taunt her?" Rav asked.

"Better question," Ely smiled. "Is it a good idea to taunt me?"

A rhythmic beat thrummed behind the clouds. Ely raised his face skyward. Jagged lightning strobed. Just long enough to peel back the darkness around three leviathan figures approaching to the drum of slow, titanic wings. Their unbound eyes glared as molten suns.

"Looks like I'm up first," Rav snarled, crouching low.

"Wait."

Ely retracted his ether exoskeleton to reach his jacket pocket. By luck or design, Ariel's talisman had gone unnoticed by the Apostle during their ruptureside chat.

Rav cast an uneasy glance at the eye and blade baubles.

"It will blind them to you," Ely said.

The vampire allowed him to coil the slim chain around his wrist.

Ely secured the clasp and pressed his hand. "Happy hunting."

Rav launched into the flurry. When the next bolt flared between the clouds, a tiny black shadow hurtled toward the seraphim. A comet aimed for a triad of bellowing planets.

Purling laughter licked his ear. Ely whipped toward the sound. It tiptoed helter-skelter between his gruesome puppets. He followed, straining for the slightest whiff of life.

"Come on out, Sister. I promise I won't bite too hard."

Shrieks howled from the storm. A blazing streak like a falling star spilled through the clouds. The seraph plunged toward the earth, plumed wings rent in bloody ribbons. Ely flung himself from the hailstorm of debris as the fallen creature stamped a crater into the ruins of Septus.

Rav leaped from astride its shoulders, painted crimson head to toes. He lifted a feral, glassy-eyed grin. Higher than a cat in an opium den.

"Two to go," the vampire crowed, then bulleted off.

"Well, at least one of us is having fun," Ely pouted.

Silky little fingers petted his arm. He turned. No one. Misty breath steamed the back of his neck. Nothing. A nibble on the earlobe. A stroke between the legs.

"Come now, Sister. You'll have to buy me dinner first."

Tremulous laughter. A glimmer of spirit. Found you.

Ely whipped death magic tendrils around a crumbling pillar. They snagged on the intruder, whisking her out of her hiding place. Sister Ignatius wriggled against the bindings. Her habit's high collar choked tight against her throat.

Her eyes swallowed his gaze, burnished gold beneath full, angled brows. Rose-stained lips a sensuous snare.

Ely swayed, eyelids cumbersome, mental cogs gummed.

"Wake up, Elyssandro!"

He blinked. The Watcher was gone. A wavering phantom stood in her place, translucent but burning lantern bright.

"Ariel?" Ely sputtered, shaking the swamp fog from his brain.

"Stop playing," she barked. "You've met this kind of magic before. Stay awake!"

A tremor folded through the casting. Ariel vanished.

A starburst blinded him, and the half-column that had sheltered the Watcher exploded into lime powder. Ely ducked as the seraph glided overhead. The backdraft from a great shifting airfoil knocked him flat.

A torpedoed blur swooped upon the wheeling mountain. The seraph stumbled backward, struggling to slow the momentum of its enormous frame. Rav struck again, gauging spraying holes in the creature's throat. The seraph clawed at its neck, flinging the vampire into open air. Its solar eyes unleashed nuclear heat. Bullseye.

"Rav!" Ely shouted, sprinting to his fallen friend.

Smog billowed a gray shroud over his body. No more than a charred, twisted mound of gristle wrapped in the cinders of an Etrugan longcoat.

Ely collapsed to his knees. Death's white haze evaporated as horror closed shackles on his mind.

Laughter. Not a girlish titter. Cold. Deep as night.

"You make it too easy."

Ely sprang to his feet. Rav leaned against the remains of a wall, lips screwed up in a sneer. When he glanced back at the blasted remains, they had disappeared. An illusion.

"Who's the boring one now?"

As the vampire moved closer, Ely saw where the mirage glamoured false. She exaggerated the eyes. Rendered them too bright and captivating. The mouth curved too wicked full. The marble skin glistened too smooth. Too perfect. A daydream.

"Alright, Sister, I see your hand," Ely rasped through torn breath.

"Oh?" Rav's evil twin crooned. "I don't think you do, tiger."

Before he could blink, nightmare Rav held him pinned to the crumbling wall, illusionary forearm grinding substantial against his sternum. A hypnotic fire flickered in the strange, artificial eyes.

The vision pressed close, teeth grazing his ear. "I could've killed you a thousand times over by now."

"But you won't," Ely grunted. "Your master wants me."

"Maybe I'm not a good little boy like Titus."

The counterfeit vampire's tongue drifted like soft snow along his temple.

"Maybe I just like to watch you squirm."

The voice shifted as the phantom lifted his head. Now Kai smiled at him, not with haunted sadness but with the youthful glow of a pirate prince unsullied by Death. Beautiful. Sinister. Hollow.

Ariel was right. He did remember this power pulsing through his mind from the roots of her prison.

"Wake up!"

He gasped, eyes opening to the wasted ashes of Septus. No evil Rav. No hollow Kai. Only snuffling effigies.

Ely twisted his fingers, tugging at the invisible wires draped through senseless animus.

"Find her."

His minions lowed and shuffled. He closed his eyes, repelling from vessel to vessel until...

Her scream crested above the moans of the dead and the bellows of battle from the clouds. Ely strode toward the sound, conducting his ranks before him as a swarming hive. At their epicenter, Sister Ignatius bowed on her knees. Skeletal hands gripped her arms and twisted her shoulders to their limit.

"They have no minds for you to torment, Sister," Ely jabbed.

The Watcher lifted her head, brimstone in her golden eyes.

"You have something of mine," he continued.

"Kill me," she spat. "You'll never find the helyx."

His finger twitched. She squealed as her captors wrenched.

"Elyssandro."

The gentle rebuke halted the wheels of time. His breath snuffed out like a candle. Heartbeats droned a century apart.

She stood among the ashes, snow gathering in her dark curls. Raiment flowing gossamer in the breeze as it had the night she returned from the tomb. Ely's knees trembled as she neared.

This isn't real.

Yet she reached to touch his face with hands warm and soft as love remembered. Spice of the incense burned beside her casket clung to her hair and clothes.

"Mother."

His voice died in his throat. She lowered her hand, eyes sweeping over him with quiet disappointment.

"What are you?" she asked. "You're not the son I loved."

Her eyes quivered. Crimson tears spattered her cheeks. Blood trickled from the corners of her mouth. Gushed in dark rivulets down the folds of her gown.

Ely sank to the ground, clutching his chest. A tremor rippled beneath his collapsed knees. The revenant blinked out. Another trick culled from his own head.

The effigies lay still and silent. Returned to eternal repose. Even his armor had dissipated, leaving the barbaric cold to shear through his ill-prepared garments.

The Watcher was nowhere to be found. He hadn't strength enough to seek her fleeing spark. It taxed all the grit left to his name to drag himself onto two legs.

"Ely!"

He blanched as the vampire joined him. This time Rav's features carried their right proportions. Gore embedded the pores and lines of his face, and his presence waxed full. Bursting with exhilaration and care. Perhaps a trifle inebriated.

"It's really you," Ely breathed,

"Of course it's me. Are you hurt?"

Ely dared a stuttered breath. "I don't know."

He stuffed his iced hands into his trouser pockets, staring out into the darkness. His fingers closed about a wedge of grainy parchment tucked inside. He frowned, lifting it free. Dainty letters flaunted pretty loops across the torn scrap.

Good game.

Chapter Twenty-Five
BLOOD AND STARLIGHT

"What in the wild, blue-balled fuck were you thinking?" Rión's eyes rained azure fire, her features flared and furrowed in a rare display of countenanced emotion. Since Rav had shot off somewhere in the glacial labyrinth to weather the effects of his violent delights, it was to be a sibling's brawl upon the Ulvebrand's upper deck.

"Running off to fight a Watcher on your own? Are you out of your shiteaten mind?"

"I wasn't on my own," Ely argued. "I had a vampire with me."

"Thank the named gods! Else you'd have been roasted alive like the limp-cocked *kladkindt* that you are."

"I'm not convinced that I would," Ely countered, still puzzled. "The Watcher had more than ample opportunity to kill me. Instead, she left me a note."

"Some beasts like to play with their food, little brother, before ripping out its spine."

"She's nothing to trifle with, that's for certain. I won't underestimate her next time," Ely vowed.

Rión's gaze sapped lime green. "Next time?"

"We still haven't rescued Nix," Ely sighed.

"Wouldn't it be so convenient if there happened to be a man aboard this ship that could lead you straight to your demon ball without having to a bait a mind-fucking holy sorceress?"

"Well, when you put it like that, it seems obvious," Ely muttered.

"I know you, little brother. You didn't want to put anyone else in danger. But we came all this way for you. I will take it as a fucking gauntlet thrown the next time you leave my axes behind."

"Understood," Ely replied with a slim smile.

The Etrugan warrior grunted, but her eyes regained a composed ruby hue.

"Go get some rest, starshine."

Rión patted his shoulder dead and left him to frost-encrusted reflection. Between his encounter with Kai and the Watcher's meddling, his head felt like a vat of melted lard.

A prodigious yawn advised him to heed Rión and seek out a bunk below deck. He climbed into a vacant alcove. Economical for an Etrugan but spacious enough for multiple humans to sleep in moderate comfort.

The moment he shut his eyes, he found himself wandering the woods. Warm light from above frolicked with serene, cool dark from below. Birds twittered in the branches overhead. Between the lichen-adorned trunks, a fawn lifted its freckled head. It twitched long, slender ears toward him then returned to grazing.

"It is so peaceful here, isn't it?"

Ely whirled toward the sylphic voice. Sister Ignatius lounged in the low, sturdy boughs of an apple tree laden with dappled fruit. Her habit, delicate white lace from head to foot, dripped a diaphanous cascade.

"Out of my head, Sister," Ely growled in quiet warning.

"Or what?" she smiled, her features delicate venom. "You'll hurt me?"

She sat up, dropping to the fecund foliage on noiseless feet.

"Go on," she needled. "Tell me all about what kind of brute you are."

"Get out," Ely repeated.

"You'll wrap your fingers around my neck?"

The Watcher drifted forward, an eddying current of lace.

"You'll pop my bones one by one? You'll hold me down and show me just what a big, strong man can do to a wicked little witch?"

Ely retreated a step, breath shuttered, confusion unfurling tangled roots.

"Why are you here?" he asked.

"I don't know, tiger," she cooed. "A little parlay before our next round?"

"Why didn't you kill me?"

Sister Ignatius giggled, eyes a gilded trap. "Maybe I like you."

She raised a hand toward him, fingers edged in mottled violet-black like frostbite. Ely recoiled.

"What's the matter?" she preened. "I thought you loved monsters. The champion of the misunderstood. Don't you want to know my story?"

"No. I don't," Ely glared.

"Come on. It's a good one. Heart-wrenching."

"Skip to the part where you hurt people I love, and I come for revenge."

"Do you mean the part where I interrogate a prisoner of war and put a leash on a rampaging beast, and then you massacre an entire town and make puppets of their corpses? That part?"

The Watcher clicked her tongue.

"Tell me why you're stalking me, Sister, or get out," Ely demanded. "Is Titus putting you up to it? Is he still alive?"

"I don't know what became of Titus," Sister Ignatius spat. "I don't care."

"Why carry on with his work? What's in it for you?"

"You assume I have a choice," the Watcher answered.

"There's always a choice," Ely said.

Sister Ignatius snorted a bitter laugh. "Do you think your bloodsucking lover boy would agree with you?"

Ely swallowed his reply. As ever, she knew exactly where to slip the knife. "Where are your chains then, Sister?"

"Inside," she groaned. "It spreads like a contaminant. His thoughts. His desires. His hate and rage."

"Titus?"

"Not that pathetic, pious pawn. You know who I mean."

"The nameless god," Ely mused.

"He wants you," she said. "He'll do anything to get you."

"I can't give him what he wants," Ely said.

Sister Ignatius gulped short, gasping breaths. "It doesn't matter. Once he gets an idea in his head..."

She groaned and clawed at the burnished clasp at her shoulder, letting the lace folds spill to the forest floor. Rings of lambasted flesh peeled and curled around her hips. Cracked along the seams of her stomach. Outlined her breasts. Ruptured her sternum. Beneath raw lacerations, fevered flames churned.

"Help me," she gasped. "Starfell. I'll wait for you. At Starfell..."

"Ely. Ely? You down here?"

A slurred whisper from the hallway jerked him back to the Ulvebrand barracks drenched in sweat. His heart thrashed in his ears.

"Where the devil are you, conjurer? Ouch. Pardon."

The bunk groaned as Rav collapsed over the edge.

"There you are."

The vampire burrowed under the blanket, unwieldy as a catnipped tom.

"Named gods, your feet are so cold!" Ely cried.

"I went for a swim in the canal. I thought you'd be pleased."

"I'm so very thrilled that you're clean, but you could've at least put on some socks as a courtesy."

The vampire's huffing nose tickled the side of his head. "Damn it all, why do you smell so good?"

"My blood, perhaps? Just hazarding a wild guess. You're still absolutely trashed, aren't you?"

"Can you see all the colors cavorting around?"

"No, but I'm starting to feel a bit tingly now that you mention it."

Snickering roots throbbed, and the image of his friend scorched to a smoking heap hovered before his mind's eye.

"No. No. No." Rav curled fjord frozen limbs around him and stroked his hair from his face. "No fretting, conjurer."

Ely sighed. "You were magnificent out there, Rav. I'm sorry I let her slip my grip. I'm sorry I let you down. Yet again. Next time—"

"Shhh," Rav burbled in his ear. "No talking. Only sleeping."

Ely patted his anchored arm. "Sweet dreams, Rav."

The vampire was already snoring.

Ely closed his eyes, mind slowly unclenching as the narcotic-laced presence chased away his sunny glen of nightmares.

Rav woke to discover his night of sanguine debauchery left him absent the customary headache and nausea. In fact, he felt more ordered than usual. As though the fragments of his mind had absorbed desperately needed nutrients. Seraph blood agreed with him. Who would have guessed?

Ely grumbled and twitched beside him. Face released from its protective smile. He was not in a nightmare. Rav knew too well the clawing dread powerful enough to drag a vampire from the black abyss of midday sleep. No, not a nightmare. Still, the conjurer felt thoroughly out of tune. How could he not after yesterday's revelations? Shocking enough just to an unwitting eavesdropper on the ice.

Rav's gaze slipped to his bedfellow's arm thrown over the pillow, sleeve peeled back to expose the shackling glyphs branded on his wrist. Stark scar sunken like a vortex at the center. The conjurer would end the world before he allowed the child born of his gift to suffer such a fate.

What would he do, then? Return to Séocwen with his pirate king to play protector from the shadows? If Kailari Novara asked it of him, he would do it in a snap of the fingers.

The thought made Rav's chest tighten. Elyssandro deserved the kind of love regaled by bards and poets. Not meager scraps flung behind the back of a misused wife.

When we free Ariel... he reminded himself.

The old plan still played out in the back of his mind. Once the two conjurers came face to face at last, that would be it. Fates sealed. Except...

"Are you just watching me sleep?" the conjurer asked, eyes still shut.

"Thinking," Rav replied. "You happen to be sleeping in my line of vision."

"What are you thinking about?"

"What comes after."

"After we've settled our quest?"

"Yes."

Ely opened his eyes. Warm autumn brown. Always welcoming. Never disturbed to find a monster peering back at him.

"I thought we decided on a townhouse. Somewhere nice, like the theatre district. I think Sir Quinn could get us in with the landlord at the Globe Flats. I may already have a few ideas for sprucing up the walls."

"You say that like you really mean it," Rav murmured.

Ely draped broiling mortal fingers over his hand.

"Of course I mean it. We adventure wherever we like. Spend holidays with the family in Fjarat. Then come home again to our quiet little undead haven. It's perfect. Unless, of course, you have other plans, my dearest Lovelace."

Rav shook his head. "I thought *you* might."

Ely dropped his gaze and his hand. Thoughts formed waves across his forehead.

"I know you heard...everything. I shouldn't have been so weak, but make no mistake, it was a fight from start to finish. I'll do exactly as I've promised. Put down the Watcher. Extinguish souls. All of that. But...no, Rav. Nothing's changed."

"Are you at peace with that?" Rav pressed.

"I'm unsettled by my sins and the shadows they've cast on other lives. It's nothing to do with you and me and our stunning balcony views."

Ely looked up again, eyes alighting on Rav's face with a tender, earnest smile. It engulfed him like beaming summer and threw his pulse sideways. He flinched. Confused by the sudden spark that fizzled through him.

A lavender face with bright eyes and bristling teeth popped over the lip of their loft. Rión's taller, louder daughter.

"Uncle Ely!" the Etrugan piped. "Oh, hi, Uncle Shiteating Vampire. Sorry if you were doing kissing."

"We were not," Ely clarified. "How can I help you, Ari?"

"Mother wants you. Come on. Get up!"

"Sure. Mustn't keep Mother waiting," Ely chuckled.

"You're right. She'll bite you," Ariadna deadpanned.

Then she disappeared.

"Well, I suppose that's all the pillow talk we have time for," Ely yawned. "Maybe you should stay and get some rest. I'll report any plans or profanities when you feel better."

"Yes," Rav agreed. "I think that would be for the best."

Ely tugged the blanket over him and pressed chapped lips to his temple.

"Sweet dreams, Rav."

The conjurer disappeared over the ledge.

Rav shifted, restless in his skin. How? After a thousand years, how was it possible to feel so human?

It will pass, he told himself.

Elyssandro deserved someone brave and beautiful and whole. Stick to the plan. Free Ariel. Fates sealed.

It will pass.

The curious collective squeezed into Rión's cabin, straddling broken blades and discarded clothing. Three Etrugans, two Skylarks, and one conjurer all gathered around a faded map laid out on the table. Yellowed, torn in places, and splotched with the blood of its former templar owner, the landscape appeared accurately drawn from what Ely could tell. Not that geography was ever his strong suit.

"Mel says the signal is weak," Victor continued. "She thinks there are anomalies interfering."

Ely drew a line with his finger and tapped a marker north of Septus where the cartographer's terse and sober-handed script read *Starfell*.

"There. That's where the Watcher told me to meet her."

"It does match the direction of the signal we're tracking," Victor commented.

"We should point out," Leanora added, "that it's not Nix with whom Mel is currently communicating."

"Nix is offline, whatever that means," Victor shrugged.

"It means she's unable to communicate over long distances," Leanora input. "If she's damaged, she might be conserving power."

"So, who are you speaking to?" Ely inquired.

"Prometheus. All the rest are dormant at present," Victor said.

"The rest?" Ely asked, curiosity pricked.

"There are five altogether according to Prometheus."

"Well, that does raise the stakes a bit, doesn't it?" Ely said, wishing now that Rav had accompanied him after all to exchange electric currents across the table.

"You know it's a fucking trap, little brother," Rión snarled.

"Very likely, which is why I'm not asking any of you to–"

"Close your cock hole, starshine." Rión slapped the map with her enormous clawed hand. "We're coming with you."

"I promised Mel we'd get her family back," Victor added.

"And I'm sure as hell not about to let Victor have all the fun," Leanora jumped in.

"The twins and I will get started on provisioning," Rión stated. "The rest of you puny humans, eat a decent fucking meal and take a nap."

They adjourned. Ely wandered to the upper deck, too restless to lay down. Too anxious to stomach Etrugan cooking.

A thermos appeared under his nose, gentle breath of mint and honey steaming his face. Ely accepted the kind gift with murmured gratitude. Leanora leaned on the railing beside him, mittened hands hugging a thermos of her own.

"Thought you might appreciate a little luxury before we rough it," she said with a nudge.

They sipped in silence until the brew restored warm humanity to souls and fingertips.

"I think I might be out of my depth with this Watcher," Ely said at last.

"Well, I'm not," Leanora answered, patting her pistol's glossy mirrorwood handle. She continued, "Creatures like that Watcher, they press upon the regions of the brain that trigger fear or pain or even pleasure. Studies suggest they are not entirely in control of what they show you. It's your own mind expelling toxins and processing data. What you need is a protective warding glyph."

"Is that among the clever little charms you've inked on your back?"

"It's not on my back, but you've certainly...appreciated it."

"I think I can make an educated guess," Ely smiled.

"I'll etch you a matching one if you like," Leanora offered. "Not permanent, of course. I don't have the right stylus for that."

"Does placement matter?" Ely inquired with a sidelong glance.

She laughed. "Not in the least. We'll keep it professional."

"Lea..." he started.

The thread snagged in a useless tangle.

"It's alright, Elyssandro. Let's save that conversation for a latte in a quaint little coffee shop. You'll find I'm a very modern-minded individual, and I suspect you have more than enough complications on this particular voyage."

Leanora relieved him of his empty thermos.

"A bracelet should do the trick. I'll have it encoded by the time we shove off. Let's see if we can't keep lurking fiends out of that handsome head of yours."

"Many thanks, Lea."

"My pleasure," she answered with a nod, then made her departure.

Rav gazed out at the silver fjord, still and pensive as he listened to the conjurer's debrief. They sat on the cross beam of a mast, shoulders leaned lightly together as they siphoned starlight between their fingers.

"Why does she have the helyxes in the first place?" Ely questioned.

"Helyxia," Rav murmured

"Right. Right," the conjurer waved grammar aside like a buzzing gnat. "It took us ages just to lose our one and only helyx. That would suggest Ignatius and Titus have been collecting them for quite some time."

"They're a rare and powerful technology. It's hardly surprising the Canon would have an interest in them," Rav reasoned.

Ely frowned, tapping his fingers against his leg.

"Do you think she really needs my help?"

Rav turned a sharp, reprimanding eye in his direction. "Damn it all, Elyssandro. You can't get chivalrous over crocodile tears and burlesque theatre."

"The nudity was utterly terrifying, Rav. You're imagining it wrong. But that's not the point. What if I had staked you instead of listening to your side of the story?"

"That was a once in a millennium fluke," Rav scolded. "It could have gone very badly for you."

"You're right," Ely backpedaled. "You're right. I didn't mean to cheapen our bond. That was terrible form, my sweet Lovelace. Forgive me."

"Forgiven. Now promise me you won't let her manipulate you into believing her some kind of victim."

"Named gods. She did almost have me believing. Am I that easy a mark?" Ely moaned.

Rav raised an eyebrow. "Would you like me to lie to you?"

"Yes." Ely sighed. "No."

"You're very trusting, conjurer. And compassionate. Kindhearted. Even in the face of great adversity."

"You forgot devilishly handsome," Ely winked.

"Omitted for brevity. Now, maybe it makes you an easy target. Maybe the corpse-fingered Watcher really does need help. That doesn't mean you owe it to her." Rav clasped Ely's face between star-kissed hands and entreated, "Please, for once, just be selfish."

Ely nodded in answer. Gaze intent. And there again. That traitorous pulse, waxing human. Curse this brilliant night sky. Except the bewitching light seemed to have the conjurer too in its thrall.

"What are you two shitbirds doing up there?" Rión's echoing growl from the deck nearly startled them from their perch. "Time to go!"

Ely turned to the shadows, aura stinging. Rav swept an arm around his waist, and they dropped through the rigging to join the impatient Etrugan below.

The hearty black longboat coasted over star-crossed waters. Dodging glaciers and ice sheets. Its intrepid crew dipped oars in silence broken only by the occasional grunt born of dying muscles and rising blisters.

Leanora and Victor, bundled up in matching fur-lined anoraks, sat among the frugal supplies packed at the bow. Ariadna and Brindle dragged oars in time, looking grown and formidable tressed up in Etrugan armor. Ari bore a gargantuan sword across her broad shoulders. Brin carried an ebony bow and quiver of thick-shafted arrows fletched with cobalt tanuba feathers. Behind the twins, Ely took up oars beside Rión. A fresh length of braided leather circled his wrist, a copper bead in the center etched with what he was assured were the most powerful of protection glyphs.

At the rear of the vessel, Kai sat poised at the rudder.

"He wouldn't take no for an answer," Rión had hissed with a glare at the pirate king. *"And he's our only hope at navigating this chilly clusterfuck."*

Ely passed him a nod and a reserved smile. The pirate king returned the gesture, on his guard as well. Neither had spoken a word since.

Somewhere in the astral sea above, Rav drifted, a fanged thunderhead. Ely caught sight of him by and by when he sailed across the moon's crescent.

They secured the longboat in a shallow cave at a fork in the canal, donned packs, and continued on foot. Victor took the lead, striking out with undaunted confidence as if he had spent his entire life in this hostile terrain.

Ari and Brin trundled behind him, ready to defend against unexpected perils but still firmly within their mother's eyeline. Kai and Leanora followed, Ely and Rión taking the rear guard. With no sun to rise and set, they tracked their progress by braying stomachs and flagging limbs.

The expeditioneers broke camp between the rugged thighs of a cross-legged crag. Kai sheltered with Victor and Leanora. Rión, with her formidable brood, raised a second shelter. Ely threw a little extra wrist flair into conjuring his harborage with an audience spectating.

He gave Ari his ration of half-frozen flatbread and smoked jerky, opting instead to join Rav for a lambent feast on the cliffside. The winking quicksilver eased oar blisters and fortified the death magic arsenal building to a crescendo within his cells. By the time they reached their destination, he aimed to be more constellation than human.

His aching mortal frame disagreed. Ely crawled into his shelter exhausted. Rav collapsed beside him, just as weary from long hours rubbing shoulders with the sky. Ely conjured them a climate appropriate blanket. They lay back to back, Rav trapping his companion's warmth, if contributing none of his own.

Nightmares convulsed Ely's sleep. The Apostle's empty eyes. The Watcher's poisoned giggle. His mother's face contorted and bleeding. Cool fingers on his brow dropped a lifeline back to safety. Rav drew him close, letting him rest against the steady thrum of his heart.

Two glorious days he skimmed the sky like a wild eagle before the seraph blood began to fade. Clouded thoughts crept in, at first a strange voice here or there, startling him. A flash of another place. Another time. Even when ravaging thunder crashed between his ears, Rav still managed to keep a pulse on their direction of travel.

Then day three.

He flashed between the frozen valley and the tranquil meadows of the late Lord Aurelio's estate. When he returned, he no longer saw his companions struggling overland below. Useless breath jolted his lungs. His heart careened. Thoughts splayed akimbo.

No. Calm. Get your bearings.

Gripping panic by the ears, he settled into his senses. The orientation of the mountains. The magnetic tilt of the earth. The direction of the stars.

Rav adjusted course, fighting the fog. He felt the conjurer's hopeful restlessness first. Then he scented a thin whiff of smoke followed by earthy Etrugans and sweet-veined humans.

Rav shipwrecked beside Ely's conjured shelter. Relief engulfed him from within and without as he crawled inside.

"You're back," Ely breathed. "You had me worried."

"I got turned around," Rav admitted, pressing a hand over his eyes.

"Your head again?" Ely asked.

"It was better," Rav sighed. "Something in the seraph blood helped, but now that it's all passed through, everything is hazy again."

"We'll find you more," Ely said, brushing soft, soothing fingers along Rav's temple.

Startling sparks. Confusion. Rav shifted to face the side of the shelter. Ely rolled onto his back, widening the trench between them.

"I'm sorry," he said. Dismay flooded around him. "I would never hurt you, Rav. I meant to be a haven for you."

"You are."

Rav turned to face him again.

"The only place I have ever felt safe is lying close with your ungodly heat seeping into my bones." He reached to grasp Ely's hand. "It's selfish of me. Feeding on your humanity with nothing but ice to offer in return."

"Have whatever you want of my humanity," Ely murmured, twining their fingers together. "I don't need it. It's been nothing but trouble."

Rav smiled, but a sharp vicious surge behind his eyes cut it short. He pinched the bridge of his nose, inhaling through the bombardment.

The conjurer waved a hand, and a small section of their shelter dissipated like smoke. He commanded a sterling trickle into his palm, offering it to Rav. The frigid sip scattered the carrion shadows in his skull.

"Seraph blood," Ely mused. "Then it seems a hunting trip will be in order. We'll get you well, dearest Lovelace. I promise."

Rav closed his eyes, letting the conjurer's naïve sunshine push away the nagging facts. Mind carved up. Soul sliced away. Oceans of blood and starlight could not make him well.

Their journey resumed in the monotonous shadows of another darkling day. Ely stumbled through deep drifts, heart and head lost to the heavens.

"Are you expecting a storm, starshine?" Rión grunted over their slogging boots.

"He's too far afield," Ely said. "I can't feel him. It makes me anxious."

"Is he getting ready to crack like a fucking egg?" Rión asked.

"He's fine," Ely replied. "Just a bit worn around the edges."

"And if it's more than that?" Rión posed.

"We have an understanding, he and I," Ely answered, jaw tense.

Rión grumbled in her throat. "I hope you never have to find out if you can honor it, little brother."

They lapsed into their thoughts. Ely returned to his vigil, searching the skies. *Where are you?*

His heart fluttered as he caught the turbulent vibration overhead. Rav scooped him up, carrying him toward one of the slopes that lined their valley path.

"There's something you need to see," the vampire rumbled over the howl of the wind.

They debarked on a ledge overlooking a sheer drop down the far side of the ridge. Below, black turrets protruded from the mountainside, barely more than silhouettes in the moonlight. They oozed corrupted death magic. Another Cosmologist landmark.

"Starfell?"

Rav nodded.

Ely blinked and rubbed at the pressure spring loading his temples. Even at this distance, the heathen conjury made his head woozy and his stomach sour. He recalled the pressing echoes from the cursed Tower ruins, but those felt tame in comparison. Starfell loomed a hulking, primordial beast. The jutting formations seemed to reach for him, dragging at his consciousness. At his magic.

"There are seraphim guarding the gate," Rav said. "Templars on the ramparts. More inside."

Ely's stomach clenched. Sweat broke against his brow, and his heartbeat sped.

"Fuck."

Rav nodded. "To put it lightly."

Chapter Twenty-Six
ENTER THE CHORUS

The crew anchored just outside the shadow of the fortress. Near enough for Mel's sensors to gather data, far enough that Ely could try to exist without violent stomach cramps. A low, rocky fold stubbled with briars afforded shelter from wind and patrolling seraphim. Ely raised his death magic yurt as far toward the periphery as safety allowed.

Victor, Leanora, and Rión hiked up the lower ridge to give Mel a closer berth for half a day's surveillance. Rav took to the skies for a bird's eye perspective. Ely stayed behind with Kai and the twins.

"Mother says we won't go with you inside," Brin signed beside their meager campfire.

Ely had crafted a ring of benches flameside, sturdy but more cushioned than their dusky appearance suggested. He had gotten bolder with form and composition in his conjurings.

"Absolute *maardon* shit!" Ari added, speaking aloud in time with her hands.

"Your mother's right," Ely signed sternly. "It will be dangerous, even out here. You must guard each other and be ready for whatever comes."

The twins took their chattering teeth inside their tent made cozy by a miniature conjured stove.

Ely scanned the stars. No shadow gliding among them just yet. He closed his eyes and let his mind flow outward. Starfell sucked at his awareness as he bent toward it. Once he bumped into the beautiful mayhem he sought, Rav gave his consciousness an indulgent squeeze.

Ely smiled and opened his eyes just as Kai dropped an armload of scrub branches beside the fire.

"Can you speak to him with your mind?" Kai asked, taking a seat on the bench opposite.

"Not like I'm speaking to you now," Ely replied. "It's almost like catching eyes across a room or hands in the dark."

"It is love, then?"

"Why are you asking, Kai?" Ely murmured, eyes taking refuge in the flames.

"I wish happiness for you," Kai replied.

"Happiness is fleeting and devious." Ely flicked a stick into the fire in a hiss of sparks. "I dread happiness. Love. Hope. Maybe hope most of all."

"Then I pray the named gods will restore your faith."

Ely looked up, chest pinched tight. "It's hard to have faith when you know the cost."

Kai watched him, gaze caring melancholy. "It costs everything just to be alive, diakana."

Ely took first watch, sending Kai for respite from the cold. As he waited, he moulded death magic into a winter helm of a design he'd been refining in iterations. A polar cat with saber teeth. Warm about the nose but not too suffocating. It was still heavier than he liked, the snarl not quite as elegant fierce as he envisioned. It would get there.

A glimmer at the edge of his periphery turned his head. Not the presence he was looking for, but timely nonetheless.

"Nice to know you're still with us," he said.

The glimmer rippled and arranged itself into feminine form, sharp, narrow features stern. Ariel claimed the vacant seat opposite him. The firelight flicked vivid on her solid form. No hints of translucence, but she left no footprints.

"I was beginning to worry something happened to you when we destroyed the rupture," Ely added.

"It's a little tricky," she said. "Conjuring into a new shape while casting. I'd forgotten. It took longer to recover than I liked."

Ely smiled. He always forgot the traces of Paxat impressed on his own pronunciations until he heard them from another expatriate tongue.

"Is that how you do it?" he asked. "Self-conjury?"

"Yes."

"Could I do it?" Ely asked.

"At your age? Don't be a fool, Elyssandro," Ariel scoffed.

"Says the millennium old geriatric trapped in the tree trunk," Ely muttered.

"I didn't come to see you sprout a tail, but I can tell you how to free a Watcher."

Ely's helm scattered into vaporized ether. "I'm sorry, I don't think I'm hearing right under there. You think I should help Sister Ignatius?"

"When a Watcher is inducted into the Sisterhood, the presiding Apostle plants a Miracle within her that grows and feeds upon her magic, slowly supplanting her soul."

"Well, that's nauseating," Ely said. "I was really hoping she was just playing with my mind because now it feels wrong not to help her."

Ariel clipped a curt nod. "If you want to survive Starfell with the keys in hand, kill the Miracle, free the Watcher. Let her take vengeance on the Canon."

"What does it entail to kill a Miracle?"

"You'll know it when you feel it. That won't be a challenge for you, except..."

"I have to break into Starfell to do it," Ely finished.

Ariel inclined her head.

"You'll need to be fast. The cosmology will begin to weaken you before you ever get inside. You won't realize how far gone you are until it's too late."

"And you're sure she'll defect to our side once I've destroyed her holy parasite?" Ely asked.

"No, conjurer, that's not a gamble worth taking," Rav's forbidding rumble declared, its owner ruffling the fire in his swift descent.

The vampire faced their apparitional visitor, straight-backed and clear-eyed as Ely had never seen. Not in this time, at least.

Ariel's expression hardened. "Now is not the time to play at caution."

"I didn't suggest caution," Rav answered. "Depending upon that creature's good feeling to hand over the helyxia and get us out of Starfell intact is a fool's errand at best."

"What do you propose instead?" Ariel demanded. "Lest we forget, your last plan got you killed."

Rav met her eyes in unflinching challenge. "And no doubt his plan hinged on misguided diplomacy of some kind. But, of course, I'm not him, am I?"

Rav eyed her with an august tilt of the head, a near-smile on his lips. Brash. Cavalier. Lordly, even. It stunned Ariel Marcellus speechless. Satisfied, Rav sat beside Ely on his bench.

"You're all vim and vinegar," Ely observed. "Have you been out hunting seraphim already?"

"Just a harmless sip, conjurer. Never even missed."

"Hm. Like a mosquito?" Ely pondered, then added quickly, "A very well-proportioned one."

Rav crooked an eyebrow, "Might I submit to your imagination a vampire, instead?"

"Yes, a much more agreeable fantasy, that," Ely grinned.

Rav resumed measured gravitas as he turned to Ariel who sat observing them with jaw tightened.

"The Watcher knows you're coming," she said, voice quiet. Expression withdrawn. Pensive. "You will have to contend with her one way or another."

"Tooth and claw should suffice," Rav answered.

"Whatever you say, Ravan Aurelio," she choked.

Ely watched the casting fade, anxious bats aflutter behind his ribs. There was no misunderstanding the shocked conclusion that had just struck her in the mouth. She saw what she should have seen all along. Why did that sit so uneasy?

"Ariel has many strengths," Rav stated. "Discerning enemies from friends is not among them."

"I think she just realized as much, *Ravan Aurelio*," Ely answered with a pointed glance.

Rav flicked narrow-eyed displeasure in his direction. "I am not him. I'm clear-minded for the moment. The moment will pass."

Ely found his breath lost as their gazes intertwined. Heart roused to aching.

"As far as I'm concerned, Ely, it is your judgment alone that matters. You see beauty in the monstrous. You see wronged souls trapped behind violent deeds. And as much as I fear for you..."

He heaved a reluctant sigh, his own argument distilling a conclusion.

"Whatever you believe we must do about the Watcher, I am with you."

The vampire stiffened and turned an ear to the Starfell side of their encampment. Scented the air. Relaxed.

"Rión."

The Etrugan soon appeared with Skylarks in tow.

"This is about to be as pleasant as fighting off a two ton gorilla that hasn't been fed or fucked in a fortnight," Rión greeted them.

"Fully operational military outpost," Leanora translated.

"And there's only one way in or out," Victor added.

"Actually," Rav interjected, "I found another way in. A drainage tunnel on the far side of the mountain. It's unguarded."

"You devil," Ely exclaimed. "Have you been sitting on that this whole time?"

"I was getting to it," the vampire replied.

"How far to climb?" Rión asked.

"Impossible," Rav answered with a sly smirk.

"Fuck off," Rión grunted. "You try to fly with me and my axes, we'll both end up impaled at the bottom of a cliff."

"Shall we make a bet of it?" the vampire jousted.

Rión bent a salty seafoam gaze in Rav's direction. "Feeling your balls tonight, are you, Aurelio?"

"You didn't answer my question, Twin Axes."

Rión's eyes glittered mirthful gold. "No bet, vampire. But tiny doctor did make some interesting suggestions on our hike, and with your tunnel, it might just add up to a wily little bastard of a plan."

Ely crouched under cover of snow-weighted pines. Mind lightyears from the calm, tranquil center he needed so desperately to grasp. The fortress walls menaced just outside his wooded sanctuary. Chipping away at his strength and resolve.

He closed his eyes, stilled his mind. Awaiting a vampiric nudge to lay his opening hand. Rav had taken Victor and Kai to the far side of the fortress where the impossible entrance awaited infiltration. Leanora and the Etrugans lay in wait at their own hidden posts. Even the twins, to their violet-eyed delight, were enlisted in the orchestration of this good old-fashioned diversion.

The seraphim had winged away to patrol the surrounding mountains and would not return for hours. Once the raiding party took position, the final game would begin.

The previous twelve hours had been spent in preparation. Rav soared off to memorize the topography and pay one last visit to the seraphim. Victor and Kai cleaned and tuned their stash of firearms while the Etrugans sharpened steel. Ely and Leanora sat huddled between two conjured lanterns as she instructed him on the sculpting of devices whose mechanics he could not begin to understand.

"I've never encoded a death magic fabrication before," she said, a manic gleam in her eye. "I'm not entirely sure which stylus..."

A few rounds of quick experimentation found the instrument intended for alloy lent itself well to petrified ether.

"Well, Elyssandro, you have a tenured position waiting for you at South Sea when you're ready to transfer institutions," Leonora said, inspecting shimmering gears and wires.

"So they'll work?" Ely asked, eyes sweeping over their collection of lettered gadgets.

"Spectacularly!" the stalwart doctor beamed.

The company retired for a final recharge. His stove's overzealous heat drove Ely to strip down to his light linen trousers while he lay tossing on his conjured mattress. Examining and cross-examining Ariel's position on the Watcher. Sister Ignatius's entreaty. Rav's exhilarating faith in his good judgment. Most of his intended repose fretted away round the maelstrom's edge by the time Rav crept into their shelter, aglow with renewed vigor.

"You should be sleeping," the vampire whispered.

"Can't," Ely murmured.

"Because you're overheated. It's like the deserts of Hell in here," Rav grumbled. "At least put a hole in the ceiling."

"Then it gets too chilly."

"Can't you just un-conjure that stove, then?"

"I'm not very good at putting out live flames," Ely admitted. "We'll get ash and cinder everywhere. I'll have to remake the entire shelter. You might catch fire. No, no, I'd rather sweat a little."

Rav grunted and added his coat to the pile of discarded clothing. Watching him shrug the shirt from his shoulders only pitched the fever in Ely's cheeks.

His eyes took pause on the death magic script that marked a target on the vampire's back. Such a glaring vulnerability in the midst of supple steel. He prayed the stake lost in the Septus implosion was the last and only in their enemies' possession.

Rav lay down beside him, infusing blessed coolness through the bedclothes.

"Alright, Elyssandro. What are we brooding about?"

Ely rested his head on his arm, facing his companion. "Have I doomed us all, Rav?"

"No more than any other Tuesday, conjurer," Rav reassured him, settling as a mirror opposite.

"Is that just the seraph speaking?"

"I've said nothing more than what gets caught up inside my muddied head," Rav replied. "Despite what you might think, I'm perfectly sober. All thoughts, words, and deeds my own."

"So, you're telling me underneath it all you're a shameless flirt?"

"I'd call it charismatic."

"Tomato, potato."

Rav shot puzzled amusement down his nose. "Have you had heatstroke?"

"Possibly," Ely shrugged. "I thought it was a saying."

"Who's intoxicated now?"

"Named gods, I wish," Ely sighed. "I haven't been proper pickled since we knocked over the temple of the horned god."

"You had me tied up in anxious knots," Rav recalled. "I thought you'd managed to hurt yourself again."

Ely angled a skeptical glance. "Anxious? Pinning me to the statuary?"

"Yes. Anxious," Rav doubled down with a toe-tingling smile. "I was already such a fool for you. It was maddening."

"Is it still maddening?" Ely asked.

"Are you sure you want to know?" Rav said, propping himself up on an elbow. "Your pulse sounds dangerous."

"That's cheating," Ely murmured, face flushed.

"Here."

Rav took his hand and held it where his heart dashed against its death magic seal.

"Yes, it is maddening still," the vampire said quietly. "Maddening. Bewildering. Paralyzing."

Ely lay stone still, endeavoring to capture notes of sinking disappointment before they played from his heartstrings...

Rav alighted at the rusted drain mouth. Victor Skylark slid from his back, unshaken by the jetting flight up the mountainside. Kai Novara waited on the ledge, solemn and stoic. A trickle of water, somehow left unfrozen after its journey through Starfell, escaped through the grate in a polluted gray waterfall. They squeezed between the iron bars, bowed apart just wide enough for a man to maneuver.

The tunnel stank of refuse and fermented death magic. A narrow berm ran along the left side of the pipe. Dangerous footing for whatever miserable soul found themselves charged with maintenance.

Taking the vampire's assurance that there were no humans afoot, Kai lit a torch. Rav much preferred the comforting cover of darkness. And since Victor Skylark used a sense far more acute than sight to navigate, the pirate king alone required illumination.

"This tunnel feeds into the central hub," Victor told them. "Keep straight, and we'll be in the heart of it soon enough."

Rav grimaced, pressing his hand against his head where a high-pitched whine drilled at his ear.

"You alright, *che'oma?*" Kai asked.

"Fine," Rav grunted.

"Mel said the frequency is inaudible to humans," Victor informed them. "She thinks it may have some nasty side effects given time."

While the humans walked the treacherous strip, Rav clambered up the tunnel wall, creeping along the rounded ceiling. It was an easy trick, defying gravity to make a floor of any surface. Mortals found it unnerving. He quite enjoyed the change in orientation. It eased the spine. A bit compressed now after carrying two men to a dizzying height. And–

Damn that sound! It convulsed between his ears like a shiv, sending blanched flashes of light before his eyes. In the blinding pulse, he caught snatches of figments and faces. Gayly costumed socialites with mouths splitting wide in scornful laughter. A harrowed soldier, battered and blood-streaked, begging for his mother as the light faded from his eyes. A shark's smile from the Council pulpit.

Rav shook his head, nearly losing his footing on the tunnel ceiling.

Not now. Stay here.

Yet the monotonous crawl restricted to a lagging human plod dragged on. The supersonic assault continued, unrelenting.

"What are you doing?" a vicious voice demanded.

No. Not you.

"Look at me when I'm speaking to you."

A vicious face disturbed the shadows.

Leave me be.

Darkness abandoned him to the harsh scorn of afternoon sun through a westerly window. He had no wish to look upon the livid beauty addressing him. But it was not his memory. Not his choice. Lord Aurelio turned toward his wife, and so he did. Dressed in alabaster, face fresh with youth, Fiona White glowered from the doorway.

"Why aren't you dressed?" she demanded. "We're expected within the hour!"

"I'm not going," he answered.

"Not again. You're exhausting, Ravan."

"I will not go watch them dance and drink and pick the bones of my comrades in arms from their teeth."

"To hell with your comrades in arms," she spat.

"Do you mean your brother too or just the lowborn rabble?" Lord Aurelio shot back.

Fiona shrieked like a stuck banshee and flung a candlestick from the desk.

"Forgive me, kitten, I shouldn't have."

Don't apologize, you fool, tear her fucking throat out!

The woman in white glared daggers and clenched her claws.

"You will put on the suit laid out for you and meet me in the carriage within the next five minutes. And when we arrive, you will smile and kiss the ring on every hand in that wretched place. Because if you don't, they'll remember the unsavory bastard you are and crucify us both in the square."

Rav growled and lunged, fangs closing about frozen shadow. Back again in Starfell's putrid bowels.

"Everything aces up there, pal?" Victor Skylark called.

"Fine. Only bats," Rav responded.

The grating intonation dragged him back toward the light.

No. Calm. Steady.

Rav craned his flailing mind to the tranquil early hours when he lay on a death magic mattress crafted in outrageous perfection of comfort. Black pillows plush as if they materialized from a sumptuous, funereal manor. Bedclothes soft as pure Marikej silk. The conjurer knew their precise thread count from the top of his head. Absurd, to coax such luxury from the ether in the midst of this savage wilderness.

Even in the safe repose of their haven, Ely's hand clasped against his heart, Rav had struggled so to make his confession. His conjurer was all too quick to read a rebuff in his words instead of the simple three that he longed to release.

I love you.

Ely reclaimed his hand, reclining on his back as though hiding his expression in profile might mask the cacophony of emotions that eddied around them. Aching desire and crushing desolation.

I love you.

"I know that you and Ariel have not had your reckoning," Ely said. "That she may change her tune when all is said and done. If that's your hope, then–"

"It isn't," Rav intercepted his thought.

"You're certain of that?" Ely asked.

"I will never be him."

Ely turned a smoky jasper gaze across the pillows. "No. You are an astonishing, valiant immortal. She will see it."

"I don't care what she does or does not see," Rav said. "She could have freed me or given me back to Death. But she didn't. She left me to torment."

His fingers worried at the blanket until the conjurer's hand closed over his, a gentle shadow on the face of the moon.

"I will not abandon her to her fate as she abandoned me, but our reckoning will not be a reconciliation," Rav finished.

Ely tightened his hand. "I understand. Truly."

Rav raised his eyes, voice somehow steady even as his heart tried to break its sigil.

"What I hope you understand is that it is not your doing when I find myself stuttered or silent," he said. "What I feel for you is not quiet. I would be bold and passionate given the chance. "

I love you.
Damn it all, say it!
I love you.

Ely slid closer. Pulse like a thunderstorm. Warmth and light overflowing the wellspring of his generous human heart. Beneath it all lingered a lonely tremor. As though he were fearfully venturing weight upon a mending wound and praying not to feel pain's return.

"Elyssandro, I want better for you than the monster that was made of me."

His conjurer caressed his face. "Dearest, as you know, our opinions on that subject are in every respect different. So, what do you want for yourself?"

Rav's view drifted from Ely's eyes, like autumn twilight, down his travel-rugged face to his lips. Further still along the slope of his throat to the naked bronze of his chest. Then back again to his waiting gaze...

"This is it," Victor said.

Rav released his hold on the shadows to balance on the thin beam below.

"Mel says Prometheus is signaling from a chamber just above," Victor told him. "If we can find a way in."

The malevolent echo raked needled claws against Rav's ear. Dr. Harald Brahm leered back at him.

No.

Rav blinked his vision clear. Victor Skylark.

"Here," called the pirate king.

His torch blaze repercussed from rusted ladder rungs ascending up through an opening overhead.

Victor turned a blind eye to Rav. "Shall we call in the cavalry?"

Rav nodded. "Yes. Best do this quickly."

Ely peered into the spangled black night. Or was it day? He had lost track in this winter darkness. His mind remained a locked vault, and still he felt the Watcher grinning from behind the fortress walls. Taunting. Tapping her grisly fingernails.

The longer he waited, the more his resolve wavered. The more he doubted his sanity and that of the disparate band of renegades now poised to assault a Canon fortress. What the hell were they thinking? Putting their trust in him.

Breathe. Just breathe. Find an anchor.

Closing his eyes once more, he directed his wavering faith inward. Back to his windblown companion watching him with sultry ocean eyes.

Ely waited. Motionless. His invitation hanging on the air. He thought he would feel a fool, venturing out on a narrow limb with a heart-shattering plunge beneath. But instead, a weight crumbled from his chest. No more turning his face to the shadows. At least he'd sung his own ballad. Absent the chorus, that was.

I love you.

I love you.

Long, cool fingers outlined his face. Traced his mouth. Finally, Rav bent forward and kissed him. Slow and fervent. Sweeping him up in the starlight that lingered on his lips. Left perfumed nebulas from fingertips traced along his jaw and stroked through his hair.

Something shifted in the vampire's presence. As though a lodged barb that kept him rigid with pain had been drawn out.

Ely sat back to read his face. Rav gazed at him, yearning and intent.

"I do want more," he said. "I want everything."

A delicious tremor skittered from Ely's stomach to the depths of his desire. "Have it, then," he entreated.

Rav kissed him again and laid him back upon their luxuriant berth. Strong but yielding arms enfolded him. Teeth nipped feather soft at his ear. Wintry kisses wetted his neck.

"Named gods," Ely moaned as Rav rocked against him like a ship in a sudden swell.

"Sweetness, put your hands on me," the breathless immortal pleaded.

Ely obliged, as undone by soft words as by satin skin grown suddenly warm to the touch. His fingers embarked on an unhurried exploration from powerful shoulders over tattooed chest. Down a long, lean torso to

Etrugan-made leather. He paused, only just daring to skim beneath the trouser waistband.

"Don't stop," Rav whispered. "I want to know your hands as intimately as your violin."

Ely unhooked barricading buttons, low feral rumbles caressing his ear as he made tender acquaintance with the hardening contours he had tried until now to ignore.

Rav unknotted the ties at Ely's waist and drew back the folded fabric, eyes all smoldering hunger. "In case you've any lingering question," he said, "I find you thoroughly enticing."

"If it wasn't quite obvious, my devastating Lovelace, the feeling is mutual."

Rav smiled, fingers brushing electrifying strokes along his thighs. He bent between, tongue tracing a bold trail. Ely clutched the bedclothes. Endeavoring to keep silent. Failing utterly in the cascade that followed...

Turbulence engulfed him from beneath the droning static of Starfell. Affectionate but urgent. Time to move.

Effulgent death lit in Ely's cupped palm. With a blasting breath, he sent it from his hiding place, a pale violet auger dancing on the frigid wind.

The somnambulant woods shuddered. Arachnid shapes swarmed through frosted pine needles.

Creaking. Clicking. Chittering.

Their gleeful artificer emerged. Her signal amplifier—conjured with some artistic liberties in the shape of a dainty black tiara—glistened in its moonlit throne of flaming curls.

"*The brain emits powerful electrical signals,*" she had claimed. "*If I can electroencephalographically tune the queen to my brainwave patterns, then I can conduct the horde.*"

"*You're a genius, Lea. I have complete faith in whatever it was you just told me.*"

"*Let's just say that Watcher isn't the only one who can exert her mind.*"

The mechanical spiders surfed death magic sprockets over the ice. They dashed in a crawly breaker against the fortress wall. Scuttled up the slopes. Spilled over the crest.

Death blinked slitted eyes and rattled their tether as horror bellowed from the battlements. Ely raised a hand, groping for spirit in the air. Still too faint.

Templars appeared in the crenulated turrets. Light from the pregnant moon glinted from their raised crossbows.

A retort like thunder and a spray of pulverized ether drove back one of the sentries. Another gun blast from a different angle. Another. Rión and Ariadna shifted positions and renewed their volley. Brin passed ready weapons and reloaded exhausted artillery.

Send us in, Death brayed, sniffing fresh souls on the loose from the ramparts.

Patience. We have to be extra—
Come on. You'll enjoy this.

They burst from his shoulders as membranous wyvern wings and beat against the frozen night. Ely lost grip on the rearing cosmic dragon. Death bore him swift and silent above Starfell's walls.

Well, shit. Not exactly the plan.

As he passed over the templars engaged in panicked combat against the spider horde, he flung fragmented death magic into the fresh-minted corpses below. Once made, the walking dead turned weapons on the living templars, rallying yet more effigies to the banner of the midnight sun.

As Death winged him onward between Starfell's forbidding towers, the stronghold's counterfeit conjury sucked at his limbs, a hungry vortex. He dipped toward the courtyard below.

Don't break my legs again, he pleaded.

Death gritted their teeth and caught an updraft, shooting them toward the moon only to send them in a spinning nosedive from an even more fatal height.

Ely's mortiferous wings recovered their bearings in narrow time to save him from painting the ground red. They set him down at the foot of a daunting staircase. A bit of a running stop but no fractures.

His implements of aviation departed in crackling violet motes, and a slow, mocking clap applauded his entrance from the top of the steps. Sister Ignatius waited between fluted columns. She held out a beckoning hand, then faded back into the shadows behind the entry arch.

Ely took an unsteady breath and mounted the steps.

The infiltrators navigated the maze of corridors and chambers with little interference. As hoped, the creeper army had lured all hands to the front gate. Stragglers met a quick end by blade or by fang. No fuss. Minimal muss.

"There's supposed to be a door there," Victor insisted, blind eyes incredulous over the flawless wall.

"Where? Here?" Rav pointed.

"Yes," Victor fumed. "Precisely there."

Rav knocked.

Echo, echo, echo.

"There's a corridor behind," he said.

Kai foraged among the chamber trappings. "Maybe a lever or a spring?"

Rav threw a shoulder against the façade. The room shook. Debris sugared the floor. A hairline crack tiptoed around the shape of an archway, and the hidden door grated inward.

"Your way is better," the pirate king laughed.

They proceeded into the drafty passage. Rav caught a familiar whiff among the musty, faded scents. Fragrant jasmine thrown into flames.

"The Watcher's been through here," he told the others.

If they responded, he heard nothing over Starfell's plaintive shriek. He passed through cobwebbed corridors in the torchlit depths of the University of Dianessa, then the gentle lamplit halls of the Aurelio ancestral manor.

Stay here. Stay now.

Or if stray he must, let it be only a few hours back when spellbinding hands woke him to throbbing desire. The first in living memory that belonged only to him.

Ely allowed him to make a slow, savored conquest. Rewarding him with exquisite sounds as Rav took his silken warmth into his mouth. That he could invoke such unadulterated pleasure woke a valor in him he thought had been extinguished. It urged him to chase the teasing angles and subtle strokes that compelled his sweet, hot-blooded companion to writhe and grip his hair. At once a cry for mercy and for more.

Rav sat back to strip away the last of their linen and leather. Ely gazed on him as though he were the most wondrous sight ever beheld. When he returned to his conjurer's lips, Ely wrapped arms and legs around him, bracing him close against burning, star-scented skin.

"Will you let me take you, Elyssandro?" he whispered.

"Named gods, yes," Ely trembled in return.

Past and future muted to silence behind the swelling symphony of the present.

Only now. Only us. Only this.

Ely kissed him with the desperation of the bitter world's end one moment and the patient nectar of timeless nirvana the next. Climbing. Sparking. Consuming. Crying his name and pulling him deeper. Slowing to stroke his face or clasp his hand.

Rav watched the subtle shift in his brow, sensed the cresting wave in his aura. Ely's eyes fell closed, tensed muscles shimmering to surrender. Rav tipped over the edge after him. Release glorious and shattering as death.

They lay in blissful quiet after their crescendo's end. While his conjurer siphoned starlight through a vent rearranged in the awning, Rav took the moment to indulge in undisguised observation. What a wonder to gaze upon features already dear and familiar with so deeply intimate an admiration. How terrifying to consider fragile mortal beauty. A candle to be snuffed out, whether by a sudden wind or the relentless march of time.

"Have I made you unhappy, Rav?" Ely asked, taking in the downturn of his thoughts.

Rav caressed his face. "No, my darling. You've made me feel alive. And I don't want it to fade."

Ely kissed him. "Whatever happens—today, tomorrow, and every day after—we'll face it together..."

"Over here."

The hidden passage drained into a cluttered den littered with hoarded rummage. Victor directed them to a large wooden trunk fitted with a heavy padlock. He produced a set of lock picks but could not seem to coerce the rusted iron to release. Kai took a turn with no more success.

"May I?" Rav asked, stepping forward.

The pirate king offered the picks, but Rav simply gave the lock a tug and snapped the shackle.

"I'm starting to see why it's convenient to have a vampire on an expedition," Victor said.

Rav flipped open the lid. Sure enough, a trove of helyxia lay nestled in a bed of straw. Two still remained in their ovoid shells. One rested silver and pristine. The last lay cracked and sooted. Rav lifted the wounded helyx, holding her gingerly between his hands.

"Nix," he murmured.

She shuddered and blinked. Her ochre mist swirled into a squinting eye.

"Fangs?" she modulated in sluggish tones. "You came to rescue me?"

Rav nearly let a smile slip his lips.

"Where's Elyssandro? You haven't lost him have you?"

"No, he's here. Teaching the Canon what happens when they hurt a friend."

"He'll show them..."

She flickered.

"Rest, demon. We'll get you to help soon."

Nix's eye ebbed away. Rav tucked her carefully in the deepest pocket inside his borrowed coat. A shame they had lost her harlequin silk. Hopefully the lining wouldn't irritate her chassis too unbearably.

During the brief reunion, Kai had gathered the two cocooned devices into a pack.

"There's one missing," Victor stated gravely. "Mel says she's called Kubernetes. The Watcher took her from the box."

"Can't Prometheus help us find her?" Rav questioned.

At the mention of his name, the chrome sphere lying among the straw vibrated and ascended into the air at face level. Swirls like flames sprouted crimson, orange, and lemonade across his surface. They shaped about a fiery blue corona, a pinpoint singularity at its center.

"You have summoned me, oh courteous master?" the mechanical drone pronounced.

Though the voice made very little tonal variance, something in the demon's blazing eye suggested sarcasm.

"I am no one's master," Rav responded. "We do need your help. Your sister, Kubernetes. Do you know where the Watcher took her?"

"Sister Ignatius required assistance."

"What for?" Rav demanded.

"To trap the necromancer."

Static squealing shattered any further explanations. Rav raised panicked eyes to find his terror mirrored on the pirate king's face.

"Where are they now?" Rav pressed.

Prometheus flashed a patterned heatmap, then answered, "The observatory. I can take you there if you wish."

Rav looked back at his companions. Icy perspiration harried his brow. Ely would expect him to complete their part of the mission regardless of any perils in which he might find himself quagmired. Better his conjurer live to express his displeasure.

"I'm with you, *che'oma*," Kai said, voice somber and rasping.

"Don't worry about me, fellas," Victor Skylark shrugged. "I'll egg sit while you search and rescue. I want to take a crack at some of these treasure chests."

Rav nodded. "Lead the way, Prometheus."

Ely banished his helmet to better marvel at the magnificent hall that lay beyond the archway. Sable colonnades stood in parallel rows, tall and noble soldiers at attention. Between them, statues the height of towering oaks glowered down. Officious looking tablets etched with knife-lettered death magic burdened their great laps. Their hands they held poised in gestures uncannily reminiscent of Apostles.

At the end of the columned channel, the ceiling curved in a monumental dome that peered through pure, unfrosted glass at the night sky above. Below, a glazed pool consumed dripping starlight into its depths.

Sister Ignatius awaited his arrival in the center of the tarn. She toasted a saccharine smile.

"Another round?"

The Watcher sat before a stately table crafted in the shape of a pentagon. Ripples spread where the central support dipped beneath the surface, gently bobbing. An empty seat waited opposite the Watcher. On the table, a Caj board begged an opening.

Ely tested the water with a wary boot.

"Have faith, Elyssandro," the Watcher cooed.

Well?

Death still panted from their flight exertion. The oppressive atmosphere seemed to have sapped them silent.

Ely took a tentative step. The yielding surface undulated, but he did not sink. In fact, he realized, this was not water at all but pure starlight captured through the dome overhead. Devious, those Cosmologists.

He ventured on until he reached the chair prepared for him, sculpted of warped ether. Its contours seemed magnetized, ready to weld to him the moment he sat. Rendering him instantly irradiated, like he'd spent hours baking in the sun.

Yes, this needed to be quick.

Sister Ignatius poured the tiles into an ivory shuffling can and dumped them out to be divided.

"Fascinating, isn't it?" she chimed, maculate fingers swiping tiles in a hypnotic dichotomy.

Yours. Mine. Yours. Mine.

"What?" Ely asked, shaking off the imminent stupor.

"The utter incompatibility between conjury and cosmology."

"Sure. Fascinating. I'm more interested in what we're playing for. This is match, isn't it? One-all?"

Sister Ignatius giggled. "Sure, tiger. In the interest of transparency, since we're such good friends now, I did throw our first hand to spring the trap."

"So, it was you in my head," Ely observed.

"I am she, and she is me," the Watcher singsonged.

"So long as the Miracle lives, is that it?"

Sister Ignatius turned flickering golden eyes across the board. Not human, that gaze. A god's eyes. Could the soul beneath even be freed this far gone?

"Someone's embarked on an education, I see," the Watcher sneered.

"Are you to start or am I?" Ely inquired.

"Guests first."

As his eyes moved through the motions of considering ravens or knights or goblets of gold, Ely conducted a hair fine probe toward his opponent.

"You'll know it when you feel it," Ariel had said.

That a Miracle held her in its haloed clutches he needed no sorcery to confirm. The air reeked of its sweet smoke. Skin and hair and animal fat caught to fire. A witch burning slowly on the pyre built within her own flesh.

"Tick tock, pudding," Sister Ignatius fleered.

Ely blinked at his tiles. They blurred and distorted before his dimmed vision. Starfell lapped up his inner resources with lupine thirst. Think faster. No time for strategies.

He laid his opening set. Sister Ignatius tutted her tongue.

"Elyssandro, if I didn't know better, I'd think you didn't care to win."

Ely hid his intentions amongst his remaining tiles. When the Watcher turned to attend her own, he prodded the noxious magic putrifying across the table. There had to be a source. A cancerous mass at the nexus of her spirit.

Sister Ignatius hummed and rearranged her tiles.

Click. Clack.
Click. Clack.

Click. Clack.

Ely's seeking thread severed. His arms dragged heavy as anvils. The ravenous chair latched onto his armor. Soldering him to its surface. Holding him fast. The restraint woke him from the trance, but now he struggled in vain.

This would be a good time for you to take over, he suggested silently.

Nothing.

Sister Ignatius rose, a gleeful gleam in her divine eyes.

"I think we can both agree you were going to lose."

The Watcher untied a leather pouch from her habit belt. Building playful dramatic tension, she loosened the drawstrings and rolled the contents into her hand. She held it aloft for him to get a gander at a dodecahedron with faces of shifting polychrome. While this did not resemble the others in the least, the spirit trapped inside the mechanism whispered to him. Helyx.

"She's special, this one," Sister Ignatius purred. "You can't imagine the trouble it was to get ahold of her. It would make your trudge across the ice seem like an idyllic jaunt."

"Do tell me when you've published your memoirs," Ely grunted, shifting focus to his misbehaving armor. Perhaps if he relaxed, it might slip loose. Or at least dematerialize.

"What exactly sets this one apart, aside from the obvious?"

Sister Ignatius giggled and slid a violet finger down one of the helyx's colorful planes. "Let's have a taste. Kubernetes, show our guest why we've invited him."

The helyx chirred and chirruped. As she glided to hover above the center of the pentagonal slab, the surrounding pool distorted, rising about them in translucent panes.

"Conjurer!" a dear and desperate shout boomed from the entry.

Rav blurred as a canon blast and crashed into the barrier. The surface absorbed the concussion in gelatinous wrinkles then flicked the vampire back into the forest of pillars.

Kai bounded forward next, peering in at him with helpless fury as geometric rime crept along the glassy barricade. The room beyond faded, and Ely saw only his own wan face looking back at him.

Then the walls and the floor blanched blinding white. Kubernetes pulsed variegated light and gridlines splayed out around them, rising into constructs that slowly rendered into familiar formations. Shelves and tables. Settees and chairs. A great hearth aroar with conjured flames.

"Ah. I see. You've wormed your way back into my head."

"Not me. Kubernetes has her own protocols, so that charming little bauble round your wrist is as good as worthless in here."

"I'd much rather have a demon digging around in my melon," Ely said. "No offense."

"This is not our destination, Kubernetes," Sister Ignatius flung in sharp command. "Put the ship on course."

The surrounding scene rolled and mutated. Dusty halls. Ghouls loitering on crumbling steps. Skeleton pedestrians thronging cobblestoned streets.

"This is brilliant, Kubernetes. Extraordinary," Ely grinned, all at once homesick.

The helyx paused her rumbling to turn a curious facet toward him. For a moment, he thought he caught a glimpse of a humanlike expression within the neon. Was that a wink?

"Kubernetes!" Sister Ignatius snapped.

"Go on, love. Show us what else you've got," Ely encouraged with a smile.

The Vale's decay retreated as jungle heat burst in humid tendrils. Blossomed perfumes enticed from the radiant canopy. Monkey chatter bandied from the branches.

"Isle of the Gods?" Ely questioned. "Whatever are you looking for here, Sister?"

The helyx angled a new face forward. The scene reconfigured to accommodate two emergent characters. One spry and svelte, the other ungainly and gaunt. A pirate prince and a diakana walking the primeval path.

"Named gods, were we really so young?" Ely exclaimed.

The jungle petrified and crumbled. All around them volcanic rock and spiraled destruction. Just ahead, a filthy conjurer dragged his lifeless companion from the rubble. Clasped him close in screaming despair. Then nothing. Just stillness. A gasp. Happy tears. An embrace.

"That can't be all of it," Sister Ignatius spat. "Show me again."

Kubernetes conducted the memory back to the entry point. Then, when no magic gestures or incantations or glyphs unlocked the secret to resurrection, the Watcher belched an angry yowl.

"Back again, Kubernetes. Further back. A child won't be able to hide the trick."

"There's nothing to see then either," Ely warned, struggling against his armor prison.

The Isle of the Gods voided white. The air turned to bone-cracking cold. Not the arctic dryness that surrounded Starfell. The damp, frigid winter of his childhood.

Ely grappled again with his restraints. Dread locked his joints. He cast a pleading glance at the helyx. Within the electric blue of her nearest plane, he saw a face fixed on him. Eyes, nose, and mouth distinct in the play of light.

"Kubernetes," Sister Ignatius adjured.

New shapes emerged. Austere stone painted amber in the firelight. A bed heaped in furs. One miserable boy looking out at the moon. No tears left to cry.

Ely closed his eyes. He didn't need to watch. He knew exactly what the little conjurer would see gazing down on the castle courtyard below. A strange shadow would move at the archway, pale moon cascading over a tall, slender silhouette. He would leap from the window seat and tear from his room, down the hall, down the corkscrewed steps, and across the slippery iced stones. She would catch him in the warm safety of her arms. And for a moment, the world would be turned right again.

Ely took a breath and opened his eyes. There she was. Dark curls flowing loose under falling snowflakes. Smile radiant and sad as she pressed her cheek to the top of her son's head.

Ely waited for the shriek from the doorway. The pallid lady in waiting who never expected to look upon her queen's face again.

"It's alright, Nadine, it's only me. Terésa. Nothing to fear."

"Devils! Witchcraft! Save us!"

Next would come the heavy thud of iron boots trampling the stones around them. The cruel grinding of metal as swords unsheathed. Shouting. Hacking. Spurting blood. All echoed inside his mind. But the only sound that followed was Sister Ignatius's rage.

"This can't be all there is!" she fumed. "Turn it back, Kubernetes. Show me again!"

Ely fixed his eyes on the Watcher. Like tempered steel quenched into its final forging, anguish hissed to sharpened clarity.

"Sister Ignatius or nameless virus within," he said, "what you're failing to observe here is the most crucial of all details. Show our eponymically challenged friend, won't you, Kubernetes?"

The helyx twisted. The construct shivered. The air bent and distorted and thickened.

"I wasn't alone on either of these occasions," Ely said.

Darkness crept at the edges, focusing and condensing. Gathering matter and anti-matter. Gathering light and sound. Space. Time. Dimension.

"No..." Sister Ignatius gasped, realizing too late what she'd invited from his mind to render.

Death stared down through twin constellations. Reached forth wormhole arms with hands of grasping galaxies whose spiraled fingers closed about the reeling Watcher. They lifted her, screeching and cursing. Opened a fathomless maw aglitter with stars and planets. Dropped her inside.

The helyx twinkled playful coruscations. Her imaginative entity persisted a moment, then it collapsed into wires and empty white.

Ely found his armor had separated itself from the chair, and he could once again stand. He moved away from the predatory furniture with haste.

"That was quite a show, Kubernetes. Well done, and many thanks."

"If it is not an excessive burden, Elyssandro, I prefer to be called Kate," a mechanical gargle entreated.

"Kate. That's lovely."

"Nix transmitted the wonder of you," the helyx harmonized. "I thought it was a bug perhaps introduced at the time of her injuries, but I see now why she imprinted."

"Thank you," Ely said. "I think?"

"It was intended to be received in the positive," Kate confirmed.

"Great."

A nearby groan set him back on guard. Sister Ignatius lay a ragged bundle on the bleached floor. Habit stained with glittering cosmic hand prints. Ely raised a defensive hand but paused, curious, as an unexpected spark tickled his senses. Soul.

"Sister Ignatius?" he asked, ether still at the ready.

The Watcher stirred, struggling to sit upright. She blinked, eyes no longer godly gilded but warm honey. Thoroughly human.

Panicked rage distorted her face, and she tore at her veil as though it were a boa constrictor coiled to kill. She cast the covering aside, freeing a close-shorn head veined with burnt ridges rapidly fading with the memory of the destroyed Miracle.

She flexed her fingers before her eyes, gasping as their mottled rot returned to unblemished skin. Tears spilled from her eyes. She ran her hands from her heart down her torso, awe on her face for whatever change she found.

"You saved me," she breathed.

"I was fused to a chair," Ely said. "It's Death you should be thanking. And Kate, of course."

Sister Ignatius shook her head, now fully healed of its wounds. "True Death would not be so kind to the likes of me."

The grim passenger stirred within his skull to nod their agreement.

"It was you," the Watcher concluded.

"So, now what?" Ely asked. "I don't know about you, but this blank room is giving me a headache."

"Oh, yes," Sister Ignatius looked up from contemplating her purified hands. "Kubernetes, will you lower the Ether Net?"

"That depends," the helyx crackled. "Are you going to transfer my controls?"

"Yes. Please initiate protocol three-one-eight. Full transfer."

Kate swiveled, streaks of color swiping across the empty walls.

"Transfer complete. I await your directive, Elyssandro."

"Sure...lower the Ether Net, is that what you called it?"

"At once."

The alabaster light vaporized like steam from window panes. Then the barrier liquified and crashed down, once again a pool beneath their feet. Stars palpitated through the dome above.

A swift descent spilled rollicking waves across the Cosmologist's pool. Rav appeared at his side, cloaked in dread. He circled. Sniffed for wounds. Then pressed his forehead to Ely's, heaving a relieved chuff.

"I'm fine, sweetheart. Really," Ely sighed, giving his hand a reassuring squeeze.

"Diakana!" Kai splashed through the captive starlight to join them.

He stopped, eyes shifting to the figure lurking behind. The pirate king drew his sword. Rav looked up and tensed, fangs at the ready.

"No, wait," Ely cautioned, quickly planting himself between his two gallants and the freed Watcher. "She's been released from the Miracle. And she's even turned over Kate here as a sign of good faith."

He gestured to the helyx, who scuttered forward and bobbed a nod or perhaps a curtsy. A little round ball of fire zoomed to greet her. Prometheus? No sign of Nix.

"Are you satisfied she's reformed, conjurer?" Rav asked.

"The Miracle is stone dead. That's all I can attest," Ely replied.

"You need proof?" the Watcher asked. "Come to the battlements. I'll hand this fortress to you on a platter. Set me loose upon the Canon, and I'll bring you the High Apostle's head."

"Now, what would I do with that?" Ely shrugged. "I like your attitude, though."

"And if she's bluffing?" Kai asked.

"Choose your instrument of revenge, Ne'mori Raka," Ely replied.

"As you command, diakana," Kai smirked, turning wolf's eyes on the Watcher.

Sister Ignatius swallowed audibly.

"So," Ely beckoned. "Shall we take the havoc outside, then?"

As the others set purposeful ripples in the Cosmologist's pool, Ely turned to the unusually quiet vampire.

"Are you alright?" he asked under his breath, too low for the others to hear.

"I don't think so, Ely," Rav murmured.

The vampire's ear wept a claret trickle.

"You're hurt?" Ely whispered, dismay crashing over him.

"That sound," the vampire winced. "It's been hounding me since we arrived."

All this time so worried about himself. Why wouldn't Starfell's cosmology prove just as brutal for a vampire? Worse, even?

Ely conjured a hasty handkerchief. Such a molehill of a spell took a mountain of effort. It seemed Starfell still leeched his death magic as fast as it replenished.

"Come here, honey. Let me."

As he dabbed gently at the blood, he glanced up to find the vampire gazing at him with perplexed warmth. Ely lifted a small, intimate smile. The chorus chimed out again in his mind.

I love you.

I love you.

But aloud, "Come on. I think we'd better be finished with this place sooner than later."

They exited the Ether Net and caught up with the others among the colonnades. Rav stumbled. His hand pressed to his forehead, face crumpled in pain.

"You alright, *che'oma*?" Kai frowned.

"Kai, stop where you are," Ely hissed in warning. "Do not move."

Rav straightened. Chest heaving. Lips curved back over fangs enlarged and vicious. Faster than a charging cheetah, the vampire pounced. Kai slammed into a pillar with a yelp.

Ely gaped senseless horror. Feet rooted to the floor.

The pirate king rolled from the vampire's grasp, saved by the column's impact on his assailant's head. He tore his pistol from its holster and fired, gunpowder sparking. Rav grunted and snarled, undeterred by the red fountain blooming over his jacket. Kai brandished his cutlass while the vampire hissed and circled.

Release us, Death leapt up. *We'll put an end to it.*

As the pirate king lunged, the vampire crouched low, roaring past like a cyclone, taking his legs from under him. Kai threw up his hands to protect his face as relentless fangs descended.

"Rav, stop!" Ely's voice ricocheted between columns and statues.

The vampire turned toward the new prey that plucked at his bleeding ear and spat two spewing fingers to the floor. Ely took a step back, unable to draw breath as Rav advanced, muzzle dripping. Eyes absent light. Presence a merciless void.

Release us. Now.

"Rav," Ely choked. "Wake up."

Slam!

Ominous popping rattled beneath his armor shell as he skipped like a stone across the starlight pool. Ely stirred with a groan. Lungs stunned and useless. Head scrambled.

A growl rumbled from behind. He turned. The vampire clawed his face with the brute strength of a striking tiger. A heated geyser spewed, and his left eye screamed, lids sealed shut. He reached for any vestiges of death magic left, but it spread too thin.

Let us have him, the legion demanded, throwing a battering ram against his tenuous control.

No!

The vampire's fangs raked Ely's forearm. They could not puncture his ether armor, but the crushing pressure set off a firework that shocked a latent reserve of death magic back into his hands. He snaked and snared viscous black around the snarling immortal. Binding him.

"Please," Ely groaned, strength sloughing away into the starlit pool.

Fast and painless. Like a rabid dog, Death cajoled.

His good eye grew murky. Charcoal sparks evaporated from his failing armor. Once left bare to those shredding teeth...

You made him a promise. Remember?

Ely let out his breath. Hope fled with it.

"I love you," he whispered.

He saw Rav go still. Blink. Eyes gleaming crystal clear just as Death's white clouds swirled closed.

Chapter Twenty-Seven

THE LIGHT AT DAWN

Ariel paced her prison, all bland emptiness. Not even a setting pried from her head. The Hollow was tired. Sickening by the day. She wondered what would happen if it failed before rescue arrived with the keys. Would she remain trapped inside her dormant body? Or simply fade to black?

Would rescue even come?

Ariel huffed a breath, pacing faster, clenching her virtual fists. Elyssandro was more than a match for a single Watcher, if only he might focus. If only the Cosmology didn't bleed him dry too quickly. If only Ravan Aurelio didn't insist on protecting him.

She knew that stubborn, unmovable look. The one that inevitably started a furious fight. The one that invariably left them tangled up and sweat drenched before she agreed to give him his way. A lump caught in her throat.

"Shocking is it?"

Ariel's eyes flicked to the smirking intruder, leaning casually on nothing. Shaped, as expected, like her fixated thoughts. A tall, cavalier figure dressed for a country ride.

"You're back," Ariel said to the Hollow. "Feeling better?"

"Oh, I'm peaches and cream, my little dove. We're talking about you. And him. And the stunning plot twist none of us ever saw coming. After you scorned him and left him to torture and defilement, he no longer loves you. And now you get to watch him make bedroom eyes at another boy."

"You're tiresome."

"And yet some sad, splintered part of you is always so happy to see me."

"Get out."

The Hollow smiled. Taunting. Heartstopping.

"I can't, honey. I live here."

It caressed her face, warmth and texture so precise she couldn't bring herself to move away.

"You brought them together through the bonds of common cause. Well done. But there's no room for you. You might as well stay with me, little dove."

Ariel looked up, impressed by the meticulous rendering. The Hollow didn't usually bother with the more intimate details of smile lines or the play of light and color around the irises. Why put in the effort today?

"You're too weak to keep me here," she realized aloud.

The Hollow glared at her. Eyes glitching electric sparks. "Perhaps. So ask yourself, do you really want the lights to go out?"

"I'll take my chances," she replied.

Ariel closed her implicit eyes, seeking instead her true body. It lay as it had for a thousand years. Immobile. Every cell embalmed. Lost to time.

Before the terror of her paralysis could set in, she cast into the oily folds of the shadow planes.

A slick film of blood coated his teeth, the heady aftertaste on his tongue. It was the lords of the Council splattered across his chin. It was Harald Brahm and Fiona White dripping from his fingers.

No. They're a thousand years gone.

What have I done?

Death struck first at the sigil on his chest. He felt their vengeful talons tearing at the inscription. Unknotting the magic that froze time in his veins.

He should be frightened. Or sorrowful. Or entreating. Instead he felt only peace. He would be freed from the coils of immortality before he learned whatever terrible truth marked his final moments.

The hand of Death, so swift and sure, faltered. Rav fell back, captive starlight lapping over him, cleansing his sins, easing his wounds.

His usurped conjurer approached. Hand raised for cataclysm. Another form swept between them. Golden light danced around her to mingle with the liquid starshine.

"Enough," Ariel intoned.

"Stand aside," the reaper's legion harmonized around Elyssandro's voice.

"Has he not given you enough?" Ariel demanded.

"What has the abomination to give us? Its every atom is an insult!" Death seethed.

"I speak of the conjurer that has entrusted you with his body and soul. Has he not shown loyalty time and again? Will you not do better than the nameless charlatan that burns his faithful to ashes for their good service?"

Death replied with a thunderous exclamation. Their unbridled presence swelled and swarmed. An eruption poised to swallow them both.

Ariel threw her arms wide, matter dissolving into a golden filament brilliant as the sun. Rav shielded his eyes. Heat and brightness wrapped around him. The vacuous pool seemed to drop away. Then a bottomless abyss.

Falling.

Falling.

Falling.

Death's gravitation contracted inward until Ely's cobbled legs pitched him into sampled sky. He groaned. It took gritted teeth and grunting effort just to pry his armor loose from the Ether Net.

Splashed starlight had calmed the flow of blood from his wounds, but he still could not open his left eye.

"Rav?" he called.

No answer. Naturally. Of course. Numb. Stay numb.

But there must be something left. A shiver of spirit in the air. An echo. A body. Something to hold in mourning. But there was nothing. No traces left behind. He was just gone.

What have you done? Ely demanded.

Silence.

Then the next wave of horror struck. Kai.

Ely swayed to his feet, choking on shock and dread and rattled bones as he stamped a trail of star-stained footprints to the motionless pirate king. Drenched in blood. Jacket shredded. Mangled hand cradled to his chest.

"He has lost two terminal digits and much vascular fluid," Kate observed over his shoulder. "If you place him in the Ether Net, it should should act as an anti-hemorrhagic."

Ely gripped Kai under the arms and dragged him to the pool with much protest from cracked bones making their debut. As he ladled handfuls of distilled starlight over Kai's lacerations, the blood ceased spilling. Kai moaned softly but did not wake.

A gentle buzz droned by his side.

"Your ocular organ is damaged," Kate informed him.

"I noticed."

Ely raised his functioning ocular organ to the helyx.

"Kate, did you see what happened...? What...what I did?"

"My instruments were temporarily disrupted by electromagnetic radiation," Kate replied. "When the phenomenon terminated, you were alone in the Ether Net."

Ely nodded and swallowed. Stay numb.

"Starshine!"

Rión sped between the columns, Victor Skylark six steps behind.

"Fucking gods!" Rión growled as she came near enough to get a view of the carnage.

"Help him," Ely entreated.

Victor knelt at Kai's side, throwing his pack from his shoulders to fetch his first aid kit. "You've really done it this time, old man."

Rión lifted a calloused gray claw to Ely's cheek, the blue sorrow in her eyes punctuated with a watery shiver.

"Oh, little brother."

Ely reached for his voice. It defected.

He signed, "I kept my promise."

Only bones picked clean remained along the battlements. The ether spiders, fat on flesh, splayed atop them. Victims of their own voracity.

The rest of Starfell's former inmates lay in the inner quadrangle where Rión said they made their last stand against one another when the Watcher planted weeds inside their heads. Then she whistled in the seraphim to roast the rest. The winged giants followed her commands like well-trained hunting hounds. At the curtain call, a seraphim set the former Sister upon its mountainous shoulder slope, and she vowed revenge on the Canon as they soared away. Fucking glorious! So declared the Etrugan warrior.

With the fortress conquered, they commandeered the infirmary where Brin could bandage up Kai and wrest him out of immediate danger. Then they raided the storehouse to provision their return journey.

They camped outside Starfell's noxious walls. Ely sat vigil by the dregs of a campfire. One eye bandaged underneath a patch of fitted ether, the other cast to the stars. Sensing. Praying. *Where are you? I should feel you out there with them.*

Kate and Prometheus slept nestled with the dormant helyxes in the knapsack at his feet.

"*Helyxia,*" Rav's quiet reminder nudged.

Ely released a shuddering breath. Push it away. Lock it up.

Nix was not among the slumbering clutch of demons. Victor said Rav had placed her in his coat pocket before rushing off to his rescue. So, she too was gone. Erased from the universe. Why? How?

Death made no account.

The hike from Starfell back to the ships dragged an endless slog through frozen hell.

Ely conjured a sled to transport Kai. Rión and Ari traded off with him to coil death magic bonds around their shoulders and haul the pirate king mile by weary mile. Brin kept Kai sedated, trickling wholesome light over his forehead when he began to stir and groan.

By the time they reached the Ulvebrand, Kai's remaining fingers suffocated black and infection set in.

"You cannot take his hand. There must be something to be done!" Ely shouted at the Etrugan surgeon over scalding tears.

"Are you ready to explain to a little child why you let her father die?" Rión snarled as she dragged him from the infirmary.

He could not outmuscle her on a good day, much less concealing cracked ribs. A headache like a roaring comet restrained him from scorching a midnight sun into the deck.

It was Ak'hila Novara, Kai's acting first mate, that gave the final word. Spare his life. Cost be damned.

"I have a colleague in the Prosthesis Department at South Sea," Leanora assured Ely with a timid hand on the shoulder. "He's the best in the field. And he owes me a favor. We'll get his majesty taken care of, I promise."

Victor passed him the ribald, skunky spliff he'd been clenching between his teeth. That, at least, let him sleep.

Ely sat in the ship infirmary while Kai shuddered through fitful rest. He had relieved a Novara cousin of his watch, to the young man's relief. Humans seemed to find the scent of healing wounds near unbearable. A lifetime in Death's Vale rendered Ely immune.

Kai took a sharp breath, groaned, and opened his eyes. Bright with pain. Ely reached for the concoction waiting at the bedside, but Kai stopped him.

"Please," he murmured. "Don't trap me in dreams yet."

Ely poured him water instead, helping him to drink. Kai lifted his remaining hand to touch the binding angled around Ely's gouged eye.

"It doesn't matter," Ely said.

"It matters, *che'miora*. I know your wounds are deeper than you'll say."

"You don't have to be kind," Ely replied bitterly. "Everyone's so maddening gentle with me. It's my fault. Don't pity me. Blame me."

"When the time comes, I'll blame the Canon," Kai grimaced. "Right now, I want nothing but to lay eyes on home."

Ely stroked his fevered brow. "I'll get you back to your family, Kai, I promise. Tell me about her. Elyssa."

Kai smiled, face sparked back to life.

Sweet Brin did her best to save his eye from utter ruin. Ely told her to keep her strength for more dire needs and left nature to limp through its course.

When he drummed up the courage to remove the bandage, he felt nothing before the glass. Gruesome. To be sure. The raw, jagged scar that sliced his eyebrow, its vicious twin embedded below on his cheek. Iris swimming in a bloody canvas. Pupil, pinched and curved into a Reaper's scythe. Appropriate. Deserved.

Pain bellowed and throbbed through commutable days and nights. He longed for a tender, cooling touch stroked against his temple. Dispelling bad dreams. Sending him to peaceful rest.

He settled for Etrugan grog and smoke rings. Victor Skylark, at least, offered no damnable pity.

"They'll get past it eventually, the poor, pitiful invalid treatment," Victor chuckled and passed the joint. "I'd be willing to bet that dragon eye of yours comes in handy too."

"It's nothing," Ely shrugged, expelling smoke in a dulling haze. "I didn't lose a limb."

Victor fixed him with his eerie blind gaze. "Kai Novara's tougher than a rusted bear trap. Trading a hand to take down a Canon fortress? It'll be a legend before we even set foot on land again."

The Ulvebrand churned through the waves, exciting heavy wake from its shoulders. Ely leaned against the railing, squinting at the skyline. Lucent shimmers refracted a rainbowed halo against his tender eye. Shapes blurred and light ricocheted in dizzying overlays around the disfigured pupil. Much easier to see with it shuttered.

The sun peered blood red over fevered dark waters. At long last, after the unrelenting dark of arctic winter.

Dawn.

BOOK II: CROWN OF RUST

The Sonata continues in the second installment, Crown of Rust, coming 2025 in print and eBook.

ABOUT THE AUTHOR

This series started as a bit of fun and relaxation while working my way through grad school. You know, to keep statistics from crushing my soul. If I'm being honest, the characters had already been talking to me for years during long oceanside commutes. Their stories finally overflowed, and I had no choice but to write them down, often in the early hours before sunrise. It's become a ritual now. Coffee, blanket, stylus. I hope you've had a good time on this wild, weird adventure and that you'll join me for more. You can find me online at ekmacpherson.substack.com.

E.K. MacPherson is a writer, software engineer, and parent. She holds a degree in Computer Science and a Master of Information and Data Science from U.C. Berkeley. A wandering streak lured her from her raising in the woods of the Emerald Triangle to the sultry magic of New Orleans to the sleepless waves of the West Coast. She and her family now enjoy the wide open green of Tennessee.